Jazzy Kitty Publications
Presents

Love Will Drive You CRAZY

JACOB SANTIAGO

Love Will Drive You Crazy

By Jacob Santiago

Cover Created by Jazzy Kitty Publications

Logo Designs by Andre M. Saunders/Leroy Grayson

Editor: Anelda Lukesia Attaway

ISBN 978-1-954425-36-1

Library of Congress Control Number: 2021922558

ACKNOWLEDGMENTS

Verily all praises and things are due to Allah.

I want to acknowledge Mrs. Anelda for helping me publish my book and having patience with me in my writing.

I want to also acknowledge my wife, Kayla, for helping me and giving me the support and love that I can't repay back in words. I want to thank you for everything you have done for me.

I want to also acknowledge my family as a whole even though we are not perfect; I know you still love me. I would shout out a whole bunch of guys, but all my guys either turned on me or the street took them.

Now that I'm 28 years old, I've learned that all you have is family, and even then, you will still be left out on your own. If it doesn't benefit the next person nine times out of 10, they are not going out of their way to help you. So whatever decision you make, put yourself first. Writing these types of books is Haram (forbidden) for a Muslim. I only really wanted to publish them to make my mom proud of me and my family. So, if you are a Muslim, I am not encouraging you to write books of this nature, but I will encourage every person who reads this to study Islam upon the Salafi.

DEDICATIONS

I dedicate this book to my son King. I love you so much King. You mean the world to me. Because of you, I don't want to live the life I used to live. I want you to be proud of me and look at me like I was Superman.

This dedication is more like a letter to you than an actual dedication, but I just want to let you know how I really feel about you; if I can't get the chance to when you comprehend what I'm saying. Due to me being incarcerated, I have left you, but I promise I will never leave you again. You the man of the house now; you got to protect your mom and your little sister when she comes.

I love you son, and I hope I make you proud. Everything I do from here on out is for you and your sister. I love you more than I can put into words.

TABLE OF CONTENTS

INTRODUCTION

Love Will Drive You Crazy is a romance with twists and turns that are exhilarating. It is full of excitement and drama.

The drama includes love, lust, romance, loss, lies, hot sex, murder, and betrayal. It is a true page-turner.

CHAPTER 1

Fairy Tale

"HUH, HUH, HUH, DON'T STOP, DADDY! DON'T STOP!" yelled Vanessa at the top of her lungs.

The love of her life, Damon, has given her multiple orgasms and hasn't stopped having them since she walked through the door. It was August 25th and it was their 8th year anniversary. As soon as Vanessa walked through her door, her man was standing in the front of the master bedroom, where you could see from the small apartment where they were living. The lights were off, and at least a hundred candles were lit throughout the whole apartment. Damon was there with a dozen roses covering his private part since he was ass naked. Dropping her keys on the floor as well as her pocketbook. Damon walked up to Vanessa, gave her the flowers, and picked her up while closing the door at the same time. Damon was not saying anything while Vanessa was thanking him up and down. Damon unbuttoned Vanessa's blouse showing her size 36-C breast wrapped under a Victoria's Secret black bra. Unzipping her skirt from the side and letting it drop to the floor. Unhooking her bra and dropping her panties, leaving her heels on. Damon picked Vanessa up and laid her on the bed. Damon started caressing Vanessa's breast as he sucked on her neck. Licking his way down to her breast, Damon moved his hands down to her vagina, which was already soaking wet. Vanessa let her eyes drop to his tongue down Vanessa's stomach passing her belly button and landing on her clit. Moving his tongue down and up, side to side, across Vanessa's lips. Spreading her lips apart with his fingers, Damon used his tongue to go like crazy on Vanessa's clit; orgasm after orgasm, Vanessa couldn't take it anymore.

"BABE, PLEASE DON'T STOP!!!" yelled Vanessa as she got to moving her body so much that Damon grabbed her ass cheeks to hold her still.

"DAMON, I LOVE YOU BABE! DON'T STOP, I'M CUMMING!!!" yelled Vanessa at the top of her lungs, pushing Damon off of her to get her full orgasm.

Damon stood tall, looking at Vanessa while she squirmed on the bed in a fetal position. Crawling backward, so her head was on the pillow, she left a puddle of her juices on the sheets. Damon was already hard as a rock getting on the top of her. Vanessa wrapped her legs around Damon's waist when he entered Vanessa, sliding right in. Damon knows his girl likes it rough, so he wasted no time pounding away. Harder and harder, he pounded Vanessa away until he felt as though she climaxed, and then he switched positions. Laying on his side, he rolled Vanessa over on her side and came close to her. Vanessa turned half of her body over to kiss Damon's lips. She grabbed Damon's dick and played with it. Going up and down Vanessa's vagina lips, teasing each other until Damon couldn't take it anymore. Damon grabbed Vanessa by the neck and started to choke her ever so lightly while he entered inside her. With each stroke, he pounded harder, making Vanessa scream louder and louder. Squeezing onto her sheets, Damon couldn't take it anymore, and he came inside of her, wishing he could get her pregnant. Vanessa hated when she couldn't get her orgasm off because she knew Damon was a quick nutter, but she loved this man with all her heart. So, she didn't care if he nutted quick or not; she was always right by his side. Vanessa was mad that she didn't get her orgasm like she wanted; knowing Damon nutted, she was about to say something until Damon stopped her.

"Hold on Babe, I got a surprise for you," said Damon getting up from the bed and opening one of the dresser drawers where he kept her present.

Damon made payments on this ring for two years and when he was finally done, he proposed to her right there.

"Vanessa…" Damon squatted on one knee next to the bed.

"Yeah?"

Vanessa wondered why Damon was on one knee because she couldn't see the black box in the dark because most of the candles were in the living room. He took the ring from the side of his back and opened the black box. A 3 9CT ring stood in front of her. Vanessa saw the ring, and for a moment, she was going to say "NO" because of her still being mad until she looked into Damon's hazel eyes, and all she could say was "YES." Damon got up and put the ring on her finger, and they both kissed and hugged each other.

The next morning was like no other until Damon woke up Vanessa and gave her breakfast in bed. Waking up to cheese eggs, bacon, sausages, fried toast, and hash browns every day was why Vanessa loved Damon so much. Grabbing the fork to eat her food, she almost forgot that Damon had proposed to her last night. Looking at the ring in the sunlight looked better than it did in the dark. It was a nice size ring for a guy that worked at UPS as a Delivery Driver.

Damon kissed Vanessa on the forehead and said, "Good morning Babe, I love you," walking out of the bedroom so he could clean the dishes before he took a shower.

Vanessa fell in love with Damon because he can make a woman feel so special inside that she feels like a queen, at least in their world she does. After Vanessa got done eating, Damon came and got her plate and took it into the kitchen. Damon got to the kitchen and heard the water running in the shower. Damon washed the dish, went to the bedroom, and went to his pants pocket where the tickets were.

"Babe," said Damon as he walked into the bathroom, "look."

"Babe, I got soap in my eyes; hold on!"

"Well, let me tell you then. We are going on a cruise to all the islands in the pacific ocean. Six days five nights, we are out, so hurry up because we catch our plane at 12:30, and it's 10 o'clock now."

"You got to be kidding me!?" asked Vanessa swinging the shower curtain open and exposing her magnificent shape.

5'10, 150, her weight went to all the right places; a caramel skin complexion with her natural hair. Some would say she resembles Alicia Keys, just a body like Megan Good.

"I'm serious, Babe, come on!" yelled Damon as he walked into the other room.

Damon is not even getting in the shower; he got his clothes on so he won't be late.

"Girl, you are lying," said Kim talking to Vanessa over the phone.

"I'm dead serious; we about to board the plane. I'm going to call you when we land. Love you Bye."

"Bye," Kim said, hanging up the phone and putting it down on the nightstand.

"Why you always stopping everything you are doing for that girl?" Aairyah said, smacking Kim on the ass as she walked past him.

"Because that's my girl, and I would do anything for her Babe, just like I will do anything for you," she said, kissing Aairyah.

Kim is walking off, showing all 26 of her tattoos. Kim was Puerto Rican and Black with hair like she was all Puerto Rican. The Blackness shows when she speaks and how she acts.

"So, what is the excitement all about?" Aairyah asked, watching Kim walk into the bathroom.

"Damon proposed to Vanessa last night and today they are flying to Florida for a cruise for a couple of days," said Kim putting on her Victoria's Secret panties and bra.

"So, where you go at last night?" Aairyah questioned his wife, who he had been married to for five years.

"I told you, me and Sabrina went to the movies last night. Why do you keep questioning me about last night? What you do last night?" asked Kim with a confused look on her face.

"Cuz you said you went with Sabrina, but I found three tickets in your jacket pocket. Who was the third person?" Aairyah asked, getting up from the bed, still ass naked from them having sex the night before.

Kim, caught in shock and didn't have anything to say, started stumbling over her words.

"It... It... It was Shanay," said Kim walking to the sink in the master bathroom.

"Shanay, huh?"

"Yeah, Shanay, why you so concerned?"

"Because you are my wife, and I need to know who you been with. Is that too much to ask?" asked Aairyah standing behind Kim.

Kim was trying to switch the subject because she knew that when Aairyah gets mad, he gets mad, and she didn't feel like hearing his shit that morning. So, she pressed her ass against Aairyah's dick. Kim knew that pussy was his weakness, so she kissed Aairyah on the lips. Then she squatted down and started to kiss the tip of Aairyah's dick. It grew instantly. Kim played with his balls with her left hand, grabbed his dick with the right, and slowly sucked on the head of his dick. Faster and Faster, Kim went stroking and sucking on his dick. Aairyah started to moan.

"OOOOOOH SSSHIIIITTTT Babe."

Hearing the sound of Aairyah's moaning made Kim go faster. Grabbing his ass cheeks now, he started stroking Kim's mouth. All the years they have been together, Aairyah still loved the sex.

After about five minutes, Aairyah picked up his wife by her armpits, sat her on the sink, and spread her legs open, showing her dark-tinted pussy. Aairyah licked away on Kim's pussy until she got wet. Getting up and entering inside of Kim, he grabbed her waist and stroked her hard, thinking of how much he loved his wife. Harder and harder, he pounded the wetter Kim got.

"OH, PAPI DON'T STOP; I LOVE THIS DICK," said Kim, grinding with her husband.

Aairyah picked her up and walked to the bed with his dick still inside her. He put her on her back and told her to turn over. She did what she was told and propped her ass up in the air. Kim stretched her body across the bed and grabbed a handful of covers waiting for the pleasure she was about to overwhelm her body. Aairyah, still standing, gets closer to Kim's body and goes inside slowly. A couple of strokes in, and Aairyah goes crazy stroking like he never did before. He put his leg up to not catch cramps to hopping on the bed with her because he got tired of standing. Aairyah kept going until Kim couldn't go anymore.

"Baby, it's starting to hurt," said Kim crawling away from Aairyah with Kim breathing heavily and Aairyah covered in sweat.

They both collapsed on the bed and fell asleep in each other arms.

"Sabrina, can you come here, please; this bitch is down here causing a problem and I don't feel like smacking hoes today," said Omar at the front door.

"I ain't a Bitch or Hoe, Nigga, so you better watch your mouth," said Shanay inviting herself inside and walking past Omar.

Sabrina walked downstairs and saw that Shanay was going to the living room.

"Shanay, come here, I'm trying to see what I'm going to wear today and I need your opinion."

"Ok," Shanay said, turning around and walking upstairs.

"You need to brush your teeth."

"You need to brush your ass and stop wearing that hairdo over and overlooking like Whoopi Goldberg fresh out the clinic," said Omar laughing at his own joke.

Shanay was Black with dreads, but she was cute with it. Then again, her body is what most men come after her for. She had an ass like Buffie and she was cute with the walk she was working with. Shanay didn't say anything but smacked her ass on the way up the stairs.

"So where did y'all go last night?" asked Sabrina, wondering what's the latest gossip.

"He took me to this bullshit ass restaurant and tried to get me drunk and then take me to Motel 6." Sabrina started laughing as soon as Shanay finished her sentence.

"You know what's funny about it?"

"What?" Shanay asked, curious to know what was so funny.

"You still gave him the pussy," said Sabrina laughing.

"Girl, it was a long story and I was faded, so it didn't matter."

"You don't know what he could have and you still fucked him?" Sabrina asked with a serious face.

"I can't do the marriage thing with the same dude all my life; it don't get boring?" asked Shanay.

Shanay was an everyday whore who don't care if she lived in the ghetto all her life or not.

"I mean, it does, but then again, it doesn't. If you truly love your man, you will stick by him no matter what," said Sabrina holding her grounds, letting Shanay know that "WHORE" was out of her vocabulary.

"Well, I'm still young; Fuck it, we are all still young. I want to try new things. I want to have fun, let my hair out without no nigga having his say so in what I do, you feel me?" Shanay said, trying to defend herself from being labeled as a whore.

"I feel you, but you got to settle down sometime," said Sabrina.

Well, I didn't have a fairytale like you, Kim, and Vanessa getting married right out of high school. I didn't find that guy yet, and how it seems I never will," replied Shanay.

Sabrina was feeling sad for Shanay for a man unwilling to take care of her for the rest of her life.

"You will find the right man; you just got to stop giving the pussy up so fast," said Sabrina in a kinda laughing matter, trying to lift Shanay's spirits.

"I try, but it seems like I can't go a day without sex. It's like I'm an addict to sex," said Shanay.

By the time Shanay picked her head up, Sabrina had looked like a million bucks. She had on this red, white, and blue Versace dress with thin black stripes, matching Versace heels, and glasses.

"Damn, Girl, where y'all going at tonight?" Shanay asked, siked to see her girl sexy as ever.

"We going out to dinner somewhere special, so I wanted to throw something good on for my man," said Sabrina looking into the mirror.

"Yeah, I got a date tonight as well. He said we were supposed to go to Red Lobster or someplace like that."

"Didn't you just come from a date last night? What he wants to take you out tonight again?"

"No, that nigga Chris is not on my level; his cheap ass called this morning I didn't even pick up."

"So, who are you going to Red Lobster with?" Sabrina asked curiously.

"Jamal."

"Jamal?" Sabrina said with a confused look.

"Yeah, Jamal, I met him a couple of days ago, and he wanted to take me out, so I ain't missing a free meal, Girl," said Shanay.

"Girl, you crazy," said Sabrina.

"Anyway, what's up with Vanessa?" Shanay asked.

"She told me she was going to the movies with her co-worker at work; hell, if I know. She said if Damon asked her if she was with me, tell him I was with her." It was like a lightbulb hit Shanay in the head.

"You don't think Vanessa is cheating, do you?"

"I don't think so. Why did you ask that?"

"Because she said she went with her co-worker, but I'm with you if Damon calls. Don't that seem strange? She's hiding something," said Shanay.

"Yeah, I know, but they been together since they were in the 9th grade; you think she would do that?"

"I don't know; he was her first." Then, suddenly, before she could say anything else, Omar walked into the room.

"I'm about to go over to the store. Do you want anything?" Omar asked his wife, ignoring if Shanay wanted it something or not.

"No, I'm good; do you want something, Shanay?" Omar gave Shanay an answer before she could say anything.

"No," said Omar and walked back downstairs.

"Why he so mean to me?" Shanay asked, not knowing why Omar always came at her for no reason.

Sabrina knew why. Omar told Sabrina that Shanay is a whore and he doesn't want me hanging around her because it might rub off on me.

"I don't know, Girl, you know he's crazy," said Sabrina, not telling her sister the truth because the truth really hurts.

"I thought y'all high yellow ass was supposed to be friendly?" Shanay said.

Sabrina started laughing at the sight of them both being high yellow.

"Shut up Bitch. I know Vanessa is going to have a ball when she gets on that boat."

"Shit, she's having a ball on the plane; I know she drunk already."

"So, she told me to buy three tickets just in case her husband finds out he won't expect nothing of it," said Cameron.

"No, she's married?" JT asked.

"Yeah, she's married and guess with who?" Cameron said, laughing on the other line.

"Who?" JT asked eagerly to know who it is.

"Kim."

"Kim, Puerto Rican Kim with the fat ass, that act ghetto as hell?"

"You know it."

"Damn, how you get her? She's been married for a couple of years now, right?"

"Yeah, met her at Kenndy Fried Chicken; she was with the Freak Bitch Shanay. She was on me from the gate, so you know one thing led to another, and we were at the movies. I mean, we didn't do anything, but you know her husband is lame."

"Who Aairyah?"

"Yeah."

"She's been with him for a minute. Wasn't he the water boy at school?" JT said, laughing after the fact.

"He might as well; he never got in the game when we were in high school," said Cameron laughing.

"Yeah, what's up with Trish?"

"What you mean... (BEEP) Oh, that's her right here. I'm going to call you back," said Cameron switching over lines before I could even say bye.

"Hello."

"Hey Honey, what you doing?" Trish asked, walking to M&T Bank, where she worked at.

"Nothing; why, what's up?"

"Just missing you, that's all."

"Girl, you left the house. What do you want?"

"Ok, Babe, can we go somewhere tonight?"

"I'm not sure, Babe."

"Come on, we didn't go nowhere in so long Babe, and I wanted to go to the concert tonight."

"I don't know, Babe."

"OMG! Babe, Ok, whatever I'm about to go in here, I'll call you on my break."

"Ok, love you."

"Love you too, bye."

"Bye," said Cameron hanging up and pulling up in his S550.

CHAPTER 2

Howard High

"You Bumpy Face Bitch!" Kim said, laughing at her own joke.

Kim had the whole class laughing. It was freshman year and the first day of school. Kim stood 5'5 with her body already very fully grown. Kim's size was 30-22-30 and she wore it with a passion. Caramel complexion looking like Cameron Diez. Kim was the only girl that had a tattoo in freshman year.

"Fuck you Kim, you always talking Shit with your Whore Ass. Don't make me tell Richard about Ron-Ron and you," said JT getting out of his seat.

"The whole classroom said, "OOOOOHHH!" Kim was embarrassed and ran out of the classroom and into the hallway.

"What you say that for? You know she is going to snap," said one of the girls in the classroom.

"It's not like it's the truth. She's always talking Shit; she gets on my damn nerves," said JT.

JT turned around when he heard the classroom door swing open, and it was Marshall Kim's brother. Marshall stood 6'0, 220 and was the high school star. Showing most of his chest with the small V-neck, he had on. Showing off his big "B" sign in the middle of his chest in red ink. Marshall was a Blood and was the same complexion as his sister. Marshall looked just like his sister, but she was a freshman, and he was a senior.

"What's that Shit you was saying now!" Kim screamed, pointing at JT.

JT heard about Marshall whipping boys' asses in school, and when he saw him, he thought of how hard Marshall was going to hit him.

```"What's that Shit you said to my sister," barked Marshall moving the desk out of his way and making his way to JT.

"Chill Marshall, it wasn't even like that," said JT walking to the back of the classroom, back-peddling until he couldn't go anymore.

"Whip his ass Bro!" Kim yelled.

"What's going on here?" asked the homeroom teacher.

Marshall looked back and said, "Hey Mr. Miles, how did the summer treat you?"

"Oh, hey Marshall, it was good. How was yours?"

"Good, just was having a few words with my friend JT here, but I will see him after school," said Marshall, patting JT on the back and walking out of the classroom.

"A'ight Miles."

"Ok, Mr. Marshall see you on the court," said Mr. Miles.

Marshall had a lot of pull in his school since he led their high school to the championship the past three years.

"We going to see what happens after school Punk," said Kim sitting at her desk.

JT was nervous as hell because he knew he would get his ass whipped at the end of the day. Lunchtime came and Kim saw her junior high sweetheart. The whole school was talking about how JT would get his ass whipped. When Kim saw her man, his face was screwed up. Before Kim knew it, Richard slapped the Shit out of her.

"So, you Fucking that nigga Ron-Ron?" asked Richard, the football star of Howard High.

Kim hit the floor hard, and before she knew it, she started crying.
```

"Babe, they are lying." Which was a lie, but she couldn't tell him that.

"He told me you did the same night you "so-called" went to the carnival."

Aairyah saw the whole thing and ran to Richard full speed; before Kim could say anything, Richard was knocked out cold on the floor. Aairyah hit Richard with all his might from the side. Aairyah grabbed Kim's hand and picked her up. Thinking he did the right thing by hitting Richard, he was the worst enemy in Kim's mind.

"What the Fuck you do that for? Kim said, snatching her hand from Aairyah's hand.

"Because he had no right putting his hands on you," said Aairyah with a confused look on his face.

"So why you do that? I didn't tell you to do that. I don't even know you, like get away from here," said Kim pushing Aairyah away.

"You okay Baby?" Kim asked, trying to wake her man up.

When Kim knew she couldn't wake him, she called for help. Aairyah took off down the hallway and was out of sight at that sound. The bell rang and the 1st lunch was over. After Richard woke up, the principal tried to ask him questions, but he forgot what had happened, so the principal sent him home.

"Girl, what happened to Richard? I heard Aairyah knocked him out cold," said Vanessa standing tall in her Steve Madden heels.

Vanessa and Kim have been friends since the third grade, and they told everything to each other.

"Yeah, some guy came over and punched Richard in the jaw."

"What he do that for?" Vanessa asked, walking to her class with Kim.

"I don't know. Maybe because Richard slapped me." Before Kim could say anything, Vanessa stopped her.

"Why you keep letting that man put his hands on you? You know I told you if he put his hands on you again, I'm going to call the cops."

Vanessa was concerned about her friend Kim because Kim used to go over to Vanessa's house with black eyes and busted lips over the summer.

"He stopped hitting me V. He found out I was messing with Ron-Ron and he smacked me," said Kim feeling sorry for herself.

Vanessa hugged her friend at the sight of Kim tearing up.

"It's okay Kim; you don't have to worry about him anymore. I'll make sure he gets locked up for what he put you through," said Vanessa hugging her friend Kim.

"No, don't do that, V. I love him; it's just he… he going to realize that hitting me is going to break us apart, and he will come to his senses."

Vanessa knew that she couldn't convince Kim to leave him alone because she would stop talking to him for a couple of days every time she tried. By the end of the week, she'll be right back with him.

"Do Marshal know about this?"

"No, and I don't want him to know about it."

"Why not?"

"Cuz, that's my man, and he can hold his own, but Marshal will whip his ass," Kim said, laughing a little bit.

Vanessa wiped the tears from her best friend's eyes before entering her classroom. When entering the classroom, Ron-Ron was all in Shanay's face yelling at the top of his lungs, calling her all types of bitches and whores with his hand all in her face. Shanay is ghetto as hell didn't give a fuck about none of the bullshit he was saying because she knew as soon as he turned his back, she was going to clock him with all her might.

"Fuck, are you doing Ron-Ron?!" Vanessa yelled.

Ron-Ron looked over and saw Kim in the doorway. Ron-Ron locked eyes with Kim, and before he knew it, Shanay choked him sending him back a couple of steps. Ron-Ron gathered himself together after he saw black specks in his vision.

"Bitch I'm gonna kill you!" Ron-Ron said, charging Shanay.

Ron-Ron choked the Shit out of Shanay, trying to kill her. Shanay, barely breathing, still talking trash to Ron-Ron and got him even madder. Vanessa ran over there and grabbed Shanay's feet because Ron-Ron tried to throw her out of the third-story school building. One hand holding the window open and the other around Shanay's neck. Ron-Ron tried to push her out of the window by her neck.

"Get the Fuck off of her, Ronald! Vanessa yelled, pulling Shanay back into the room.

Ron-Ron only cared about two people in his life, his mom and sister Vanessa. Ron-Ron was a ladies' man, but he tends to want to live the street life and be down with the Urban lifestyle. Vanessa pulled Ron-Ron off of Shanay and pushed him.

"Fuck is you doing disrespecting my brother Bitch?!" Kim yelled, walking up to Shanay.

"If he is really your brother, you wouldn't be Fucking him! Shanay said, calling Kim out in front of the whole school.

Kim wondered how the whole school knew already, and it was the first day of school. What Kim didn't know was that JT was having sex with Shanay on the D-L without nobody knowing.

"You lying Bitch!" Kim yelled, rushing Shanay and tackling her to the ground.

Both girls were scratching and pulling each other's hair until Vanessa grabbed Kim off of Shanay.

"Let the Bitch go Kim," said Vanessa after trying to pull Kim off.

Kim still had a hand full of weave in her hand.

"Fuck this Bitch; she wants to make false statements about me; she going to get her ass whipped," said Kim, still trying to attack Shanay by swinging at her making Shanay get the worst headache in the world.

After Vanessa got Kim off of Shanay, they headed out of the class before the teacher came in after his lunch break.

"Why people saying you Fucked my brother?" asked Vanessa in the girl's bathroom, where Vanessa was trying to clean up the scratches on Kim's face.

"People are not saying it. Shanay is saying it, and I don't know, maybe she's jealous because she wants me to get mad or something," said Kim, but Vanessa knew better, and she also knew when she was lying, but she didn't say anything.

"Vanessa looked back at the times when Kim always wanted to go to her house when Ron-Ron was there, and she also wondered why she caught Kim sneaking out of her bedroom at nighttime. But she didn't think anything of it. She just wondered why her best friend didn't want to tell her that she was having sex with her brother." Too deep in her thoughts, she didn't even hear Kim call her name.

"Vanessa, Vanessa, hello?"

"Oh Shit, my bad Girl, I was somewhere else; what were you saying?" Vanessa said, blinking her eyes to step back to reality.

"I said, what are you thinking about?"

"Oh, nothing in particular."

"Yeah, Ok, what's up with you and Omar?" Kim asked, throwing away the wet toilet paper in the sink and looking in the mirror."

"Who said I ever messed with Omar?"

"People talk, and they said they saw you in his new car on summer break."

"Girl, he gave me a ride. I hate when people get things screwed up with their twisted mines; it's not even funny," said Vanessa.

In actuality, Kim was right Omar has been on Vanessa's mind all day and that's how she has been looking so good in these new Steve Madden heels that Omar bought.

"Yeah, yeah, so what's up with Damon?" Kim asked, now walking out of the bathroom with Vanessa behind her.

"I don't know; he's a sweet guy, but he just not my cup of tea. You know what I mean?" Vanessa said as they walked through the hallways.

"No, I don't know what you mean; he is the football team star, and he's sexy; Girl, you better get at him?" Kim said with a look like are you going to because if you don't, I will look on her face.

"No, you know I go out with Alex and it will break my papi's heart; If I did that to him," said Vanessa going back inside the classroom where Shanay and Kim were just fighting.

"Hey, Ummmm," said the teacher motioning his name to give them their names.

"Vanessa and Kimberly," said Vanessa walking to the back of the class.

Vanessa sees Ron-Ron in the back of the class and he's laughing and pointing at Shanay's head. Vanessa looked and saw a couple of tracks pulled out of Shanay's hair from the back. So, Vanessa, Ron-Ron, and Kim started laughing. Shanay really didn't want any smoke because she wasn't from around there, she's from the other side of town, but she wasn't scared to throw down.

"So, what's up with that Bitch? Is she coming or what, because I don't got time to wait for her," said Damon complaining as always.

"I don't know, but she is not going to get me kicked off of the team messing with her," said Aairyah walking out of the school's back door.

"So, what happen nigga?" Damon asked, walking to the locker room.

"That bitch ass nigga Richard slapped Kim in the face and when I saw it, I just went off."

"She don't even know you exist," said Damon laughing at Aairyah's stupidity.

"Yes, she do, and if she don't, I know Kim do like I'm the man of the field," said Aairyah showboating.

"No, I'm the man; you are the second man on the field and what's up with Kim's sexy ass?"

"Yeah, whatever, and I don't know, wasn't you messing with her?"

"Trying to, but you know she likes bad guys and shit like that."

"I didn't know that, but is Richard still in here? Or did he go home?"

"Somebody told me that his mom picked him up after he woke up."

"Oh, you know he is cool with Omar, and Omar ain't nothing to play with out in the streets," said Damon telling Aairyah to be careful with them dudes.

"So, I'm not scared of none of them niggas man. Do I look scared?" Aairyah asked with a confused look on his face trying not to show how he really felt.

"Dog, I knew you since 2nd grade; I know you is scared. But you know I'm riding with you man," said Damon shaking Aairyah's hand.

Damon and Aairyah went up to the football locker room and tried to open the door but couldn't' because it had a chain lock around it.

"What the hell is this for?" asked Aairyah picking up the master lock on the door and dropping it, letting it hang from the door.

"So, I heard you Fucked up Richard punk ass for my sister," said Marshal walking up to Aairyah and Damon.

"Yeah, you know he smacked her… and… and I did what was best," said Aairyah strutting at the looks of Marshal.

Aairyah heard about Marshal when he was in middle school and he knew Marshal was all about his work. Marshal gave Aairyah a handshake and Damon as well.

"So, what you want to win my sister over or something?" asked Marshal.

Aairyah put his hands up as he prayed with fear in his eyes.

"No, no she not no game I respect her, I mean I like… I love… she's cool peoples that all," said Aairyah, stuttering over his words.

"You don't got to be scared man, you're cool, but I don't want her with that Bitch Ass Nigga anyway, so I will allow you to talk to her if she wants to talk to you, that is if you got game with you or not," said Marshal cracking a smile.

"That boy don't got no game at all," said Damon laughing at his best friend.

"Yes, I do. I got your cousin, didn't I," said Aairyah.

Marshal started laughing, giving dap to Aairyah.

"Chill y'all before it gets out of hand," said Marshal giving Damon dap so he wouldn't feel left out.

"What's up with the locker room? Why is it locked? Marshal asked.

"Hell, if we know we tried to get in our damn self," said Damon looking over Marshal's shoulder.

"There she go, there she go," said Damon, pointing at one of the baddest girls in school.

"Who the hell is that?" Marshal asked, licking his lips at the sight of her.

"That's Sabrina, she transferred from some other school. I overheard her talking to the principal when we were getting our classes assigned to us. I think he said Sabrina or Sabria something like that, but she sure is bad," said Damon.

"Oh, that's who you were talking about?" asked Aairyah.

"Yeah."

"So, how old is she?" Marshal asked, looking at Sabrina like a T-bone steak.

"I think she's a junior or sophomore. I'm not too sure," said Damon.

"Well, I want her sexy ass; tell her to come here," said Marshal.

"You tell her I don't know her," said Damon.

"You know so much about her; tell her to come here, or I'm going to put my foot in your ass," said Marshal looking at Damon now.

Damon didn't have to get told twice because he knew when Marshal meant something that 9 times out of 10, he was going to do so without any hesitation. Damon screamed Sabrina's name. Sabrina looked over and couldn't recognize who it was, so she kept on walking.

"You asshole, you scared her off," said Marshal hoping she had a change of heart and came walking towards them.

"My fault," said Damon.

"Fuck it; I'll catch her another time; hopefully, she is going to be a cheerleader so she can see me play."

"She probably will be," said Aairyah.

"Oh, where are you going at?" Ron-Ron asked, walking down the hallway after Omar.

"I'm trying to skip class if you not so damn loud," said Omar.

"It's the last class anyway, Fuck it, I'm with you."

"You didn't see no Bitches; matter fact, did you get any numbers today?" asked Omar.

"Why you trying to play me? You know the boy got a number."

"Yeah, who?" asked Omar walking out back of the school.

"Yeah, I do, don't worry about that; just know I got a number and I think they are going to suspend me for choking Shanay's ass," said Ron-Ron.

"What you choke Shanay for?" Omar asked, lighting up a cigarette.

"Because she tried to play me and said I gave her an STD," said Ron-Ron lighting his cigarette off Omar's cigarette.

Omar started laughing and choked on his cigarette. After he was done choking and concluded that Ron-Ron was infected with an STD, he said, "So, what did you give her?"

"She said I gave her Gonorrhea and that I was cheating on her. The crazy thing is I never went out with her. We got drunk, got high, and had sex; that was it," said Ron-Ron.

The bell rang and the school began to let out. Omar and Ron-Ron went to the front of the school and saw everybody come outside. The bus drivers had the wrong memo because they were a half-hour late, thinking they were going to be a half-hour early. All 500 students were outside the school waiting for the buses to come.

"Look at all these girls, man. I thought I would never..." were the last words that Ron-Ron said before getting knocked out cold by Richard.

Omar had no hesitation in punching Richard in his face. Omar started Punching Richard in his face, punch after punch, until Richard ducked one and swung a huge uppercut that landed on Omar's chin, sending Omar down for the count. A full crowd sounded Richard and the bodies that were at his feet. Aairyah and Damon were the first ones to go over there and see what had happened. After they saw what happened, there was a loud scream on the other side of the yard. It was JT and Marshal fighting. Marshal had JT by his collar and was punching the lights out of him.

"Stop, Please, Marshal, please!" Shanay yelled, hoping Marshal would stop hitting him.

Out of nowhere, Cameron came and kicked Marshal off of JT. Marshal got up and squared up with Cameron. By the time Richard got over there, Marshal was whipping Cameron's ass. Cameron was on the floor in a feeble position, trying not to get kicked in his face by Marshal's size 12 Timberland boot. Richard swung at Marshal, making him stumble from the blow. Cameron got up and they both squared it up with Marshal. Richard swung, Marshal ducked, and Cameron caught Marshal.

After about 5 minutes, they had Marshal punching and kicking him on the floor. Aairyah and Damon were just watching as they whipped Marshal's ass. When Aairyah saw Kim running through the crowd, he tapped Damon and told him to jump in it with him. Aairyah stole Richard first because he thought he could knock him out again. Richard stopped kicking Marshal and turned towards Aairyah.

"I been looking for you the whole time Punk!" barked Richard while Richard squared up with Aairyah.

Damon tackled Cameron towards the floor and started punching Cameron. Richard didn't see Aairyah when he knocked out Ron-Ron and Omar. Marshal got up and kicked Cameron in his mouth while Damon was on top of him, busting his lips. Damon was still punching Cameron while Marshal got behind Richard. Richard didn't see it coming; Marshal gave Richard a haymaker sending him to the floor yet again for the second time in one day.

"What the Fuck is going on out here?" Kim asked, putting her hand over her mouth as if she was in shock.

"Vanessa, I think you want to go across the yard because your brother is probably still out cold," said Aairyah pointing to where a small crowd sounded them over the yard.

Vanessa ran over to the crowd and saw that Mr. Miles was trying to wake up Ron-Ron and Omar, who were woken up by some ice water. Mr. Miles threw ice water on Ron-Ron and he woke up instantly.

"Wha…What happen?"

"We got knocked the Fuck out," said Omar laughing a little bit at the incident.

"Who knocked us out? Damon, what happened?" Ron-Ron asked, not fully getting what really happened.

"Come on Ronald; we are going home. Damn Bro, your eye is Fucked up, man," said Vanessa feeling sorry that her brother's eye was shut.

"I'm going to whip your man ass," said Aairyah.

"No, Aairyah, please don't... Oh Shit, I got to see if he is Ok," said Kim running off to where Richard was laying.

"I'll meet you at the house." That was all you heard from Kim as she ran over to the man of her life.

The buses showed up and the whole time they were fighting, none of the teachers helped except Mr. Miles and he came too late. Buses came and people left like nothing had ever happened.

"Go ahead and take everything off. I'll make sure my baby is okay," said Kim grabbing the ice pack off of the counter and putting it on Richard's lump that was on the side of his face.

"I'm going to kill that nigga," said Richard, snatching Kim's bag as she jumped suddenly.

"Don't say that, Babe," said Kim, strip teasing Richard until all her clothes were off.

"I am watch, you'll see," said Richard grabbing Kim by the waist and making her get on her knees.

Kim didn't say anything because she was used to be used and abused of her body, and she really didn't know what love felt like. She unzipped his pants, pulled out his penis, and started kissing and sucking it until he got hard. Then she started sucking his dick non-stop. Saliva dripped off of the head of his dick after she got done sucking him off. Knowing his favorite position and damn near the only position, Kim got on the bed and got on her hands and knees. Richard got out of his shirt and dropped his jeans as he got behind Kim entering inside of her raw. Kim always liked how Richard fucked her, but she knew that she was one of plenty of girls he messed with. Richard was her first, but after she found out multiple times that he kept cheating on her that she slept with Ron-Ron off and on. Kim was in love with Richard, but she couldn't get enough of Ron-Ron's dick. If only Richard knew that Kim had sex with Ron-Ron a few days ago, he would be even more piss than what he was with her.

"SMACK MY ASS DADDY!" Kim yelled back on Richard's dick as he strokes away.

"KEEP GOING BABY! DON'T STOP!" Richard goes even harder and faster.

"OOOOOHHH SSSHHITTT RICHARD, I'M CUMMMMING!" Kim yelled, climaxing over Richard's dick. Richard pulled out and nutted on Kim's back and ass cheeks only seconds later.

"I told you I didn't like that Babe; why you keep doing that?" asked Kim getting off of the bed and walking to the bathroom.

Richard pulls his pants up and walks to the kitchen downstairs.

Marshal walks into the house after telling all his homeboys to be on the lookout for Richard, JT, and Cameron. Richard looked back with a full cup of juice in his hand and saw fire in Marshal's eyes. Richard makes a run for it after seeing three of Marshal's friends come into the house with red flags around their wrists and heads. Richard ran faster than a crack head that stole something. All three friends chased him while Marshal went upstairs to Kim's room.

"Kim!" yelled Marshal after seeing that she wasn't in her room.

Kim didn't even know that Richard just got chased out of the house and that Marshal was in the house, so she came out of the bathroom ass naked. Kim was shocked to see Marshal standing by her room door.

"What the hell are you doing here?" asked Kim going back into the bathroom.

"Why the Fuck you got this nigga in mommy's house after I just fought his ass and you got the nerve to be having sex with the guy!" yelled Marshal walking to the bathroom door, "I should whip your ass!"

"He's my man Marshal and I do what I please." Marshal was so mad at his sister that she could be so stupid at times.

"You know what? I got something for his ass," said Marshal leaving the house.

"Mom, look at Ronald's eye," were the first words that came out of Vanessa's mouth when the brother and sister came into the house.

"Oh My Gosh, what happened to my hijo?" asked their mom, speaking Spanish with a thick accent.

Their mom Mellisa was from Puerto Rico and moved to the United

States when Ron-Ron was born. Hoping to find a better life for her and her children, she found out that her life was ruined when she met their dad in Puerto Rico. The father came to the United States with Mellisa and his son Ronald who is a Jr., to come to have a better life with his family. After Mellisa had Vanessa, five years later, the abuse started to kick in on Mellisa. Ronald Sr. became a heavy drinker after he found out that his family got killed in a tsunami in Puerto Rico. Mellisa knew and felt his pain; she wished he didn't take it out on her as much.

"He was knocked out by Kim's boyfriend because he wants to sleep with her," said Vanessa feeling betrayed that Ron-Ron or Kim didn't tell her they were having sex.

"Are you okay?"

"Yeah, I'm good Mom, trying to just chill and go to my room," said Ron-Ron walking up the steps to his bedroom.

"Some girl name Shanay called for you a couple of minutes ago," said Mellisa.

"Shanay?" asked Ron-Ron, confused, wondering how she got his number.

"So, what's up with you, Sis? How was the first day at school?" Sabrina asked, talking to Shanay as she headed to the bathroom.

"It was crazy all day today. I swear I just wanted to kill someone today," said Shanay with hatred in her voice.

"Why, what happened?" asked Sabrina, missing half a day because Sabrina had got on her period, and it stained her favorite white pants.

She was so embarrassed that she walked all the way home by herself.

Shanay gives the rundown about the whole day to her getting choked by Ron-Ron, getting her ass whipped by Kim and all the fights that went down after school.

"Damn, that's crazy, so where is Ron-Ron at? Wasn't you talking to him in the summertime?" asked Sabrina.

"Nope, I'm not dealing with him. I'm waiting on…"

BEEP, BEEP, BEEP.

"Who's that?" asked Sabrina.

"My ride," said Shanay looking out the window.

"Tell mom I'll be home tonight, don't wait up for me," said Shanay throwing herself out the door.

When Sabrina looked out of the window, she saw some guy come pick her up and JT in the passenger seat. Sabrina already knew what was up and felt ashamed of what Shanay was doing. Sabrina grabbed the cordless phone, called her cheerleading friends, and told them to come over and chill with her because she was lonely. About a half-hour later, 3 or 4 of the friends from the cheerleading squad came over and started to gossip about guys in school. Sabrina started the conversation because she wanted to know a little more about Omar.

"I really can't see myself with none of the boys in school; they are not my type," said Sabrina.

"Well, I can. I want to just jump on Marshal's dick and ride that shit like a horse with no saddle!" said one of the cheerleaders while everybody started laughing.

Everybody agreed that Marshal looked good, even Sabrina.

"I heard Ron-Ron had a little dick," one of the cheerleaders said.

By this time, one of the cheerleaders, including Sabrina, was in the living room watching the Music Channel.

"I heard the same thing," another cheerleading said.

"Richard is cute in his own way, but what's that boy name that is cool with Ron-Ron?"

Sabrina knew that this was her time.

"Omar!" blurted out Sabrina before anybody could say something.

Everybody looked at her like she was crazy.

"Somebody must know of Omar," said one cheerleader.

"No, I just know that they are cool with each other, and they play football together, I think," said Sabrina.

"Yeah, yeah, well, I really don't hear about Omar's name like that until today when he got knocked out by Richard."

"Yeah, me neither. I think he's a good choice for you, Sabrina," said one of the cheerleaders.

"Yeah, he's cute; we'll see, we'll see," said Sabrina reminiscing about Omar.

"Do Marshal got a big dick?" asked the same cheerleader that said she wanted to ride his dick.

"You Fucking Freak," said Sabrina, all of the girls started laughing.

CHAPTER 3

The Good, The Bad and The Ugly

"You Mother Fucker!" Was screamed through the phone when Shanay picked up the phone; Shanay knew who it was when he said it.

"Bitch! What did you do to me?! My dick is burning!" yelled JT.

"Who you calling a Bitch!" said Shanay, not mentioning JT's other comment.

"Look, listen, come to my house, and we will talk about it. I'm around too many people to talk about that shit," said Shanay hanging up the phone.

Shanay was still burning, but she was taking pills for it. Shanay found out a couple of days ago and thought that Ron-Ron gave her Gonorrhea, but in all actuality, Shanay was messing with an older guy on summer break right before school started. She had sex with the older guy the same night she had sex with Ron-Ron.

Ten minutes later she got a phone call and it was Ron-Ron.

"Hello."

"These pills are not working and I'm burning Bitch."

"Listen, go to the doctor and let them know; they will take care of it, so stop calling my phone and stop calling me a Bitch, Bitch," said Shanay hanging up the phone.

Two seconds later, the phone rings.

"I told you to stop calling my Fucking phone Nigga! What?" Shanay knew it wasn't Ron-Ron from the voice over the phone, "who is this?"

"This is Cameron."

Shanay was wondering who the hell is Cameron. A long pause came upon them and Cameron spoke up.

"The boy that picked you up with JT."

Then Shanay realized that she just had a threesome with this guy and barely knew him.

"Oh, what's up, Cameron?"

"That's Fucked up how you burnt me like that; you could have warned a dude first," said Cameron.

"How could I warn you if y'all both was drunk? Y'all wouldn't have cared anyway."

"You don't know that."

"You wouldn't, especially when you were smacking my ass so hard."

Shanay was a sex addict and couldn't get enough of it. Shanay totally forgot that her sister and all her cheerleading friends were over at the house. She turned around to see if anybody had heard the conversation she had been having. When she turned around, everybody was looking at her. Shanay regretted going to the store for her mom and got the old school phone instead of the cordless her mom told her to get just so that she could have a couple more dollars in her pocket. Shanay felt so embarrassed that she wanted to cry right there.

The doorbell rang and broke the silence.

"I got to go; call me later," said Shanay hanging up the phone and answering the door; it was JT.

Shanay walked outside the house with JT and started walking up the street.

"Hold up, let me get something for you, and I will be back," said Shanay running back to her house.

All she heard was laughing when she went inside the house and as soon as she entered the laughing stopped. All eyes were on Shanay as she ran upstairs and got the pills; she came back downstairs and left the house. Shanay came out and gave the pills to JT.

"So, what's up?" asked Shanay.

"I'm burning; that's what's up. Damn that shit hurt."

"Yeah, I know," said Shanay tripping over her feet while they were walking.

"Oh shit." They both laughed and looked into each other eyes.

"Why do you do this?" asked JT with sincerity and love in his voice.

Shanay already knew what he was talking about.

"I don't know. Honestly, I'm lost. Every dude is the same. I figured I don't have no man, no feelings."

Shanay started to tear up and so did JT. Shanay didn't want to show her feelings to no man, so she stepped off.

"I'll talk to you later," said Shanay walking back to her house.

In all actuality, they both liked each other more than sex but could never say it to each other.

"Bye," said JT watching Shanay walk off, leaving him lonely.

SMACK! SMACK! SMACK! SMACK! SMACK! SMACK!

"I knew you Fucked him!" SMACK! "You really going to burn me tho Bitch!" SMACK! "Get the Hell out! I don't want you here; you lucky I don't kill you Bitch!" Richard yelled, trying to kick Kim out of her house.

Richard, so furious, didn't even realize that he was kicking her out of her own house until Marshal popped up from around the corner. Marshal saw Kim's face all bloody and Richard over top of her, smacking her repeatedly. Fire lit in Marshal's eyes as he grabbed the gun that one of his Blood friends gave him, and he shot one time, hitting Richard in his chest and making him fall on his back.

"NOOOOOO!" Kim yelled at the top of her lungs.

Kim looked around and saw her brother holding the gun in the air.

"Why did you do that?!" Kim hollered.

Kim leaned over Richard's body and began screaming for dear life, hoping her man didn't die.

"Help! Help! Somebody Please Help Me! Mom!!!" yelled Kim.

At the sound of that, Marshal ran and fled the scene. Neighbors came outside of their houses at the sound of the gunshot. One of the neighbors saw Marshal fleeing the scene and called the cops.

"I'm sorry," were Richard's last words before closing his eyes forever.

"Please, Babe, wake up. I can't lose you!" The neighbors surrounded the body as well as Kim.

After ten minutes of screaming and hollering, the paramedics and cops came to the scene. The cops had to pull Kim off of Richard's dead body. The paramedics tried their best to bring Richard back to life, but the bullet hit his heart directly in the middle of it. The cops questioned Kim after they calmed her down and called her mom. Kim was on the back of the ambulance truck with blood all over her. Non-stop crying, she kept playing the scene in her head.

"So, what happened here, Misses?" asked the detective, trying to get Kim's name.

"Can't you see she's still in shock of what happened? She is scared to death," said one of the paramedics that were trying to clean her face.

"I am obligated to question her before she leaves this scene."

"Well, she looks to be too young anyway, so wait for her mother to get home." The detective was mad that a paramedic was telling him what to do.

Five minutes later, Mellisa came running to the paramedics.

"Oh My God! What happen Baby?" Mellisa yelled, running over to her daughter's arms.

"Mom, he didn't mean to put his hands on me. He promised, he loved me… I should have never cheated," sobbed Kim, crying in her mother's arms.

"What happen Baby? Richard put his bands on you again? I told you don't mess with him. Where he at? I'm going to whip his ass myself," said Mellisa.

"No, Mom. He's dead," said Kim crying even more with a monster headache.

Mellisa had a surprised look on her face, not noticing all of the blood on her daughter's clothes.

"Where's Marshal?" asked Mellisa knowing that Marshal would have been home by now.

Kim didn't say anything. The detective came over and started questing Kim.

"How you doing Ma'am? I'm Detective Smith and I have a few questions for your daughter."

"Can you hurry up, please? My daughter is drained and she needs to be in the house."

"Okay. Can you just tell me what happened, please?" asked the detective holding a pen and pad in his hand. The detective was an old White guy with glasses and a suit on.

"Well, me and my boyfriend were arguing in the house and then we started fighting. One thing led to another and we were on the front porch and…" Were the words that she last spoke when she heard.

"There goes the shooter right there," said one of the neighbors, pointing at Marshal trying to get inside his house without being seen.

Marshal looked across his shoulder and saw the neighbor pointing at him. The cop ran over to where Marshal was at. Marshal ran and left the cops a couple of blocks away until one of the cops came up beside him, tossed him from the car, and locked Marshal up.

"So will you or what?" Damon asked, hoping that Vanessa would say yes.

Vanessa was under pressure because she was attracted to Omar but knew that Damon was just as good-looking as him, if not better.

"I don't know. Maybe, I mean, don't get it wrong, your hot, it's just that…"

"That you are taken or what?" asked Damon, getting aggravated that Vanessa was not trying to budge.

Damon has been trying to get with Vanessa since junior high, but he never had the courage to ask her until now.

"Never mind, I guess you are; I'll step," said Damon walking off down the hallway.

"No, wait," said Vanessa grabbing Damon's arm.

"Listen, you are a good guy; it's just that I mess with Alex, and I don't want to break his heart," said Vanessa letting go of Damon's arm.

"Well, when you feel like I'm worth your time, then come holla at me, but for now, can you just leave me alone?" asked Damon walking down the hallway, leaving Vanessa where she stood.

Vanessa leaned up against the lockers and started to think of which guy was best for her.

"Alex was her junior high sweetheart, and she always had love for him, but he never could please her like she wanted to be. He never gave her flowers and candy-like Damon did in junior high, and he never bought her anything like Omar did in the summer break." With all the thoughts running through her mind, the bell rang.

The classes let out and the first person that ran up to her was Alex.

"Hey Ma'am, what you doing?" Breaking Vanessa's train of thought.

Vanessa concluded that Alex wasn't the one for her because every time they see each other, Alex barely hugs her and he never kisses her in public as much as he does when they are alone.

"Hey Alex," said Vanessa in a dull voice.

"What's wrong mammy? Why you seem like you don't want to talk to me or something."

"Because I don't," Vanessa blurted out, not even meaning to say that out loud.

"Oh, you don't," said Alex with a look on his face as he didn't care.

"I do, but…," said Vanessa lost for words.

"No, you don't. You probably Fucking that nigga Omar, huh. Like I didn't see you in his car or something. You know what, I'm glad you broke up with me now. I don't have to lie to my real girlfriend anymore," said Alex walking off, leaving Vanessa at the lockers like Damon did.

Even though Vanessa didn't want to be with Alex anymore, she still cried because she still had feelings for him. Vanessa opened her locker and saw the picture of her and Kim on the inside of her locker door. Vanessa put her head inside her locker so no one could see her as she cried. Vanessa wondered where her best friend was when she needed her.

Vanessa seemed like she couldn't take it anymore when somebody put their hands in front of her eyes and said, "Guess who?"

Vanessa turned around and saw Omar smiling in her face. However, when Omar saw Vanessa's eyes all puffy and red, his smile turned upside down.

"What's wrong, V.?" Omar asked, wiping Vanessa's eyes with his shirt.

"Vanessa thought it was crazy that all the boys she thought of popped in her face back-to-back."

"Nothing," said Vanessa, lowering her head so that Omar couldn't see her face.

"Something's wrong; you are crying," said Omar picking Vanessa's head up with his two fingers and kissing Vanessa on the lips.

Vanessa's lips tingled as Omar kissed her.

"Everybody! Marshal killed Richard yesterday; it's all over the news!" yelled one of the students that went to Howard.

Vanessa was out of her fantasy that fast.

"Oh Shit, I got to go to Kim's house; I'll talk to you later," said Vanessa leaving Omar at Vanessa's locker.

"Wait. I'll take you," said Omar running after Vanessa.

Omar put the pedal to the metal, trying to get to Kim's house as fast as possible. Finally, Omar got to Kim's door, walking right into her house without knocking. Kim was in the middle of the living room talking to her mother when Vanessa rushed in, ran, and hugged her best friend. Tears ran down both of their faces as they embraced each other. Vanessa knew that her best friend was in pain losing her boyfriend and the one responsible for the murder was her brother. Vanessa knew that that was a hard pill to swallow. Richard had to have put his hands on Kim because she saw the busted lip, scratches, and black eye when Vanessa pulled back from her. Omar came into the house a few seconds later, and Kim had a surprised look on her face.

"So, what you think?"

A few weeks flew by and Kim was still depressed as ever. She was not coming outside of the house and not even going to school. Aairyah came to Kim's house every day with a dozen roses for the past three weeks. This was his 22nd day and he was not leaving without a fight. For the past three weeks, Kim would close the door in his face and shout, "LEAVE ME ALONE!" through the window. Or sometimes, she wouldn't even open the door. Her mom would try to cheer her up and all she would do was lock herself in her room. Kim's mom needed help, so she went to Vanessa, Kim's best friend, for help to try to cheer her up. Vanessa would come over sometimes if Kim would answer the door. Vanessa tried everything in her willpower to cheer Kim up, but Kim will not budge. Vanessa was all up Omar's ass and vice-versa that Vanessa stopped coming to Kim's house as frequently.

KNOCK, KNOCK, KNOCK, KNOCK, KNOCK.

Aairyah heard footsteps coming down the steps, but nobody answered the door. So Aairyah knocks on the door even harder.

BOOM! BOOM! BOOM! BOOM! BOOM! …A long pause startled Kim before she opened the door.

Aairyah bum-rushed into Kim's house without her saying any words.

"What are you doing?" asked Kim, stumbling backward.

Kim didn't really know Aairyah like that, but Aairyah didn't care. Kim knew that Aairyah was a sweet guy through all the little notes he had left on her steps inside the flowers. The "**I wish you come back to school**" notes or the "**Hope you feel better**" notes what was keeping Kim going as well. But Kim knew that she had been caught off guard wearing an XXL Nike t-shirt on that was Marshal. Nothing on underneath, Aairyah caught her at the right time for what he was about to about to do. Aairyah threw the flowers in her hand and closed the door behind him. Aairyah locked the door and looked in Kim's face as he grabbed her aggressively up off of her feet and into whatever room he assumed to be hers.

While going to the room, Kim screamed, "Get off of me! Help! Help!" Kim yelled, hoping Aairyah wasn't here to rape her, "please, Aairyah, don't rape me, please!"

Aairyah didn't care about what she was saying; he was going to come with what he thought that he deserves. So Aairyah threw Kim on the bed and when she tried to jump up, he held her down.

"Just stop; I'll show you," said Aairyah.

At this time, Kim was crying.

"I been through enough, can you..." That was all Kim said before Aairyah's head was down in between Kim's legs licking on her lips.

Kim never had her pussy licked, let alone her clit being played with, with nobody's tongue like Aairyah is doing now. The tears dried up and moaning became the noise of the empty house. Legs shivering and moaning coming out of her mouth, it wasn't long before Kim orgasmed all over Aairyah's lips and chin. Kim felt that just for those couple seconds, she orgasmed that she didn't feel any pain, hurt, or struggle. Kim felt like she was on top of the world and she felt some relief for a quick moment until Aairyah started licking some more and she closed her eyes even tighter. Crawling back from the tongue action that Aairyah gave her, Aairyah grabbed her legs and pulled her closer.

"OOOOOOOHHHH DAAAAMMMMMMMMMMM!" Kim shouted for yet another orgasm back-to-back.

Kim wanted Aairyah in her so bad that she pulled his head up from between her legs and up to her face and kissed him tasting her own juices for the first time. Aairyah, already hard, had no problem entering inside Kim's wet pussy. When Kim told him to take his pants off, Aairyah wasted no time taking his pants off and getting on top. Kim was used to just having sex, and sometimes she might climax here and there with Richard or Ron-Ron, but Aairyah had already put Kim in a world she had never been in. Aairyah entered inside of her and stroked her ever so softly, making her feel every inch of his manhood. Faster and faster, Aairyah wanted to orgasm, but he stopped and told her to get on her side. Aairyah got on the side of her and lifted her leg. When Aairyah does that, you can see the juices flowing down Kim's leg as Aairyah goes inside of her. Kim holding her leg up, Aairyah choked her ever so lightly. Stroking away faster and faster, Kim climaxed the same time Aairyah did.

Laying there in sweat and out of breath, Aairyah asked, "So, are you going to school?"

The following Monday, Kim walked down the hallway with Aairyah hand and hand.

"I'm kind of nervous, Aairyah."

"Why?"

"Because people might think of me differently. Like… I don't know, I'm just nervous," said Kim tightening her grip on Aairyah's hand.

"It's okay Baby, as long as you got me, you don't have to worry," said Aairyah kissing Kim on the lips.

Kim fell in love with Aairyah the same night he made her orgasm. Kim loved that Aairyah was there for her no matter what, which was one reason she fell in love with him so fast.

"Kim, if you don't feel well after first period, come talk to me. I'll be in Mr. Miles's class; just come get me and I'll be there for you," said Aairyah giving Kim another kiss.

"Okay A., I will.

"Okay," said Aairyah walking to his classroom.

Kim walked to her class, but before she got there, she saw Damon at his locker getting his books out for class.

"Hey Damon," said Kim leaning up against one of the lockers.

Damon, not paying her no mind and said, "Hey."

"What's wrong? Are you okay?" When Damon looked up, he saw Kim, and it opened his eyes.

"Damn, hey Kim, how are you?" Damon asked, hugging Kim.

"I'm good; how are you?"

"I'm good, I'm good. I heard you were coming to school today."

"Yeah, yeah, I had to."

"So where is my best friend at? You know I didn't see him in like a week or something?"

"He's in Mr. Miles's class. But, hey, did you see Vanessa?" That triggered fuel in Damon and brought back why Damon was mad.

"Yeah, I saw her. Omar just dropped her off in front of the school. You probably catch her in front waiting for Omar to park his car," said Damon with hate in his voice.

"Okay, I'm going to try and catch her; I'll see you later," said Kim walking to the main entrance.

"Okay, bye," said Damon walking to the end of the hallway watching as Kim went up and hugged Vanessa when they met at the door.

Damon hated Omar for stealing the girl he loved, but he had a plan to win Vanessa over.

"Hey GIIIIIIRRRRLLL, what the Fuck is up?" Vanessa asked, hugging her best friend.

"Nothing much; what's up with you?"

"Nothing, just happy to see you. About time you got out of the house. So, I'm guessing all them damn roses took up so much space that you had to leave the house," said Vanessa remembering all them damn roses she saw every time she would go over there.

"Yeah, something like that," said Kim smiling at her friend like she had something on her mind.

"SOOOOOO," said Omar.

"Oh, my fault Babe. Kim, this is Omar, Omar this is Kim."

"Yeah, I know her," said Omar telling Vanessa.

Omar remembered the story's that Ron-Ron used to tell him about her.

"How you know me?" asked Kim.

"Well, I don't know you, but I heard about you."

"Oh, okay, so what's up with you V.? What you been doing?" asked Kim.

"Babe, I'll catch you later; I'm going to walk Kim to her class," said Vanessa giving Omar a hug and a kiss before she walked off with her girl down the hallway.

"Look, Kim I'm sorry for not being there for you, but I've been stressing over this mother fucker Kim. Like people keep telling me that he mess with that cheerleader Bitch Sabrina and…" Vanessa paused for a little bit because she felt herself getting ready to cry.

Kim felt her pain because she knew how it felt when Richard cheated on her and she couldn't leave him because she was madly in love. Kim just thinking about Richard made her start to get emotional and seeing Vanessa starting to cry wanted Kim to cry, so Kim just hugged her.

"It's going to be okay, V., I know how you feel. You just… you just got to let him go if it's true. Don't be like me, V., learn from my mistakes," said Kim, still hugging Vanessa with tears coming down her face.

"But I know it's true; somebody put pictures in my locker with Omar and Sabrina kissing, and who knows what more they did," said Vanessa crying on her best friend's shoulder.

"So why didn't you show them to Omar and break up with his ass," said Kim breaking apart from their hug and looking Vanessa in her eyes, "don't be stupid like me, V., you deserve better. Don't be around here messing with the next man Bitch."

"He not the next man Bitch; he's my man," said Vanessa drying up her eyes.

"You thought he was your man; you don't need him V.; leave him alone; all he going to do is bring you down," said Kim grabbing the bottom of her t-shirt and wiping Vanessa's eyes.

Vanessa thought about what Kim said and knew her best friend was right.

"You're right; I'm done being lied to; it's time for a change," said Vanessa walking down the hallway with Kim.

"If he really loves you, he would have told you the truth; Fuck him V. I just don't want to see you go through the pain I went through," said Kim stopping at her class.

"Okay, I'm going to confront him after school; Kim, I'll catch you at lunch," said Vanessa.

"Ok Bitch," said Kim.

"Bye, Hoe," said Vanessa with a smile on her face walking down the hallway.

When Vanessa walked to her class, she had a letter and a bear with a heart in its hand saying, "I Love You." Vanessa went to her seat and picked up the letter.

Dear, Vanessa, I just wanted you to know that you will always be in my heart even though you are in love with Omar. I still got feelings for you a lot, and I was hoping when you are done with that dude or stuff doesn't work out, just know that I'll be here with open arms.

Sincerely yours truly, Damon.

Vanessa had to read the letter to fully understand the letter. She always knew that Damon was a sweetheart but never gave him a chance because she was always with Alex and now Omar. Damon was on Vanessa's mind all day that day and was waiting for the end of the day so she could confront Omar and let him know that she was done with him. A couple of periods flew by, and Vanessa saw Omar and confronted him right in the middle of the hallway.

"What's up Babe?" asked Omar.

"Look Omar we are done. Don't call me, don't text my phone or nothing; go be with that cheerleading Bitch!" Vanessa said and stormed off.

"Hold on, wait," said Omar, grabbing Vanessa's waist and pulling her closer to him, "what are you talking about?" asked Omar, thinking about how Vanessa found out about Sabrina.

"Follow me," said Vanessa.

Vanessa walked to her locker and Omar followed. Vanessa opened her locker and got the pictures that were from him and Sabrina kissing.

"Here, you cheater," said Vanessa with tears falling down her eyes, throwing the pictures at him and walked away.

Omar picked up the pictures and knew he was caught red-handed.

"He just wondered if Vanessa was really taking pictures of him or was it some dude or girl. Does Sabrina know about this? How will she act if she finds out?" A million questions ran through Omar's mind.

A month flew by and Vanessa took Damon up on his offer. After seeing Omar walk the hallways with Sabrina, Vanessa had to get some type of getting back at him. Every time Sabrina and Omar walked down the hallway, Vanessa would put Damon's hand on her ass and would kiss him in front of him so he would get jealous, which he did. It used to build a fire inside of Omar, knowing that Damon was having sex with Vanessa, knowing Damon should have been with her.

"Hey Vanessa?" Shanay asked, walking up to Vanessa's locker.

"Hey," said Vanessa wondering what Shanay wanted.

"I just wanted to say that it's no hard feelings between us," said Shanay holding her hand out to Vanessa.

Vanessa looked at her hand, thought about it for a minute, and then shook her hand.

"No hard feelings."

"Well, thank you because I'm in love with your brother Ron-Ron," said Shanay.

"You what?"

"Yeah, I'm in love with him, like he really knows how to treat a female," said Shanay.

Vanessa remembered her mom saying that Shanay had called for Ron-Ron before but thought nothing of it. Shanay talked Vanessa's head off that whole day about Ron-Ron and when the day was over, you heard Shanay call Vanessa, sis, at the end of the day. Kim overheard what Shanay said and wondered what she meant by saying that.

"She said sis to you?" Kim asked, walking behind Vanessa and going onto the school bus.

"Yeah, she talking about her messing with Ron-Ron and other bullshit."

"Oh, so what's that, your sis now?" Kim asked, catching feelings that Shanay was having sex with Ron-Ron and that she fought Shanay at the beginning of the school year.

"She cool, she a'ight."

"Oh, okay, if you say so," said Kim, still having feelings about Shanay.

CHAPTER 4

Virgin Island

"Damn Babe, this is so freaking beautiful. How did you know to bring me here?" Vanessa asked, getting off of the cruise ship.

"Well, you talked about going to an island for the longest why not go to five islands all in one week," said Damon grabbing Vanessa's hand as they walked across the sand in their sandals.

"So, what we going to do today?" asked Vanessa locking fingers with Damon.

"You'll see when we get there," replied Damon.

Vanessa and Damon walked down the beach and saw how the sunset looked so beautiful. After walking about 10 minutes, Vanessa saw a fire on the beach up ahead.

"Damn Babe, what you think happened up there?" Vanessa asked, squinting her eyes to see what it was that was up ahead.

"I don't know; let's go find out?" asked Damon looking curious to find out as well.

When Vanessa got close to the burning fire, all she could do was hug Damon because what was burning was charcoal that spelled, "I LOVE U VANESSA."

Vanessa was in tears of joy when she said, "I love you too Babe," getting guided by Damon.

A table was set up with a fancy white tablecloth over it with red roses in the middle on the other side of the fire. When they sat down, a woman and guy came from out of one of the restaurants that sat right on the beach. All Damon thought about was this was going so perfectly.

"Damn Babe. you did this for me?"

"Yeah, you mean the world to me Babe, and I am so glad that you are by my side, and I couldn't choose nobody better than you," said Damon leaning over the table and kissing Vanessa on the forehead.

Vanessa thought that she couldn't be in a better place.

"We have your two lobsters steamed like you asked," said the woman waiter.

"And here goes your fresh salad with a bottle of our finest wine," said the male waiter moving the flowers from the table and putting them on the floor, then placed the bottle of wine in the middle of the table.

"Thank you," said Damon tipping both of the waiters.

Damon didn't say anything the whole time he had the lobster in his face. They watched the sunset go down while their toes were in the sand; Vanessa loved it. After about a half-hour later, they heard the cruise ship's horn telling the passengers to board the boat.

"Come on, Babe, before they leave us," said Damon, throwing the money on the table, grabbing Vanessa's hand, and walking off to the boat.

"So, where else are we going?" asked Vanessa getting on to the cruise ship that holds up to a thousand people.

"Next trip is St. Thomas and believe me, we are going to have a blast. This whole week is about you; everything that you ever told me you wanted to do, we are going to do," said Damon.

"But how did you pay for this?"

"Don't worry about it Babe, just know I got this and can you do me a favor, please," said Damon giving Vanessa the room key.

"Anything for you, Daddy," said Vanessa getting the key from

Damon.

"It's getting colder out here; can you go get our coats while I order dessert for us?"

"Sure, Baby, I will," said Vanessa walking to the front of the boat where Damon had the Presidential Suite.

When she got in the room, she grabbed the coats off of the bed and saw a note on the bed before she headed out that said, "Babe, open the closet, and you will get your next clue."

All of this excited Vanessa and she went straight to the closet. When she opened the closet, there was a sexy red and black lingerie with her name sowed into it. Vanessa took off all her clothes, grabbed the lingerie off the hanger, and dropped another note. Vanessa bent down and grabbed the note.

The note stated, "So, I'm guessing you found the lingerie. Go to the refrigerator and your third clue will be in there."

Vanessa couldn't hold back her emotions; she was grinning from ear to ear. Vanessa grabbed the lingerie and put it on. When Vanessa looked in the mirror and posed, the lingerie had Vanessa's name sowed in the middle of her stomach, and her breast was cut out, showing her perky breast. The lingerie stopped at the bottom of her navel, showing off her well-groomed vagina. Vanessa went to the bed and opened the fridge that was the size of two microwaves stacked on top of each other. It was a bowl filled with chocolate and a can of whip cream next to it. Under the whip cream bottle was another note.

"It is strawberries inside of the chocolate bowl; put everything on you want me to lick off of you and put it where you want me to lick it off."

Vanessa was aroused at the situation and how her man put this together for her. Vanessa grabbed the chocolate and smeared it all over her breast as well as her vagina. Then squirting the whipped cream on her breast as well as her vagina and placing the chocolate-covered strawberries on top of the whipped cream as she laid down on the bed.

Anticipating his arrival, Vanessa started to feel butterflies in her stomach, knowing that Damon would be here any minute to lick all of this whipped cream off her body. As Vanessa expected, Damon came into the room and went right to work. Vanessa had her arms spread out like she was saying, *"What you going to do with this."*

Damon didn't say a word with his erection already from popping a vagina. Damon took all of his clothes off and jumped right on top of Vanessa, kissing her on the lips. Kissing her neck and down to her breast. Juices were already coming out of Vanessa's cookie from Damon licking the whipped cream off Vanessa's breast and eating the strawberries. Vanessa could feel Damon's hard erection going across her leg as Damon was licking the last bit of chocolate off Vanessa's breast. Vanessa's pussy was screaming for Damon's dick to go inside her, so she grabbed his manhood and put it inside her soaking wet vagina.

Vanessa's pussy was still covered in chocolate, whipped cream, and strawberries, but Vanessa didn't care; she wanted him in. Damon didn't ask any questions at all; what he did was put Vanessa's legs on his shoulders and started stroking away, sending whip cream everywhere. Vanessa never felt Damon this hard and it made his climax as fast as he nutted. Vanessa pushed Damon on his back and grabbed one of the strawberries that were on the bed that fell off of her vagina and put it in her mouth. Vanessa's mouth was full of strawberry juice; she put her mouth on Damon's head of his dick and let the juice pour down his dick. Vanessa grabbed the whipped cream and sprayed it over Damon's dick and threw the whipped cream. Vanessa licked all of the cream off of Damon's dick and started to suck the tip of Damon's head while playing with his nuts.

Letting the saliva flow down his dick, Vanessa began to suck Damon's dick, bobbing her head back and forth while still playing with his balls. Vanessa had the bed cocking how fast she was sucking Damon's dick by this time. Damon grabbed Vanessa's head after 10 minutes because he didn't want to nut in Vanessa's mouth.

Cum went up in the air and landed on the bed. By the time the cum touched the covers, Vanessa was on top of Damon, riding him with her ass slamming on Damon's dick up and down. Vanessa grabbed Damon's legs as she swung her ass up and down. Damon grabbed her ass cheeks and looked at the tattoos covering her body. When Vanessa saw Damon looking at her tattoos, she turned towards him and started riding him from the front. Damon grabbed Vanessa towards him and bear-hugged her. Damon positioned himself to Fuck Vanessa's brains out, which he did, stroking faster and faster while holding Vanessa to his chest, so she doesn't move. Vanessa climaxed again and again in the same position until her pussy started to ache in pain rather than pleasure.

"Babe hold on," said Vanessa feeling exhausted and dehydrated.

When Vanessa said that, she passed out in Damon's arms, full of sweat. Damon didn't say anything but put his head back and went to sleep.

"Hi, how are you doing?" asked an unknown man walking up to Vanessa from behind.

Vanessa turned around and her panties got moist from the look at this man's body in which he had his shirt off.

"Yes?" asked Vanessa blushing.

"Will you like to take this dance?" Holding his hand out for her to come to the dance floor.

It was nine at night and Vanessa was on the top floor. The cruise ship was having a party on the top floor and on the floor right below it was a casino which Damon was at. Damon took a tour around St. Marks for Vanessa today and thought about partying at night. The only thing was Damon didn't make it upstairs yet because he had been gambling for about an hour already, telling Vanessa he would meet her up there.

"Ummmmm." Vanessa thought about it and came up with her answer after looking at her ring.

"No, sorry, I'm waiting on my husband to come up here," said Vanessa showing her ring off.

"I been across the room and seen you been sitting here for the longest; you sure he coming?" Vanessa couldn't keep her eyes off of this guy's body and he noticed that already.

"Yeah, he's coming," said Vanessa looking around the room for her man.

"Well, can I get your name then, Mrs.?"

"You can call me Vanessa; Mrs. is not there yet; we're engaged."

"Oh, okay, my name is Jermaine."

Pumping his chest one by one, then both at a time. Vanessa always thought that was funny to her, but she never saw it in person.

"You can touch it; it won't bite," said Jermaine.

"I don't think that is a good idea," said Vanessa taking another sip of her Moscato.

Jermaine grabbed her hand and rubbed it against his ripped abs, making her touch every muscle on his stomach. Damon came upstairs and caught her in the moment of her touching his abs.

"So, what's going on over here?" asked Damon with a bottle of Corona in his hand.

When Vanessa heard the sound of her fiancé's voice, she immediately grabbed her hand back.

"It wasn't like that, Babe, I swear," said Vanessa getting up from the chair she was sitting in.

"Why the Fuck you got your hand on this nigga body?" Damon said, getting madder and madder at the moment.

"Hey man, stop cussing at her," said Jermaine putting his hand up to tell him to stop.

Damon smacked Jermaine in the head with the Corona and punched him in the face sending him to the floor. Security guards broke up the fight before it could even start, throwing Damon out of the club part of the cruise. Vanessa followed the security guards out of the top floor not before looking back and seeing Jermaine holding his head and looking at Vanessa.

"I'm sorry," said Vanessa running after her man.

The security guard came back inside and Vanessa went out, trying to catch up to her man.

"Babe! Babe! Can you please stop!" Vanessa yelled, tripping over her heels, "it wasn't like that, like what the Fuck!" said Vanessa grabbing Damon's hand.

"Then what was it like than V.?" Damon asked with tears coming down his face.

"Babe, he grabbed my hand and put it to his body. I didn't do it on my own."

"So, what's that supposed to make a difference? I saw you smiling from ear to ear when you were touching him; you must of liked it," said Damon.

Vanessa wiped the tears from Damon's eyes and said, "Babe," picking Damon's head up and looking into his eyes, "nobody will come in front of you. Nobody."

"I... I... I." In between sobbing like a girl.

"That doesn't make it okay for you to do that," said Damon walking off to the bedroom, and Vanessa followed.

Damon knew he couldn't break up with her even if he wanted to. He put too much money on this cruise and relationship alone that he can't break up with her. Damon got in the room and got in the shower. Vanessa tried to go into the bathroom behind Damon, but he closed the door in her face. It startled Vanessa, making her jump. Vanessa took off all her clothes and got in bed naked. Damon took so long in the shower that he saw his soon-to-be wife sound asleep when he got out. Damon cried in the shower and felt relieved that the weight was off his shoulders, but he never forgot all the little shit that Vanessa put him through. Damon walked to their bed and went fast to sleep. Damon woke up to catch himself moaning. Vanessa was sucking his dick to wake Damon up. Vanessa was out of the shower fully dressed, sucking Damon's dick. Making the loudest slurping noises turned Damon on.

"You like that Shit, Daddy?" Vanessa asked, catching her breath as she continued to jerk and suck Damon's dick.

Damon didn't say anything but released his kids in Vanessa's mouth.

"Babe," said Vanessa after running to the bathroom to spit out her man's semen.

"That shit is nasty."

"Sorry, can I get some ass?" Damon asked still horny.

"No, then we got to take a shower again, and the next island is about to come up…"

"Attention all passengers. We have pulled up to Jamaica and you have 6 hours on this beautiful island before we take off to the next island. Thank you and have a wonderful time." It was over the cruise intercom. Damon forgot about last night and got up from bed.

"Come on, Babe, I got a surprise for you," said Damon throwing on his clothes and going out the door faster than a crackhead that just got beat, pulling Vanessa's hand to come along.

Damon and Vanessa got off the cruise boat and headed to the first taxi parked for visitors to come off of the boat. They got in the taxi and Damon pulled a piece of paper out.

"Take us to Galloway Parkway," said Damon putting his piece of paper back in his pocket.

"Where are we going, Babe?"

"You'll see when we get there," said Damon, a little nervous about what was coming up because neither one of them did this, but Vanessa always asked Damon about doing it but never had the chance to do it.

Now was their chance to do it and Damon was going to get it done no matter how much fear he had. He was going to make his wife's dream come true. The taxi pulled up to an empty field with an airplane in the center of it. Damon tips the taxi and gets out of the car.

"What are we doing here?"

"You'll see," said Damon with a grin on his face.

Vanessa and Damon got on the airplane and flew in the air thousands of feet.

"You remember what your wish was to do?"

"I know we are not about to jump off this plane?" asked Vanessa.

"Yup," said Damon with a smile on his face.

"Babe, it was just a wish. It wasn't for real. I'm too scared to jump off," said Vanessa. Damon was also scared, but he didn't pay this money for no reason.

"You are going to be fine," said Damon as he and she got strapped to one of the professional skydivers.

"Babe come on, please don't make me do this," said Vanessa.

"You're going to be fine."

The door opened and the wind started to hit their face. Vanessa went to the door and looked down, and when she did, Damon tackled her and the professional skydiver out of the airplane door.

"BAAAABBBBBEEEEE!" said Vanessa with her hands in the air like superman. Vanessa never stopped smiling the whole time in the air.

"Babe, I fucking love you!" said Vanessa acting like she was swimming to go to Damon. They locked hands and kissed.

"I love you too!" said Damon; after about a thousand feet left, the parachute went up, and Damon told Vanessa to look down.

When Vanessa looked down, she saw how beautiful Jamaica really was. She saw the beautiful clear water on which the cruise ship was setting on. She saw the buildings that were set in the heart of Jamaica. When she saw what she was about to land on made her even happier. In red roses spelled "I LOVE VANESSA." Vanessa landed right on the heart and so did Damon. When Damon dropped, Vanessa ran over to Damon and grabbed his face.

"I love you Babe," said Vanessa kissing Damon.

"I love you more Babe. Do you want to go on the boat, or do you want to chill here on the island a little bit longer?" asked Damon looking into Vanessa's eyes.

"Let's do whatever you want to do?" asked Vanessa letting go of Damon's face and grabbing his hand.

"Okay, come on," said Damon taking off his shirt and running to the ocean.

Damon ran into the ocean and started swimming. Vanessa took her shirt off, showing her Victoria's Secret lingerie. Swimming to wear Damon was, Vanessa went underwater, pulling Damon's shorts down. Damon pulled Vanessa back up.

"Babe, this water is clear people can see you," said Damon looking around.

"Oh, I didn't know," said Vanessa getting the water out of her eyes.

"This feels so good, Babe. Just floating in this beautiful water and with my soulmate, you know what I'm saying, Babe."

"Yeah, I just wish..."

BBBBBBRRRRNNNN! BBBBBBRRRRNNNN!. The sound of the cruise ship blasting through the air.

"Come on, Babe, before we get left," said Vanessa, swimming back to the shore.

Damon didn't even finish his sentence because of the horn. He met Vanessa on the shore, and they grabbed their clothes and headed to the cruise ship. On the cruise ship, Damon and Vanessa took a shower and sat back to watch a movie in their room until Damon's phone went off.

"Hello."

"Hello, Mother Fucker. I been calling you for the past two hours; where the Fuck are y'all?" asked a female voice that sounded familiar to Vanessa, but she couldn't really hear because Damon got up from the bed and went to the bathroom.

"My fault, we went sky diving but can you set it up for me because that's a girl thing and pick what kind of dress but make sure it's the same color as mine tho," said Damon after hearing what the other person said over the phone.

"Okay, bye. We will be there tomorrow morning; just make sure that you are going to get it done okay." After a couple of seconds went by, he said goodbye and went to the room.

"Who was that?" said Vanessa leaning up from the bed.

"Can't get," said Damon in a Chinese voice.

"Can't get?" asked Vanessa confused, laying on Damon's chest as he laid down.

"Can't you get out of my business," said Damon, chuckling.

"I'm serious; who was it?"

"Your mom," Damon laughed again.

"Okay then," said Vanessa thinking Damon was playing, but he was dead serious.

Damon and Vanessa fell asleep to the movie American Wedding. Damon woke Vanessa up by licking her pussy like a cat drinking milk. Spreading her lips with his finger, Damon played with Vanessa's citreous with his tongue untiled she jumped back from him, exploding all over the sheets and laying in a fertile position, trying to get that tingle sensation last.

"Bring your ass over here and let me get some of that Daddy Dick," said Vanessa grabbing Damon's pants and pulling him onto the bed.

"Hold on, let me take my clothes off," said Damon getting up from the bed.

"Ahaa, Ahaa, nope, you did it to me yesterday, so I'm doing it to you today. Bring your ass on; I got a surprise for you all day," said Damon.

"You suck," said Vanessa.

"Next stop Bermuda and it looks like we stopped, so put your clothes on, and I'll be waiting for you outside. Oh yeah, make sure you leave any devices in the drawer like we did yesterday because we will be getting wet," said Damon walking out of the room and closing the door.

Vanessa got up, put her clothes on, and put her cell phone in the drawer. After looking at her cell phone, Vanessa noticed that she didn't have any calls or texts while on the cruise. Vanessa grabbed Damon's phone out of the drawer and looked in his call log.

She saw her mom's number and thought to herself, *"Why they were talking in private."*

Keeping a mental note about it, Vanessa sat her phone down and headed out the door, where she saw Damon putting on a life jacket. Vanessa came down the ramp and greeted the instructor, who told them the rules. Vanessa was overwhelmed because everything that she wanted to do for fun; this man had done in a week.

"Thanks Babe, I appreciate everything you did for me and I hope you can forgive me for anything I ever did to you."

Damon didn't want to be emotional, so he just said, "Your welcome," and handed her the keys to the jet ski and told her, "the last one to the jet ski is a rotten egg."

Vanessa loved Damon because he always knew how to have fun and be funny at the same time. Vanessa ran past Damon and Damon tackled her in the sand and ran for the jet ski.

"You lose," said Damon bouncing around and pointing at Vanessa, who was still on the floor.

"I see how we are playing it," said Vanessa getting up and going to the jet ski.

"I still love you."

Kissing Vanessa and smacking her ass as she steps out of her clothes and into her bathing suit.

"Come on, Babe, the pink one is yours; we are going to be jet skiing today," said Damon hopping on the jet ski next to hers.

Vanessa hops on the jet ski and starts it.

"Babe, it got a little kick to it, so when you start it be careful," said

Damon starting his jet ski and taking off a couple of feet ahead and turning around so his fiancé could catch up.

Vanessa hit the clutch on the jet ski and flew past Damon.

"The last one to the store and back is a rotten egg," said Vanessa laughing the whole time.

There was a water ice stand in the middle of the sea not too far out from the shore where people who were driving jet skis got a free water ice. The water ice stand was held on logs of wood with a rope ladder that hung down from it. Two jet skis were parked beside it that the workers drove. Vanessa went around the water ice stand and back to shore. Damon didn't catch up to her until he got to shore.

"You cheated," said Damon getting close to Vanessa.

"You always cheat, so I don't care," said Vanessa peeling off and going to the ocean again.

Damon and Vanessa were riding the jet skis all day and eventually stopped and got water ice.

"So, what's the plan for tonight?" asked Vanessa eating the water ice on the jet ski slowly going to the shore.

"You'll see," said Damon doing the same as Vanessa right beside her.

"Are we staying on this island are what? Because I heard over the intercom that we were staying overnight."

"Yeah we are. As a matter of fact, we got to get in the shower and get dress because I got a surprise for you," said Damon pulling up to the shore.

"Okay," said Vanessa getting off of her jet ski and going towards the cruise ship.

"Let me get your key, so I can turn our jet skis in."

"Okay, Daddy," said Vanessa throwing her keys to Damon and waking towards the cruise ship.

"I'll meet you inside, Babe," said Vanessa; Damon nodded his head as he went to the booth to return his keys.

When he came back to the cruise ship and inside his room, Vanessa was in the doggy-style position with whipped cream over her vagina. Vanessa looked back and smacked her ass to tell Damon to come and get it. Damon walked over and started to eat Vanessa's pussy from the back. Licking all of the whipped cream off, Damon stuck his finger in Vanessa's ass while eating the pussy.

After about 10 minutes, Vanessa felt her orgasm coming, and her legs got weak. Damon went faster, forcing Vanessa's legs to give out on her as she dropped to her stomach. Damon got on top of her and spread her ass cheeks as he entered inside of her. Wearing Vanessa out for what seemed like a half-hour, Damon ejaculated inside of Vanessa. Damon kissed Vanessa and smacked her ass as he got up from the bed.

"Come on, Babe, let's take a shower," said Damon going inside the bathroom.

Inside of the shower, Damon told his secret.

"Babe, what if we get married tomorrow? What would you say?"

"We can get married whenever you want to, Babe; just know my girls got to be there, so tomorrow can't happen, but if we could, I would love that."

Damon didn't say anything else and neither did Vanessa they got out of the shower and got dressed.

"So, where we going at now?" asked Vanessa.

"You ask too many questions. Babe, just come on," said Damon handing Vanessa her phone and grabbing his as he left the room.

Damon grabbed a taxi and went to the best hotel Bermuda has to offer; entering inside it, Damon had a registration for two already. Both of the rooms were on the same floor.

When they got to their floor, Damon handed her the key and said to her, "Your surprise is across this door. I love you and see you tomorrow."

"Tomorrow? What are you talking about?" asked Vanessa, confused as ever.

"You'll see. Trust me. I love you," said Damon walking down the hall as he gave her a kiss.

Vanessa opened the door and turned on the lights.

"Surprise!" Everybody in the room screamed.

Vanessa had water coming down her eyes as she saw everyone in the room. Sabrina, Shanay, Kim, Mellisa, and a couple of her high school friends were in the room.

"O.M.G., what the hell are you guys doing here?" asked Vanessa, blushing and putting her hand over her mouth.

"We're here to celebrate your bachelorette party and your wedding tomorrow," said Kim, the first one hugging her.

"Don't worry; I was the one who picked your dress out. Well, you picked it out. I just remembered which one you liked," said Kim.

Vanessa went around and hugged everybody. Vanessa still had a grudge against Sabrina for messing with Omar but forgot about it over the years.

"Cut the small talk; let's get the party started," said Shanay dimming the lights and cutting the music on.

Kim grabbed Vanessa's hand and sat her down on the couch.

Two male strippers came out of the backroom with police uniforms and firefighters. One of the males was a dark chocolate man who looked like Tyrese, the singer, and the other male was brown skin which he looked like Chris Brown. Both of the men were extremely built, taking off their clothes. The female surrounded the men throwing dollar bills at them.

"You guys are crazy," said Vanessa putting a dollar bill in one of the men's trousers.

"This is the shit, man. We all the way on the island with these island bitches throwing money, getting drunk, and having fun," said Ron-Ron wrapping his arm around Damon.

Ron-Ron was drunk before the party started and the party started way before Damon even got there.

"Ayo, you crazy as hell for getting married, my nigga. You sure you want to do this?" asked Aairyah.

"Yeah, man, you know that's my heart. I'll do anything for that girl, plus if Kim proposed to you, I wouldn't have said no," said Damon throwing the money at the stripers and clapping her ass on the floor.

"Yeah you right. I just hope she don't ask. Anyway, which one you Fucking tonight?" asked Aairyah.

Damon looked around the room and saw Omar throwing money and Ron-Ron smacking the other girl's ass.

"My girl will kill me if she found out that I had sex with one of these girls," said Damon throwing more ones.

"She not going to know."

Damon second-guessed it and concluded, "Nah, man, I can't do it. I'm in love with Vanessa, man; she will kill me."

Aairyah picked one of the girls off the floor and handed her to Damon. The stripper looked like Jennifer Lopez with a body like Pinky, the porno star. The only difference was that the stripper was 5'11. The stripper had a white one-piece see-through tight-fitted suit on. You could see her nipples and in the back of the suit was a thong instead of covering her ass. She had a tattoo that said, "GIVE IT TO ME DADDY" on her ass when she turned around to Damon. The stripper grabbed Damon's hand and pulled him to the bathroom.

"So, you getting married, huh?"

"Yeah, I am," said Damon.

"Well, let me show you what you going to be missing the whole time with your sexy ass," said the stripper kneeling down and unzipping Damon's pants.

Pulling Damon's dick out from his pants, the stripper started sucking Damon's dick, getting him rock hard. Grabbing Damon's dick from the head, the stripper licked from his balls up to the top of Damon's dick. Putting his dick back in her mouth and started sucking some more. After about five minutes more, the stripper got up and went to the sink. She put her leg up on the sink and told Damon to come here. Damon did as he was told and the stripper grabbed Damon's dick and put it inside her already wet pussy, pushing the suit to the side so Damon could enter inside her.

Damon got inside of the stripper and started stroking. Damon stroked even faster, grabbing the leg that was propped up and the other hand grabbing her breast.

Damon thought to himself, *"this was the best pussy he had since high school."*

Damon stroked and stoked until he nutted and hurried up and pulled out of her before he nutted inside of her, busting on the stripper's ass and smacking it after he was done.

"Thank you," said the stripper.

"No, thank you," said Damon zipping his pants back up.

"So, what you going to do after this?" asked the stripper wiping the semen off her ass.

"Go to sleep. What you going to do?"

"Hopefully, go to sleep with you," said the stripper.

"What if my girl finds out? She will kill both of us," said Damon in a serious voice.

"Y'all can't see each other until y'all say I do. She not going to find out. I promise I will make it your dream come true."

"Okay then," said Damon going to the living room where Ron-Ron was passed out, and Aairyah and Omar were in the other room with the other stripper.

"You want to join them?" asked Damon talking to the stripper as they looked in the other room and saw Omar pumping the other stripper from the back while Aairyah was getting some head.

Sabrina walked into the room and saw Vanessa laid up with the stripper that looked like Tyrese. Sabrina couldn't believe it, but it wasn't her relationship, so she didn't say anything. Sabrina woke Vanessa up and told her to come and get her ass up. Vanessa forgot that she had passed out and went to sleep but didn't know how the stripper was lying next to her. Vanessa got up and saw that the stripper was naked, but Vanessa wasn't. Sabrina, Shanay, and Kim woke up at the same time and were up and ready before Vanessa was even up. Vanessa came out of the room and saw everybody eating breakfast.

"Hurry up Girl, we all got an appointment at the nail salon up the street in 10 minutes," said Shanay eating her breakfast.

By the time Vanessa was done brushing her teeth and washing her face, they were out the door. After getting their eyebrows and nails done, all the girls went to the massage parlor after the nail salon. The girls were lined up in a row, getting a massage as they talked.

"So, Girl, are you ready for this shit?" asked Shanay taking the towel off her head and getting on the bed next to the other girls.

"Yeah, I'm ready. I think," said Vanessa.

"You think?" asked Sabrina.

"I mean, I know I love this man and all, but it came too fast. He proposed to me a couple of days ago and we getting married already. Like it was just too fast."

"It isn't too fast; you just got to know when and how long is it going to take you been with this guy eight years, right? So, what you got to think about? He did all this for you. It ain't too many good men out there, Baby," said Mellisa.

"She's right," said Kim.

"I know, I know I'm just… I'm young."

"You young, yeah, but what you want to do keep partying and partying until you catch something and lose everything," said Mellisa.

"Maybe you right, Mom."

"I am right; you love this man, right?"

"Yeah, you should know that."

"So, what are you questioning yourself for?"

"We got are cuts, are tuxes, and we down to for," said Aairyah going to the limo.

"You a Clown," said Omar laughing.

"You, we only got 30 minutes to get to the wedding hurry this shit up," said Damon.

The limo driver put the pedal to the floor and went to the wedding in 10 minutes flat. There was no wedding rehearsal that everybody went to, so they played it out however they wanted to. Everybody was set up because the only person in the audience was Mellisa. Everybody else was either behind Damon or behind Vanessa.

The vows were given, and before Damon said, "I do," Aairyah blurted out sucker, and it was Damon's best man, so only Damon could hear. Aairyah chuckled and so did Damon before saying, "I do." Damon and Vanessa kissed, and Mellisa took pictures as they kissed.

"We going on our honeymoon now," said Vanessa.

"Yeah, after we hurry up and catch that cruise before they leave our ass," said Damon laugh grabbing Vanessa's ass as he kissed her one last time.

CHAPTER 5

Men Lie, Women Lie

"Hey Beautiful," said JT going up to Trish and giving her a kiss and a hug.

"Hey," said Trish with a huge smile on her face.

"What are you so happy about?" asked JT letting go of Trish and walking her up to M&T Bank from the parking lot.

"Just happy to see you, that's all. I just wish we can stop doing this shit and live life like a normal couple," said Trish holding hands as they walked into the bank.

"You know we can't, Cameron will kill us both, and I'm not even supposed to be doing this." When Trish said that, JT automatically backed off.

"So, you not man enough to stand up for the woman you so-called love, but you will rather live like a coward and hide behind his back. You do love me, right? Right?" Trish faced forward up because JT didn't respond fast enough.

"Do you?"

"Yeah, you know that it's just that this is my best friend since I could remember and we both are going behind his back," said JT letting go of Trish's hand as they entered the bank.

"You don't think this is wrong?" asked JT.

"Yeah, it is, but I think about you all the time and I can't get you out of my mind. Every time me and Cameron are having sex, I close my eyes and think about you going inside me," said Trish with her eyes watering up.

"What, I'm not good enough. Am I ugly to you are something?" asked Trish wiping her eyes.

JT knows that she was nowhere near ugly. Standing at 5'9, caramel complexion with a smile like Kim Kardashian and a face like Amber Rose. Not to mention her sizes were 38, 30, 36. Weighting 170, all the weight went to all the right places with a flat stomach.

"No, you just…" JT paused and looked around and saw everybody at Trish's job was looking at them.

"We will talk about it later. Call me on your break," said JT kissing Trish and heading out of the bank.

JT knew he couldn't do that to his best friend, but he was already screwing her for the longest now, and Trish got too much involved than what JT expected. As soon as JT got in his car, his phone rang.

"What's good Nigga?" It was Cameron on the other line.

"What's up Homie? What you doing?"

"Shit, I just came back from that cruise ship with my co-workers. But tell me why Trish found them movie tickets."

"Yeah."

"Yeah, man and you know my plan to do with these niggas we fought in school."

"You was telling me, but I was distracted. What was the plan?" JT was distracted because Trish was giving JT head.

"You will soon find out. I got close to Vanessa, but that nigga Damon got next to us too soon."

"He didn't recognize you?"

"Nah, it was freshman year when I left. I doubt if he will remember, but the dude hit me in my head with a glass bottle."

"Damn, why what happen?"

"Because I had his girl touching my stomach. It's a long story, but he split the top of my head open a little bit."

"Damn, you good? Did Trish see the split in your head?"

"Yeah, I'm good and Trish didn't see it yet."

"Oh, that's good then."

"Yeah, me and Kim got a date at Red Lobster, and she said it was going to be worth coming for," said Cameron.

"Yeah."

"Yeah."

"Alright, that's all it is. Call me and tell me how that go."

"Alright one," said Cameron.

"One," said JT hanging the phone up and leaving the bank parking lot.

Going to the state penitentiary where JT was a sergeant, JT got a text message that said, **"I want some Daddy."** The text message was from Shanay.

After all these years, JT was still in love with Shanay. JT knowing she gets around town quite frequently, he would still put the ring on her finger and go to another state where nobody knows them.

JT texted her and said, **"I'm just now pulling up to my job. Baby, can you wait for me?"**

JT didn't get a response, so he knew that the waiting game was out of the picture. JT didn't hear a response all day from Shanay, but he did get a call after he got off of work.

Not even looking at the caller ID on his phone, JT picked the phone up, saying, "Hey Baby."

"Hey Babe. You seem happy to hear from me?" It was Trish.

Trish knew when JT got off work and what time he got in the house.

"Yeah, of course I'm happy to hear from you. Why wouldn't I be?" asked JT wishing it was Shanay on the other line.

"Because of the argument we had this morning."

"Oh Nah, I'm not worried about that; it's okay," said JT, hearing a beep in his ear. Looking at the phone, it was Richard's brother Ryan.

"Oh ok, well, where you going now?"

"I'm going home now. Why?"

"I'll meet you there then," said Trish hanging the phone.

JT clicked over to the other line.

"YOOOOO," said Ryan.

"Yo, what's up?" asked JT.

"You seen that bitch ass nigga Marshal in there today?" asked Rayan.

"Nah, I didn't see him today. He in the hole for beating up one of my guards," said JT.

"Oh yeah."

"Yeah, he suppose to be coming home soon too. He only had 10 years."

"Yeah, I know. I can't wait to see him."

"Yo, let me call you right back. My other line is going off like crazy."

"A'ight Nigga peace."

"Peace," said JT.

Nobody was on the other line; JT just didn't want to be in any type of violence. Especially nothing to do with murder. JT pulled up to his house and saw Trish parked on the phone in front of his house. JT opened the driver's door of Trish's car while she was on the phone.

"Okay, Babe, I'll be home in a half-hour damn. Where the hell is you?" asked Trish on the phone.

"What you mean, don't worry about it? You know what you got it… Okay then bye… Love you too," said Trish hanging the phone up.

"Hey, Baby," said Trish getting out of her car and hugging Jt.

Trish loved when JT had his uniform on. It always turns her on.

"Hey Babe," said JT grabbing her hand and walking to the front door and opening it.

As soon as they walked into the house, JT's phone rang. It was Cameron.

"It's your man," said JT.

"Well, pick it up," said Trish.

JT picked the phone up and said, "What's good Nigga?"

"Shit, I need you real quick."

"What's up?"

"Matter of fact, I'm about to pull to your crib now. Open the door." JT's heart dropped.

"How you know I'm home?"

"Because I'm looking at your car and I'm getting out of mind."

JT hung the phone up and ran upstairs. JT ran to his room and saw Shanay ass naked on the bed with her legs wide open.

"I been waiting for this dick all day," said Shanay patting her pussy after licking her fingers and spreading he pussy lips showing her bright pink pussy.

JT was stuck wondering how Shanay got into his house, forgetting that he had given her a set of his keys.

"Hold on, I'll be right back," said JT going out of the room and closing the door behind him.

BOOM! BOOM! BOOM!

Trish ran up the stairs and met JT in the middle of the hallway.

BOOM! BOOM! BOOM!

"What you want me to do?" asked Trish with fear in her eyes.

"Go in the bathroom and hide. I'm going to see what he wants."

"Okay," said Trish running into the bathroom.

JT went downstairs and opened the door.

"Damn, nigga what took you so long?" asked Cameron, letting himself in.

"Because… I got company, that's why." Shanay came downstairs with a towel on.

"Oh, hey Shanay." Cameron put his arm around JT and turned their back on Shanay so he could whisper in JT's ear.

"Why you didn't tell me you was still fucking Shanay? Let's have a threesome for old time sakes?"

"She not like that no more Cam, and you never asked if I was fucking her."

"What you mean she not like that? Once a whore, always a whore," said Cameron turning around.

"Do you remember me?" asked Cameron looking at Shanay.

"Yeah, JT talks about you all the time."

"Oh really. So, what's up?"

"Nothing much same old same old."

"So let me cut to the chase. What do you want to do with me and my bro right here right now?" asked Cameron, pointing at JT.

"What you mean?" asked Shanay, knowing exactly what he meant.

"What's up with a threesome again for old times?" asked Cameron.

"Damn, I didn't see you in how long and you already talking about sex?"

"Like, come on, Shanay, you know what it is," said Cameron.

Shanay was feeling Cameron way more than JT, but JT was her baby, and she would do it if JT didn't have a problem with it. Shanay looked at JT and so did Cameron. JT didn't want to be labeled as a sucker because if he said no, Cameron would clown him for falling in love with a "Hoe," so he struggled his shoulders and looked at Cameron, then at Shanay. That's all Shanay needed to see and the towel went off, showing Shanay flawless chocolate skin that she lotioned down before JT came home. Dreads coming down her back were the first thing Cameron reached for.

At the sight of this, JT became furious inside, like his blood began boiling when she took her towel off. Smacking her ass and pulling her hair so she can be face to face with Cameron crouch. Cameron pulled his dick. Shanay, with Cameron's dick still in her mouth, rose from the crouching position to bending over and sucking Cameron's dick. Cameron smacked her ass and started putting his two fingers in her pussy, and looked up at JT.

"What's wrong, man?" Cameron saw that JT was mad as hell just by his demeanor.

JT didn't notice it because he had blacked out. JT heard Cameron's voice and snapped back to reality.

"Oh, nothing, nothing, just thinking about something."

"Think about this pussy that's in your face and stop playing with it," said Cameron smacking Shanay's ass again.

"Hold on; I got to use the bathroom real quick. I'll be back," said JT running upstairs. JT went to the bathroom and closed the door. Trish was inside the tub with the curtain closed so nobody could see her.

"Trish," JT said her name in a whisper.

"What's going on down there? I thought I heard a girl's voice? Did he leave yet?" asked Trish getting out of the tub.

"It's a girl downstairs, and no, Cameron didn't leave yet."

"Where she come from? Did Cameron bring her here? Don't lie to me," said Trish getting a little hostile and raising her voice.

"SSSSSHHHH, be quiet and no, he didn't bring her here; she was already here."

"You're lying. I'm telling you this now if…."

"Yo, we going to your room. Hurry up to nigga; what you taking a shit?" said Cameron passing the bathroom door and going to JT's room.

"I hope he not. Take a shower if you do," said Shanay laughing a little bit.

"Fuck y'all, I'll be there," said JT, ensuring that the bathroom door was locked.

"Listen, I'm going to go into the room and close the door behind me. When I close the door, you come out of the bathroom and leave. Okay," said JT, whispering.

"For what so you and him can have a threesome with her, huh?"

"No Girl!" JT raised his voice, accidentally looking at the door to see if anybody heard him and began whispering to Trish again.

"Can you please just do what I say? I'll call you later and see what's up. I just don't want him to find out," said JT, kissing Trish on the lips, leaving the bathroom, and closing the door behind him.

When Trish heard the bedroom door close, she made her move. Sneaking out of the bathroom and going downstairs, Trish saw the towel that was on the floor.

"Dirty SCANK," said Trish as she walked by it.

Trish left out of the door quietly and left in her car. About 10 minutes later, Trish decided to call Cameron. Cameron answered the phone out of breath.

"What's up Babe."

"Hey, what's up? What you doing?"

"Nothing just got done playing basketball."

"Yeah with who?"

"That's a dumb question. Who else?"

"JT," said Trish in a laughing matter.

"Yeah, Babe JT."

"Oh, okay, so when you coming home?"

"I'll be home in a couple of hours because I'm going to take a shower at JT's house, then go and see if I can get some makeup work done at the office."

"If you say so. Okay then Bye."

"Bye. Love you."

"Love you too."

"Let me get the steak meal with garlic and fried onions on the steak, please," said Cameron.

"And you?" asked the waiters.

"The same thing he's having," said Kim, still on the phone.

Aairyah. Kim was arguing on the phone for a while until she got off.

"Look, I been married to my husband for five years. He's my high school sweetheart, and I love him to death. My girl got married not too long ago, and we all went to the island so we can be there for my girl's wedding. Well, my girl's brother, the one that's getting married, told me that Aairyah told him that they had a fivesome with the two stripper girls and that my husband was the main one that was involved."

Cameron thought to himself, *"This bitch talks too much."*

"Tyrone! Tyrone!" said Kim looking at how Cameron was dozed off.

"Yeah." That was said after Cameron got to reality.

"You not even listening to what I'm saying. I forgot all guys are the same."

"I was listening Kim," said Cameron letting a big breath in and out, reaching across the table and grabbing Kim's hand.

"Look, Kim I understand where you coming from, but I feel some type of way when you speak about your husband," said Cameron making up a lie because he didn't know what Kim said.

"I'm telling you my problems. Damn, Tyrone, why can't you just listen to me? Like what the fuck."

"I do listen to you; why you think we are here at Red Lobster so we can talk."

"I told you it will be worth your time to come. That's why you came here."

"I came here to talk to you are married; my mind frame isn't even on that type of time."

"Yeah you right. I am married; what the hell am I doing here?" asked Kim getting up from the table and walked away.

"Hold on, wait," said Cameron walking towards Kim.

"Your right, Tyrone. I'm not suppose to be here," said Kim putting her ring finger in the air and pointing at it.

"I'm married... I mean, we still can be friends," said Kim putting her hand down.

Cameron was like Fuck this Bitch, but he remembered why he was doing this. Thinking about that gave flashbacks to when Cameron was at the pep rally for his singing act; Damon, Aairyah, and Omar pulled a prank on Cameron that left him crying for days. When Cameron began to sing in front of the whole school. Damon cut off his microphone and got on the intercom. Aairyah came behind him and pulled his pants down while Marshal put Cameron in a full nelson so he couldn't pull his pants up. Omar put the projector on and had the tape rolling.

"What we have here is Cameron. This guy is a pervert; he likes boys, and if you can see in this video here, this guy is masturbating in the schools' bathroom." All the kids were laughing at Cameron the whole time.

"OH YEAH, OH YEAH, THIS FEELS GOOD. HOW YOU LIKE THAT!? HUH! TAKE THAT, YEAH! OH YEAH, OH YEAH, I'M ABOUT TO CUM! OOOOOOOHHHHH SHIT!... DAMN GIRL, YOU KNOW HOW TO MAKE A DUDE FEEL GOOD," said Cameron on the videotape. The whole school laughed in tears from what they saw on the projector. Marshal let him go and he ran off of the stage of the auditorium and ran all the way home.

"Yeah, we still can be friends," said Cameron knowing if he blew this, he would lose his chance of getting at Kim.

"I'm glad you understand, Tyrone. It's just too much to cheat on this man. He been with me from thick and thin."

"I understand where you coming from and I respect you more for doing that, so go ahead and go get your man," said Cameron walking back to his table, feeling low.

"Don't worry, things will be okay," said Kim leaving the restaurant.

Kim couldn't see herself with anybody else but Aairyah. Kim has been through too much with Aairyah to let him go and see another girl with him. So, Kim called Vanessa, and she didn't pick up, so she called Sabrina.

"Hello," Kim said after the third ring.

"What's up, Girl," said Sabrina.

"Nothing much; I just got to talk to you in private. Where you at?"

"I'm at the house; come over. Is everything okay?"

"Kinda, I'll talk to you when I get there; it's something I heard," said Kim.

"Okay then I'm home."

"Be there in 20 minutes. Bye?"

"Bye."

"It always been me and you nigga. What's up? Why you keep

procrastinating? What's up?" asked Omar.

"Well, I'm still in love with Kim. I mean, I still got feelings for her," said Ron-Ron.

"Nigga you fucked her in high school and didn't even care about her. Now all of a sudden, you are in love with her?" asked Omar.

"Yeah, it's confusing," said Ron-Ron.

"Ok, you say this to say what?"

"I say this to say I told my sister that everybody had a fivesome with the strippers at the island." Omar had rage in his eyes as soon as Ron-Ron said it.

"Why the Fuck you say that for!?"

"Because I wanted to get Kim back, and I figured that if I tell my sister, my sister will tell Kim, and Kim will leave Aairyah alone," said Ron-Ron slumped in his chair where they were sitting at.

"You know that's going to fuck my relationship up with my girl; what the Fuck is wrong with you? Do you know you are a cold-blooded sucker for that!? Like, who do shit like that? Damon just spent all this money to make your sister happy, spoil the hell out of her, and marry her. Do you know that's probably the only nigga that will do some shit like that for your sister? Then you turn back on me because you know word going to go back to Sabrina."

"I know, I know man. I'm sorry, it's just that… I don't know man."

"Just know I'm going to whip your ass if I lose Sabrina. I'm letting you know now," said Omar getting out of his seat and grabbing his McDonald's bag.

"Come on, I'm about to go home now," said Omar.

Ron-Ron felt so low he couldn't even say anything to his best friend. Omar left the McDonald's and went to his house; when Omar got inside, he saw Kim and Sabrina talking in the living room.

"Hey Babe. What's up, Kim?"

"Let me talk to you Nigga," said Sabrina.

Omar already knew what it was going to be about. Ron-Ron sat down next to Kim as Omar and Sabrina went upstairs.

"Listen, Kim. I told my sister that so you can break up with Aairyah because I can't stop thinking about you. I know we went our different ways, but I still got feelings for you," said Ron-Ron.

"So, it's not true?"

"Yeah it's true. But I told so I can somehow be in your heart like I use to in high school," said Ron-Ron putting his head down, hoping she felt sorry for him and she could feel sympathy for him and take him back all these years.

"You're lame for that. Like who does that? You're breaking perfect relationships. I don't know about them, but I'm sticking by my man side no matter what. I'm just that to mines," said Kim getting up from the couch and walking out the door, leaving Ron-Ron on the couch.

Ron-Ron heard Omar and Sabrina arguing upstairs.

"Hey, we finally meet again," said Cameron, intentionally bumping Vanessa at Victoria's Secret in the mall.

Vanessa didn't recognize the voice until she turned around and saw the guy that was in front of her.

"Oh, hey, what's your name again?" asked Vanessa.

"It's Jermaine beautiful, but what are you doing in here? Hold on, is your man with you?" asked Cameron looking around and ducking like somebody was going to hit him.

They both laughed as he did an impression of how he was ducking from the bottle.

"No, he's not with me. Actually, me and him are going through something right now." That was music to Cameron's ears and he knew this was his chance to shine.

"Oh, I'm sorry to hear that, but hey, life goes on. I umm… I know it's probably too soon to ask you this but will you like to go to the club with me tonight? I'll treat if it helps," said Cameron with a smile on his face.

"I don't know. Maybe it's too early for that and I still mess with my husband. We got married the last day of the cruise."

"Oh, okay, I see, but it won't hurt nothing; maybe it will get your mind off of things, and it's not like we are doing nothing," said Cameron.

Vanessa thought about what he said and took his advice.

"Yeah, maybe you are right."

"Okay, so you are coming with me?" asked Cameron, happy and eager to hear her response.

"Yeah, I'll go with you," said Vanessa.

"Okay, here goes my number. I'm kinda in a rush; it's my sister's birthday today. That's why I'm in Victoria's Secret, if you was wondering."

"Yeah, I figured you wasn't shopping for yourself."

"Oh, so you got jokes? Okay," said Cameron.

"Nah, I'm playing. Well, I got your number now, so I guess I will call you tonight, and you can tell me where to meet you."

"Okay that's cool. Just call me; I'll be waiting," said Cameron as he walked away.

"Jermaine."

"Yeah," said Cameron looking over his shoulder.

"Never mind, I'll call you."

Cameron wanted to go back to Vanessa, but he knew Trish was around here somewhere because he was shopping with her.

"Damn nigga you got big as shit over the years. What you been eating horses?" Joked one of Marshal's cellies.

"Nah, I just been working out all these years since I been in here."

Marshal and his celly Killer J were looking at pictures his mom sent him a couple of years ago.

"Yeah and who is that?"

"That's my sister. Here go her getting married a couple of months ago," said Marshal showing him his recent pictures.

"Damn, she bad nigga."

Marshal couldn't really say anything because Killer J got two life sentences, and if things came to a comedown, Killer J wouldn't stop until Marshal was dead.

"Yeah, I know. It's crazy that she been messing with the same dude since I got locked up."

"How long you got left anyway?" asked Killer J.

"I got a year left if they give me all of my good time."

"Damn, your time coming real short."

"Yeah man, hopefully, things come together, and I go home."

"I'll be praying with you."

JT walked past Marshal's cell and said to him, "Damn, you been here for a minute; my nigga is you good?"

"Yeah, I'm good until your dumb ass guards try to put their hands on me. Then I had to whip their ass."

"I know I heard. What time is you looking at?"

"Like 12 months left."

"Damn time flies. They got you on the lifers' pod. Why they move you over here?"

"I don't know. I just got out of the hole yesterday."

"A'ight, I got you; I'm going to see if I can get you on work release your last year. Let me see if I can, but I think I got you, so you can go home and try to get a job while you are there."

"A'ight man, good looking."

"No problem, I'm going to holla at you tomorrow."

"A'ight, man, but let me ask you a question?"

"Yeah, what's up?"

"Why are you doing this for me if I killed Richard?"

"I mean, Richard was cool peoples, but I never really got involved with him like that. Omar was cool with him more than I was."

"Oh, a'ight nigga holla at me."

"A'ight," said JT, walking off and going towards the door so he could get let out of the pod.

CHAPTER 6

When Pleasure Becomes Pain

"My name is Mitch and yours?" asked Cameron.

"Sabrina, why, what can I help you with?" asked Sabrina.

Sabrina worked as a nurse at the state hospital and worked on a client. When she stepped out of the patients' room, Cameron introduced himself. Sabrina and Omar were still going through it, but she couldn't leave Omar. They still lived together, but she wanted Omar to feel the same pain that she felt and she wanted revenge. After all the years Sabrina was loyal to Omar, she felt as tho she could go with another person without being called a "Whore" or a "hoe." Sabrina never cheated on any man she dated, even in junior high, but she knew that she didn't have enough guts to cheat. She was too loyal to her man, and she knew she didn't roll that way, but it wouldn't hurt to make Omar jealous.

"Oh, well, I was here to help my grandmom, and I saw you, and I just thought that I saw the most beautiful girl I ever seen, and I had to stop and speak to you." That comment made Sabrina blush a little bit, and she gave in on Cameron's comment.

"Oh, thank you."

"I'm sorry to ask, but do you have a husband?' said Cameron looking at Sabrina's ring.

Sabrina thought Cameron looked familiar but didn't really press the issue.

"Why you ask that?" asked Sabrina.

"Well, the rock on your finger tells it all."

Sabrina started to fiddle with her ring and thought to herself, "*What an idiot of me."*

"Oh yeah, going through rough times right now."

"Sabrina, we need you in rooms 1-11," said a nurse coming out of one of the hospital rooms.

"Okay, here I come," said Sabrina turning her head towards the nurse who said it and back.

"Well, don't let me keep you up. I guess I'll catch you another time."

"Yeah, I guess so," said Sabrina turning around and walking towards the room where she was called to go to.

Cameron didn't want to end it like this, so he said, "Hey, Sabrina."

"Yeah?" Cameron hesitated before asking.

"Can I get your number? I mean, I will like to see you again, and I don't want to end it like this."

"Yeah. You can have it, but you got to make sure you call me on my working hours because my husband will snap if he finds out."

"Okay, I got you," said Cameron as they exchanged numbers and walked away, saying their goodbyes.

Sabrina was thinking about why she gave her number out to a random guy, and she felt guilty doing so. After work, Sabrina went home to see Omar in the living room watching T.V.

"Hey Babe," said Omar as Sabrina walked in and closed the door behind her.

Sabrina dropped her keys on the coffee table near the door. Sabrina still had this gut feeling about giving her number out, so she sat next to him and said, "Hey, Babe."

If Sabrina never felt guilty about giving her number out, she would have walked past Omar and didn't say anything to him like she had been doing for the past week. Omar was surprised she said something, so he knew his wife best and knew something was up.

"What you do?" Sabrina loved and hated that Omar knew her like the back of her hand.

"Nothing; why you say that?"

"What did you do?" asked Omar.

"Nothing Babe, I'm just tired of us arguing, that's all. I want us to be back to how it use to be," said Sabrina.

Omar knew something was up, but he rolled with the punches.

"Oh, okay. So how was work?"

"Good, good, just too many people getting hurt, but other than that, it's been okay. How have your business been doing?"

"I got the three cars last week, but I only sold one, and the other two I can't get rid of."

"Oh okay. Well Babe, can we…"

Sabrina's phone rang, and her heart dropped when she looked at it. The look on Sabrina told it all to Omar. Sabrina didn't pick her phone up and that was unusual to Omar to see.

"Who was it?" asked Omar.

"Nobody. Somebody at work." Omar reached for Sabrina's phone and took it.

"Give me my phone," said Sabrina jumping on top of Omar, trying to get her phone back.

Omar was too strong to let Sabrina get the phone and the phone rang again. The first ring, Omar picked it up.

"Hello," said Omar.

"Hello, is Sabrina there?" asked Cameron.

"Who the Fuck is this?"

"The person your girl gave her number to," said Cameron knowing this will piss Omar off.

"Well, stop calling this Fucking number because she married," said Omar handing up on Cameron.

"So, you giving nigga's your number?" asked Omar; Omar's blood was boiling.

"I just gave him my number, that's all. You the one Fucking stripper's Nigga!"

"So, what you think it's cool to give your number out, huh?" Omar raised his hand to hit her and Sabrina covered her face with her arms.

"I should whip your ass, but you know what? I'm out; you can keep everything I'm out," said Omar jumping off of Sabrina and heading towards the door.

"Babe, I swear I didn't do nothing with him. I was just trying to make you jealous," said Sabrina jumping up from the couch and running towards the door.

"Well, you did a damn good job," said Omar pulling Sabrina away from the door so he could leave.

"You had sex with a stripper like what the fuck. I just gave him my number today," said Sabrina jumping back in front of the door.

"Well, you should have did it."

Sabrina didn't know what to do, so she did what she knew. It hurts Sabrina to know that her husband is in pain. Sabrina swung on Omar, punching him in his face and jumped on him, bear-hugging him so he couldn't get her off of him. Sabrina had so many mixed emotions inside she didn't know what to do.

"I don't feel like arguing with you; can you please get off of me," said Omar trying to pull Sabrina off of him.

"NOOOO," said Sabrina hugging Omar tighter.

"Can you please stop?" asked Sabrina crying on Omar's shoulders.

Omar felt bad and knew he was in the wrong the whole time.

"We can talk later; let me just get my mind straight first," said Omar in a whisper.

Omar's muscles relaxed when he said it, and all the pressure and anger were off his back at the sound of his wife crying.

"NOOOOOO. You staying here," said Sabrina unlocking her legs from Omar and grabbing his hand.

"Come on Daddy," said Sabrina sounding like a little girl.

Omar didn't say anything but followed her lead. Sabrina grabbed Omar's hand, locking their fingers together so Omar wouldn't leave her sight. Sabrina got into their room, positioned Omar in front of the bed, and pushed him down on the purple silk sheets that Omar bought to match the Chinese purple drops she had hung up. Sabrina turned the surround sound on and turned it to Maxwell, fortunate. Sabrina went in front of Omar and undressed herself, showing all of her high yellow 36 C breast and her shaved pussy that was looking too good for Omar not to get an erection. Sabrina took Omar's sneakers off one by one, as well as his socks. Pulling his pants down after unzipping his pants, Sabrina saw that Omar's dick was pumping to get into her.

Sabrina still went slow, grabbing Omar's hands so he could sit up so she could take his shirt off. She did just that. Sabrina then took Omar's boxers off, slowly watching Omar's dick bounce back to him after the boxers went across his dick. Omar scooted up the bed so he could lay flat on the bed. Sabrina went to the side of the bed and positioned herself to where she was on top of Omar with her pussy in his face as she sucked Omar off. Sabrina wrapped her lips around the head of Omar's dick and started to play with it with her tongue. Omar spread Sabrina's legs so she could sit on his face. Omar spread her ass cheeks and went like no tomorrow. Omar used his thumbs to spread Sabrina's lips away from each other as he entered his tongue. Licking from her pussy to her ass whole did it all. Omar stuck his finger in Sabrina's ass as he wrapped his lips around Sabrina's couch, sucking the juice out of Sabrina. Omar knew when Sabrina was going to have an orgasm because her legs started to shake and her dropped pussy was all in Omar's face, damn near suffocating him. Omar laughed a little. Sabrina was still jerking Omar off while she was trying to get herself together. Sabrina picked her head up and looked back after the tingling feeling went away. Sabrina smiled and turned around, kissing Omar's dick and facing him. Sabrina kissed Omar tasting the juices from her pussy on his lips. Sabrina got on top of Omar and started riding him. Sliding on Omar softly and then slammed down on it. Sabrina leaned forward, putting her hands on Omar's chest and arched her back. Using her thighs to go up and down riding Omar. Omar slapped her ass as she went down.

After about 10 minutes, Sabrina got up, and Omar looked at his dick and saw that Sabrina climaxed all over it. Omar grabbed Sabrina and pulled her back on top of him. Omar spun Sabrina so her ass was facing him and threw her and her side. Sabrina arched her back so her ass was out. Omar grabbed the ass check that was not on the bed and spread it out as he entered in. Sabrina's juices were still all over her pussy and even her asshole was covered in white cum. Omar entered inside Sabrina's asshole and Sabrina screamed.

"AAAAAAAAHHHHH, SHIIIIITTTT HOLD!"

Omar covered Sabrina's mouth before she could say anything. Omar thrust even harder, hitting Sabrina's G-spot. Juices flew down Sabrina's pussy as Omar stroked. Sabrina never felt a dick inside of her ass until now. Omar pulled out and went inside of Sabrina's pussy. Omar now had one of Sabrina's legs in the air as he stroked. Omar couldn't take anymore after Sabrina started to rock her body back and forth to Omar as he was pumping away. Omar put all 9 inches inside her and released his semen inside Sabrina. Sabrina turned around and kissed Omar when he had his eyes closed.

"Promise me you will never leave me," said Sabrina looking into Omar's eyes.

"Promise me you won't give no guy your number."

"I promise," said Sabrina.

"I promise," said Omar kissing Sabrina and thinking to himself that Sabrina said I couldn't cheat.

"You know what? I'm tired of this shit; you not going to keep putting me through this," said Vanessa crying her eyes out.

"Putting you through what?" Damon wondered what Vanessa was

talking about as he entered the door to their apt.

"What was you doing last night?" asked Vanessa, still crying.

The water from her eyes messed up the mascara that she had put on earlier that morning.

"Me and Aairyah went and had a couple of drinks and chilled; what's the point?" asked Damon, confused about how much she really knows.

"So, you didn't go nowhere else?"

"No."

"You Fucking Liar! Shanay saw you and Aairyah in the hotel room last night, and y'all went in there with two females!"

"That Bitch is lying."

"Yeah she lying. You right, huh," said Vanessa in a low tone and then started to yell again.

"You Fucking Dumb Ass, she had a room next to yours, Asshole! She heard the girl screaming your name!" said Vanessa going to the bedroom and grabbing her bags.

"Babe, she lying!"

Damon saw Vanessa take her bag out to the living room and drop it by the door.

"Where you going at Babe?" asked Damon softening up his voice and praying she doesn't leave.

"Babe, I'm sorry." Vanessa grabbed the door and opened it.

"Can you please move?"

Damon was standing in the middle of the door, so she couldn't open it all the way. Damon grabbed her hand.

"You promised me you would never touch me in any type of way that

I didn't want to be."

"But Babe, can we talk?"

"Can you let go of me?"

Damon let go and got away from the door. Vanessa grabbed her bag, went out to the parking lot, placed it in her car, and returned to the apartment.

"I'm leaving to my mom's. When you figure out that I'm all you need, then come talk to me. Other than that, don't call or text my phone."

"You are the only one that I need Babe."

Vanessa remembered something that her mom said to her as a little girl. Don't never let a man think he owns you. If he did wrong, let him feel it. Never think that he can always come back to you when he, please.

"Matter of fact. I'll call you when I feel as though I can talk to you. For now, don't call me because I won't pick up."

Everything that Damon was saying was going from one ear out the other the whole time Vanessa was walking to her car.

All Vanessa heard was, "Is you even listening?" asked Damon as Vanessa got in her car.

"No," said Vanessa and closed the door to her car and started her car.

"I'll call you when you stop lying and tell me the truth," said Vanessa as she pulled off from the parking lot.

Five minutes later, Damon was blowing Vanessa's phone up. Vanessa looked at her caller ID and saw it was Damon and threw her phone on the passenger seat and turned her radio up that was playing Keyshia Cole's "Love."

"This shit had to be on," said Vanessa.

Tears started to come down Vanessa's face as she thought about Damon.

Vanessa said to herself, thinking about turning back, *"I got to let him learn a lesson. I can't be going through this all my life. Or will he cheat on me again? He just said he was sorry. Maybe I should go back. He did do everything that I wanted to do and married me too. Should I. No, Vanessa, stay focused. Go to mommy's house and think things through."*

Vanessa kept debating in her head on what she should do but decided that she was going to her mother's house. Pulling up to her mom's house, Vanessa grabbed her bag and knocked on the door. Sasha answered the door.

"Oh My God, Baby, tell me what happen?" asked Sasha grabbing Vanessa's bags as she entered the door.

"Damon… Damon cheated on me Mom," said Vanessa crying again on her mother's shoulder after Sasha dropped her bags.

Sasha hugged her daughter and felt her pain because their father did it to her.

"It's okay, V.," said Sasha rubbing her daughter's back as the tears fell on her neck.

"I did everything mom. What did I do wrong?" asked Vanessa wiping her tears on her mom's sweater.

"You didn't do anything wrong Sweetie. Come on, let's sit down," said Sasha.

After Vanessa stopped crying, she told her mom everything that had happened to her and Damon's relationship after they came back from the cruise. After about two hours of talking Vanessa felt relieved but not fulfilled. Like something was missing and she knew what it was.

After about a week, Vanessa got tired of watching movies and eating ice cream with her mom. Vanessa talked to Marshal twice since she had been there and wrote to him to send him pictures and apologize for not being there for him after all those years. Vanessa would text Jermaine throughout the week and figured one night out wouldn't hurt. After all, she hasn't been out in a while. Vanessa got a phone call from Jermaine on the 8th day.

"Hello," said Vanessa.

"Hey stranger, how are you?" asked Cameron hoping she was in a good mood.

"I'm good; how about yourself?" asked Vanessa, not telling him how she really felt because she didn't want to talk about Damon right now.

"I'm good. Could have been better if you would have never stood me up that night when we was suppose to go out."

"I know. I'm sorry. What you doing tonight?" asked Vanessa, hoping he had something to do.

"Nothing exactly. How about we go to the club tonight. Before you say anything, let me talk. Everything is on me. It's Saturday and you don't got nothing to do."

"Ummmmmm… I don't know. Maybe another time Jermaine."

"Come on V. I promise we won't do nothing out of the ordinary and I will have you home by 12."

Vanessa thought about it, and maybe a drink or two wouldn't hurt her.

"Okay, I will go."

"Okay, I will come pick you up at 9."

"Okay, I will see you then."

"Okay Bye."

"Bye," said Vanessa hanging up the phone and walking to her mom's room.

"Mom, I'm going out tonight, and I need your opinion on what I'm going to wear tonight," said Vanessa running to her room.

"Where you going at?" asked Sasha getting off of her bed and going towards Vanessa's room.

"I'm going to have a few drinks with some friends," said Vanessa going through her closet as Mellisa walked into the room.

"Oh, ok, well, have fun," said Sasha.

Sasha was happy that Vanessa was going out; she didn't care who she went out with, as long as she was going out.

"Hold on Mom; you didn't even look at what I was going to wear."

"Oh, I'm sorry," said Sasha turning back to her door and seeing Vanessa holding an all-white tight fitted dress.

"Should I wear these heels with it? Or these ones?" asked Vanessa holding up a pair of black and white Steve Madden heels in the air next to the dress.

"Wear the black and white heels that looks more better," said Sasha.

After picking and choosing which pocketbook she was going to wear with her outfit and heels, she took a shower. Getting out of the shower and lotioned herself down, Vanessa couldn't stop thinking about Damon because this was his job to do after she got out of the shower. Vanessa's phone rang, and she picked it up after seeing it was Damon.

"Hello," said Damon after Vanessa didn't say anything.

"Hello," said Damon again. Vanessa still didn't say anything but just heard Damon breathe over the phone.

"Listen Babe. I know you are mad at me but just hear me out." Vanessa still didn't say anything.

"Look, I'm sorry, okay. It's like you took my soul with you when you left. I can't function right. I lost about 10 pounds already. I barely can eat. The more and more I go without, the harder it is to move are even go to work. I love you Vanessa, and I would never let you go. I'm sorry, and I love you bye," said Damon and hung the phone up.

Before Vanessa could say anything, she heard that tone hit her ear. Vanessa wanted to call Damon back, but she started crying. After an hour of crying, Vanessa got another phone call. It was Jermaine on the caller ID when Vanessa looked at her phone.

"Hello."

"Yeah."

"I'm sorry I'll be running late. I'll be there at 9:30. Because it's 9:00 now, and I just got on the highway." Vanessa lost track of time from crying and realized that it was 9 o'clock.

"Okay, that's not a problem. You remembered where I lived at?"

"No, you never told me; you just said get on 95 North."

"Okay well, I'll text you the directions."

"Okay," said Jermaine and hung up.

Vanessa texted Jermaine the directions and got herself together after all the tears cleared up from her face. Vanessa threw her panties and bra on and then slithered herself in her white dress. Vanessa put her heels on and looked in the mirror. Vanessa knew she still had it in her to take any man home by showing herself off in the mirror.

"That's what I like to see," said Mellisa seeing Vanessa smile at herself in the mirror.

"Go head, Mom," said Vanessa posing in the mirror.

"Go Girl," said Mellisa. Over the year, Mellisa's thick accent still was there.

"I get it from my momma," said Vanessa laughing and walking over to her mom and hugging her. Vanessa's phone rings.

It is Jermaine; she picks up the phone and says, "You are outside?"

"Yup."

"Okay, here I come," said Vanessa hanging the phone up.

"Okay Mom, my ride is outside. I love you. I will be back by 12."

"You not taking your car?"

"No, because I'm going to be drinking a little and I don't want to drive home alone," said Vanessa walking out of the room and walking to the front door.

"Is they going to be drinking?"

"I don't know. I love you, bye," said Vanessa leaving the house before her mom gave her a lecture that she didn't want to hear.

The door closed before Mellisa could say bye. Vanessa got into Cameron's S550 Mercedes Benz and said, "Hey."

"What's up?" asked Cameron after pulling off.

It was very little talk during the whole way to the club. You could hear the music in the parking lot, and it was a long line sitting out front of the club.

"Damn, it's packed in there; you sure you want to go in there?" asked

Vanessa getting out of the car.

"Yeah, you going to have fun; come on," said Cameron closing his door and locking it.

Cameron went in front of the line and paid the bouncer two hundred dollars to get in for him and Vanessa. Going inside the club Young Jeezy and Gucci Mane's "So Icy" song blasted through the speaker. Cameron grabbed Vanessa's hand because she couldn't hear him through the speakers blasting through the air. In the club, there were two floors. When you entered the club, you were on the second floor where the VIP was, and there were a whole bunch of stools and tables where people were sitting at. Cameron got a table, went to the bar, and ordered some drinks. Coming back to the table with two shots of patron and two drinks mixed with pineapple juice and Cîroc. Cameron gave Vanessa a shot and the drink.

"On one, we going to take the shot," said Cameron putting the shot glass in the air.

"What is it?" asked Vanessa putting her shot in the air touching Cameron's shot glass.

"One."

Cameron took the shot, and Vanessa hurried up and took it behind him. Vanessa's chest was on fire when she put the shot glass down.

"Drink the pineapple juice," said Cameron, drinking some of his cup.

Vanessa drank some of her cup, and it didn't help, but it didn't burn like the last shot did.

"Come on, let's go downstairs," said Cameron grabbing Vanessa's hand and taking her downstairs.

Downstairs was the dance floor and bathrooms. Cameron basically dragged Vanessa to the dance floor because she didn't want to dance.

"Vanessa, you got to let your hair down. Stop thinking about whatever you are thinking about and just let your hair down," said Cameron, two-stepping in front of Vanessa and grabbing her hand to dance along with him.

Vanessa heard her song and went off. Mystical Danger came on, and Vanessa returned to her senior year in high school. In school, the thought about her blew her mind off all the stress she was put under. Forgetting what she was even mad about, Vanessa started moving her hips to the song and then after a while, she let her body loosen up, and she and Cameron danced to three more songs after that until Vanessa started to break a sweat.

"Let's go back upstairs to get a drink! It's getting too hot in here!" Yelled Vanessa over the music to Cameron.

Cameron and Vanessa went back upstairs and sat down on one of the stools that were next to her old table. Cameron returned to the table after going to the bar with a serving tray; 4 shots, 4 beers, and 2 mixed drinks.

"Damn, what the hell you doing with all these drinks?" asked Vanessa as Cameron sat the tray down.

"We going to drink them."

Cameron got the shot first. Vanessa grabbed one as well.

"Grab the lemon off of the Corona and when we take the shot, bite it and drink the mixed drink."

Cameron started it off; he took a shot, bit the lemon, and drank the whole mixed drink.

"You can't beat that," said Cameron in a laughing manner.

At this time, Vanessa's mind was blank; she didn't have a care in the world. Vanessa took the shot of Patron, bit the lemon, drank the whole mixed drink, and took the other shot. Vanessa slammed the shot glass on the table and squinched her face up.

"You can't beat that," Vanessa said, throwing her hands in the air like she had accomplished something.

"Damn I can't do that. You really are a drinker."

"I barely drink. This is something new, but you know what?"

"What? That it looks like you are about to throw up on me," said Cameron looking at Vanessa's face.

"No, I just felt like I had to burp, but you know what time it is." Cameron checked his watch and saw that it was 11:30 pm.

"Can we finish these drinks, please?" asked Cameron, picking up one of their beers and started drinking it.

"But we got all these drinks that I paid for and I don't want to throw them away."

Cameron takes another sip. Vanessa had in her mind that she really didn't care if she went home at 12. She just promised her mom that she would be home at 12. Damon wasn't even on her mind at the time as she took the other shot of Patron. Vanessa picked up one of the Corona and started to drink it.

"I guess we can," said Vanessa feeling tipsy as she took a sip of the Corona yet again.

"So do you want to dance?" asked Cameron after Vanessa drank the Corona.

"Yeah, come on," said Vanessa getting out of the chair and following Cameron down the stairs to the dance floor. It wasn't until Vanessa went downstairs that she felt the drinks hit her.

"Damn, I can't do this Jermaine; I got to go home," said Vanessa stumbling on the dance floor.

Cameron saw how tipsy Vanessa really was and grabbed her hand to leave the dance floor. Going back upstairs, Cameron went back to their table and grabbed his beer and her beer.

"I'll take this," said Vanessa slurring her words.

Vanessa grabbed the shot and took it back. Cameron gave Vanessa a beer and they both drank it at the same time. Cameron grabbed Vanessa's hand and walked her outside of the club. Walking to the car and getting inside, Cameron thought about where he was going to take her at because everything he needed was in the car. Cameron saw that Vanessa had her head back and her eyes closed as soon as she closed the passenger door. Cameron made his move, put his hands on Vanessa's leg, and slipped it up her dress. Vanessa felt her pussy tingle as Cameron's hand slid up her thigh. Cameron felt the moisture of Vanessa's panties as he touched them. Looking around to see if anybody was out of the club, Cameron lifted one of Vanessa's legs apart from the other and turned half his body, so he was looking at Vanessa's panties face to face. Cameron slid his head between Vanessa's legs, licking his way up her leg. Biting the thread of Vanessa's panties and sliding them down her leg. Cameron then had both of his legs in his hand and pulled them up, sliding Vanessa down from her seat. Cameron began eating Vanessa out sideways. Vanessa didn't even open her eyes the whole time. Cameron held both her legs up with one hand and was fingering her with the other one while he was licking Vanessa's juices. Vanessa rocked her body back and forth to Cameron's finger and by this time, Vanessa's pussy was throbbing with anticipation. Cameron heard people coming out of the club, so he stopped.

"Keep going," pleaded Vanessa as her body rocked back and forth.

"People are coming out of the club," said Cameron starting the engine.

Vanessa opened her eyes immediately and pulled up her panties. Cameron pulled off and didn't look back. Vanessa figured that Cameron was taking her home to her mother's house, so she put her head back, still tipsy off the drinks. Vanessa wakes up to Cameron pulling her out of the car's passenger seat.

"Where are we?" asked Vanessa, not seeing the big Motel 6 sign over top of her.

"At the motel. Come on." Vanessa stumbling over herself, couldn't think with a clear mind. They went into the room and Cameron slammed Vanessa on the bed. Vanessa's pussy began to throb again as Cameron pulled down her panties and began his tongue work again.

"OOOOHHHH SSSSHHHIITTT Jermaine, don't stop," moaned Vanessa grabbing Cameron's head to keep going.

Cameron wrapped his arms around Vanessa's thighs as he ate her out. Vanessa's pussy was drenched after Cameron got done. Vanessa's pussy was beating for Cameron's dick now. Cameron got up and went by the TV that sat directly in front of the bed. Cameron took his shirt off and placed it on top of the TV.

"You remember me?" asked Cameron to the TV and headed towards the bed.

"What you say?" asked Vanessa taking her panties off.

"Nothing, I was talking to myself," said Cameron.

Cameron grabbed Vanessa's hand and pulled her to her two feet. Lifting her dress up over her head and throwing it on the floor, Cameron turned Vanessa around and pushed her onto the bed. Vanessa slid her knees up the bed, arching her back. Cameron got behind her and slowly went inside of her.

"Who got a little dick now?" asked Cameron stroking Vanessa harder and harder.

Vanessa didn't hear what Cameron said but threw her ass back against Cameron's dick as he stroked her hard.

"AAAAHHHH SHIT DAMN, AAAAHHH!" Vanessa was moaning loudly.

Smacking her ass brought thoughts to Vanessa, knowing only one man smacked her ass while fucking her and it was Damon. Reality done checked in on Vanessa and memories of Damon popped in her head of when they were children, then when they were saying their, I do's. Cameron felt Vanessa's rhythm stop, but he kept going. Vanessa completely stopped and her drunkenness went away. Vanessa jumped out of bed and ran to the bathroom. Cameron got off of the bed and went to the bathroom.

"What's wrong?" asked Cameron, knocking on the door.

"I can't do this; take me home," wept Vanessa behind the closed door.

"Okay, I will," said Cameron going over to the bed and putting his clothes on.

Vanessa came out and saw Cameron putting something in his book bag. Vanessa didn't think anything of it. Vanessa went to the bed, grabbed her panties from the floor, put them on, and did the same with her dress. Vanessa still had her heels on while she was having sex, so she didn't have to find them.

"Can we go, please?" asked Vanessa crossing her arms in front of her chest.

"Yeah, we can come on," said Cameron opening the door for Vanessa to leave out.

During the whole ride to Vanessa's mom's house, there were no words.

Pulling up to the mom's house, Vanessa said, "Listen, I'm sorry. This shouldn't of never happen; I have a husband and I shouldn't have done this," said Vanessa opening the door.

"It's okay, I understand."

"And can you please don't call or text me no more?"

"I got you," said Cameron putting his car in drive.

Vanessa got out of the car and Cameron peeled off.

The next day Vanessa went to her house and parked out front of the house behind Damon's car. Vanessa put her key in the door and heard females moaning; Vanessa's heart dropped. Vanessa ran upstairs and her bedroom door was wide open. She ran inside of the room and saw Damon with a picture of Vanessa next to him with a porno on. Damon was asleep with a bottle of lotion next to him and all she could do was laugh. Vanessa turned her head and saw the porno and laughed again because it was the same porno that she and Damon used to have sex to. Vanessa turned the

TV off and went to the bed. Damon had a picture of Vanessa next to him and one cuffed up under his arm. Vanessa went downstairs to cook breakfast for her man.

Vanessa thought to herself, *"I got to make it up to him even tho he don't know. He probably still thinks I'm mad at him and he going to do whatever I tell him. No, what if he finds out. He won't find out. Will he? Probably not. Hopefully, he don't. Let me cook this food."*

Vanessa cooked the food in 20 minutes and fled upstairs. Vanessa got ass naked, stood over top of Damon, and placed her foot on his stomach so he could wake up. Damon woke up and jumped when he saw his wife over top of him. Damon looked down and saw his pants were off, and the lotion bottle was in his hand. Damon threw the lotion bottle at the wall with a shocked look on his face. Vanessa walked further up the bed and crouched down till where she could feel Damon's hot breath touching her pussy.

"Which one you want to eat first?" asked Vanessa with a smile on her face.

Damon grabbed Vanessa's ass cheeks and stuck his tongue in Vanessa's pussy. Vanessa rode Damon's face with the plate of food still in her hand. Vanessa got up, placed the plate of food on the nightstand, jumped on the bed, and grabbed Damon's dick. Vanessa rubbed Damon's inner thigh shooting Damon's dick rock hard. Vanessa licked the bottom of Damon's nut sack to the head of his dick, wrapping her lips around Damon's head. Vanessa placed her hands on the inside of Damon's hips and rocked her head back and forth. Damon didn't have any sex in a week and a couple of days, so he orgasmed early and just as fast as he got soft, just as fast as Vanessa got him hard. When Vanessa got him hard, she jumped on top of him and laid on his chest. Damon pulled his feet up the bed and positioned himself. Vanessa wrapped her arms around Damon's head and squeezed her body against his. Damon grabbed his dick and went inside Vanessa. Damon grabbed Vanessa's shoulders and pounded away. Every time Damon moved his hips back, he would pull her shoulders down on his dick, stroking faster and faster. Damon nutted inside of her at the same time she climaxed.

"I promise you, Babe, I won't hurt you no more," said Damon lifting Vanessa's head to look at her in her eyes.

"Okay, Babe," said Vanessa laying her head on Damon's chest, trying to erase the memories she had last night.

CHAPTER 7

Love is Blind

"If you don't tell him, I will. I'm not going to keep living my life like this, JT. I'm not know whore!" said Trish putting on her panties and bra.

"Whoever said you were a whore and I told you that I'm going to tell him when the time is right and right now is not the time," said JT putting his pants on.

"So, when is the right time? When he catches us red-handed?" asked Trish throwing her dress over her head and letting it slide down her perfect frame.

The past month, JT knew Shanay wouldn't change her ways, even after pleading to Shanay that he would take her out of the hood and move to another state, but Shanay wasn't trying to hear that. Shanay was going to stay true to herself as she says because to her, every nigga was the same and that no nigga was good enough for her. From that day on, JT knew that putting a ring on Shanay's finger was out of the picture because he knew she wasn't changing her mind. So, JT figured that his relationship with Trish could come to play, but he knew that he couldn't go with his best friend's girl. Every time Trish brings up that question or Cameron's name, JT would feel guilty, but every time he looks into Trish's eyes, he forgets about Cameron. When JT knew that Shanay would just be his, JT felt miserable every day and the only person that cared was Trish. JT began to show his true feelings towards Trish and showed her that he was really feeling her. JT didn't know what to do or even how to tell his best friend that he had been screwing his girl for the longest, but he would have to find a way somehow.

"He's not going to catch us red-handed, and I told you I will tell him; just give me some time," said JT putting his boots and shirt on.

"Like I said, you better tell him before I do," said Trish putting her heels on and combing her hair in the mirror.

JT rented a room for a couple of hours so he could have sex with Trish without Cameron finding out.

"What, you don't love him no more or what?" asked JT heading out of the hotel room.

Trish went behind him and closed the door on her way out.

"I mean, yeah, I love him, but I'd rather be with you," said Trish grabbing JT's hand and locking her fingers as they walked up to the motel's front desk to sign out.

"Why you ask me that?" asked Trish.

"No reason," said JT.

"You wouldn't have asked me that if it wasn't something behind it. So, what's the reason."

"I said no reason."

"It must be a reason, so what is it?" asked Trish with hostility in her voice.

"You really want to know why I asked you?"

"Yeah, I do."

"Because I'm not sure if I want to spend my life with you. That's why," said JT opening the door to the motel's office.

Trish let go of JT's hand and ran to her car that was in the parking lot. JT chased after Trish and caught her in the middle of the parking lot. Grabbing her arm Trish was too weak to pull away from JT, so she punched on JT's chest as he bears hugs her. Trish cried in JT's arms as JT hugged her and rubbed her hair with the palm of his hand.

"Why can't you love me for me," said Trish in a low tone of voice, sobbing as she spoke.

"I do love you for you; you know that. It's just… It's just hard, okay. Like Cameron is my best friend, and I don't want to keep betraying him."

"Well, you been doing it this long. Why you keep coming back? Why you keep having sex with me, huh? Why? Why you keep doing this to me? Why JT? Why?" asked Trish, now hugging JT tight like it was her lifeline.

JT really didn't have an answer for Trish; he was just in love with her pussy, until time caught up with him and his emotions started to feel for Trish even more.

"Because I love you." That was all JT could say.

Trish looked up at JT's face. As Trish's face was buried in JT's chest, she left mascara on JT's shirt as well as tears.

"So why can't we be together, JT? I love you too. You know that. So why can't we just live our lives like I told you time after time?"

"We will Trish one day," said JT as he kissed Trish tasting the tears off of her lips.

"When JT, when?" asked Trish.

"Soon real soon."

Trish knew she had to take it into her own hands if she would be with this man for the rest of her life. Trish grabbed JT's hand and headed to her car. Trish unlocks her car and reaches for her phone out of the middle console.

"So, what now?" asked JT looking at Trish playing on her phone and then putting it to her ear.

"I'm calling Cameron and telling him that it's over and that me and you are dating. Hello"

"Hello." JT heard Cameron over the other line and he immediately reached for her phone and hung it up.

"What is wrong with you?" asked JT.

"Either you are going to do it, or I am," said Trish putting her hand out as to say, give me my phone.

"I'll do it; just give me until tomorrow, and I will do it," said JT, heart beating as he gave Trish her phone back.

"Look JT, I'm in love with you, and if you don't do it, I will," said Trish sitting inside her car.

"Okay, I got you."

Trish's phone rang; she picked it up and it was Cameron on the other side of the phone. So, Trish put it on speaker and said...

"Hello," said Cameron.

"Hello," said Trish.

"You called me?" asked Cameron in an uplifting voice.

"Yeah, where are you at?" was Trish managed to say.

"Just got off of work. You should know that. Why where you at?" asked Cameron.

"On my way home."

"You not there yet?" asked Cameron, knowing that his wife got off at 3 o'clock and it's 6 o'clock now.

"No, just a lot on my mind. I figured I go for a joy ride to ease my mind and get some stuff off of my chest," said Trish lying.

"Is everything okay Babe?"

"Yeah, everything is fine. I'll meet you at the house," said Trish in a hurtful voice.

"Okay, Babe go straight to the house. I'm on my way over there now," said Cameron.

"Okay bye."

"Bye. Love you."

"Love you too," said Trish and hung up.

Trish put her phone on the passenger seat and looked at JT.

"I guess we will see what happens tomorrow," said Trish getting out of her seat and kissing JT on the lips and sitting back in her car.

"I guess so."

Trish closed her door and started her car. As she rolls her window down, JT's phone rings and it is Cameron.

"Hello."

"Yo nigga please tell me you at your crib?" asked Cameron like he was eager to say something.

"Nah, I'm not even there. Why what's up? JT said, looking at Trish.

"Because I got to tell you something, meet me at your house in 10 minutes."

"A'ight, I got you. I'm coming now," said JT kissing Trish on the lips and throwing up the peace sign to say bye as he walked to his car that was on the side of hers.

"I'll call you later," said JT opening his door.

"Okay. Love you." JT hesitated for a few seconds and really meant what he was about to say.

"I love you too," said JT hopping in his car.

JT left the parking lot and went straight to his house. Meeting Cameron at his house, Cameron was already parked in front of his house with the radio loud as hell. JT got out of his car and went inside of Cameron's car. Cameron turned the radio down and looked at JT.

"So, who was you fucking just now?" JT's heart dropped as he looked at Cameron, eyes wide open.

"Ummm… Why you say that?" asked JT, trying to figure out a lie.

"Because you got all that make-up shit on your shirt," said Cameron, pointing at JT's shirt.

"Oh, uuuummmm Shanay. Yeah, Shanay, you know how that bitch is," said JT wondering if Cameron only knew somehow that he was having sex with his girl.

"You still be fucking that Bitch? Nigga your dick going to fall off. I can't believe you still be fucking her she old news for real," said Cameron.

"Hey man, you got to get it how you live," said JT loosening his body up and slouching in the seat. Cameron reached over, opened the glove box, and pulled out a red box.

"Look at this shit," said Cameron closing the glove box and opening the red box that he pulled out.

"You think she will like it?" asked Cameron showing JT the ring that Trish picked out years ago when they first started dating. JT felt even lower than what he already did. Cameron looked at JT's face and saw a shocked look on his face.

"You thought I would never get married, huh? I thought I wouldn't either, but Trish has been good to me ever since we have been going out. I had to wife her," said Cameron closing the box.

"Yeah man, that's what's up," said JT, still with a crazy look on his face.

"Damn man, I thought you would have been happy for me?" asked Cameron.

"I am happy for you Man. I just got a lot on my mind," said JT feeling dizzy at the fact of everything that's happening.

"You better be because you are my best man and I need you there with me," said Cameron.

"No doubt, I got you. But let me get inside here so I can take a shower and shit," said JT dapping Cameron up as he opened the door.

"A'ight, man, I'm going to holla at you in a little bit. You know I'm going to propose to her tonight?"

"Yeah," said JT shocked.

"Yeah man, I really think she is the one for me," said Cameron turning up his radio.

"Yeah man, I think so too," said JT closing the car door behind him and walking to his house.

"Yo, I'll come over here later because I got a surprise for you."

"A'ight nigga," said JT opening his house door and watching Cameron ride off.

JT got in the house and hurried up and called Trish. Ring after ring, Trish was not picking up the phone. *Damn what is she doing?* Thought JT as he kept calling and calling. After the seventh time, JT stopped calling and then went to take a shower and think about what was going to happen.

As soon as JT got out of the shower, his phone rang.

"Hello."

"Yeah, you called me?" asked Trish.

"Yeah, why the hell you didn't pick up my phone call earlier?" JT asked with a little anger in his voice.

"Mmmmhhh, I like an aggressive man. I was in the shower Daddy, getting all of the sweat you created on me. I want some more Daddy," said Trish in a little girl voice.

"I can't right now. Look listen. Cameron is going over there now and her…." That was the last thing he could say before Trish cut him off.

"Cameron just came in the house. I'm going to have to call you back. I love you, bye," said Trish hanging up on JT without him being able to say anything back.

The dial tone was all JT heard when Trish hung up on him. Trish hurried up and deleted JT from her call log, and went to the master bedroom, which was connected to the bathroom. Cameron walked into the room and Trish was lotioning herself down.

"Why you take a shower in the middle of the day for?" These were the first words that came out of Cameron's mouth.

"Because… I been thinking about too much shit and I figured that the shower would be a stress reliever," said Trish taking her towel off and showing her body.

"Oh, okay, well, I got a surprise for you. We going out tonight, and I got to take a shower.

"Where we going at?"

"You'll see when we get there," said Cameron taking his clothes off and walking to the bathroom.

Trish was surprised when Cameron said it and got excited when he said it. Trish walked into the bathroom when Cameron was in the shower.

"So, Babe, where are we going?" asked Trish picking up Cameron's boxers and smelling them.

Trish smelled a scent on them but couldn't tell if it was a female scent or not.

"We going out; wear something casual and classy at the same time. You know you look good in whatever you throw on," said Cameron turning the water off and getting out of the shower.

Cameron stood in front of Trish's ass naked and Trish hands couldn't stop from touching Cameron's body. Trish loved Cameron for everything he did for her. Trish also went to Howard and was a cheerleader as well. That's how Cameron knows where Sabrina, Vanessa, or Kim will be at because Trish would tell him about her friends, but she didn't know that she was giving her boyfriend information that would tear their relationship apart

Trish grew up in a non-stable home. Her mother was a drug user and her father had life. Trish didn't have any brothers or sisters, so she had to do everything on her own until Cameron came along and gave her everything she had till this day. Trish still would talk to her friends from high school, but they didn't have a close bond like the rest of them had. Trish was only close to Sabrina because they were on the cheerleading squad together, and Sabrina would tell Trish about Vanessa and Kim's relationship, and that information would trickle down to Cameron.

"You will want me more after tonight," said Cameron grabbing Trish's hand off of his body.

Trish had flashbacks to where Cameron used to treat her like a queen, doing everything under the sun for her.

"Running over here and there to please every need. Trish's lips sparked like the first time they kissed. Trish felt so special to him, thinking about everything he did for her. For that moment, Trish could see herself with Cameron for the rest of her life. Until Trish thought about all the bad and hurt he put her through. Trish wondered to herself, was this all it took for him to take me out to fall back in love with him? Or was I already in love, just mad at him because of what he did?" Trish's thoughts got interrupted when Cameron spoke.

"Babe, it starts at 8 o'clock; we are going to be late," said Cameron getting out of the bathroom and to the master bedroom.

Cameron hurried up and got his clothes on and jumped in his boots. Cameron grabbed his keys and hopped in his S550. Pulling up to the stadium, Trish was surprised. All in all, Trish wanted to go to a game and didn't care who was playing. Handing their tickets in and heading for their seats, Cameron told Trish to sit down; he was going to be right back. Trish sat down and watched as the person over the loudspeaker called the players to the floor. The New York Knicks was playing the Los Angeles Lakers. Cameron came back with two hot dogs and two sodas half an hour later.

"Damn, it took you long enough Babe. Where was you at?" asked Trish feeling lonely at the first quarter.

"I'm sorry, Babe, I got a surprise for you. You'll see," said Cameron handing the hot dog and soda to Trish as he sat down.

The first quarter was over and the second one was over just as quick. Kobe Bryant was doing his thing as he did every game and then halftime came up.

"Babe, I will have never thought I'd have this much fun at a basketball game."

The lights went out in the whole stadium and people started hollering until the spotlight was on Trish. Trish didn't know what was going on until she saw Cameron on one knee in front of her. Trish looked up and saw her face on the monitor as well as the scoreboard.

"Trish will you marry me?" asked Cameron.

Trish's stomach turned a million times before she said…

"Yo, you are really creeping me out Ron-Ron. I told you already that I'm sticking to my man, so can you please stop stalking me," said Kim getting inside her black Land Rover.

"Don't make it seem like that."

Kim jumped right in his mouth before he could say anything else.

"It is like that. You been showing up at my job for the past two weeks. Even my lunch breaks. My co-workers thinking, I got another man, you got to stop that shit before I tell Aairyah," said Kim, walking to her car in the Bank of America parking lot.

"Can you just hear me out?"

"No, I can't hear you out; Ronald get away from me," said Kim hitting her car alarm to unlock her car door.

"So, I'm guessing there is no chance then, huh?" asked Ron-Ron stopping in front of her truck.

"There isn't a chance at all. It was high school shit, Ron-Ron get over it," said Kim jumping into her Land Rover.

Kim left Ron-Ron in the parking lot helpless. When Kim went on I-95, she decided that this was getting out of hand, but she didn't want to get Aairyah involved, so she called Vanessa.

"Hey Sis," said Vanessa after she picked up the phone.

"Hey, I got to talk to you. Do you got time?" asked Kim taking the exit off to Vanessa's house.

"Yeah, anytime, Girl; what's the problem?"

"I'm coming to your house now," said Kim hanging the phone up and getting off the exit.

Kim arrived at Vanessa's house in no time and knocked on the door. When Kim looked up after rambling through her purse, she thought she saw a ghost.

"Listen, I'm sorry, okay," said Ron-Ron.

A million thoughts went through Kim's head. *How did he get here before me? Is Ron-Ron that obsessed with me?*

"Are you okay?" asked Vanessa coming to the door, moving Ron-Ron out of the way.

"Yeah, can I talk to you outside?" asked Kim walking to her truck.

"What's up Kim? Why you acting strange?" asked Vanessa, following Kim to her car.

"It's your brother. He keeps stalking me at my job on my lunch break and shit. Then I meet him here when he was just at my job," said Kim.

"Why would he be stalking you?" asked Vanessa.

"Because he still wants to be with me after all these years, and I told him that it would never happen because I'm married."

"Do you think that after all these years that he still wants you is freaky," said Vanessa biting her bottom lip and raising her eyebrows in a sexual way?

"No, it's not freaky; it's creepy and I want him to stop that shit he is creeping me out V."

"Okay, I will talk to him," said Vanessa turning around and going to her house.

"Thanks, V.," said Kim as she got in her truck.

"No problem and oh yeah, we are going out tonight. Do you want to come?"

"Who is we?" asked Kim.

"Me, my man, Sabrina, her man, and Trish and her men. I'm not sure." Kim took a while to respond.

"Come on, Kim, it will be fun," said Vanessa.

"Okay, I'll go," said Kim, "hey, where are we going at anyway?"

"I'm not sure Trish said she was going to pick it out."

"I didn't know you even still talked to that girl. I didn't see her in a couple of years," said Kim.

"Yeah, we still talk here and there. She said she wanted to go out, so I told her that we all was going out and why no with our mans?"

"Oh, okay, Mrs. I have secrets, but okay, I guess I have no choice."

"Nope, you don't, so I better see your ass there."

"I am going to be there, but who do Trish mess with?"

"I'm not sure I think Cameron still if I'm not mistaken. We don't really talk about relationships like that, but I think she told me she was going to break up with him, so I'm not sure if she did are not."

"Oh, okay Bitch I'll see you there," said Kim closing her door and starting the Land Rover.

"Trish going out, but I'm not. I probably go by myself and sneak up on them if anything," said Cameron putting on his clothes.

"What I need you to do is go meet Trish at the club and see what she is up to. See if she not meeting know nigga at the club," said Cameron putting on his boots.

"A'ight nigga I got you; just tell me when to go up there and I will," said JT.

"Go up there in a half-hour because Trish leaving now," said Cameron grabbing his keys.

"Okay, I'll call you and let you know what's up," said JT hanging the phone up. JT left his house as soon as he got the word that Trish was leaving. Trish's phone rings as she pulls up at the club.

"He Babe," said Trish as she answered the phone.

"Hey, what club you going to?"

"How you know I'm going to a club?"

"UUUUMMM, your boyfriend is my best friend, you know and we kind of talk here and there," said JT sarcastically.

"OOOOHHHH, we going to Club 723. Why you going to meet me there or something?" asked Trish.

"You'll see," said JT hanging up the phone and driving to the club.

JT got there in 15 minutes and had to wait 10 minutes to get in. When JT got into the club, they had exotic dancers in oversized bird cages. All the different color lights inside of the club as well as the VIP were full.

They had a dance floor that took up most of the club that was smack dap dead in the middle. On the outskirt of the dance floor were booths that could hold up to 10 people. JT looked around and saw Trish and a couple of other people at a booth, so he walked over there.

"Hey," said JT louder than usual, tapping Trish on the shoulder as he went over there. Trish smiled so hard that she thought she was doing an orbit commercial.

"Hey Babe," said Trish getting up and hugging JT.

"Everybody, this is my man JT. JT this is everybody."

JT noticed everybody sitting at the table. On the opposite side was. Vanessa, Damon, Sabrina, and Omar. The side that him and Trish were on was Kim, Aairyah, Trish and himself. JT gave everybody dap or a handshake and the first person that recognized him was Kim.

"Now I know you. You was in my class in high school, right?" asked Kim staring at JT.

"Yeah, that is me," said JT.

"Y'all don't remember this guy?" asked Kim talking to everybody at the table.

Everybody either struggled their shoulders are said no except for Damon.

"He looks familiar."

"This is JT. The boy ass y'all whipped in high school. When y'all fought Rich… And the other boy, I forgot his name," said Kim. Saying Richard's name is still a hard pill to swallow for Kim.

"Cameron," said Aairyah and started laughing.

"Yeah, that's him," said Omar.

"So, how you feeling JT?" Aairyah asked.

"I'm good," said JT looking at Trish.

Trish was surprised that after all these years, they still knew JT, even Cameron, but Cameron was already gone before Trish entered Howard.

"Oh, shit, you remembered what we did to Cameron?" asked Aairyah, bagging up.

Damon and Omar laughed as well. Kim, Vanessa, and Sabrina even chuckled at the fact. JT and Trish were the only ones not laughing and felt like the eyeballs of the bunch. Cameron or JT didn't tell Trish about the incident with Cameron at school, so Trish was lost and didn't know what everybody was laughing at until Damon said, "I'm cumming, oh yeah, you like that Shit Bitch." Imitating what Cameron did in the bathroom. More laughter feels in the booth as Trish and JT feel stupid. Kim told Trish about what happened and Trish damn near laughed herself.

"Yeah, that was some funny shit," said Damon.

Trish looked at JT and asked, "Why you never told me that?"

"You didn't ask?" said JT. Time flew by and bottle after bottle went up in the air.

"Come on, let's dance," said Omar getting out of the booth, grabbing Sabrina's hand and taking her to the dance floor with the drink still in her hand.

One couple after another, everybody got up and started to dance. Laughing, grinding, and acting a fool all took place on the dance floor. JT knew that Cameron was somewhere in the club, so he couldn't be too open to Trish like he usually is.

"Hold on Babe. I'll be right back; it's too hot," said Kim in Aairyah's ear.

Aairyah nodded to his girl as he kept dancing to the song by himself. Everybody was tipsy that came to the club and only Kim was the one trying to sweat it out.

"Hey bartender!" Kim yelled, still tipsy from earlier.

"Hey Kim," said Cameron in Kim's ear. Kim turned around and saw Tyrone.

"Oh, hey Tyrone," said Kim giving him a hug.

"What you doing here?" asked Cameron.

"I'm with my friends and my husband," said Kim looking back at her husband and friends on the dance floor having fun.

"Oh, that's what's up. I tried to call you, but you didn't pick up, so I figured you was done being my friend," said Cameron making sure his back was turned to the dance floor, praying nobody came over.

"You called me when my husband was around and he doesn't approve of me having boys as friends. I don't know why but I got to respect it," said Kim forgetting she called the bartender over.

"Yeah, can I get a double shot of Hennessy," said Cameron waiting for Kim to respond.

"And a bottle of water. I'm dehydrated," said Kim fanning herself.

The bartender came back with the shot and the bottle of water.

"So, when can I see you again?" asked Cameron.

"Why you say that what you going somewhere?" asked Kim drinking her water.

"Yeah, I got to run, sorry, but can I take you out for lunch on your lunch break Monday?" asked Cameron seeing Vanessa walking towards them.

"You can't take me out, but we can have lunch," said Kim taking another sip of her water.

"Okay, I'll call you," said Cameron leaving the area before Vanessa could even get close.

Vanessa came up and saw that Kim was talking to somebody.

"Who was that?" asked Vanessa, pointing in Cameron's direction and grabbing Kim's bottle of water at the same time.

"Oh, that was Tyrone. One of my friends," said Kim.

Vanessa looked at Kim with a look on her face to say she was lying.

"Yeah whatever. You never told me about no Tyrone," said Vanessa drinking some water.

"Because it's none of your business," said Kim taking her water bottle back and drinking it.

"Whatever, but I'm about to go home and take my man with me because it's starting to get too hot, and I'm sweating," said Vanessa.

"Yeah, me too; let's go get our mans," said Kim walking to the dance floor.

CHAPTER 8

Deep Dark Secrets

"He tried to propose to me; what should I do?" asked Trish, out of breath.

"What did you say? Where you at?" asked JT.

"I just ran out of the basketball stadium. He tried to propose and I ran," said Trish, still out of breath.

"So, where you at now?"

"I'm in the parking lot."

"I tried to tell you that he was going to do it, but you hung up on me, but this what you do. Stay by the car; when he come out, tell him that you are not ready to get married… And that you didn't know what to do, so you ran," said JT, thinking of a way to get her out of it.

"Trish! Trish!" said Cameron hollering in the parking lot, looking for Trish.

Trish was a couple of cars down, hiding behind a truck.

"Cameron is calling me Babe. I'll call you and let you know what happens. Okay. I love you. Bye," said Trish and hung up the phone before JT couldn't say anything back.

Trish came from behind the truck and met Cameron in the empty space where cars were still looking for a parking space. When Trish saw Cameron's face, she felt sadder than ever. Cameron's eyes were watery when Trish appeared from behind the truck.

"Look, I'm sorry." Trish's eyes began to water as she walked toward Cameron.

"I'm just not ready, Cameron. I'm sorry."

"So, when are you ready? We been together for years on in. When will you be ready Trish? When?" Tears rolled down Cameron's eyes and pain in Trish's heart came when she saw Cameron cry for the first time.

"I-I-I'm sorry. I ran so you wouldn't be embarrassed."

"Embarrassed. Everybody in that stadium was laughing at me. People that were watching the game were probably laughing at me. You-you." More tears come down as Cameron starts to sob.

"You hurt me to the fullest. Like, is there somebody else?" asked Cameron wiping his eyes with his shirt. Trish wrapped her arms around Cameron and hugged him until he stopped crying.

Trish then looked him in his eyes and said, "No, there's nobody else." Trish's voice was raspy when she said it.

It seemed like Cameron could look right through Trish on how much guilt she was carrying.

"I'm sorry. Can we go home now?" asked Trish.

Cameron looked inside Trish's eyes one last time and said, "Yeah, come on," said Cameron walking to his Mercedes Benz with his head down.

Cameron got in and drove off to their house, not saying a word. Pulling up to the house, Cameron got out and so did Trish. Cameron felt so low that he couldn't even function right inside the house, so he went straight to bed. Trish got in the shower and when she came out, Cameron was sleeping with the remote in his hand, watching "The Price Is Right."

Trish turned the light that was in the bathroom and the one in the room as well. Trish walked to Cameron, grabbed the remote out of his hand, and turned the TV off. Trish then walked to her side of the bed, dropped the towel she was covered in, and hopped in bed butt naked. Sliding under the covers, Trish went on Cameron's side and started to fondle with Cameron's dick as she whispered in his ear.

"Daddy can I get some," said Trish, now playing with his balls.

Cameron didn't respond, so she took it upon herself to go under the covers and suck Cameron's dick. Trish still didn't get a response until she was about to pick her head up, and Cameron shoved Trish's head down to keep going, and that's what she did. Cameron grabbed Trish's head and made her go faster and faster until he came in her mouth. Trish swallowed it on accident and smacked Cameron's stomach to tell him to get off of her head. Cameron let Trish go, and Trish came up gasping for air.

"Why did you do that? You know that shit is nasty," said Trish, looking at Cameron's figure because she can't really see in the dark.

Cameron didn't say a word but turned to his side and put the cover over his face. Trish was shocked because usually, Cameron will run a mile to get some pussy, but now he's not even budging. Trish didn't say a word but went to her side of the bed and laid on her side to be back-to-back with Cameron. Cameron heard Trish crying on the other side and turned around. Cameron got up behind her and got close. Flashbacks ran through Cameron's head of all the shit that they had been through and including tonight, and it made him shed a few tears. Trish felt the tears touch the back of her neck. Cameron grabbed Trish's lower stomach and propped her to arched her back. Cameron entered inside of her. Cameron picked Trish's head up and laid his arm out so her head was on his biceps. Cameron then wrapped his arm around her neck as he began to thrust inside her. Trish felt warm, complete, and loved that moment. Rocking her body with Cameron and all until JT slipped her mind. Then all the body movement stopped, and Cameron could feel it.

"What's wrong?" asked Cameron stopping his penetration.

"Nothing keep going," said Trish acting like nothing had happened.

Cameron knew something was wrong but didn't want to stop having sex because his orgasm was about to come up again. Cameron went harder and harder as he squeezed her neck and released his kids inside her. Cameron kept his dick inside of her as he fell asleep. Trish finally went to sleep an hour later, wondering what JT was doing.

"Hello," said Kim.

"Hello," said Vanessa driving to Kim's house.

"Yeah, Girl, what's up?" asked Kim bending over the countertop, ready to get her ass plushed by Aairyah. Kim heard sobbing in the background.

"Do you have a minute?" asked Vanessa.

"Yeah, what's wrong Girl?" asked Kim getting ready to lean back up, until Aairyah came behind her, grabbed her neck and slammed her back down, sending juices down Kim's thigh because roughness turned her on.

"I'm coming over," said Vanessa.

"Can you…" Those were the last words Kim said before Vanessa hung the phone up.

Ten minutes later, she was parking in front of Kim's house. Going up to the door. Vanesa thought she was entering a porno shoot with all the noise Kim was making. Vanessa overheard Kim moaning, yelling, and screaming Daddy until she knocked on the door. The sound of the knock automatically stopped the moaning. A long pause came before.

"Here I come V.," said Kim.

A couple of minutes later, Kim came to the door, hair wild with nothing but a dress on. Vanessa didn't care; she was in tears when Kim opened the door.

"What's wrong V.? Is everything alright?" Kim asked, opening her arms.

Vanessa fell right into her arms and started to cry even more. Kim grabbed Vanessa, brought her into the house, and sat her down on the couch. Kim sat next to her and rubbed her back.

"What's the matter? Did Damon do something?" asked Kim, still rubbing her back.

Vanessa was still sobbing and nodded her head no.

"Did something happen to Sasha? Ron-Ron?" asked Kim pulling Vanessa's hands away from her face.

"Where's Aairyah?" asked Vanessa looking around the house.

"He's upstairs in the shower. Why, what's up Girl?"

"Look, don't judge me on this, okay? You remember when me and Damon split up for a little while?" asked Vanessa, saying like it was that long ago.

"Yeah why?"

"Well, I met this guy, right, and he was cool at first. But I didn't plan on doing nothing. I swear. Then after a while of being bored at my mom's house and neither you are Sabrina had time for me, so the guy called my phone and said he wanted to go out. So, I didn't have nothing to do, so I said yeah, and we went out. To make a long story short, I slept with him," said Vanessa.

"You what!" said Kim louder than a usual tone.

"I know, I know."

"Why did you do it? I mean, neither one of us is a golden child, but that shit is high school days V., We are married now. We vowed ourselves to this one person, and you broke it," said Kim.

"Are you with me, or you with them?"

"My bad, sorry I got carried away, but what happened? What made you do it?"

"I don't know Kim, like I was drunk, going through something's with Damon, and I was kinda horny," said Vanessa looking at Kim like she was disgusted.

"That doesn't make it right to cheat on your husband. I mean, I see where you coming from, but that's y'all problem. Hopefully, he forgives you. Do you think he will?" Vanessa looked at Kim like she wasn't her best friend for years.

"Damn, Kim you don't even have my back," said Vanessa getting up and walking to the door.

Kim got up and grabbed Vanessa's arm.

"Hold up V. Look, you know I got your back no matter what. It's just going to be a hard pill to swallow for Damon, and you know I keep it 100 with you no matter what, and that's why I said it like that. I'm not trying to be ignorant, but that's how it is V."

"I know it's just that every time me and Damon about to have sex, I will think about that night, and… and…" Vanessa paused.

"And what, V.?" asked Kim in a concerned voice.

"And it turns me off. Like my pussy gets dry and everything."

Kim wasn't prepared for that, but they told each other everything, so she just held Vanessa again.

"I think he's catching on Kim. I don't want to lose him; he's been good to me all the way around the board. I mean, he cheated, but besides that, I didn't mean to cheat on him," said Vanessa crying on Kim's shoulder once again.

"If he really loves you, he will take you back V."

"He don't want to hear that bullshit Kim. He told me the only way I will break up with you is if you cheat on me, and he was dead serious Kim," said Vanessa.

"Well, don't tell him then V."

"What's if he finds out Kim. Then what?"

"Then I don't know V. Maybe you tell him in the future. Like a couple of years from now. Then what he going to do?"

Vanessa thought about it and knew she didn't have any other choice to go with.

"But it's killing me inside tho. Like every day, I think about it at least once out the day."

Aairyah came downstairs with a towel on.

"What's going on down here?" asked Aairyah looking at Kim and Vanessa at the front door.

"Oh, nothing Vanessa had to talk to me, that's all, Babe." Aairyah walked over closer to them.

"V., you okay?" Vanessa's hands were covering her face.

"Yeah, I'm good, A. Thanks for asking," said Vanessa grabbing her shirt and drying her eyes.

"I'm here if you need me," said Aairyah walking back upstairs, "and for you. Daddy wants to see you upstairs when you are done," said Aairyah walking up the steps.

"Okay Daddy, I'll be there," said Kim.

"Look, I'll talk to you later Kim. I'm going to see what's up with Damon and let you know," said Vanessa opening the front door.

"You sure, V. It's okay; you can stay here."

"Nah, it's okay. I'll call you and let you know what's going on."

"Okay Girl, love you and make sure you call me," said Kim hugging Vanessa.

"Love you too, and I will," said Vanessa walking to her car after leaving Kim's house.

"Sabrina! Sabrina!" Omar yelled as he walked into the house. Omar just had come from work on a Sunday and he was dead tired, especially after going to the club the night before.

"Yeah, Babe!" Sabrina yelled from upstairs.

"Just seeing if you was here, that's all."

Sabrina's phone rang and it was Shanay.

"Sabrina, your phone is ringing," said Omar looking at Sabrina's phone that was on the coffee table near the front door of the house.

"Pick it up. It should be Shanay!"

"Hello." That is what Omar said as he answered Sabrina's phone.

"Who is this? Where my sister at?" asked Shanay, knowing who it was, just ignorant as she can be.

Shanay was in her car, bumping Trina in the background.

"You know who this is. What do you want?" asked Omar walking up the steps to Sabrina.

"I want my sister. Nobody don't want your ugly ass boy," said Shanay, now laughing a little bit at her own joke.

"Yeah, your sister like it, and if I wasn't married, you would like it too," said Omar entering the master bedroom where Sabrina lies in the room ass naked, holding her feet in the air showing her well-groomed pussy.

Sabrina was in the room watching a porno, playing with herself. Omar saw the juices glossing down and around Sabrina's pussy in front of the bed. Omar threw the phone at Sabrina and went straight to licking the pussy. One hand holding a foot up and another grabbing the phone on the bed.

Sabrina put the phone to her ear, and all she heard was, "This pussy."

"What you say?" asked Sabrina. Covering the mouthpiece after letting a moan out.

"Nothing, just your husband being ignorant as always, but what you doing?"

"Nothing," said Sabrina breathing hard over the phone.

"Oh, okay, but guess who called my phone talking about he bought me a new car, and he wants to put a ring on it?" Sabrina has been waiting to hear this for years.

Sabrina kicked Omar's shoulders so he could get off of her. She turned on her stomach so he could stop and she could have a clear mind. That didn't stop Omar from sticking his dick inside of her.

"Who?" asked Sabrina, eager to know who it is.

"Chris."

"Chris? Who the hell is Chris?" asked Sabrina as she felt Omar's bare skin touch hers as he got on top of her.

Omar rubbed his dick against Sabrina's ass as he waited for her cue to go in. Sabrina lifted her hand and had one finger up as to say one minute.

"The Chris I shitted on. The one I said his cheap ass; the one who took me to the motel," said Shanay driving to where Chris said to meet her.

"Oh, okay, now I remember, so why he buy you a new car for?"

"Because he is pussy whipped or something. Maybe he just want to spend all his money on me," said Shanay hype over the phone.

"Well, what, he hit the lottery or something?"

Omar's dick was beating and pre-cum was coming out of his dick, anticipating to get inside of Sabrina's pussy. Omar smacked her ass to tell her to get off the phone. Sabrina put up her index finger again to tell him to hold on in an angry way.

"Yeah, he hit the lottery, but I'm not sure for how much just know your sister is going to be balling."

Omar grabbed Sabrina's waist and placed her ass in the air.

"Well, you know that AAAAHHHHHHH. I'm going to call you back."

Omar rammed his dick inside of her as she was on the phone. She has one handing holding her up and the other around Omar's neck as her body is twisted, looking at Omar.

"DAMN, DAAAADDDDDDY!"

Moaning Omar as she throws her ass back and forth on Omar's dick as he strokes her harder and harder. Smacking her ass repeatedly, breaking more than a little bit of sweat. Omar pushed Sabrina off her and watched her body lay on the bed. Omar turned her over and watched as white cum from Sabrina climaxing all over his dick. Omar grabbed Sabrina's feet and slid her body down the bed. Sabrina's legs were now dangling from the bed as Omar leaned over and picked her up off of the bed. Sabrina wrapped her legs around Omar's lower back and her arms around his neck. Omar picked Sabrina up by her shoulders and lifted her off the bed. Sabrina went in between their bodies and grabbed Omar's dick. Sabrina then went and slid Omar's dick up and down her lips.

"So, this is what you want?" asked Sabrina, still not entering inside of her flooded pussy.

"Yeah, Babe come on, put it in," said Omar, eager to penetrate his love of his life.

Sabrina then entered his dick inside her and slid down on it. Sabrina held on to Omar's neck and rocked back and forth, sending Omar to the wall. Sabrina went faster and faster now. Sabrina swung on Omar next like a swing smacking her body against his. Sabrina was so wet that Omar had juices coming down his leg because every time their body would meet up, Sabrina's juices would get on Omar's leg and thigh, and it would run down his leg.

After about 10 minutes of Sabrina throwing it on Omar, her orgasm came and she went wild. Juices were now dropping from Omar's balls and landing on the floor, leaving a little puddle of Sabrina in between his legs. Omar then grabbed her waist and slammed on her even harder, sending her to her highest point and exploding all over Omar's dick. Omar orgasms at the same time as Sabrina making his knees weak and dropping to the floor and landing in the puddle that was on the floor underneath him.

"Guess what?" asked Omar after they laughed at Omar's legs giving out on him.

"What!" said Sabrina kissing Omar.

Sabrina was an inch apart from Omar's face; lips almost touched it as he said, "My ass is drenched fucking with you."

They both laughed and Sabrina rested her head on Omar's shoulder as she dozed off with Omar's dick still inside her.

Kim's phone notifies her, saying she has a message from Tyrone.

"Hey Kim, I was wondering if we are still up on our date at lunchtime."

Trish immediately erased the text and texted Tyrone back and said, Hey Tyrone, I told you already it's not a date, but yeah we can have lunch together. How about we meet up at T.G.I. Fridays? It's only a couple of blocks from my job.

A couple of seconds later, Kim got a text message back saying.

"That will be fine. I'll see you there at 12:00."

Kim didn't respond to the text message; she just closed her phone and kept doing what she was doing. Lunch break came. Kim headed out the door and ran to her car because she was late leaving out. Getting in and starting her car, Aairyah pulls in front of her car so she can't leave the parking space. Aairyah jumps out and Kim's phone begins to ring. Aairyah had a big smile on his face as he walked up to her car. Kim hangs the phone call up and puts it on silent. Kim rolls the window down as

Aairyah approaches the car.

"Hey Babe," said Kim as Aairyah leaned over the window and kissed him.

"Hey, didn't expect me to show up here, huh?"

"No, what the hell are you doing here?"

"I told my boss to let me take an extra hour off so I can have lunch with you."

"Awwwww, that is sweet."

"I know, I know your husband is the man I know," said Aairyah laughing a little, "but seriously, bring your sexy ass on so I can eat; I'm hungry," said Aairyah walking to his car.

Kim thought about taking her phone but thought otherwise and left her phone in her car. Kim locked her car door as she got out and jumped in Aairyah's car.

"So, where are we going?" asked Kim.

"I was thinking about T.G.I.F.," said Aairyah speeding out of the parking lot.

"No," said Kim as soon as T.G.I.F. came out of Aairyah's mouth.

Aairyah looked at her like she was crazy.

"Are you okay?" asked Aairyah.

"Yeah, yeah, I'm okay. I just don't want to go there."

"Okay…" Aairyah was reading Kim's body language and knew something was up.

"Soooooo, where do you want to go?" asked Aairyah.

"It really doesn't matter, just not there?"

"Why not? What is there a person you don't want to see that's there or something?" asked Aairyah, looking at Kim as he says it.

Kim thought about telling Aairyah about Tyrone but knew Aairyah would put things in the wrong way and snap.

"No, I just don't want to go there, that's all."

"So, where was you going at before I showed up at your job? Without even thinking, Kim said, "T.G.I. Fridays."

Before Kim could take back what she said, Aairyah was going down her throat with a million and one questions.

"Now we going to T.G.I. and we going to see who is down there!" said Aairyah knowing Kim is hiding something.

A couple of minutes went by and Aairyah was pulling up inside T.G.I. Fridays.

"So, is you coming or what?" asked Aairyah, parking and getting out of the car.

"No, I told you I don't want to go inside of there." Aairyah got outside the car, went to the passenger side, and opened the door.

"I'm not going in there," said Kim with her arms crossed around her breast.

"Oh yes, you are," said Aairyah yanking her out of the car and basically dragging her to the front door of Friday's.

"Get your ass in there," said Aairyah pushing Kim in the front door.

"I hate you sometimes," said Kim walking inside.

"I love you too. Now get your ass in there," said Aairyah.

Tyrone was in the far corner and as soon as he saw Kim, he got out of his seat. Aairyah came behind her and Tyrone went right by her, knowing Aairyah was his girl. Tyrone saw the look on Kim's face and knew something was up.

"Hey everybody! Does anybody here know this girl right here!" Aairyah raised Kim's hand, and everybody looked over at them.

Kim felt so embarrassed she snatched her hand from Aairyah and stormed out of the restaurant. Aairyah chased after her and met her at the car.

Kim thought to herself, *"That was a close one. Should I just tell him that I have guys that are friends? No, he's going to snap."* Kim was facing her back to Aairyah as he approached her from behind.

"Something is up and I know it is," said Aairyah.

"What the Fuck is wrong with you? You fucking embarrassed me. Now I can't even go in there no more," said Kim with tears coming down her face.

Aairyah felt bad about what he did but kept a mental note.

"I'm sorry, but it seems like you are hiding something from me," said Aairyah grabbing Kim and hugging her.

"Okay, I love you. I'm not hiding nothing from you," said Kim wrapping her arms around Aairyah and placing her hands on his shoulder blades.

"Okay come on then Babe. Let's leave," said Aairyah opening the door for Kim.

Aairyah got inside and pulled off.

Kim dried her eyes and said, "I'm hungry." Aairyah looked at Kim and laughed, and so did Kim.

"Let's go to McDonalds," said Kim.

"Ba da ba baaa, I'm loving it," said Aairyah doing the theme song to

McDonald's.

Kim laughed again as Aairyah chuckled. Kim loved this man and she knew that Aairyah could always make her laugh, cry, and feel like the most beautiful girl in the world. Kim knew hanging with Tyrone would be trouble, so she decided that hanging with him was done for. Aairyah went to McDonald's and ate it at Kim's job parking lot.

"So, what we doing tonight Babe?" asked Kim eating her French fries.

"I don't know. Do you got something in mind?" asked Aairyah.

"No, not really. Vanessa wanted to go out tonight to get some stress off her chest."

"Is this incident is going to be like the one we just had?"

"No, Babe, I promise," said Kim kissing Aairyah.

"Hold on; it's Monday. Who the hell goes out on a Monday?" asked Aairyah looking at Kim.

"Vanessa said she just wanted to have a drink. That's all. You can come if you want to," said Kim eating more of her French fries.

"Omar might be there and Damon, I think, so I'm not sure. Well, not Damon, but Omar might be there," said Kim.

"I'll see tonight if I go," said Aairyah.

"Okay, well, let me get in here before my lunch break is up," said Kim kissing Aairyah and getting out of the car.

"Love you," said Aairyah.

"Love you too," said Kim going to her job.

Aairyah pulled off and when Kim saw him out of the distance, she went back to her car to get her phone. She had seven missed calls and five text messages when she got her phone. Kim deleted the text messages, the missed calls, and Tyrone's phone number from her phone so Aairyah wouldn't see if he was ever to look through her phone.

After work, Kim went straight home and got ready so that she could go to the club with her friends. Aairyah was already ready when Kim stepped in the door.

"Oh shit," said Kim as she saw her man Gucci down to the socks.

"Look like somebody is going somewhere tonight," said Kim walking up to Aairyah and hugging and kissing him.

"Yeah, I don't got nothing else to do and neither of us go to work tomorrow, so why not?"

"Okay, I hear you," said Kim going upstairs.

Hours later, Kim and Aairyah left the house and went to the club. Kim noticed that entering the club was like a high school reunion. Everybody was in Club 723. Ron-Ron, Omar, Damon, JT, Vanessa, Sabrina, Shanay, and Trish were in the club when Kim and Aairyah walked in. The club had all different color lights going on with everybody on the dance floor. Kim and Aairyah went to the bar and got a mixed drink of Hennessy and Hpnotiq.

"I thought nobody was going to be here," said Aairyah.

"I didn't know all these people was going to be here," said Kim.

Aairyah noticed that Damon was on the dance floor, waving his hand to tell him to come over there. Vanessa walked up and Damon walked off.

"Babe, I'll be back," said Damon as he stepped off.

"Hey, Girrllll!" said Vanessa giving Kim a hug.

"Heeeyyyy!" why the hell you didn't tell me that all these people was going to be here?"

"I didn't know all these people was going to be here. When I came, everybody showed up."

"Damon, long time no see," said a man whispering in Vanessa's ear.

Vanessa remembered the voice but couldn't pinpoint it. Vanessa turned around and saw her junior high sweetheart Alex.

"Hey Alex," said Vanessa hugging Alex.

"Damn, you look good," said Alex admiring her frame.

"You don't look too bad yourself."

"Can we get a dance?"

"No, my husband is here and he wouldn't appreciate it," said Vanessa taking a sip of her Incredible Hulk.

"What, you can't speak to nobody?" asked Kim.

"Oh, my fault Kim; you know I didn't mean it. How you been?"

"Yeah, yeah. Sike Nah, I'm good, but how are you?"

"I'm good."

"Look, V., I'm sorry for them high school days. I never had a girlfriend when I was with you, for the record. I may have cheated for the wrong reasons, and I think that was my biggest mistake in my life. Couldn't you ever forgive me?"

Vanessa felt where Alex was coming from, but she knew that she was married and nobody could come between her and Damon. Damon saw from afar that somebody was trying to hit on his wife, so he approached them.

"I'm sorry, but I'm married; maybe if we could have made it through high school and college, we would have made it, but now it's too late," said Vanessa trying to let him down without hurting his feelings.

"But…" Alex felt a top on his shoulder and saw Damon breathing down his neck.

"Oh, shit, long time no see," said Alex with a smile on his face.

Damon couldn't put the name with the face, but all he knew was he was all up on his girl.

"You don't remember me?"

"I don't give a Fuck who you is. You better get the Fuck away from my girl." Aairyah came behind Damon and said to him.

"What's the problem?" Kim automatically grabbed Aairyah's hand and said to everybody.

"We are dancing; there isn't a problem."

"It's a high school friend Babe. Nothing major, come on," said Vanessa, following Kim and Aairyah lead to the dance floor and leaving Alex in his tracks.

"What was that all about," said Damon in Vanessa's ear as Vanessa grinded on Damon.

"It wasn't even serious. Babe chill out."

Damon didn't say anything about it, but he walked off. Vanessa grabbed Damon's hand.

"Where are you going?"

"I got to use the bathroom," said Damon in a hostile voice.

"Well, can you at least say something?"

Damon walked off and didn't say anything at all. Kim and Aairyah were dancing, and Sabrina and Omar danced side by side.

"That boy is drunk; look at him Babe."

Aairyah looked over and saw Omar's arms wrapped around Sabrina, basically hanging over her whole body.

"Babe, you are Fucking drunk. Can you stop," said Sabrina trying to get Omar off her.

"Stopppppp…Whyyyyy," said Omar slurring his words and smelling like he had just drunk a gallon of Hennessy.

"Get off of me!" said Sabrina pushing Omar off her.

"Come on, Kim this nigga is getting on my nerves," said Sabrina walking off of the dance floor.

Trish and JT didn't touch the dance floor the whole time they were there. Ron-Ron didn't even get close to Kim that whole night, and he was pissy drunk right with Omar, but he was sitting at the bar the whole time. Sabrina and Kim came up to the side of Ron-Ron as they sat down.

"What the hell was y'all drinking?" asked Sabrina, sitting on the stool next to Ron-Ron.

"Cîroc and Hennessey annndddd Goose annndddd Goose annnndddd Hennessey annnddd Goose." Sabrina just looked at Ron-Ron like he was stupid, and Kim didn't even want to look his way.

"We got to get his sister because he's too drunk to drive," said Sabrina.

"Where is she at anyway?" asked Kim.

"Oh, shit, look at these two on the floor," said JT with his arm around Trish.

Trish was happy as she could ever be. Like she could let her hair done and not watch over her back for Cameron. She was with the man that she wanted to be with all night. She was tipsy, and she didn't get any unexpected calls from nobody.

"Oh Shit, Damon is going to snap. Where is he at? Where the hell is Sabrina at?" asked Trish as she took a shot of Cîroc.

JT and Trish had the perfect view of what was going on, but JT wasn't paying attention to that. JT's eyes were on Shanay the whole night. Watching her dance with multiple guys giving them her number and letting them buy her drinks. Now she was sitting at a couple of tables in front of JT and Trish, and he was madder than ever. Trish watched as Damon came out of the bathroom, stepped for a second and ran over to where Omar and Vanessa were dancing. Damon approached Omar and said something that led to something else and Damon stole him, sending Omar back a couple of feet. Sabrina and Kim ran over there, and all they heard was…

"What the Fuck wrong with you nigga pressing up on my girl like that?"

"Fuck you nigga. She was my girl first. You stole what was mind. I was suppose to get married to her, not you. You was the one the one that broke us apart. Yeah, what you think? Nobody told me that you slid them pictures in Vanessa's locker, you hating Mother Fucker!" said Omar.

Damon was in shock and when he looked at Vanessa, she had the same impression as Damon.

"So, what the Fuck you trying to say? You want to be with her nigga?" asked Sabrina, heartbroken ready to break down in tears.

"Yeah, I want to be with her," said Omar, not knowing what he had just said out loud, "I didn't mean that," said Omar realizing what he said. Sabrina ran off the dance floor and out of the club. Omar chased after her. Aairyah watched as Vanessa stepped off on Damon and left the dance floor as well.

"Babe come on, we leaving," said Kim grabbing Aairyah's hand and walking off of the dance floor,

When Kim left the club, she saw Tyrone coming inside the club. Her heart dropped, hoping that he wasn't going to say anything while Aairyah was right there. They made eye contact and kept it moving. When Kim and Aairyah got to the parking lot, they saw Omar and Sabrina arguing. Damon came right behind them, speeding past Kim and Aairyah, going to his car where Vanessa sat at.

"I'll holla at y'all. Drive safe," said Damon as he went to his car.

Sabrina left Omar in the car and walked up on Kim and Aairyah.

"Can I stay with y'all tonight? I'm not trying to go home with him," said Sabrina, tears rolling down her eyes as she said it.

"Yeah Girl, you know that, come on," said Kim walking to her car and getting in.

Omar walked up to Aairyah's car and grabbed Sabrina before she could get inside the car.

"Get off of me Omar."

Omar would not budge; he just grabbed her tighter and tighter. Sabrina tried to get in, but Omar yanked her arm so she could get away from the car. When Omar yanked her to him, Sabrina slapped the shit out of Omar in his face making a loud noise you could hear from the other side of the parking lot. That brought rage in Omar's eyes as he cocked back and punched Sabrina in her eye, sending her to the floor. Aairyah flew over Sabrina and started whipping Omar's ass. Damon saw what was going on and ran over there. Aairyah had Omar on the floor by the time Damon came, so they both started kicking him on his ribs, head and stomach. Sabrina was on the floor crying holding her eye. Kim ran around the car, helped Sabrina on her feet, and put her in the back seat. Vanessa ran over and was confused about what was going on.

"What the hell happened?" asked Vanessa.

"I'll tell you later; get Damon off of Omar and go home. I'll call you when I get home," said Kim grabbing Aairyah and telling him to stop.

Aairyah and Damon stopped kicking Omar and left him there in the street. Aairyah jumped in his car, and Damon and Vanessa did as well.

"Oh shit, there go Cameron," said JT getting up from the table and walking off.

"Hold on wait. What you want me to do?" asked Trish, grabbing onto JT's shirt as he was about to leave her there.

"Stay here. I'm going to be back." JT walked off and went to Shanay's table.

"Excuse me can I talk to you for a minute?" asked JT grabbing Shanay's arm.

Shanay was at the table with two other guys. Shanay jerked her arm back when JT tried to move her from the chair.

"Look JT, I'm doing me right now. I don't got time for no bullshit."

"I just want to talk. That's all," said JT, kinda mad, but guilt crept over him for being there with Trish.

"Why don't you go over there with that Bitch you was with all night?"

"Come on Shanay. It's not even like that."

"Yeah whatever. I'll see you when I see you," said Shanay.

JT saw Cameron approaching them faster than he expected. JT had to do something because Trish was only a couple of tables down by herself, and it would look strange that she was by herself at the club when she told Cameron that she was going over to Sabrina's house. JT grabbed Shanay by her dreads, got her out of her seat, and threw her a couple of feet in the opposite direction. Cameron rolled up on him when he did it.

"What the Fuck is going on over here?" asked Cameron.

"This Bitch keep disrespecting me and I'm tired of it. You know what. I'm out Fuck you Shanay. Yo Cam, you chilling here?"

"I guess so."

"A'ight nigga this Bitch got me mad as shit. I'm going home Man," said JT as he gave dap to Cameron and walked off.

Cameron looked at Shanay and kept it moving to where Trish was at.

"What the hell is you doing here?"

"I came here with Sabrina and them, but I don't know where they went?" said Trish, trying to play it off.

"Yeah, I just seen them leave when I came in. Where your car at?"

"It's at Sabrina's house. I caught a ride with her."

"So, what they left you? And you never told me you was going to no fucking club," said Cameron, pissed off that Trish didn't tell him where she was going.

"She better have not left me and Babe. I didn't even know that she was taking me here," said Trish trying to get the drunkenness out of her system.

Cameron just laughed and said, "Let me find out." And walked out of the club with Trish following behind him.

CHAPTER 9

Enough is Enough

Damn, what the hell happened to me? Why the hell am I in so much pain? How did I get here? Shanay asked herself a million questions as she lay on the hospital bed.

"She will be fine. She's in a slight coma right now, but everything will be fine. Her injuries aren't that bad, so she wouldn't be there for too long. If you have any questions, be free to ask me. My office is down the hall to the right. She can hear everything you say, so feel free to talk to her if you please," said the doctor.

"Okay, thank you Doc," said Sabrina holding Shanay's hand as she spoke.

Then, the doctor left, leaving Sabrina and Shanay alone.

"Hey Sis? What the hell happened? Last thing you told me was that you was going with Chris and he bought you a car and hit the lotto or some shit."

Everything popped back into Shanay's head when Sabrina said Chris's name.

"Well, if you could see my eye is black. Omar punched me at the club and he was drunk. You know what he told me? He said he wanted to be with Vanessa. Yeah, his high school sweetheart. I know they was Fucking in high school and he was cheating on me with her in high school, but I still took him back. After all these years, he still wants to be with her. Fuck that; he can have her. I'm not worried about it. Fuck both of them." Shanay could hear Sabrina crying and tears sprinkling on her hand.

"Don't cry Sis; everything is going to be okay. Just watch; everything is going to be alright.

"Sis, I need you more than ever right now. I'm lost without you. I been staying at Kim's house the whole time. Vanessa and Omar been blowing my phone up. I just want to know what happened. Like damn, this shit hurt both of us." Sabrina's phone rings and she looks at it.

"It's Omar; should I pick it up?"

In Shanay's mind, she said, *"Yeah, see what he got to say."* Shanay could hear the phone still ring as it went off.

"Nah, I'm going to let him think about some shit before I even talk to him. He hurt me Shanay. Bad like I'm still hurting from that, and now this shit happens. I don't know, but I'll be back around six because I got to go to work at 10. I promise I will. Kim and Aairyah might come here at 3 or 4; they came the last two days. Chill Girl, you been in a coma only three days, and yes, you still look good. I don't know if you was up the last two days when everybody was here, but I don't know. Maybe I'm talking too much. I just hope that you will be okay. The doctor said he would release the information when all the lab work comes back. I'm running late so I'll see you at 6. Love you," said Sabrina giving Shanay a kiss on the forehead.

"No, hold on, I got to tell you what happened."

"Oh yeah. The guy that Trish to out with JT. He's been here every day too. He actually came more times than I did. His name is all over that visiting list. He brought you those red roses that are by you. He said he was a good friend. I don't know, but I'm going to tell Trish about it or not. You can tell me when you get out of the coma. Love you, and I'll be here at 6. Bye," said Sabrina walking out of the room and down the hallway.

Damn man, only if she can hear me. Flashbacks of the night with Chris came up in her head.

"So, where's the car at?" asked Shanay as she came and pulled up on Chris.

"Damn you, a gold digger for real. I can't get no hi or how you doing?"

"I'm sorry Baby. How you doing?" asked Shanay with half of her body out of the window.

"I'm good but follow me, and I'm going to show you the surprise I got for you," said Chris as he pulled off and headed to the local Motel 6.

This nigga is still driving that bullshit Ford Focus and he won the lottery. He better not be on no bullshit. JT pulled up to the side of Motel 6 and Shanay screwed her face up. Shanay parked on the side of him and said.

"What the hell are we doing here?"

"You are going to see. Stop getting mad like you can't get your ass whipped," said Chris jokingly.

"If you say so," said Shanay getting out of her car and going to the motel room.

Chris handed Shanay the key to open the door.

"Here, go ahead in. I forgot something in my car."

Shanay didn't think anything of it and opened the door as Chris went to his car. As Shanay stepped in, somebody hit her with a bat on her back, making her drop instantly. Shanay back felt like it broke. Shanay couldn't even move if she could. Again and again, the masked guy hit Shanay in her back. Shanay knew from then that the dude was trying to paralyze her.

Chris stepped in the door and saw the other two masked men kicking her in her stomach, face, and ribs.

"Hold on, chill, chill," said Chris closing the hotel room door.

"Throw her on the bed."

All three masked men picked up Shanay and threw her on the bed. Shanay screamed as they picked her up. Crying and praying that somebody would come to her rescue. Chris dropped 3 E-pills in her mouth as she screamed and made her drink some water.

"That's for the pain."

Chris and the other masked men took off Shanay's clothes and turned her on her stomach, showing her fat ass that was oh so round.

"That's what I like to see," said Chris taking his pants off.

"Listen, I'm going first, then you, then you, and Buckey, you going last because you are going to give it to her," said Chris as the men laughed.

Shanay couldn't even move because of the pain in her back. Shanay's body felt numb as she tried to move her body. Chris jumped on top of her and spread her ass cheeks. Chris threw his condom on and entered inside her as he pounded away. Shanay didn't even know who was fucking her until somebody whispered in her ear.

"You going to like this dick." Shanay knew it wasn't Chris and from then on, Shanay passed out from the pain and pills.

Damn, what else happened as Shanay tried to remember what happened to her. Trying to figure out what happened, Shanay heard somebody enter the door.

"Hey beautiful." Shanay knew the voice but couldn't put the name with the face.

"It's JT. I tried to bring you more flowers, but the nurse said you got too many roses. But how are you holding up." JT sat in the chair next to the bed that Sabrina was sitting in.

"I see Sabrina was up here not too long ago. Well, let me see what's new. Oh, Marshal should be coming home soon. You know I be talking to him sometimes. Oh, shit, I don't think I told you, but Sabrina's eye was damn near shut yesterday. I didn't ask what happened. I just made sure she was cool. She probably told you already. I'm getting a promotion too. Yeah, don't hate," said JT laughing a little bit.

Shanay laughed in her mind and thought about all the fun times she had with JT. Shanay heard JT blowing his nose and going to the bathroom. JT came back and Shanay heard sobbing as JT spoke.

"Look Shanay. I love you. You should know that by now and it's killing me inside, that you keep doing this to yourself. The doctor told me that you must have got raped because the DNA was still inside you when you were found all beaten up, and I just wish you could settle down, Babe. All the shit I try to do for you all the times I said we can move to a different state. Like why can't you just love me for me? Why you got to Fuck around with all these dudes for? Why?" asked JT crying even harder, holding Shanay's hand.

If Shanay could cry, she would have cried in JT's arms, but she couldn't. Shanay just felt pain in her heart as JT kept on talking.

"Look, my promotion is going to make me leave the state. I don't know when it is, but it's going to happen and I want you to leave with me. Please."

"I will JT, I will. I'm sorry for all the stuff I did to you. I'm sorry. Can you please forgive me?"

"I don't know what else to say, but I prayed that shit like this wouldn't happen to you. Fuck it it's over with. I'm still here right by your side."

"I'm sorry I love you, JT as well. I knew you loved me too when you gave me your house key that day and told me to come over when I please and I took you for granted. I'm sorry, Babe, I love you."

"But Fuck it, you probably go back out there and do the same thing over again anyway, so I'm probably wasting my breath and time."

You not wasting your breath or time; I love you. Shanay was getting mad because she couldn't talk to anybody except in her mind.

"I don't know, but hopefully, you come out of this shit soon; until then, I'll come see you tonight and every night until you wake up. I love you and I'll be talking to you tonight," said JT kissing Shanay on her forehead.

"Wait, don't go; I need you here with me. Can't you just call off and stay with me all day? Why are you leaving? You about to go to Trish's house or something?" Shanay had anger inside of her now.

"I love you; Shanay I'll see you tonight," said JT kissing Shanay again.

"I'll come here after I get off of work," said JT as he walked out of Shanay room and went to the front desk to sign out.

"So, what you love this Bitch or something?" asked Trish walking behind JT as he signed out.

"What are you talking about? Why is you even here?" asked JT walking to the elevator.

"You know what I'm talking about. You already know."

"Know what? What are you talking about?"

"So, you want to play dumb. Sabrina told me you came to see this Bitch more than her. Every hour you get, you come up here. You don't even got time for me like what the Fuck."

"Look, you know I love you, and I will do anything for you, but I love Cameron just as much as you. He's like my brother Trish and you know that," said JT stepping into the elevator and going down.

"You keep saying that, but that doesn't stop you from Fucking me from time to time. Now does it? You Fuck me more than Cameron do, but now all of a sudden, you don't want to go through with it no more. I thought we already had this discussion already, huh?" asked Trish, furious that JT was trying to ignore her.

"You know what Fuck that, I'm going to tell Cameron everything," said Trish rushing out of the elevator as it stopped and the doors became open.

"Wait Trish," said JT as he followed Trish.

"No, I'm tired of this shit. One day you are going to be with me, and then the next, you are not. I don't got time for this Shit; I'm out," said Trish leaving the hospital and walking to her car.

"Then what huh? Then who you going to be Fucking with, huh? You lose me, and when you tell Cameron, you lose him too. Think about it," said JT closing the driver's door as Trish tried to open it.

"Why are you going to break up with Cameron in the first place?" asked JT, now leaning against the car.

Trish paused for a moment that said, "Because of you! That's why. I

Fucking love you, but you don't love me like I love you," said Trish, now crying.

JT got up from the car and wrapped his arms around Trish.

"Why can't you love me for me," said Trish, still crying.

"I do Babe. I do," said JT grabbing Trish's keys from her and opening the door.

JT reached into Trish's car and hit the unlock button to open all the doors. JT opened the back door and placed Trish in the back seat of her car.

"What are you doing?"

JT didn't say anything but grabbed Trish's legs and threw them in the air, making Trish's body fall backward. Trish's white sunflower dress slid to her stomach as she fell backward. JT pulled her yellow and white panties down and balled them up in his hand.

"Hold on, stop its people out here," said Trish.

JT pushed Trish back and went in between her legs, tongue first. Trish's head hit the car door as JT licked her clit and sent her running as he always does. JT's body went further inside the car as she went further back. People walked past and saw JT's legs hanging out of the car and Trish's head from the back window moaning out of control.

"OOOOHHH SHIT DOWN DAMN DADDY, YOU LOVE THIS PUSSY!" moaning loudly, that the parking lot could hear her.

Trish forgot where she was at as she was about to reach her orgasm. With the excitement and JT's tongue going on Trish's clit, Trish's juices burst out of her and covered JT's face like icing on a cake.

"You still love me?" asked JT putting Trish's panties between her legs and sliding them up.

Trish was out of breath, trying to speak. JT kissed Trish's pussy before sliding them all the way up. JT grabbed Trish's hands and slid her out of the seat and up on her feet.

"Yeah, I love you, Babe," said Trish kissing JT on the lips and tasting her juices at the same time.

Trish wiped the juices off of JT's face and said, "Can you promise me that you are going to be with me and love me."

"Yeah," said JT knowing he won the battle.

"No, you said it too fast. Promise me you are going to marry me and tell Cameron it's over," said Trish looking into JT's eyes.

"I promise."

"That was the only way I could get you from him. I wasn't like it was a lie." Pleaded Damon as he was following Vanessa around the house. Vanessa still was ignoring him as he followed her.

"So, what, you can't fucking speak to me. It's been three days like damn. Is it that fucking serious?" asked Damon hoping Vanessa would say something to her.

Since the incident that happened between Omar and them, Vanessa didn't say anything to him the whole time.

"I want to know why you did that?" asked Vanessa putting her clothes on.

"Because I was in love with you just like I'm in love with you now. Babe, I love you unconditionally. You don't realize that. I didn't put the ring on your finger for nothing. I love you. The only reason why I did it was because I wanted to marry you and grow old with you like we are doing now. Babe, can you please stop getting mad at me please. I hate when you are mad at me," said Damon looking into Vanessa's now watery eyes.

"I'm sorry for being mad at you," said Vanessa hugging Damon and putting her head on his shoulder.

"It just felt like our relationship was a lie or something. Like I been lied to for all these years," said Vanessa hugging Damon tighter.

"It wasn't Babe."

"I know, I know I'm sorry. I love you."

"I love you too Babe." Vanessa's flashback came to her when she had sex with Jermaine.

"Come on, let's go see if Shanay is alright like we planned to do."

"Okay, Babe," said Vanessa loving the fact that Damon is by her side no matter what.

"Why do you want to go so bad?" asked Vanessa looking at Damon in his face.

"Because most likely Sabrina might be there, and y'all can talk it out and to support you going to see your friend. Is that too much to ask?" asked Damon.

"No, just wondering," said Vanessa kissing Damon.

Damon got dressed, and he headed out of the door with Vanessa in hand. Pulling up to the hospital and getting out, Damon saw Trish pulling out of the parking lot.

"There go your friend leaving," said Damon pointing at Trish.

"That ain't my friend; that's Sabrina's friend or Kim's friend. I mean, she cool, though."

Damon parks and gets out of the car with Vanessa. They walk into the hospital, go up to the desk, and sign in. Vanessa saw the visiting list and saw that Sabrina was there and JT was listed as her fiancé.

"Oh Shit, Babe," said Vanessa pointing at JT's name and its relationship with her.

"Somebody going to get caught up, but we just saw Trish leave tho."

"I don't know what's going on, but something is going on," said Vanessa as they walked to Shanay's room.

Damon opens the door and Vanessa walks in.

"Damn, what the Fuck happen to her," said Damon loudly so Shanay could hear them.

Shanay already knew who it was. *Fuck you Damon.*

"Shut up Babe. Damn Shanay, who the hell did this to you?" asked Vanessa walking to Shanay and feeling over her bumps and bruises on her face.

"Whoever did this, Shanay, I promise I will whip their ass," said Damon.

"It's going to be alright, Nay-Nay," said Vanessa laughing, remembering when Vanessa first gave her that name at the end of high school.

Shanay remembered it like it was yesterday; it brought a smile within herself.

"You know the boy JT put fiancé on his visiting slot. Yes, he did, Girl, but you know he mess with the girl Trish. I don't know; something is up."

A light bulb popped in Shanay's head when Vanessa said Trish. *Hold up. Cameron messed with Trish because when JT gave me the house key that day, Trish pulled up and he said it was Cameron's girl and that he didn't have anything to do with her. So, JT is showing Trish off as his girl, then what the fuck is Cameron doing? Unless Cameron doesn't know that they are going behind his back? Is Cameron plotting on somebody? Or something? Whatever it is, I'm going to get to the bottom of this.*

"So, Shanay, it's me, Damon; how you holding up?" asked Damon as Vanessa went to the bathroom and closed the door behind her.

"Look, listen, you know I'm in love with Vanessa, but I'm in…."

Kim and Aairyah walks in the door and Damon gets out of his seat.

"Damn, there goes my Baby," said Kim walking up to Shanay's bed and kissing her forehead.

"So, I went to your apt and got you set up, cleaned it and everything, so hopefully you wake up tomorrow. I can't believe you're even in a coma. Forget it tho. I just want you to know I was here with you every step of the way."

Damon backed up and dapped Aairyah up. Aairyah pointed at Kim and made his hands as a mouth and made it go up and down, as to say Kim talks too much.

"I would have never thought that I would have cared so much when we was freshmen. Yeah, you remembered I whipped your ass." Kim was laughing so Shanay could hear her.

"I'm playing Girl." Vanessa got out of the bathroom and saw Kim.

"Heeeyyy," said Vanessa running up to her friend Kim.

They both hugged each other and Vanessa's phone rang. Vanessa picked it up and said, "What's up Bro… yeah, she's good…

just me, Kim, Damon, and Aairyah… Why don't you want to come up?... A'ight well, I'll talk to you later," said Vanessa hanging up the phone.

Kim already knew who it was and looked at Aairyah. A couple of hours passed, and everybody left Shanay, leaving her in the bed, as lonely as ever.

After what just happened to me, my mind is still on sex. What the hell is wrong with me? Shanay could feel her pussy tingling. *What the hell is going on? Why do I got to keep wanting sex? What the fuck? Maybe if I go to sleep, I won't feel it.* Ten minutes later, Shanay fell asleep and dreamed about JT having sex with her.

The next morning Shanay woke up and her eyes were wide open. She could see everything in the room; she was in the bed, the bathroom, and Sabrina was sleeping on her side. Shanay pulled the blanket from over the top of her and tried to get up, but she couldn't move her legs. Shanay couldn't even get out of bed. Shanay couldn't even move her body; all she could do was move her arms.

"WHAT THE FUUUUUUUUCCCCKKKKKKK!" Shanay yelled at the top of her lungs.

Sabrina woke up instantly.

"What's wrong?" asked Sabrina.

Shanay grabbed Sabrina's hand and held it tightly.

"I can't move my body at all. What the Fuck." Shanay started to shed tears down her face.

A doctor came in and asked, "What happen?"

"She woke up screaming. I don't know."

"I'll go get her doctor," said one of the doctors.

"You going to be Okay, Sis; calm down," said Sabrina.

Shanay was lost in words when the doctor stepped in.

"Hey, Ms. Flowers, I'm Dr. Glover, and I've been running tests on you. Can you tell me what happen that night?"

"Fuck that night; what is wrong with me?"

"Oh, I'm sorry, I'm not your Dr. I'm filling in. Did you just wake up?"

"Yeah, Doc, she just woke up. Can you tell us what's wrong with her?" asked Sabrina, holding Shanay's hand dearly.

"I'm sorry, Mrs. Flowers, I thought you was aware of your circumstance."

The doctor had a white trench coat on, some slacks and casual shoes on and a clipboard in his hand.

"Well, Ms. Flowers, it seems like from your waist down is paralyzed. With treatment, your legs will come back in no time, depending on how hard you work. Now when the lab test came back from the person's semen, it was a guy named Brandon Wise. Do you know this person?"

"No, I don't."

"Well, I know him. Actually, he is one of my clients and he is positive for HIV."

"What?" asked Sabrina and Shanay at the same time.

"Yeah, I'm sorry. He was born with it. It was passed down from his mother and he was the one who was behind this. The cops are looking for him now."

Shanay or Sabrina couldn't even speak. Sabrina just went over and hugged Shanay with all her might.

"The top of your body is fine. You can move it; it's just probably cramped up, so you can't move it now," said Dr. Glover tapping on his clipboard, "well, I'm going to give y'all sometime to talk. Just tell one of the nurses that you want to speak to me if y'all have any questions," said Dr. Glover stepping out of the room.

Shanay closed her eyes, hoping that this was a dream and she could finally wake up, but she couldn't.

"I promise I won't tell nobody that you have HIV. I mean, everybody knows that you are going to be paralyzed."

Shanay cried some more and Sabrina felt her pain. Shanay and Sabrina didn't say anything for what felt like a whole hour.

"Sis, can you go get that wheelchair over there and bring it close to the bed."

Sabrina ran and grabbed the wheelchair, wheeling it to the side of Shanay's bed.

"Pick me up and put me on there," said Shanay.

"You can't leave the hospital for another week Shanay. The doctor said that you are very weak."

"That doctor don't know nothing. Help me sit up."

Sabrina could see the pain that Shanay was in and didn't question her from that point on. Sabrina tried to pick Shanay up and she started screaming.

"AAAAAAAAHHHHHH. Okay hold on. My back really does hurt. On 3, push me up at a 90-degree angle. Even if I scream, keep pushing," said Shanay taking deep breaths and preparing herself to get out of the bed.

"1, 2, 3… AAAAAAAAAGGGGG SHIT… That felt good a little bit," said Shanay, now sitting upright.

Sabrina grabbed Shanay's legs and turned them facing her. She then pushed the wheelchair closer so she could slide Shanay on there. Sabrina tried to pick it up, and it was a no-go.

"Girl, I can't pick your Big Ass up. All the weight is coming down on your ass," said Sabrina laughing a little bit.

"Girl come on."

"A'ight, if you fall, it's not my fault," said Sabrina trying to pick Shanay up.

Sabrina slid Shanay off of the bed, and Shanay grabbed the wheelchair and swung herself on the chair.

"Damn, that was a close one," said Shanay as they both laughed.

"Now come let's leave."

"Girl, you don't got no clothes on."

"So, what come on," said Shanay trying to wheel herself out of the room by herself.

"Okay, hold on," said Sabrina grabbing the back of the wheelchair and heading out of the door.

Going past the doctor's office and a few nurses, Sabrina was well on their way to the elevator. Stepping inside the elevator and heading out of the hospital, Sabrina saw Omar's car, but Omar was nowhere to be found. Sabrina got Shanay in her car and drove off to Shanay's house. As they pulled up to Shanay's 2-bedroom, 1½ bathroom home, they saw JT planting flowers in front of her house.

"This guy is something special. He is your backbone, I'm telling you. He paid your bills for the next three months. Help me clean the house up and he is now planting flowers in front of your house. You better marry this dude," said Sabrina bragging about JT.

"But he mess with Trish like come on now."

Sabrina looked at her like she was crazy and said, "Girl, you ain't no damn passion fruit, you better get his ass why you got him," said Sabrina, parking the car and getting out before Shanay could even say anything.

Sabrina got her wheelchair out of the trunk, and that's when JT looked and saw Shanay in the passenger seat. JT got up and ran to the car.

"What the hell are you doing here? Are you okay?" asked JT opening the passenger's door.

"Why the hell do you got a wheelchair? Are you okay Babe? Do you need some help?"

"One question at a time, JT. You know she is weak as hell, so she needs our help," said Sabrina pushing the wheelchair to the passenger's door to JT.

"That's not a problem," said JT helping Shanay out of the car and into the wheelchair.

JT rolled Shanay to the house and up the steps to her master bedroom, where she preferred she rather be. Inside of the bedroom, JT fixed the whole thing up. Pictures of JT and Shanay were up everywhere, new silk sheets and blankets. Instead of the 40-inch TV that Shanay had, he got her a 60-inch TV on the wall. Shanay wasn't buying any of it. She loved the way she decorated her room.

"Oh Shit, you never told me you change it around," said Sabrina jumping on the bed, "isn't it nice?" asked Sabrina.

"Yeah," said Shanay cracking a halfway smile.

"I just want to chill and relax. My body is in pain real bad, and I'm starting to get a headache," said Shanay grabbing her forehead.

"It's okay, I got you," said JT wheeling Shanay to her bed and getting ready to pick her up when Shanay said.

"Jay, can you get me some water? I'm dehydrated as shit."

"Yeah, I got you," said JT running at Shanay's command.

When JT left, Shanay said, "You don't think all of this shit is creepy? Like who the hell does this? He's starting to get on my nerves already," said Shanay.

"You never had a person that catered to your every need. That boy love you got damnit. Why can't you see that? I wish Omar treated me like that," said Sabrina helping Shanay out of the wheelchair and onto the bed.

"Look, everything will be fine. I got to go to work, and JT going to be here with you. Just call me at my job. Here you can have my cell phone while I'm gone," said Sabrina, handing over her cell phone.

Shanay grabbed it and put it under her pillow. JT ran up the steps and into the room. Sabrina said bye and went on her way to work. JT handed Shanay the water, and she sat it down.

"What's wrong?" asked JT sitting by Shanay.

"Nothing," said Shanay as she closed her eyes.

Week in and week out, JT has been bathing, clothing, entertaining, and comforting her every single day. Trish has been blowing his phone up and going to his house every day for the past couple of weeks, trying to find out where he was. Even Cameron didn't know where he was. JT spent most of his days taking Shanay to therapy, getting Shanay her depression pills, and taking her to a massage parlor every couple of days. Shanay used to wake up in the middle of the night and cry to JT just thinking about being paralyzed until one night, JT heard what he had always wanted to hear his whole life.

"JT," said Shanay waking him up out of his sleep.

"Yeah, Babe," said JT, half asleep.

"I want to say thank you for all you done. I Love you, and I wouldn't have nobody else but you. I'm really glad you in my life," said Shanay, wrapping her arm around him halfway.

JT turns to Shanay and sheds a few tears.

"I love you too." As he cuddles up with her.

CHAPTER 10

Confused and Suffering

Omar was in his room crying tears, looking at pictures of him and Sabrina. Even though what he said was wrong, part of it was true. Omar would do anything to get Sabrina back, but she wouldn't pick any of his calls up and reply to his texts, so Omar figured that Sabrina was done. Omar knew that a couple of words wouldn't finish their damn near-decade relationship deep down in his heart. It had been two days since Omar hadn't texted or called Sabrina's phone and it felt like two months. Omar wondered what Sabrina was doing every day.

Ron-Ron told Omar that Shanay got raped and might be paralyzed a few weeks ago, but when he got there, she was gone. Omar seemed like he could never catch up with her, only at work. When he did go in there, Sabrina would tell one of the other nurses that she was not there. Omar went so far as to wait for Sabrina to get off work. Sabrina would see him and tell one of her friends to take her to her sister's house. Omar would be waiting all night for Sabrina.

Then one day, Omar just gave up on trying to get with Sabrina and just left her alone. Omar would know when Sabrina would come to the house because some things would be out of place in her closet and lesser and lesser clothes would be taken. Sabrina wouldn't take all her clothes, just a few outfits at a time. Omar couldn't even think about any other female. All Omar did was work, come home and eat, watch TV, and go to sleep.

One day Omar got a call and jumped up to answer it, hoping it was Sabrina. The second ring, Omar picked it up.

"Hello."

"Yo, what's up nigga? What you doing?" asked Ron-Ron.

"All shit, man, I ain't doing nothing, player. What's up with you?"

"All man let me tell you who I saw today?"

"Who?"

"Kamiyah," said Ron-Ron smiling over the phone.

"Kamiyah?" asked Omar in confusion, trying to get her picture to pop up in her head.

"Yeah Kamiyah. Half Chinese and half Black. She was on the cheerleading squad with Sabrina, and she was asking about you. You remember she was cute, but she didn't have nobody, so niggas was stunting on her little ass."

It popped in Omar's head when he said half Chinese and half Black. Kamiyah was one of the most beautiful girls in Howard, but she was a late bloomer. She couldn't get any play from none of the high school stars.

"Now I know who you are talking about. Yeah, what she say?" asked Omar, eager to find out what Kamiyah had to say about him all these years.

"She said she was going to Club 723 tonight, and she wants you to be there," said Ron-Ron.

Omar seconded guessed it because he wasn't fully done with Sabrina, and he knew in her mind that Sabrina wasn't fully done with him either.

"I don't know man…

"What you mean you don't know? I'm not going to let you stay in that house all miserable and shit. Look, that body she got now is to die for. She still got that innocent look on her since high school man; she's the shit. Like I said before, you are going if you like it are not, so get dressed. I'm going to fly by your crib at 10. Holla." said Ron-Ron and hung up before Omar could say anything.

Omar just looked at his phone and said, "Ain't that about a Bitch." Omar laughed to himself and hung the phone up.

After the phone call, Omar felt good knowing females were still jocking his ass after all these years. Omar took a shower and got ready for tonight. Omar just knew he was single for tonight.

"My shift is about to be up and I still got two more clients I got to do," said Sabrina hoping that Cindy (Sabrina's co-worker) would do it.

"It's okay, Sabrina I got you. I just started my shift and I barely got anything to do today. Unless somebody comes in here today," said Cindy taking two folders of the two clients Sabrina was supposed to be doing.

"Thanks, Cindy you're a lifesaver. I appreciate it," said Sabrina, ready to jet out the door and go to sleep because she was extra tired catering to Shanay's every need and going to work afterward.

JT took night shifts at this job so he could be there for Shanay in the day and Sabrina would be there at night.

"Oh yeah, I almost forgot it's a guy waiting for you out front."

"It's not Omar, right?"

"No, I remember what you told me if he comes. It's some other guy and he's kinda sexy too," said Cindy looking at Sabrina like I'll let him hit this ass.

"Okay," said Sabrina.

Sabrina walked into the front lobby and saw Mitchel get out of his seat when they both locked eyes.

"Hey Sabrina," said Mitchel walking up to Sabrina.

"Hey, what are you doing here?" asked Sabrina, admiring Mitchel's swagger and how he kept his body in shape.

"I know, I'm sorry for coming at your job like this, but I been dying to tell you something. Yes, I know you told me that you had a man and to never call or text you, so I respected your wishes. That's why I came here and talk to you in person."

"Okay, so what did you have to tell me?" asked Sabrina, hoping to go out on a date or something because Shanay was getting pm her last nerve even though she felt bad for her sister still.

"Well…" Mitchel paused and looked around and saw a lot of people around in the lobby, "can we finish this conversation another time over dinner or something? I mean, if you don't have plans?" Mitchel asked.

"That sounds like a plan to me," said Sabrina questioning herself if she should go are not.

A flow of guilt went through her body as she spoke those words.

"Okay, then here you go and call me when you are ready," said Mitchel handing Sabrina his number.

"Okay, I will," said Sabrina taking the number and putting it in her pocket.

"Okay then, bye," said Mitchel walking out of the hospital. Sabrina went to her car and drove home.

Going inside the house, Shanay watched TV in the living room, waiting for JT to bring her food out.

"Hey Sis, how you feeling?" asked Sabrina dropping her keys and pocketbook on the coffee table.

"I'm okay, but I just wish you could be right by my side."

"I am Sis. I had to work." Sabrina knew that Shanay was in her depression stage again.

"I know that; it's just hard, you know? Like I can't have sex and what if JT finds out I have HIV? Do you still think he is going to be with me?" asked Shanay putting her head down.

Sabrina was at a loss for words because she didn't know how JT would respond to it. Sabrina just sat on the couch next to her and hugged her tightly.

"I don't know what to do?"

"Has he asked you for sex yet?" asked Sabrina.

"No, but I know he wants some because his dick be as hard as a rock when we are in bed. If he don't get it from me, then I know he going to get it from Trish. She been blowing his phone up like crazy."

"How you know she been blowing his phone up?"

"Because he let me see that he not picking her phone calls up or texting her back, but I know a man if he doesn't have no pussy in a long time that he's going to find some," said Shanay burying her face on her sister's shoulder.

JT walks into the living room with two plates of grilled hamburgers and French fries.

"I'll be back with your drinks."

Sabrina loved that JT was there. Every time she got off work, there was food ready to be eat-in.

JT came back and placed their Pepsi on ice on the table in front of them and said, "Enjoy. I'm about to go upstairs and take a shower and get ready to go to work. Do you need anything, Babe?" asked JT looking at Shanay in her eyes.

"No, I'm okay, Babe," said Shanay grabbing a French fry and placing it in her mouth.

JT then ran upstairs and got in the shower.

"So, what do you think I should do Sis?"

"About what?" asked Sabrina biting her burger.

"Going about having sex? Should I tell him before or after I have sex with him?"

"Girl, you know you can go to jail if you have sex with a person and giving them HIV? Why would you mess his life up for your mistake? Don't do that. If he don't care then by all means, give it to him."

Shanay was kind of her at what her sister said, but all she could do was say, "Okay," before her throat got dry ready to cry.

JT pulled up at his job, parked the car, and got out. His phone started to ring, and when he saw who it was, he put it right back in his pocket. JT would be with Trish if she weren't his boys' girlfriend and if Shanay wouldn't want to settle down. He always told himself-everything happens for a reason; as he shuts his car door, he turns around and sees Trish standing in front of him. Hair not done, eyes puffy and red, and mascara coming down her face; she almost scared JT when he looked at her.

"So, this is what he Fuck we doing!?" yelled Trish with a knife in her hand.

"You better not cut me with that Fucking knife I'm telling you now," said JT backing up from Trish as she got closer.

"Or what JT, huh? What you going to do?"

"Look can we talk first?" asked JT trying to cool Trish down.

"I been trying to talk, but you never answer my phone calls or reply to my text messages. You don't even stay at your house no more what you been ducking me this whole time?" asked Trish holding the knife as tight as she could.

"Listen, you have a man, okay? And most definitely, you are the shit, but I just can't do it no more; it's killing more than it's killing you." JT thought he handled it pretty smooth, but he thought wrong when Trish swung the knife at him, barely missing his ear.

"You cut me I'm going to whip your ass," said JT, ready to punch Trish in her face.

"Well, go ahead and do it. I don't care," said Trish swinging the knife again.

JT opened the back door to use it as protection. Trish swung the knife again, and this time, JT grabbed her hand and twisted her arm backward, causing her to drop the knife. Tears came to Trish's eyes as he twisted her arms. The smell of strawberries struck JT's nose as he got close up on her.

"You're hurting me! Stop it!" said Trish knowing she couldn't get her arm away from JT.

JT did miss Trish more than ever, especially since he hadn't been able to fuck Shanay due to her injuries. JT grabbed Trish's neck with one hand and lifted her skirt with the neck, showing her white and pink see-through panties. JT pulled her panties down and spread her legs, watching her panties drop to her ankles. JT let go of Trish's neck and bent down and spread her ass cheeks as he stuck his tongue in her pussy and up her ass, then again in her pussy. JT could not stop licking her pussy as if he were going to win a gold medal. Juices were flowing down Trish's legs as JT went and licked it up. JT saw Trish's legs shiver as she moaned uncontrollably.

"JAAAAAAYYYYYY TEEEEEEE, AAAAHHH." Trish's legs gave out on her.

JT grabbed her before she could go all the way down. JT blew in Trish's pussy, sending her back on her feet. He then placed the top half of her body in the truck and wrapped her legs around his back. JT smacked her ass and she turned around.

"Do you love me?" asked JT.

"Yes Daddy."

JT entered inside Trish as he grabbed her shoulders and pounded her away. JT then grabbed her hair and pulled it as he stroked her aggressively. Smacking her ass and pulling her hair excited Trish to the fullest. JT knew Trish's body better than Cameron. That is why Trish fell so in love with JT. Trish climaxed over JT's dick, and her legs dropped to the floor. JT flipped Trish around and moved her up the truck. He then grabbed her legs and placed them on his shoulders. He gave her a kiss and she grabbed JT's dick and entered it inside of her. JT stroked harder and harder until he couldn't take it anymore. Every time their bodies meet, it sounds like somebody is stepping into a puddle. The noise of Trish moaning and her juices flowing everywhere, JT busted inside Trish. Trish hugged JT and whispered in his ear.

"I thought you promised me we were going to move to another state and live our lives?" asked Trish.

JT saw water coming down her eyes as he got up.

"We are Trish, we are. I promise. Let me just handle a few things and we can leave."

JT knew Trish couldn't get enough of him, so he kept her at bay.

"But how long? How long do I have to wait to see if I can live my life like a regular human being? Why do this got to happen to me?" asked Trish, still laying in the back of JT's truck.

JT got up and pulled his pants up, which, in the heat of the moment, he didn't even remember dropping them down. JT picked Trish's panties up and realized where he was at when he heard a familiar voice call his name out loud.

"Yo JT, what you don't Fuck with nobody no more?" asked Cameron as he pulled up to his car that was parked parallel.

JT was lucky there was no parking beside him because Cameron would have seen his girl's legs wide open and her pussy in the air. JT threw the panties in the car, closed the door, walked up to Cameron's car, and gave him dap.

"What's good nigga? What you doing around here?" asked JT, giving Cameron some dap.

"Came to see if my nigga is cool, that's all. Why don't you pick your phone up nigga? Everything alright?"

JT knew that Cameron knew something because he had this devilish grin on his face.

"Nah, everything good trying to get this promotion, so I been at work 16 hours a day lately," said JT lying and hoping he didn't see all this sweat coming from his forehead.

"Oh, a'ight than nigga, call me so we can got out or something tonight man."

"A'ight, that's a bet. I get off at 11 o'clock tho."

"Fuck it; we go at 12. The party end at 3."

"A'ight bet," said JT as he walked off to enter the state penitentiary.

When JT saw that Cameron was out of sight, he returned to his truck and saw Trish still had her legs wide open and playing with her pussy.

"What are you doing? You know that was Cameron, right?"

Trish stopped playing with her pussy and put her finger in her mouth, the same one she played with her pussy with and said, "So, I want some more."

JT thought she was crazy and that he had to go to work but saw the juices glowing off of Trish's pussy. JT fed into it, literally putting his face in Trish's pussy once again in the parking lot.

"Babe, this is so romantic. Why did you do this to me?" asked Vanessa.

"Because I thought you was still mad at me for what I did in high school, and I hate when you are mad at me," said Damon looking into Vanessa's eyes as he fed her a strawberry.

Vanessa and Damon were on top of a hill where the family does bar-b-ques and other family gatherings. You could see the sunset from this hill coming down as well as the whole city that they were in. Damon laid out a blanket, a basket of fruit on top of it, and a cooler of water on his side. On the Vanessa side of the blanket was a basket full of chips and sandwiches. Damon had it set up for 12 people to eat, but only two were there. With the car doors open and the radio turned up loud but not too loud, Vanessa knew that Damon loved her with all his heart. As Damon fed her another strawberry, tears fell from Vanessa's face.

"What's wrong Babe?" asked Damon as she bit the strawberry.

Damon quickly wiped both of Vanessa's eyes with his thumbs as he grabbed her head. Images now popped up in Vanessa's head that night she had with Jermaine.

"I love you Damon," said Vanessa.

"I love you too V.," said Damon as he hugged her.

They both hugged each other for a little while as the sun vanished from their side of the earth. It was dark outside now. Damon was ready to leave when Vanessa laid him on the blanket and unzippered his pants, pulling out Damon's dick and started to suck on it.

"Why you doing it out here? Wait."

Vanessa didn't pay Damon any mind but started sucking his dick even harder. Vanessa unbuckled Damon's pants and slid them all the way down to his ankles so she could get a better flow of sucking her husband's dick. Licking it from top to bottom while playing with his balls. Now sucking one ball at a time while jerking him off, Damon closed his eyes. Vanessa licked her way up to the top of Damon's dick and started to suck on its head, letting her saliva slide down his dick. When Vanessa felt he was about to blow, she started sucking his dick faster. Damon couldn't take it anymore and exploded in his wife's mouth. Vanessa didn't care about that anymore; she felt as though she owed Damon her life. Vanessa kept jerking his dick even after he let loose. Damon loved that Vanessa could keep his dick hard. Vanessa got up and took off her yellow shorts and dropped them down to her sandals as well as her panties. Vanessa stepped over them and got on top of Damon. Vanessa laid on top of Damon first and Damon could feel the heat coming from Vanessa's pussy.

"I love you so much, Babe," said Vanessa before grabbing Damon's dick and balancing herself on her knees.

Vanessa rode Damon's dick for what seemed like a ½ hour; in all actuality, it was on 15 minutes. Vanessa got up and turned around, now in the squatting position. Vanessa leaned back and placed her hands on his chest.

"I don't know. I was trying something new." They both laughed and Vanessa fell on Damon's stomach.

Damon got up and said, "Assume the position."

Vanessa did as follows and got on her stomach. Vanessa then got on her knees with her ass in the air, stretching out her back like a cat. Vanessa grabbed a handful of grass and anticipated for her husband to come and get her. Vanessa looked between her legs and saw JT's head was there. Damon got on his back and started eating Vanessa out. Vanessa had never had her pussy eaten like this before. Damon fingered Vanessa as he played with her clit. Vanessa was in total shock and gave her best orgasm yet. She fell on top of Damon's face. Damon laughed when he got up and saw Vanessa laid out.

Damon grabbed Vanessa by her hips and pulled her up. Damon saw Vanessa squeezing her pussy tight every five seconds, waiting for Damon to go in. Damon went inside of Vanessa and she locked her pussy onto Damon's dick. Damon stroked slowly and picked up his pace when he heard Vanessa start to let out a moan. Damon went harder and harder, trying to bust his nut. Vanessa climaxed, again and again, making her drop on her stomach. Damon dropped with her and kept on going stroking harder and harder. What once was pleasure became pain as Damon stroked so hard. Vanessa was ripping grass out of the earth because Damon was going so hard. Damon kept stroking and stroking non-stop until he busted inside Vanessa.

"Damn, Babe, you made my pussy hurt. What the hell gotten into you?" asked Vanessa, still on her stomach as Damon laid on top of her with his dick still in her.

"I... had... to let you know... who's the boss around here," said Damon, out of breath. They both laughed and left when they caught their breath.

"Damn you look good. Where the hell are you going at tonight?" asked Shanay as Sabrina walked down the steps and into the living room.

Sabrina had this all-black see-through dress on that fitted her nicely, some yellow shorts, a yellow bra, and yellow and black heels on with this all-black Louis Vuitton pocketbook with a yellow strap.

"I'm going to dinner with a friend. You like?" asked Sabrina, switching from side to side as if she was a model.

"Yeah, I like. Who you going to dinner with?" asked Shanay, admiring her sister's style.

"A friend," said Sabrina, not trying to have Shanay all up in her business.

"Okay, what's his name?"

"His name is Mitchel and he is pretty cool."

The horn hits two times as Mitchel pulls up to the house. Sabrina looks out of the window and sees Mitchel pull up in his S550.

"Damn Girl, he look good in that Benz," said Sabrina walking to Shanay.

"Let me see what he looks like?"

"Girl go head. We are just friends, nothing more and nothing less," said Sabrina giving Shanay a hug.

"Do you need anything before I leave?"

"No, I'm good. I'm going to sit here and watch BET till I fall asleep."

"Okay, love you Girl," said Sabrina as she left out the door.

Shanay watched as Sabrina left and pushed power to the DVD player, turned the Chanel to 3, and waited until the movie came on. Shanay pulled down her pants and panties and positioned herself so she could be able to finger herself. Shanay pushed play and the porno began. Shanay skipped a couple of scenes where some porno star was getting her back blown out. Shanay stuck her fingers into her mouth and started to play with her pussy. Fingering herself in and out while the other hand was playing with her clitoris, Shanay was going wild. This was the first time Shanay was ever having sexual contact with herself.

Shanay told JT to put one of the blank DVDs in before cooking lunch. Shanay turned the DVD player off before the movie could get on. JT didn't say anything, so Shanay didn't either. Shanay now had two fingers inside of the pussy going in and out while her other pussy was still playing with her clitoris. Shanay busted before she could even begin. Letting her mind be free as her hormones took over her world. Shanay kept her eyes closed and let everything fall in place. Out of nowhere, she couldn't hear any more moaning or anything until she felt herself drift off to sleep.

JT was the first one to find Shanay on the couch with her pants to her knees and the porno still playing. JT knew what Shanay was doing. JT went close to Shanay and got on his knees. He put his head in between her legs, placed them on his head, and placed them on his shoulder. JT then pulled Shanay closer, and when his tongue hit Shanay lips.

Shanay woke up, and JT went hard. Shanay tried to push JT's head back, but he will not budge. JT went harder and harder. Now with one hand spreading her pussy lips and the other hand fingering her while JT's tongue ran in circles around Shanay's clit, Shanay couldn't get enough. When trying to push him back, Shanay now pulling him in and went crazy. Shanay felt herself about to orgasm and tried to push JT off of him, but he was too powerful. Shanay exploded, and JT licked every single drop up, even the juices that were sliding to her ass crack. When Shanay looked down, JT's had a smirk on his face as he picked her up. Shanay was still in a daze after her orgasm.

JT had her in his arms while walking to the bedroom. JT ate Shanay's pussy the whole time, going up the steps and into the bedroom. JT still had her in the air, eating her pussy while they were in the bedroom. Shanay went crazy, never had her pussy eaten while in the air turned her on even more. Shanay orgasmed again, shivering her body as she exploded over JT's face. JT placed her on the bed and took her jeans and panties off. JT knew that Shanay couldn't feel her legs, so he put her legs behind Shanay's head and kissed her pussy. *If he really loves me, he wouldn't care what I got, right?* Shanay thought as JT entered inside of her. Shanay felt JT's whole dick inside of her and screamed in joy. Shanay didn't have any dick since the night she got raped and what she is feeling now was incredible. JT stroked harder and harder, seeing the bright pink pussy walls come up after each stroke that he brought out. JT pounded and pounded like no tomorrow sending Shanay on one of her wildest rides. JT then moved her legs to the side, lifted one of the ass cheeks up, and pounded away harder and harder. Shanay didn't know how many times she climaxed, but she knew that JT couldn't go anywhere if he wanted to.

JT then flipped Shanay on her stomach and spread her ass cheeks. JT thought about putting it in her ass but thought otherwise and decided not to. JT entered inside her wet pussy and stroked harder and harder. JT saw that Shanay was grabbing on the pillow for dear life, knowing she was about to give in again. JT stuck his whole dick inside of her and let his kids start swimming as he dropped on top of Shanay. JT rolled over to his side and kissed Shanay as he saw tears run down her face.

"What's wrong Babe? Why you crying?" asked JT lost in words wondering what's wrong.

"I..." Shanay thought about telling JT then said, "I love you JT." It was music to JT's ears.

"I love you too Shanay," said JT getting up for round two.

CHAPTER 11

Welcome Home Party!

"Oh My Fucking Gosh! Girl guess who just called me and told me to go pick him up tomorrow?" asked Kim extra hype over the phone.

"Who Bitch?" asked Vanessa, eager as hell to know who Kim is all hype for.

"My fucking brother Bitch! He comes home tomorrow!" said Kim hype as ever.

"No, you are lying," said Vanessa, who couldn't believe her ears as Kim told her a lie.

"I'm dead serious now. I need you to call up some strippers tell them to be ready at 9 o'clock tomorrow."

"I don't know strippers, Girl. What you want me to do?"

"Bitch do something. Oh My God, Oh My God, I'm so Fucking hype. Well, you call everybody you know and tell them to come to the party it's going to be at my house! Tell everybody to bring a bottle; it's going to be on and cracking!" said Kim screaming every word that came out of her mouth.

Vanessa felt the happiness over the phone and she felt good herself that Marshal was coming home. *I wonder what he look like now?* Vanessa said in her mind before she spoke to Kim again.

"Okay Girl, I got you."

"Make sure you call every girl you know over there! My baby is coming home! Oh My Gosh, I can't wait! I'll call you tomorrow! I'm going to get everything ready for us!" Kim said, hanging the phone up before Vanessa could say anything.

Kim called every strip club she could find and told them she needed the baddest strippers money can buy. After Kim got the strippers, she paid for a strip pole to be delivered to her house overnight.

Kim thought to herself, *"What would a guy want after ten years in jail? I don't know besides pussy,"* a light bulb flashed in Kim's head, "probably a cellphone," Kim said out loud.

Kim went to the nearest T-Mobile store and got him the new sidekick. After leaving the T-Mobile store, Kim went to her house to tell Aairyah the good news. Kim got to her house and Aairyah was not there. Kim decided that he would be there sooner or later, so calling him was no point. Kim sat down on her couch, thinking about what else can I do for him when he came home. *"Maybe hire a prostitute? No, what if she got something. I know what I can get him, a car. Yeah!"* Kim thought.

"Why did the chicken cross the road?

"Why?"

"To chase his Baby mom." They both started laughing at the table.

"You so stupid," said Sabrina laughing at Mitchel's joke.

Mitchel knew a way to get to a girl's heart and making them laugh was one of them. This wine got a girl a little tipsy. What the hell did he put in here?

"So, where do you live at?"

"Where you picked me up at the last three times. I live with my sister Shanay and her boyfriend JT."

Sabrina looked at Mitchel when she said it, and Mitchel's face was all screwed up.

"Why is that a problem?" asked Sabrina with a smirk running across her face.

"No, no problem, just thought you lived by yourself, that's all, but what are we doing after dinner?" asked Mitchel, not trying to bring up her husband.

"I don't know what you got planned?"

Sabrina looked at this handsome man and only wondered how good he was in bed. Only two people touched this pussy she wanted to say but thought otherwise. The only person who had been touching her body for the last decade in a half was Omar. Sabrina wondered how another man's touch would feel like. She has been fucking Omar so long; that's all she knows.

"Well, I been wondering if we can go to the Sheraton in one of my suites," said Mitchel grabbing Sabrina's hand from across the table.

That sent chills down Sabrina's body, making her shiver.

"Well, I guess we can do that," said Sabrina, not trying to feel it was too easy to get in her panties.

Sabrina and Mitchel were sitting on the rooftop of one of the finest restaurants in the city. They were looking straight at the ocean because the restaurants were so close to the shore. Mitchel noticed that Sabrina still had her ring on when she married Omar. Sabrina and Omar got married fresh out of high school. Mitchel knew that and also knew that he couldn't bring up her husband because lost memories would fill her head, and he will lose her just as fast as he got her.

"So, where do you live at?" asked Sabrina taking a fork full of spaghetti.

"I live by myself. Right around where your sister live at. Not too far," lied Mitchel.

"Oh, okay, so why don't we just go to your place?" Mitchel had to make up a lie and fast before she thought he was lying.

"UMMMM… I want it to be romantic." Mitchel said after sipping a glass of wine.

"Oh, okay," said Sabrina feeling special.

Sabrina and Omar's relationship was going sour, but she knew that she was still deeply in love with her husband. She was just waiting for him to come to his senses and know what he did was wrong and that she could leave at any time, so he knew not to stop treating her like a queen. Sabrina knew that she had to have Omar's back, but she was still trying to have fun while she was gone. Mitchel tried to get Sabrina drunk as he does with all of his victims. Mitchel ordered another bottle of wine and poured Sabrina another glass. Glass after glass, Sabrina and Mitchel were taking them back. Now Sabrina was really feeling it and she was seeing two of everything now.

"I think you should take me home. I'm not feeling myself right now. My head feels like it is spinning," said Sabrina getting up from her chair.

"Hold on. I don't want you to fall off the roof," said Mitchel grabbing her hand and holding her tight.

Mitchel and Sabrina went down the stairs and into Mitchel's car. When they got in, Mitchel's started the car and pulled off.

"Can you take me home now," said Sabrina with her eyes closed and laid back in the seat.

Mitchel's dick was busting out of his pants just thinking about going inside of Sabrina. Mitchel drove straight to the Sheraton and went to the front desk.

"Hi, can I get my room key 206? I left it here so I don't lose it. Here's my ID," said Mitchel handing her his ID.

"Here you go Mr…"

"We don't need to say all of that; just call me Mitch. That's what my friends call me," said Mitchel, cutting the secretary off what she would say.

The secretary couldn't see where they got Mitch from but didn't ask any questions.

"Okay Mitch. Here you go," said the secretary giving Mitchel his ID and room key, "have a nice day," said the secretary looking at Mitchel leave the hotel and come back with a female that was halfway pasted out.

"Is she okay?" asked the secretary with a concerned look on her face.

"Yeah, she's okay, just a little drunk, that's all," said Mitchel holding on to Sabrina.

Sabrina didn't know where she was at and tried to snap back to reality but failed to do so. When they entered the room, Mitchel laid Sabrina on the bed and he got undressed. Sabrina lay on the bed and was dazing on and off as she only remembered bits and pieces of what happened that night.

"So, how were you going to get me to come here if I don't know my way up here."

"That's why I picked you up. Damn, you asked the dumbest questions, man. So, what you think about doing?" asked Ron-Ron, knowing that

Omar was skeptical about fucking another girl because he was so in love with Sabrina.

"I don't know if she still wants to mess with me," said Omar getting out of the car and going to the club where Kamiyah awaits for him.

"I told you she was on you Dog," said Ron-Ron hype because he wanted Candy, Kamiyah's best friend.

"That's not if you don't run your fucking mouth again."

Remembering when Ron-Ron told on Aairyah about the strippers they had on the island.

"Nigga I'm not. I slipped up that one time," said Ron-Ron lying about him slipping up.

Omar knew that Ron-Ron was lying as well. Omar knew that Ron-Ron still wanted Kim and thought she would leave Aairyah for him, but that was not the option Kim had in mind.

"Yeah, a'ight you called them already?"

"Yeah, they in there now waiting for us," said Ron-Ron looking at his phone.

Omar and Ron-Ron paid the bouncer and walked into the club. As soon as they walked in, they saw Kamiyah and Candy at the bar drinking a Margarita. Omar couldn't believe his eyes when he walked up to Kamiyah. Kamiyah was brown skin, curly shoulder-length hair, and lips like J-Lo. She wore this black and green designer dress that hugged her curves everywhere she moved. She looked so innocent that it turned Omar on even more. Candy was as sexy as Kamiyah; it was just her occupation was being a stripper and Omar wasn't fucking any more strippers after the last stripper at the bachelorette party was trying to put a finger in his ass.

"Damn, Omar you look good now as you did before," said Kamiyah giving Omar a passionate hug.

"You don't look too bad yourself. What are y'all two sexy ladies doing tonight?" asked Omar, trying to be as smooth as he could.

"So, what's up with you?" asked Ron-Ron, looking into Candy's green eyes.

"We're trying to have a good time tonight after the club. What do y'all want to do?" asked Kamiyah reaching for Omar's dick as she saw it bulging out of his pants.

"Shit, we trying to do the same thing y'all trying to do," said Ron-Ron blurting out.

"Okay then, let's just have some fun for right now," said Kamiyah taking Omar's hand and walking to the dance floor.

"So shall we?" asked Ron-Ron holding out his hand and hoping Candy would take it.

Candy looked at Ron-Ron's hand and said, "I guess so," with a hint of attitude.

"It's been a long time since I seen you. How have you been?" asked Kamiyah, grinding up on Omar.

"I been a'ight. Just been..." Omar thought about speaking Sabrina's name up and said to himself, *"This is only a one-nighter."*

"Just been what?" asked Kamiyah dropping it low and bringing her ass back up, making sure she could feel his dick as she came up.

Omar's dick got harder when Kamiyah got him against the wall and started throwing her ass back on him like they were fucking. Omar's kick dripped pre-cum, making him want to fuck her more and more.

"Just been complicated with my wife and me?"

"Your wife?" asked Kamiyah turning around and looking Omar in his face.

"Yeah, my wife," said Omar knowing he messed his chances up with Kamiyah.

Kamiyah didn't really care if Omar had a wife or not because her next move set it off. Kamiyah lifted her dress up to her waist, showing her glow in the dark green thong that she had on.

"Don't be scared; it's not going to bite you," said Kamiyah grabbing Omar's hand and placing it on her ass.

Kamiyah bent over and started to make her ass clap. Omar kept seeing the glow in the dark thong every time her ass would open. Omar slid his fingers in between Kamiyah's ass and felt her wetness as his hand slid through it. One cheek after another, Kamiyah lifted it up. Omar started smocking Kamiyah's ass, and Kamiyah got wetter.

"So, is you going to beat this pussy up or what?" asked Kamiyah getting out of her stance and leaning on Omar.

Omar's dick got hard from Kamiyah saying it. Omar didn't get a response, so Kamiyah squatted down in front of Omar and unzipped his pants. Ron-Ron got on the side of Omar with Candy and Omar picked Kamiyah up before she could pull out his dick.

"What's up nigga?" asked Ron-Ron holding Candy.

Omar knew not to do anything in front of Ron-Ron anymore, so he stood to his plan. However, Omar could see in Candy's eyes that she didn't want anything to do with him.

"Shit," said Omar turning Kamiyah around and pulling her dress back down.

"Don't tell me you hit in the club?" asked Ron-Ron with his hand over his mouth.

"No, nigga what's wrong with you?"

"Why you pull me up? My friend, don't mind."

"I don't want you doing this in the club. I see how you act after the club and then you might be able to taste this dick," said Omar with a smirk on his face when Kamiyah turned around.

After a few more dances, Kamiyah, Omar, Ron-Ron, and Candy sat at the bar and had a few drinks.

"So, Candy when you going to stop fronting on a nigga and let me feel on that pussy?" asked Ron-Ron putting his hand on Candy's leg.

Candy looked at Ron-Ron with a look of discuses on her face.

"Nigga you would never even smell this pussy," said Candy grabbing Ron-Ron's hand and flinging it off her thigh.

"So, when are we leaving because I'm ready to taste that dick," said Kamiyah grabbing on Omar's pants after her fourth shot of Hennessy.

"Whenever you are ready?" asked Omar taking a shot of Hennessy as well.

"Okay, well, let me use the bathroom real quick and we can leave after that," said Kamiyah getting out of her seat and going to the bathroom. Candy followed her to the bathroom as well.

"Man, this Bitch on some bullshit she not even trying to let me hit. I'm about to dip on these bitches," said Ron-Ron taking a sip of his water.

Omar knew Ron-Ron was always a cock-blocker but never like this.

Omar thought to tell Ron-Ron that Kamiyah was going to let him fuck but thought otherwise and said, "So now you going to dip? That shit kills me. Come on then Dog. Don't ever try and take me nowhere else with you again," said Omar stepping off from Ron-Ron and walked out of the club.

Omar knew that he couldn't fuck Kamiyah while he was with Ron-Ron anyway and if Kamiyah really wanted to fuck she would call and get his number. Omar thought if he could fuck Kamiyah tonight, he knew he could fuck her tomorrow without Ron-Ron present. Kamiyah called Ron-Ron when she got out of the bathroom and Ron-Ron sent her to voice mail.

Marshal got out of the state penitentiary at six in the morning and the first person he saw was Kim and Mellisa. Marshal could see their eyes light up at the sight of him walking up to the car. Marshal worked out every other day for the last five years of his bid. Marshal was out on parole and had 10 years back up to follow it. Kim was the first person to run to Marshal. Marshal was now 6'3, 265 pounds, all muscle. Marshal was cut up like a bag of dope and nobody could see him.

"Oh My Gosh Bro you got so Fucking big," said Kim with tears of joy coming down her face.

Marshal picked his sister up in the air while he hugged her. Mellisa came out of the car and water-filled her eyes as well. Marshal put Kim down and went straight to his mom.

"Hey Mom!" said Marshal giving his mom a huge bear hug that warmed her heart every second.

"Hey, Baby," said Mellisa giving Marshal a hug as well.

Marshal then got in the car and they drove off. Kim gossiped about everything she could think of that had happened in the past 10 years that Marshal had been locked up. Even though Marshal was happy to be home, he was still in depression from the news that his mom told him when he was locked up. Marshal thought that Kim didn't have a care in the world about their mom's health because she wouldn't have been so happy all the time, or at least he wouldn't. Even though Kim kept in contact with Marshal here and there, it wasn't the same as his mom. Mellisa did everything under the sun for Marshal when he was locked up and for that, Marshal was thankful. Kim knew in her heart that she wasn't there for Marshal like she should have been; that's why she was trying to do her best to do everything he wanted. Kim pulled up to Mellisa's house and everybody went inside. Mellisa didn't waste any time in cooking for her son. Kim and Marshal sat at the table in the kitchen, talking while Mellisa was cooking for them.

"I got a couple of surprises for you that you are going to like very much," said Kim flipping her phone open and dialing a couple of numbers.

"So where is it at?" asked Marshal, eager to know what it is.

Marshal saw Kim get up from the table as she talked on the phone. Ten minutes later, she returned, and he heard a horn beep three times.

"Well, there goes one of your surprises," said Kim walking to the front door.

Marshal followed behind her and was shocked when he looked out the front door. Aairyah pulled up to the curb with an all-black GMC truck with 24-inch rims on it. It had a red ribbon over top of it.

"No, No, No, you are bullshit'n, right?" asked Marshal walking outside of the house and to the truck.

"Nope, it's all yours," said Kim following behind him.

"What's up nigga!" Aairyah said as he hopped out of the truck and hugged Marshal.

"What's good nigga," said Marshal Bear hugging Aairyah.

"Damn nigga you strong; you need to let some of that shit out of you," said Aairyah as he unbraced.

All Marshal could do was stare at the truck that was in front of him.

"Here nigga it's yours," said Aairyah handing Marshal his keys to the truck.

Marshal grabbed the keys and hopped in.

"Come on, let's go for a spin," said Marshal rolling down the window.

Aairyah hopped in and they sped off without even saying bye. Marshal and Aairyah rolled around the city for about an hour until Kim called them back and told them that the food was done. Marshal and Aairyah got out and went to the house.

After eating the food, Marshal told his mom that he would be back and that she didn't have to stay up for him. Mellisa already knew what Kim had planned for Marshal, so she really didn't care what time he came back.

Kim took Marshal shopping buying him all new clothes and sneakers. After that, she took him to her house and he took a shower there. Marshal didn't even want to get out his new truck; he was so hype.

After Marshal took a shower and chilled for a little bit, Aairyah told him lets go get some liquor before it gets too late. Marshal was with it and they left. Kim told Aairyah to keep him out for at least an hour. Kim got everything ready. When Marshal got back, she had the strip pole set up, the strippers were all there, and everybody showed up one by one. People Kim didn't even know showed up to celebrate Marshal coming home. Kim had everybody get in position, so when Marshal gets there, they all will be ready.

"Hello," said Sabrina, not even feeling herself.

"Yeah Girl, it's me."

"Hey, K. What happen?" asked Sabrina hoping Kamiyah had some bad news so that she wouldn't feel so guilty.

"Nothing happen, Girl that man is in love with you. He wouldn't even let me taste his dick, and he had a nerve to say that he got a wife."

"He said he got a wife."

"Yeah Girl, I tried everything. I couldn't get him to fuck me at all, and he left me and Candy at the club. I think he did that, so he won't be able to fuck me. Girl, you got a keeper. Go get your man Girl," said Kamiyah.

"I will, I am. I'm going to see him tonight. Marshal's welcome home party is tonight. Do you want to come?" asked Sabrina, feeling guilty that she went with Mitchel out on a date and who knows what they did at the Sheraton Hotel.

"Marshal? The one that killed Richard?" asked Kamiyah, trying to pinpoint all the Marshals she knows.

"Yeah, it's my friend brother; he came home today."

Kamiyah's panties got wet at the moment Sabrina said yeah. Kamiyah loved bad boys and knowing that Marshal didn't have any coochie in all that time made Kamiyah an obligation to go to the party.

"Damn right, I'll go. When are you going?"

"Whenever Kim say come over."

"Well, how about I meet you at Shanay's house and I follow you there."

"Sound like a plan."

"Okay Girl, I'll see you there tonight, bye."

"Bye," said Sabrina hanging up the phone and telling the taxi to stop at the house coming up.

Sabrina felt so guilty that morning that she hoped Omar fucked Kamiyah so they could be equal, but she knows now that she owes Omar big time. Sabrina tried to remember what happened to her last night, but all she remembered was waking up in the morning ass naked and room service waking her up. She knew something had happened, but she just hoped nothing did happen. Sabrina paid for the taxi, got out, and went straight inside Shanay's house, where she heard moaning and the baseboard smacking the wall upstairs. Sabrina closed the door and went upstairs.

"FUCK ME HARDER! SLAP MY ASS! THAT'S IT, DADDY, THAT'S IT!"

That was all Sabrina could hear as she walked past her door and into her room. *"I hope JT knows that she got HIV because that's going to break his heart,"* thought Sabrina as she got ready to jump in the shower and go to the party.

"Yo," said Cameron.

"Yo, what's good nigga?" asked JT.

"Shit chilling, they said Marshal home."

"Yeah, he got released today and that he having a party at his sister's house."

"Oh yeah, you going?"

JT was hesitating to say his answer because not even 5 minutes ago, Trish called him and threatened him if he didn't go; she would tell Cameron that they had been having sex behind his back.

"I don't know. I might because Marshal asked me to."

"Marshal asked you to go over there?"

"Yeah, Marshal. You know me and him use to bust it up while he was locked up."

"Yeah yeah, well, let me know if you do go because Trish told me that Sabrina called her and told her to come so you can watch Trish for me. I don't know what it is, but Trish been acting funny for the past couple of months. I mean, you know I proposed to her and she didn't even accept it. Do you think she got another nigga?" asked Cameron with curiosity in his voice.

"Nah man, that girl loves you. You just got to give her time, that's all. Maybe she waiting on that special moment or something. You know how females are," said JT trying to encourage his best friend.

"Oh yeah, I almost forgot. You didn't tell me that you was living with Shanay."

"How you know I was living with her?" asked JT, wondering how Cameron knew his every move.

"Don't worry about it; just know I know, and you know you can't turn no hoe to no housewife."

The last comment Cameron made, made JT's blood boil, but he knew the old saying and didn't go by that.

"Nah, man it ain't even like that. I was just helping a friend out. That's all," said JT.

"Yeah, yeah, but let me know if you go to the party, a'ight."

JT thought about it and said, "You know what? I am going to go and Fuck your girl." JT thought with anger because of him calling Shanay a hoe.

"A'ight, I'm going to take her there; let me know everything she do. I'm telling you she messing with somebody I just don't know."

"A'ight homie, I got you and stop stressing over that girl; she good."

"A'ight man, you right, you right," said Cameron hanging up the phone.

JT knew Cameron knew something because of the way of his voice every time he talked to him. Whenever they talked, Cameron would always ask him, you think she is messing with somebody or do you know if she is messing with somebody? JT didn't really care anymore because, in a couple of weeks, his promotion was coming up, and he wouldn't even be living in the same state as him. JT got up from the bed that Shanay was laid naked in and picked Shanay up.

"What do you want Babe? I'm tired," said Shanay with her eyes still closed trying to go back to sleep.

"Nope, get your ass up. We going to take a shower and you going to your appointment for the doctor."

"No, I don't want to. I want to sleep." JT picked Shanay up and started walking to the bathroom.

"Babe, you are damn near walking again. You came a long way. You keep on walking with the doctors and you will be walking in no time. I promise," said JT sitting Shanay down on the covered toilet seat.

"Oh yeah, and you got to get ready to go to the party tonight," said JT, knowing Shanay would say she wasn't going.

"I'm not going to no damn party Babe. I can barely walk down the hallway without my legs collapsing on me."

"So what? You still can go."

"Uuuuummmm… no, I'm not going," said Shanay.

"Okay, if you say so."

"Are you going to go?"

"Yeah, I'm going; that's why I wanted you to go, but if you don't want to go, then it's fine with me," said JT turning the water on and filling the bathtub up with warm water and bubbles.

"So, you going to leave me here all by myself?" asked Shanay with a little attitude in her voice.

"Babe, I promise Marshal I was going to go tonight."

"Forget Marshal; he not in our relationship."

"He just came home from doing 10 years. Ten years, at least I can do is show up at his party." JT lied; knowing Marshal, he probably doesn't even know about the party.

"So why did my sister say it was a surprise party. Meaning Marshal don't know about it?"

"He does know. He acting like he don't know about it," JT lied again.

"Oh, okay, well, you know what?" JT picked Shanay up and placed her in the bathtub.

"I'm going to go to the party with you tonight." JT was in shock and had to find a way to get out of the mess he had just made.

"Why you want to go now?"

"Because I want to be with you tonight."

"You know it's going to be strippers there and people going to be up and dancing."

"So, I sit in the back and watch. It's okay, Babe I trust you enough that them strippers don't mean nothing to you and that you are all mines," said Shanay giving JT a kiss as he washes her up.

"Damn nigga her ass fat as shit. Who is that?" asked Marshal, looking at a female as they drove past them.

"It's a lot of girls out here, Man, I'm telling you. I got this broad for you to her name is Candy. My sister Kamiyah's friend," said Aairyah pulling up to Aairyah's house and walking to the door.

"Yeah, do she taste like candy?"

"Between me and you, yeah," said Aairyah letting Marshal get in the house first.

Marshal walked into the house and all he heard was "Surprise!"

Marshal was in total shock as he saw everybody get out from their hiding spaces. Marshal looked around and saw majority of females and only a couple of guys.

"Just the way I like it," Marshal thought to himself after Kim came over and grabbed his hand so he could meet everybody.

"Marshal, this is Kamiyah. That's Aairyah's sister."

Kamiyah came up and gave Marshal a hug and whispered in his ear, "I'm going to have fun with you tonight," said Kamiyah licking his ear afterward.

"This is Candy," said Kim pointing at Candy.

Candy came over and gave Marshal a hug as well but grabbed for Marshal's dick as she bent in to hug him. Kim saw what she did and looked at Marshal's face, which had satisfaction all over it.

"Okay, that's enough, come on," said Kim grabbing her brother's hand and heading him to where Vanessa was at.

"Do you remember Vanessa and Damon?" asked Kim pointing at Vanessa and Damon.

"How could I forget," said Marshal giving Vanessa a hug.

"I'm happy that you are home," said Vanessa when she and Marshal embraced.

Damon didn't like that Marshal hugged his girl with so much passion, but he knew that Marshal didn't know they had been married all this time.

"What's up nigga!?" asked Damon, giving Marshal some dap and a brotherly hug.

"Shit, man just glad to be home, that's all," said Marshal.

Sabrina came up to Marshal and them, and Marshal's eyes almost popped out of his head.

"This is Sabrina," said Kim introducing Sabrina when she approached them.

"I remember you. You look just as good as you did in high school," said Marshal giving Sabrina a hug.

Sabrina showed Marshal her ring to let him know that he was married.

"Damn is everybody married in here?" asked Marshal with a sense of humor.

"What's up, my nigga?" asked Omar when he approached Marshal from behind.

Marshal gave Omar a hug from the rip. Marshal was always closer to Omar for some reason.

"Damn Nigga I didn't see you in a minute," said Marshal.

As they embraced, Omar's eyes were stuck on Sabrina's eyes. As they both locked eyes, Sabrina started to walk off. Omar embraced Marshal and grabbed Sabrina's hand. Omar noticed Sabrina still had her ring on when he grabbed her hand.

"A Marshal, let me introduce you to my wife," Omar said as he pulled Sabrina ever so lightly towards him.

"Yeah we already met. That's crazy; after all these years, all you guys are still together," said Marshal looking at Kim, Aairyah, Omar, Sabrina, Vanessa, and Damon.

"I know, right," said Kim grabbing Marshal's Hand and sliding him away from the crowd.

"We will be back," said Kim walking him to where Shanay and JT were sitting.

As soon as Marshal approached them, Shanay panties got moistened.

"What's good nigga glad to see you on the other side of that wall," said JT as he got up and gave Marshal a dap and a hug.

"Yeah I know, right."

Shanay struggled to get up and hug Marshal. Shanay knew Marshal already because she had sex with him back in high school.

"I know that ain't Shanay," said Marshal. Shanay blushed and covered her face.

"Yeah, it's me," said Shanay with a big smile giving him a hug. Marshal looked down and saw that Shanay's ass was even fatter than before.

"Damn, she phat," Marshal thought to himself.

"So y'all two are a couple or something?" Marshal asked because he had to get with Shanay once again.

"Yeah," said JT. Shanay didn't say anything but sat back down.

"That's what's up," said Marshal.

"Okay, a few more people and then you are on your own," said Kim grabbing Marshal's hand and going towards the strip pole.

"Girls!" said Kim.

The two strippers got down and walked toward Kim and Marshal.

"Marshal, that is Juicy and the other one is Fruit."

Marshal looked at the two chicks in front of him and thought they came out of a Don-Diva Magazine. Juicy was 5'7, 145, Butter Pecan Rican, and looked like Kim Kardashian. Fruit was identical.

"So, are you two twins?" asked Marshal.

"We don't look like each other for no reason."

Marshal saw that Juicy had a tattoo of cherries on her navel and Fruit had strawberries on hers.

"So, what the tattoos stand for?"

"You'll see tonight," said Juicy, getting back on the strip pole.

"How bad do you want to see what's under these strawberries?" asked Fruit with her finger in her thong.

"Real bad." That was all Marshal could say.

Fruit grabbed Marshal's hand and led him to the back.

"He's in good hands now," said Fruit talking to Kim.

"Where the hell is he at?" asked Trish out loud to herself.

Trish was in her car in front of Kim's house. Trish called JT 10 times and he didn't pick up his phone. Trish got out of her car and walked to Kim's front door.

"You know what? I'm going to tell Cameron about this relationship we got as soon as I get home," Trish thought to herself as she entered Kim's house.

Trish was surprised to see everybody at the party and the music almost busting Trish's ears as she walked in. I had to be at least 30 people in the living room at the same time. Trish saw the original people she knew and wondered who all these other people were. Trish's eyes were glued to the two strippers that were clapping their asses on the pole; she didn't recognize Ron-Ron coming behind her.

"Hey beautiful. I hope you don't have a man?" asked Ron-Ron, getting up close to Trish.

"Yes, I do, and he suppose to be meeting me here tonight."

"So, who's your man?" asked Ron-Ron with a Corona in his hand.

"JT."

"What that JT sitting with Shanay?" asked Ron-Ron, pointing at JT and Shanay sitting on the stool next to the homemade bar Kim got in her living room.

"Well, if that's your man, he's already taken by Shanay. Matter of fact, he was the one who brought her here," said Ron-Ron spilling the beans.

Trish didn't say anything and went over to where JT and Shanay sat at.

JT saw Trish walking over, hurried up, and got up from his seat and walked to the kitchen. Trish followed him to the kitchen. A door to the basement and a back door was in the kitchen where the laundry room was presented.

"So that's what we doing? You lying Mother Fucker. You going to choose that Black Ass Bitch over me? Is you serious?"

"It's not what you think. I'm helping a friend out. She is paralyzed from the waist down and she asked for my help."

"You lying Son of a Bitch. You been staying at her house. Every time I go to your house you are never there. I call you 10 times a day you only pick up once. So, is that the Bitch you cheating on me with? That's the house you be staying at?"

"No," JT said bluntly.

"I think you are lying. Let's go ask her."

"There is no reason for that."

"Well, I'm going to ask her," said Trish walking off.

JT hurried up and grabbed her.

"You can't be serious. Me bringing the girl I'm so-called cheating on you with to the party I'm meeting you at. You got to think sometimes like, come on Trish. You know I'm in love with you. I been working 16 hours a day, I be tired. I'm doing this all for you, for us. You can't see that?" asked JT, thinking he should have won a Grammy.

"So, where you been staying at?"

"In my car at the parking lot in front of my job."

"Your car. See, you are Full of Shit. I'm going to ask that Bitch," said Trish trying to storm off.

JT grabbed her and took her in the back room. JT had her mouth covered with one hand and pulled her by the other. JT opened the door and all he saw was one of the strippers bent over the dryer and Marshal stroking her from the back. JT hurried up, closed the door, and took Trish to the basement.

"I know you are lying because every time I go to your job, your car not even there."

JT didn't hear anything that Trish was saying. JT put Trish on the couch that was in the basement that Kim and Aairyah didn't use anymore and lifted her skirt up.

"It's crazy how you keep hurting me and all I want to do is be with you." JT pulls Trish's panties down now and spreads her legs.

"Like you know, I want to be with you and you still... you still..." Trish's body starts moving in motion as JT's tongue guts going.

"And you still... AAAAAAAHHHH... you not... you not... listening... OOOOOOOOOOHHH... I want to... talk... AAAAHHH!" Trish couldn't complete her sentence because she was too into JT's tongue game.

JT always knew how to shut Trish up and this was the best way. Trish dug into JT's waves as she slammed JT's head into her pussy as he tried to come up for air.

"DON'T STOOOOOOOOOPPPPPP!" Trish yelled; Trish's body kept going in motion as JT put her at her highest point.

"AAAAWWWW, JAAAAAAAAYYYYYY TEEEEEEEEE!" Trish moaned as her legs shook and she organism over JT's mouth. JT got up and wiped his mouth.

"Turn your ass around!" JT demanded.

Trish had a terrified look on her face, but JT demanding her to do something made her pussy tingle. Trish turned around and put her ass in the air. JT didn't play any games as he got behind Trish and rammed his dick inside her.

"Not so hard Daddy," Trish said in a little girl voice.

"Shut up!" said JT as he thrust even harder and harder with every stroke he did.

"I'm still Full of Shit? Huh?!" yelled JT as he smacked her ass.

"NO DADDY NOOOOOO! YOU'RE NOT FULL OF SHIT, YOU NOT FULL OF SHIT! DADDY AWWWWW, IT HURT, DADDY IT HURT!" Trish said, moaning.

"Shut up! You going to listen to me now!"

"YES! DADDY, YES!" yelled Trish as she climaxed over JT's dick and JT kept stroking.

"Look, I'm sorry Babe, okay. Like I don't know where to begin at, I'm sorry. Why do I have to suffer from not being with you after all this time? I said I'm sorry," Water filled Omar's eyes as he began to speak again, "I'm sorry for what I said. I was drunk; I didn't mean it. You know you are the only person who has my heart's key. I love you Sabrina."

Sabrina's eyes began to water as she hugged Omar. Omar gave her a kiss as tears ran down their face.

"Can you come stay at home now Babe? I'm depressed without you."

Sabrina looked into Omar's eyes and knew that he was sincere in every word he said. Sabrina shook her head "YES" because her that throat was so dry that she couldn't speak.

"Thank you Babe. I love you," said Omar giving Sabrina a kiss on the lips and wiping her tears away, "now, let's get back to the party," said Omar wiping away Sabrina's tears and walking out of the bathroom.

Omar and Sabrina walked downstairs and saw everybody having a good time dancing, singing along to the song, and throwing money at the strippers.

"Here Babe."

Omar dug in his pocket and pulled out a knot of one-dollar bills.

"Let's give back to the community and give back to these hoes," said Omar guiding Sabrina in front of the strippers that were on the pole.

Omar didn't know that Candy and Kamiyah were up next to strip when Juicy and Fruit got off of the stage. Omar didn't even know they were at the party. Omar confessed up from the gate when Kamiyah and Candy got on the pole.

"Look Babe, I got something to tell you. When we went our separate ways for that length of time, I went to a club and met these two broads that are on stage now. I promise I didn't do nothing with them Babe. I promise."

"You know what Babe? I believe you," said Sabrina throwing money at Kamiyah and Candy.

Omar left it at that and started throwing money as well.

"Where the hell is JT at?" asked Shanay talking to Vanessa.

Vanessa looked around and didn't see him as well.

"I don't know Girl, he probably around here somewhere. Maybe he's in the bathroom, or he's in the kitchen," said Vanessa taking a sip of her Parrot Bay cooler.

"Damon! Damon!" said Vanessa calling Damon, whose eyes were on the strippers.

"Babe, all I was doing was looking nothing else," pleaded Damon before Vanessa said something. Shanay and Sabrina started laughing.

"I'm not talking about that stupid. I don't care about that. Did you see JT because Shanay is ready to go home?"

"Nah, I didn't see him," said Damon.

"Oh, okay," said Sabrina. That's all Damon needed to hear, and he left the area and went back to watching the strippers.

Marshal was damn near pissy drunk when the party was over as everyone scattered out one by one. Kim called a taxi and gave Marshal 200 dollars so he could get to a nice motel.

Can y'all please take care of my brother? I don't want nothing to go wrong; he is already drunk and he still got a beer in his hand," said Kim, concerned about her older brother.

"I got you Girl, don't worry, he is fine with us," said Kamiyah and hugged Kim.

Kamiyah grabbed Marshal by the hand and headed out the house.

"Bye Bro, I'll see you tomorrow," said Kamiyah as she and Candy walked out of the front door.

Marshal couldn't even say anything because he was so drunk; all he did was give a head nod as he left Kim's house. Kim and Aairyah looked around the house and saw the mess that had been given to them.

"It's a lot of trash we got to pick up," said Aairyah looking at Kim.

"I know, don't remind me."

"Whatever happened to them, two strippers? How the hell did they leave before everybody?"

"Because Marshal couldn't hold his hormones and got one of them in the laundry room. She came back out and started dancing, and when she did, she came on her period. So, she left and the other one didn't feel comfortable dancing by herself, so I let her go with her friend."

"But didn't you pay them to have sex with Marshal?"

"Yeah, they said they still going to do it. Just not today," said Kim picking up a couple of bottles of Coronas.

"Oh, okay and what's up with Vanessa and Damon? They still messing with each other, I see."

"Yeah, they just was not talking for only a couple of days. That's old news; I thought Damon would have told you that."

"I didn't mean to say Vanessa and Damon; I meant to say Sabrina and Omar."

"Yeah, I know you seen them tonight. Throwing money together and everything. What the hell is up with them two?" asked Aairyah.

"I don't know; Sabrina left before I could say anything," said Kim.

CHAPTER 12

It's All or Nothing

"Let me go; I can do it," said Shanay walking down the hospital hallway with nobody's help at all.

"I knew you could do it Babe. I told you could do it," said JT, meeting Shanay at the end of the hallway.

Thanks to JT, Shanay could finally walk with nobody's help at all. JT pushed and pushed Shanay harder and harder every day so she could be able to walk just once more. JT gave Shanay a hug and they started walking out of the hospital.

"Thanks, Doc. I really appreciate it," said Shanay as she walked to the main door.

"No problem. Just remember you can't run or jog for a little while, so be mindful."

"Okay Doc," said Shanay knowing her legs were still weak.

Shanay and JT met Sabrina at the main entrance. Sabrina saw her sister and hugged her as she walked to her with open arms.

"Oh My God, Girl look at you," said Sabrina giving Shanay a big hug.

"I know Girl I can't believe it," said Shanay letting go of her sister and looking at her legs.

"So where are y'all about to go at?" asked Sabrina.

"Where do you want to go at Babe?" asked JT looking at Shanay when he said it.

"Uuuuummmmmm… Puerto Rico," said Shanay laughing after she said it.

Sabrina laughed as well and gave Shanay a high five.

"Puerto Rico it is then," said JT with a serious voice and look. Shanay and Sabrina stopped laughing and looked at JT.

"You can't be serious," said Shanay looking at JT.

"I'm dead ass serious. We can pack up tonight and leave tomorrow," said JT.

Shanay wanted to jump up and down but knew she couldn't; all she could do was say, "I love you and gave JT a hug as a tear came down her face as they embraced.

"Nurse Sabrina, can you come to Dr. Watson's office. Nurse Sabrina can you come to Dr. Watson's office. Thank you." That was all you heard over the intercom.

"Well, that's me, so I guess I'll see y'all tonight because I got to get the rest of my stuff from y'all house," said Sabrina as she walked off.

"Okay Sis, call me," said Shanay.

"Babe, I love you, but how are we going to be able to afford all that stuff. I don't got no money or a job, and I can't keep relying on you all the time," said Shanay.

"With this promotion, we are going to be good and you can rely on me all you want because I love you and because I love you," said JT kissing Shanay and walking out of the hospital hand and hand.

JT and Shanay drove away in JT's car and went to Olive Garden. Sitting down and ordering their food, Shanay started talking.

"Babe, there is something I got to tell you before our relationship go any further."

Shanay was scared to tell JT the whole truth about her life and that she has HIV.

"What is it Babe?" asked JT looking directly into Shanay's eyes.

Shanay got nervous and began to sweat as the words came out of her mouth.

"Well, it's this guy name…" Shanay was cut off when Cameron approached the table with Trish in his hand.

"Hey my friend. What are you guys doing here?" asked Cameron looking at JT and Shanay.

"Oh, what's up Cam? What the hell are you doing here?" asked JT looking at Cameron and then at Trish.

Trish had this evil look on her face as to say, I'm going to kill you.

"Oh, me and my wife Trish here is just leaving. I didn't see y'all come in."

"We just got here. Me and Shanay having lunch to gather, that's all nothing major," said JT trying to act like nothing was going on between him and Shanay.

"What's up Trish? How are you?" asked JT looking at Trish's face knowing she was mad.

"I'm fine; how are you?" asked Trish turning her head sideways as to let JT know she was mad.

"He's fine. Thanks for asking," said Shanay knowing that JT fucked Trish without Cameron knowing and to let her know that JT belongs to her.

"Oh, okay then, I guess I'll holla at you another time player. I see your hands is full," said Cameron giving JT dap.

"Matter of fact, do you work tonight?" asked Cameron. JT could see that Trish was staring Shanay down and Vise-Versa.

"Yeah, after I leave here that's where I'll be going at," said JT.

"A'ight call me when you get off."

"A'ight than nigga I'll holla."

"A'ight," said Cameron as he walked off.

Trish didn't even say bye as she stepped off with Cameron.

"You still must be fucking her, huh?" asked Shanay, looking at JT in his eyes now.

"Whoever said I was fucking her?"

"Is you still fucking her or not?"

"That's my best friend girl. Why would I fuck her?" asked JT wondering how Shanay knew he was fucking Trish.

"Because you got a dick and she got a pussy," Shanay paused for a second and kept going on, "I saw you and her go in the back of Kim's house at the party. I'm not fucking dumb," said Shanay, angry as hell.

JT knew he was caught red-handed, so he pleaded his case.

"Yeah, I was still fucking her. I was, but I didn't fuck her at no party. I did before, but now I'm not, okay. I have you," said JT.

The waiter brought their food over and there was no talking from thereon. After they ate, Shanay still pretended as if she were mad in all actuality; she did so much dirt. How could she be mad, but a side of her was still mad at the fact that she was really falling in love with JT. They ate and left Olive Garden and got on the road.

"Can you take me home so I can get in my car," said Shanay, not looking at JT.

"You can use my car Babe and come pick me up later after work," said JT trying to make eye contact the whole ride to the state penitentiary.

"Okay." JT and Shanay pulled up to JT job and JT got out.

"I'll call you when to pick me up. Make sure you go home and pack your stuff up because I'm going to book the flight while I'm at work," said JT.

"Okay." That was all Shanay knew once she sped off down the street.

Shanay knew once she was able to walk again that, she had to go see one person before he comes to see her.

"Look before we go in here if I see that Mother Fucker do or say something sexual to you. I'm going to whip his ass," said Damon.

"Babe, he was the one who set this up so everybody can be friends again," said Vanessa as she walked into the bowling building.

Sabrina and Omar just sat down with their bowling shoes and a plate of nachos and cheese.

Vanessa and Damon walked over and said, "Hey guys," Vanessa said with a high-pitched voice.

"Hey, Girl," said Sabrina giving Vanessa a hug.

"Hey Damon," said Sabrina giving Damon a hug.

"What's up V.," said Omar giving her a head nod.

"What's up D.? Help me come get the rest of the stuff from the snack bar," said Omar as he walked to the snack bar.

When they approached the snack bar, Omar said, "Look, my nigga my fault for the shit that happened at the club. I was drunk and I didn't mean it," said Omar reaching his hand out to Damon.

"They say when you drunk, the truth comes out, but as long as you keep your boundaries from my wife, we cool," said Damon as he gave

Omar some dap.

Omar didn't want to comment on what Damon said, so he just said, "You got that. So, we cool?" asked Omar, grabbing the two pitchers of Pepsi.

"Yeah, we cool," said Damon grabbing a pan full of hot dogs with chili and cheese on it.

"A'ight good because I got some shit to tell you," said Omar walking to the table.

"What's up?"

"You remember those strippers, right?"

"Yeah what about them?"

"Well, the broad Kamiyah was going to let me fuck, but I didn't want to fuck her because I had loudmouth Ron-Ron with me. So, what I'm telling you is I need somebody to go over there with me."

"Kamiyah is Aairyah sister."

"Word."

"Yeah, and Kamiyah work at the strip club at nighttime, but she work at the hospital with your girl."

"How do you know all this?"

"Because I overheard Kim talking about it with Vanessa and Sabrina, and now I put the pieces together that was probably a set-up."

"Word."

That was all Omar could say when he got to the table at sat the pitchers down.

"You're up first, Omar," said Sabrina eating one of the nachos. Omar went up and started bowling.

Damon sat next to his wife and she said, "So, are you guys cool now?"

"We a'ight," said Damon as he stuffed his face with one of the hot dogs.

"Okay Babe, as long as you are okay, then I'm okay," said Vanessa as she got up and to ready to bowl.

As Omar watched Vanessa swing the bowling ball down to the pins, Damon cut his eyes at Omar.

"So, what you looking at now?" asked Damon in a mellow tone.

"Come on man, that's done and over with. I'm watching her bowl," said Omar as he started to eat one of the hot dogs.

Omar was really daydreaming about when he use to fuck the shit out of Vanessa in high school. He could only imagine how good it is now than what it was in high school.

"It's your turn Babe," said Vanessa sitting down and taking a sip of her soda.

Sabrina knew that Omar still liked Vanessa after all those years, but she never knew that it would have gotten that far, to say all of that at the club. Sabrina knew she couldn't leave Omar if she wanted to. The period that they were not together was killing her deep inside, but she still had nightmares of what happened to her that night she went out with Mitchel.

Marshal stood in the motel where Kamiyah and Candy took him on the night he came home, but this time he was with Fruit and Juicy. Marshal was at the end of the bed, butt naked, looking at Fruit and Juicy kissing.

Marshal thought to himself, *"These Bitches is nasty they are both sisters, twins at that, and they sitting here tongue kissing each other."*

Marshal's dick grew by the moment. Everything he was thinking about went out of the window as his dick jumped in eagerness. Marshal motioned for the twins to come over to him and they did. Marshal couldn't tell which one was which and that they both looked exactly like Kim Kardashian. Both of the twins didn't have anything on but their heels. Juicy had cherry red heels on that matched her cherries near her navel. Juicy's theme was cherries because she had cherries coming down her legs as well. Fruit had nothing on as well except her dark red heels on that matched her strawberries near her navel. Fruit had strawberries on the back of her neck, on her ass cheeks, as well down her leg. Marshal fell in love with these two hoes. He knew it because this was his third time tricking since he had been home with them two. Juicy came over first and looked directly at Marshal's dick as if his dick was staring at her. Juicy grabbed his dick and put her lips around its head as she started to play with it with her tongue.

Fruit came over and got on the floor in between Juicy and Marshal and started sucking on Marshal's balls. Marshal knew that his first nut would come quick because these two twins were professional at what they do. Fruit then got up and started sucking Marshal's dick. Juicy in the front of Marshal's dick and Fruit sucking on the side of Marshal's dick while playing with his balls. Marshal couldn't take any more as he loaded in Juicy's mouth. Juicy swallowed every bit of cum that came out of Marshal's dick.

Juicy then laid back on the bed and started playing with her pussy. Juicy had a light tint coating her pussy, but the inside of her pussy was bright pink. Fruit then got up and started sucking Marshal's dick. Fruit swallowed, spit, and sucked on Marshal's dick until it was rock hard and saliva was dripping off of it. Fruit then laid next to her sister and started playing with her pussy as well. Marshal got on the bed, and Juicy turned to her stomach and propped her ass up, and Fruit got in front of her sister. Juicy started eating Fruit out when Marshal stuck his dick inside of her. Marshal loved to hear both of them moan at the same time; it turned Marshal on as well as it turned them on.

Marshal grabbed Juicy's waist and started stroking her with all his might trying to break her walls with each stroke. Juicy couldn't take it and stopped eating her sister out as she moaned louder and louder, grabbing the sheets for dear life. Marshal could feel Juicy legs getting weak, so he went harder, making Juicy climax on his dick. Marshal then got up and saw Fruit come towards him. Fruit jumped on Marshal and wrapped her arms around his neck and her legs around his waist. Marshal grabbed Fruit's shoulders and entered inside Fruit. Marshal then started stroking Fruit. All you could hear were loud moans and body's slapping each other. Marshal threw Fruit's body into his with each stroke.

"OOOOOOOHHHHHH, DADDY, PUT ME DOWN, PUT ME DOWN!"

Fruit couldn't take it anymore; she climaxed three times and her arms would give out on her. Marshal got close to the bed and watched as Fruit's body dropped on the bed. Juicy, who was on the bed, started to get up until Marshal pushed her down. Marshal got on top of Juicy and lifted her legs up. Marshal went inside of her and started stroking her constantly. Marshal loved how Juicy's face would squint up and her legs tremble when she was about to orgasm. Fruit got up and pushed Marshal off of her making Marshal fall on his back. Fruit jumped on top of Marshal and started riding him. After Juicy caught her breath, she sat on Marshal's face and started riding his tongue as he began to eat her pussy. Marshal grabbed Juicy's hips as he motioned her to stop and started to eat her pussy like he wanted to. Juicy's head fell back as he gave Juicy her orgasm once again. Fruit was still bouncing on Marshal's dick and Marshal loved it. Fruit then did a 180 on Marshal's dick, now with her ass facing Marshal. Marshal bent her back towards him as he now began to stroke her. Juicy went on the other side and watched as Marshal's dick went in and out of Fruit's pussy. Marshal stopped for a little bit to catch his breath and Juicy took his dick out of his sister's pussy and started sucking it. Marshal felt like he was in Heaven. Juicy kept sucking Marshal's dick as she fingered her sister at the same time.

After a couple of minutes, Juicy then stuck Marshal's dick back inside of her sisters' coochie and watched as Marshal pounded Fruit away. After about five minutes, Fruit got up off Marshal and started sucking Marshal's dick. Juicy and Fruit took turns sucking Marshal's dick until he exploded in both of their mouths. They both took Marshal's come inside their mouth and swallowed it.

Fruit and Juicy laid up with Marshal on both sides of him and said to him, "How do you like us now?"

"I'm in love with y'all," said Marshal as they all laughed and went to sleep.

"Babe, I wonder what Marshal is doing?" asked Kim, curious because Marshal didn't come back home yet.

Kim was ass naked, getting dressed to go to dinner with Aairyah.

"Babe, he is fine; he out having fun. Stop worrying yourself over him; he's a grown man," said Aairyah getting out of the shower.

Aairyah's phone rings, letting him know he got a text message. Aairyah goes to the nightstand near his bed and looks at the text message. When he opened it, it had a picture of Candy playing with her pussy. Under the picture, it said, "Come get some Daddy; I'm waiting on you." Aairyah hurried up and closed his phone and sat it down.

Kim walked to the bathroom to finish her makeup and said, "Who was that Babe?"

"It was uuuuummm… Damon telling me he had to go work out." Aairyah lied, sounding dumb and he knew it.

"He texted you to tell you he had to work out?" Kim said in a curious voice.

"Yeah. I mean, we was suppose to go work out today, but I told him we was going out, so he told me that he was going to go work out anyway," said Aairyah trying to sound convincing.

"Yeah… right," said Kim being sarcastic and funny at the same time.

"I'm serious."

"I believe you. So, where we going at anyway?" asked Kim, curious that Aairyah got Kim from her job made her call off the rest of the day.

Brought her homemade passionate, wild, crazy sex with her all for what Kim wondered.

"We are going to the comedy club. It start at 1 pm and ends at 4 pm. That's why we got to hurry up."

Aairyah felt guilty because he had been fucking Candy for the past couple of months, and last night he was at Candy's house, tearing her ass down. Every time Aairyah leaves Candy's house, he would somehow put it in his mind that he owed Kim. So he would take Kim out every time he had sex with her.

"Who is suppose to be going there?" asked Kim.

"I don't know, but can you hurry up and get dressed please, so we can go."

"Okay, okay, here I come Babe," said Kim in an innocent voice that makes Aairyah love her evermore.

Aairyah's phone rings and he picks it up. He didn't recognize the number, so he answered it.

"Hello."

"Can we please go one more round Daddy? My pussy is calling your name and I need you so bad." Aairyah's erection grew thinking about last night.

"What about Johnny?" asked Aairyah, talking about Candy's dildo.

"Johnny is not real. I need the real deal Daddy; come over, please."

"I can't right now. I'm in the middle of doing something with my wife."

"Oh, so I can't get none of your time, but your wife can get all of it, huh?" asked Candy getting angry that Aairyah didn't want to fuck her lights out.

"Yeah," said Aairyah, not trying to get into detail because he knew his wife could hear his conversation.

"Oh okay, I see how it is. What if your wife find out that me and you are fucking? Then what? Is she still going to have some of your time then nigga?" said Candy damn near yelling through the phone.

"That's the game you going to play?"

"Yeah nigga, so is you going to come over here and beat this pussy up or what!?" asked Candy.

"I'll be over there," said Aairyah hanging up on Candy.

Kim got out of the bathroom and asked, "Who was that?"

"Babe, we got a change of plans."

"What? Why?" said Kim catching an attitude from the rip.

"Something happened at my job and they need me," said Aairyah grabbing his keys and heading out the room.

"Why can't Johnny work for you?" asked Kim.

Aairyah was in shock for a moment and turned around.

"What?"

"Johnny, you said something about Johnny."

Oh, I was trying to see if he can work for me, but he called off sick," said Aairyah lying again.

"So, you made me call off of work and you not even taking me out? What type of shit is that?" asked Kim.

"It's an emergency Babe. I didn't know my damn self," said Aairyah opening the front door.

"Look Babe, I'll see you when I get home; it shouldn't be that long. I promise," said Aairyah as he walked out of the house and kisses Kim.

Kim stomped her feet and closed her front door. Kim saw Aairyah move so fast to go to work. A light bulb flashed in Kim's head as she grabbed her keys and ran out the front door.

CHAPTER 13

Past, Present, Future

"Oh Shit, look at this shit. You got to be kidding me," said Shanay getting out of the limousine.

Shanay stood in front of the beach with her pink and white polka dot swimsuit. JT followed behind her and watched Shanay's ass jiggle as she walked in front of him. JT had his mind made up; he had to go all the way with her. JT knew he was in love with Shanay but couldn't know why he was in love with her, he questioned himself every day, but he still couldn't come up with the answer. He just knew he had to have her all to himself and he only knew one way he could do it and coming here, he knew that he was going to lock all the way in with Shanay. Shanay interrupted his train of thought when she grabbed his hand and whispered in his ear.

"Babe, you know we can't be in the sun too long. I'm already Black as it is." Shanay laughed a little. JT couldn't help but laugh with her.

"Babe, your skin is flawless. You're beautiful."

Shanay always felt beautiful when she was with JT because he always knew what to say to her that made her feel funny inside as she likes to say.

"Yeah, yeah," said Shanay knowing that JT would compliment her again.

"You are Babe and don't let nobody tell you that you aren't," said JT with sincerity.

Shanay couldn't do anything but kiss JT on the lips. JT looked at his watch and wondered why the airplane took so long. Shanay was enjoying herself the time she had been in Puerto Rico, even though it was her second day there. Shanay had a full day at the spa, went go-cart riding, and swam with the dolphins, which she loved and always wanted to do. It was 3 o'clock in the afternoon and everybody was at the beach when they arrived.

As JT set up both of their lawn chairs and umbrellas, Shanay said, "Babe look," as she pointed to the ocean.

JT looked up and saw a boy too far from the shore and it looked like he was drowning.

"Babe do something!" Shanay said as she bit her fingernails.

JT ran and jumped in the ocean, swimming to the boy that was drowning. JT swam all the way towards the boy, and like that, he couldn't see him anymore. Out of breath and arms tired, JT swam underwater where he saw the boy going under. JT felt like he was going to drown as he hurried up, grabbed the boy, and swam to the top. Out of breath, all JT could hear was people screaming and yelling. JT looked at the shore and saw people pointing at him. JT held the boy that was no more than 10 on his back all the way to shore. When he got to shore, he put the boy on his back and performed CPR. It was at least 50 people surrounding him and the boy as he performed CPR.

"Come on papi, you can make it wake up," said a woman, "please, Baby wake up," said the same woman as JT did CPR.

As it looked like JT couldn't save his life and he was about to give up, the little boy spat out water and began to cough.

"Oh My God, my baby is alive. Thank you God. Thank you!" yelled the woman as she hurried up and got by his side.

When JT got up, everybody started yelling a chanting, "Hero! Hero! Hero!"

JT smiled and was lucky he was a summer lifeguard when he was in high school. When the lady got up, JT thought he saw the most beautiful thing he had ever seen.

"Thank you, papi. My name is Carmen and I owe you my life for saving my son. Is there any way I can repay you for this?" asked Carman.

Carman was a cinnamon complexion with her long blackish, brownish hair stopping at the middle of her back. Her eyes were green and her body was bananas. Carmen's legs were nice and long, and her feet were well done. Carmen looked like Jennifer Lopez, but some people say she looks better.

"You don't have to pay me nothing. I'm just glad I can help."

Carmen knew JT wasn't from there and she knew this could be her ticket out of Puerto Rico. Carman loved that JT was in shape and that he was from America and also thought he looked good as well.

"Please let me help you with something, anything," said Carmen raising her eyebrows.

JT didn't think she was saying what he thought she was saying, so he thought that his mind was in the gutter.

"No, it's okay, you don't have to worry about it, it's okay," said JT getting ready to walk off.

Carmen grabbed his arm before he turned all the way around.

"Please tell me where you are from?"

"I'm from the United States of America," said JT.

"Well, how long are you going to be in Puerto Rico." JT loved her thick accent already and it was turning him on.

"For a couple of days. Why you ask?"

"Well, take my number down and call me tonight papi and I will make it worth your while."

JT's dick grew hard as she said papi. JT thought about putting his dick in between those sexy ass legs and wondered, how good can an island girl pussy be. JT took Carmen's number from her as he looked at her up and down.

Carmen gave JT a hug and a kiss on the lips and said, "Damn, your lips taste sweet. I wonder what else taste sweet?" As she grabbed JT's dick from his swimming trunks.

Carmen didn't say anything else and walked off. JT was about to walk off when one of the people that was chanting hero said, "Yo, my man."

JT turned around and saw a short Puerto Rican guy with black shades on say, "Yo, that girl you just kissed is Pablo's girl; he runs PK and if he finds that out, you are a dead man."

"A'ight," JT said, not caring.

JT turned back around only to see Shanay near the limousine crying.

JT walked up to her and said, "What's wrong Babe? Why are you crying?"

"I saw you kiss that girl and I know you think she look better than me," Shanay wined.

"Babe she kissed me. I didn't have no control over that. I saved her son. I told her I had a girlfriend," JT said, sounding like a little kid, "babe, you got to believe me. I will never see that girl again. You are my girl Babe. I came with you not her. I don't even know her." Shanay knew he was telling the truth but didn't want to admit it.

"I just… I just don't… want to lose you," said Shanay out of the sobs of her crying.

JT felt heart broking and hugged his girl.

"Babe, you not going to lose me. I promise you are all I ever want," said JT trying to cheer her up.

"You promise?" asked Shanay wiping her eyes.

"Yeah, I promise," said JT looking Shanay in her face as he picked her chin up so they could be face to face.

"I love you Shanay," said JT kissing Shanay. JT overheard somebody say.

"Who the hell is Shanay?"

JT looked over and saw the airplane with the flagger in the back that said, *Shanay, will you marry me?*

JT opened the limousine door, grabbed the ring on the door role and told Shanay to look in the air. Shanay saw the sign and looked at JT that was now on one knee. Shanay couldn't believe it.

"Shanay, will you marry me?"

Shanay was in full shock and all she could say was, "Yes!"

"No, you got to be kidding me?" asked Cameron talking to Ryan, Richard's cousin, in front of 8-Ball Pussy House, as Ryan likes to call it.

"Yeah, that Bitch is a prostitute for 8-Ball and has been for the past couple of years," said Ryan, puffing on a Newport.

"I knew she was a whore, but I didn't know she was like that," said Cameron in confusion.

"Yeah, that Bitch is a prostitute. I heard Chris and them niggas raped her and I heard that one of them niggas had HIV," said Ryan hitting his

Newport while looking at his watch.

"How true is that?"

"Is what?"

"That the boy had HIV when he raped Shanay?"

"It's in his bloodline, and to make matters worse, she came over here a couple of days ago and fucked 8-Ball."

"Do 8-Ball know she had HIV?"

"No, and I'm not telling him. That Fat Mother Fucker owes me money. I want to kill him, but I'll let the infection kill him slowly," said Ryan.

"So, she still prostituting till this day, huh?" asked JT in complete shock.

"I'm guessing, but I know for a fact that she fucked 8-Ball a couple of days ago. So, she just might be prostituting still."

"How you know she fucked 8-Ball?"

"Because, when I went in the Pussy House, I went to 8-Ball's office and he had her bent over fucking the shit out of her," said Ryan.

"Damn that's crazy. I hope JT is not infected."

"JT is fucking her?"

"Yeah, I didn't tell you?"

"Hell no, what happen with that?"

"Man, this nigga living at her crib and all."

"NOOOOOO!" said Ryan with sarcasm in his voice.

"Word, I told him he can't turn no hoe into no housewife, but he wouldn't believe me."

"That dude is crazy; you got to tell him that a.s.a.p. and tell him that she got HIV and she is prostituting," said Ryan.

Cameron called JT and there was no answer. Cameron called him again and forgot that he told him that he was going to Puerto Rico.

"Man, I totally forgot."

"What's up man."

"This nigga is in Puerto Rico with this broad."

"What? Do you know if he had sex with her since she got raped?"

"I don't know man. He might've."

"Well, don't stop calling his phone until he picks up. I'll do the same," said Ryan pulling his cell phone out and dialed JT's number.

"FUCK THIS PUSSY… AWWWW SHIT YEAH… YEAH I LOVE THIS DICK! I LOVE THIS DICK!" Candy is yelling at the top of her lungs as Aairyah strokes her from the back.

Aairyah's noticing himself fucking Candy more often than he was fucking Kim. Not that he wanted to, but because Candy told him to. If he didn't come when she called, she would tell on Aairyah to Kim that they were fucking and that's the last thing Aairyah wanted to do. Aairyah had Candy bent over the bathroom sink in McDonald's.

"AWWWW SHIT, DADDY I'M COM… MMMING!" Candy moaned as her legs began to shake.

Candy climaxed over Aairyah's dick and saw the whiteness around his dick now as he stroked in and out. Aairyah nutted not too long after all on Candy's bare ass. Aairyah looked at his watch and saw what time it was.

"Fuck I'm going to be late again. Yo, I'm telling you if I get fired from my job, I'm going to whip your ass," said Aairyah pulling his pants up.

"If you get fired, you can always live with me," said Candy wiping the nut off of her ass and pulling her skirt down.

Aairyah gave her a look like she was crazy.

"Bitch I wouldn't dare live with your hoe ass," Aairyah thought to himself but said something different out of his mouth.

"Yeah right."

"I'm serious, Aairyah. I love you." Those three words hit Aairyah like a bag of rocks; Aairyah knew he had to get out of there and fast.

"Look, I got to go I'll see you," said Aairyah dipping out of the men's bathroom and leaving McDonald's parking lot.

On his way to work, Aairyah called his sister up, Kamiyah.

"Hey Bro, what's up," said Kamiyah as she answered the phone.

"Your girl is what's up. What's wrong with that Bitch?" asked Aairyah heading towards his job.

"What you mean, what's wrong with her?"

"The Bitch is crazy; you got to get her the fuck out of my life."

"Why, what's the matter with her?"

"The Bitch keep wanting me to fuck her and if I don't fuck her, she is going to tell my girl that we had sex."

"See, I told you don't fuck her in the first place. Now is you going to listen to me now?"

"Yeah yeah, whatever, just get the Bitch off of my ass and tell her I got a wife and to leave me alone."

"Okay, I got you, but I can't promise you nothing. She's her own woman. Maybe she really likes you," said Kamiyah laughing a little bit.

"No shit. This shit ain't funny Kamiyah; this is my life I'm talking about," said Aairyah in a panicked voice.

"A'ight, I got you; we both stripping tonight. I'll see her at the club tonight, but like I said, I can't promise you nothing A."

"Okay. Thanks Sis," said Aairyah hanging up and going to his job where his boss cussing him out again.

"Hey, Beautiful, you remember me?" asked Jermaine, slowly sliding behind Vanessa.

Vanessa turned around and thought she saw a ghost.

"Hey Jermaine," said Vanessa, terrified of Jermaine because she wished that night she had with Jermaine was a nightmare but knew in all actuality, she knew it was real.

"So, what's up? You don't Fuck with me no more?" asked Jermaine, saying fuck louder than every other word that came out of his mouth.

"Look Jermaine, the thing we did is in the past. I was having trouble in my relationship, but now me and my husband or back together. I have a husband, so can you please leave me alone now," said Kim leaving the Footlocker store in the mall and heading to the food court.

"Can we talk about this over something to eat?" asked Jermaine.

"No, we can't. I just told you I have a husband. What don't you understand?"

"It didn't stop you before," said Jermaine trying to pick up his pace to keep up with Vanessa.

"Look, Jermaine that night wasn't suppose to happen between us. I was in the wrong, so can you just leave me alone and go on your way," Vanessa said to the Subway line.

"Well, it did happen, and I would like another round. How about you?"

No, you would never taste or even see this pussy again," said Vanessa in an angry tone.

"Damn that's not nice. How would Damon feel if he found out me and you had sex?" Jermaine asked. Vanessa turned around and was in shock that he knew that her husband was Damon.

"How did you know my husband name?" asked Vanessa.

"I know more than you think. So, is you going to let me get another round or what?" asked Jermaine with a devilish grin.

"Fuck you Jermaine. I already told my man that I did it to you when we was separated. Like a man, he still took me back," said Vanessa, then ordering her food.

Jermaine laughed out loud hysterically so it could get on Vanessa's nerves.

"You told Damon? The same Damon that went to Howard? The Damon that gets jealous even if he see us talking right now he going to want to kill me and you?"

Vanessa knew Jermaine was right but wouldn't let him know it.

"If you really want to know we are not talking right now because of that, so can you mind your own business?" asked Vanessa grabbing her food and walking off after she paid the cash register.

"Oh really? That's why you drove his car up here and got his key chain too."

Vanessa didn't know how the hell Jermaine knew all this stuff and wondered if he had been stalking her.

"What you been stalking me?" asked Vanessa as she turned around and looked at Jermaine in his eyes.

"Nope. Just know I'm closer to home than you think I am. Now, if you don't want your deep dark secret to the light, then I suggest you stop playing and meet me at Motel 6 at 10 and don't be late," said Jermaine walking off, leaving Vanessa in a daze.

Vanessa felt like her whole world was crashing down on her. She didn't know what to do, who to call or what to expect from Jermaine. All of a sudden, Vanessa lost her appetite and threw her food in the trash and left the mall. Wondering if she should go and see Jermaine tonight. Inside her car, Vanessa thought long and hard about how her life would be ruined if Damon found out that she fucked another guy.

Hey wassup Kim? I know it's unexpected but can I call you? I got to talk to you.

That was all Kim read as she went through her text messages on her lunch break. Kim decided to call Tyrone to see what was so important that he had to call.

Kim thought to herself, *"We are just friends, right?"*

"Hello," said Tyrone in a deep voice that always tickled Kim's ear every time she heard and him over the phone.

"Yeah, what's up Tyrone?"

"Kim, I was wondering if we could go out to see a comedy event tomorrow night?"

Kim thought about it and was going to say yeah but she thought about it and knew how Aairyah would act if she asked him.

No! No! Hell NO! Don't make me fuck you up Kim! Kim could see Aairyah's face in her head saying all of thee above.

"I'm going to have to cancel on that Tyrone. Did you forget I am married? I know my husband would snap if he even found out I was even talking to you, let alone go on a date."

"So why are you talking to me now?" asked Tyrone hitting Kim unexpectedly.

Kim thought to herself, *"Why was she still texting and calling Tyrone if she was married."* Kim couldn't come up with any reason, so she said the first thing that came out of her mouth.

"Because we are friends. That's why," said Kim seeming clueless.

"That's right. Friends Kim, friends. Nothing more, nothing less. I just like your presence Kim. Just kicking it with you makes my day. You remember the first time we met at Kenndy Fried Chicken. You was mad at your husband over something and you gave me the chance just to take you out to the movies was okay. I just love being around you Kim and I wouldn't do nothing to jeopardize your relationship with your husband. I know how much you love him and I respect that. Just one night at the comedy club. I got two tickets and I don't want them to go to waste."

Kim thought about it and wanted to go to the comedy club with Aairyah, but Aairyah couldn't take her because he had to go to work.

Kim knew that they were just friends and said to herself, *"What's the worst that can happen?"*

"Yeah I'll go with you. On one condition tho," said Kim.

"Okay, what's that?" asked Tyrone, eager that he got her to come with him.

"That you promise me you won't be on no sexual type stuff."

"We are friends Kim. Why would I do anything sexual with you? You're the one with the mind in the gutter," said Tyrone.

"Promise me," demanded Kim.

"I promise," said Tyrone.

Ron-Ron is sitting on one of the bar stools in the Pussy House, talking to 8-ball about some business.

"So, do you really think that Bitch is going to stop fucking me? Shit I own her. Everything she got is because of me. Her car, her crib, and her life. I made her nigga," said 8-Ball with a bit of attitude.

"I'm just saying nigga. The boy JT wifed her up and to the looks of it, she ain't going no were," said Ron-Ron running his mouth like a girl like always.

"So, what does that mean? I can still fuck her any time I want."

Ron-Ron's phone rang.

"Hold on… Hello," said Ron-Ron walking away from 8-Ball hearing.

"Yo, where you at?" asked Omar.

"I'm around; why, what's up?"

"Yo, you is not going to believe this shit."

"What? What happen?"

"The nigga Marshal just knocked Ryan out for trying to pull a gun out on him," said Omar.

"No, when was this."

"Just now. The nigga Ryan is on the concrete as we speak. Marshal just pulled off in his truck. Yo man, I wish I had a camera that shit was too funny, my nigga," said Omar laughing in the background.

"Damn, where you at now?"

"I'm out front of the Pussy House."

"Here I come now," said Ron-Ron.

Ron-Ron walked out of the Pussy House and saw Ryan stretched out on the floor.

"I told that nigga Marshal ain't to be fucked with," said Omar standing over Ryan taking pictures on his phone.

"What happen? How did it all go down?"

"Me and Marshal was at Vanessa's house. Sabrina is at work and so is Vanessa. Marshal tried to get these two stripper broads he said he met. They was bullshit'n, so I said fuck it; I got a spot, follow me. We came here to fuck some bitches, but when we got there, Ryan started talking crazy. Talking about I should kill you right here. Calling him all types of bitches and shit. So, Ryan reached for his gun and it only took one hit to knock Ryan out. Marshal then hopped in his truck and left."

"Hold on… Why you in the Pussy House?" asked Omar.

"I was talking to 8-Ball about something."

"Why you coming to the Pussy House?" asked Ron-Ron putting his cell phone in his pocket.

Even though Ron-Ron was his man, Omar realized he still had a loudmouth.

"I just told you to take Marshal here so he can get some pussy. Duh," said Omar trying to play it off. 8-Ball came out of the Pussy House and saw Ryan stretched out on the floor.

"Damn, what happen to him?"

"He got knocked the Fuck out," said Ron-Ron trying to intimidate Chris Tucker on Friday.

"Damn that's fucked up. Oh shit, what's up O.," said 8-Ball noticing Omar beside Ron-Ron.

"Damn, I didn't see you in a minute. How you been?"

"All man, I'm chilling with wifey trying to stay out of trouble."

"Yeah, ain't nothing wrong with that. Matter fact, I need you to deliver a message for me. Tell your wifey sister, Shanay, to get at me. She owes me some paper, but I can't get a hold of her. Her phone off. Now I don't want to go to her crib and smack me a bitch, but I will," said 8-Ball.

"A'ight I got you, but what she owe you money for?" asked Omar, curious as to why Shanay would owe him money.

"You don't want to know."

CHAPTER 14

Hope, Wishes and Dreams

"Damn, this nigga knows how to treat a bitch good."

We just came back from our vacation. I had so much fun. The spa, the beach, the tour, everything was so much fun. Even when we went to the carnival, and I threw up because liquor and rides don't mix, I still had fun. The best of it all is that he proposed to me like; what more can I ask for? And through it all, he was right by my side the whole way, except when he went to play poker and I was too tired to go. I still wonder where I'm going to have the wedding at. I just got to tell him about 8-Ball and my past and that I got HIV and gave it to him. Is he still going to be with me? If he really loves me, he would, right? What about 8-Ball? I got to get him off my ass first. What if he stops messing with me? What am I going to do next? Prostitute all over again? Open my legs to every nigga that got a dick? I'm tired of that shit. How long would it take for JT to find out that I got HIV? That I'm a prostitute for 8-Ball? That I been working at the Pussy House since I was 17? That I might get my head split if I don't pay this man his money? All these questions are giving me a headache. What is taking JT so long anyway? Maybe I should just go to sleep and wait till he comes back.

Shanay was lying ass naked on the all-white king-size bed set watching TV in suite 500; from her room, she could see the whole city. Shanay loved the Quality Inn and everything in it. Shanay drifted off to sleep as soon as she closed her eyes. Shanay was woken by JT's tongue going in and out of her pussy. Shanay arched her back and her legs began to curl up as well. JT knew how to make Shanay orgasm five times in one and Shanay loved it. JT was finger fucking Shanay with one hand while the other one pulled back the lips of her pussy so JT's tongue could lick Shanay's clitoris. Up down, side to side, JT licked Shanay's clitoris like ice cream. JT sucked it so hard he wanted to swallow it if he could. Shanay arched her back even harder, grabbing onto the sheets with a tight fist full. Shanay's body rose up in the air as she moaned.

"I LOOOOOVVVVEEEEE YOOUUUUUUU!" yelled Shanay coming all over JT's mouth, lips, and face. JT went at her again non-stop.

"NO, HOLD ON BABE... WAIT... STOP... AHHHHHHH!" said Shanay trying to run from JT's tongue game but got stopped by the headboard. JT pulled her by her things closer to him and began again.

"AAAAAHHHH JAY JAY TEEEEEEEE, AHHHHHHHH!" Shanay moaned.

JT always knows how to take Shanay to another world. Shanay never had a guy to take her time with her and actually make love to her. All the men she dealt with did the same thing to her over and over. All they did was either ask for some head or ask for a back shot or both. Shanay loved JT even more by the second, minute, and hour of the day that's in the month of the year. Shanay could feel herself orgasming, again and again, making her body weak as hell. Shanay just laid on the bed, catching her breath as JT got on top of her.

JT kissed Shanay and said, "I love you Shanay," said JT kissing her again. Shanay never knew what true love felt like until now. Shanay shed a couple of tears, not because of the pain but because of the enjoyment and love she had for JT. Shanay wrapped her thick chocolate legs over JT's back as he slowly stuck his dick inside Shanay's drenched pussy. Inch by inch JT slowly went inside Shanay until he couldn't go anymore. Shanay pulled JT closer and wrapped her arms around his muscular back. JT swiftly moved his hips up and down, not trying to go fast but not trying to go slow either. JT felt Shanay fingernails dig inside him, making him go faster now. JT still wasn't going as fast as he wanted to let Shanay feel every inch of him slowly. JT tried to make love to her the best way he could, as he turned Shanay to her Sid as he did the same. JT wrapped his arm around Shanay's chest. As her shoulder, Shanay arched her back so JT could enter inside of her.

"Do you love me Shanay?" asked JT whispering in Shanay ear ever so softly as he went inside her. Shanay head went back and turned the top half of her body so she could see JT's eyes.

"I love you JT'," said Shanay and kissed JT on the lips and turned back around.

JT grabbed Shanay's shoulder and pulled her down every time he stroked her. Not too long after, Shanay climaxed as JT nutted inside of her.

"I want you to have my Baby Shanay," said JT as he kept his dick still inside of her.

"I would love too," said Shanay turning around and cuddling under JT's arms as if she was a little girl.

JT or Shanay didn't say anything as they fell fast asleep.

"What the hell am I going to do? He knows Damon but how? Where would he know Damon from? Only from the cruise incident, and my Baby whipped his ass. What if he do tell Damon what is Damon going to do? Is

he going to believe it? Or whip his ass again for lying as I would have told Damon? Or should I tell Damon about the incident before he tells him and get it over with? Shit, Damon ain't trying to hear that shit; he is going to whip my ass and Jermaine's ass if he finds out."

Vanessa was at the movies waiting on Damon to come back to their seats with the popcorn and soda. This is the same night when Vanessa was supposed to meet Jermaine at Motel 6, so it was on Vanessa's mind the whole night. Damon came back with a big bowl of popcorn, 2 large Pepsi's, and 2 large Snickers in his hands. As Damon sat down, he could see that something was wrong with Vanessa, as to say got a lot on her mind face on.

"What's wrong Babe?" asked Damon as he handed Vanessa her soda and candy bar.

"Nothing wrong," said Vanessa feeling guilty as soon as he said those words.

"Something wrong with you. Are you okay?" Vanessa knew that she couldn't hide anything from Damon if her life depended on it.

"I'm cool. Nothing wrong Babe," said Vanessa knowing that Damon knew something was up.

"Okay, whatever you say," said Damon.

Vanessa's mind kept drifting off to what Jermaine said in the mall *"how would Damon feel if he knew me and you had sex."*

Vanessa looked at Damon and said to herself, *"I can't let Damon find that out. I'm in love with this man. He did everything for me. How could I have cheated on him? Why?"* Tears started to form as she thought about Damon leaving her and messing with somebody else.

Damon could feel and see Vanessa looking at him in the corner over his eyes. As Damon turned to see Vanessa, Vanessa turned her head and watched the movie with tears coming down her face. Damon grabbed Vanessa's chin and moved her head so they could be face to face. Damon kissed her and wiped her tears from Vanessa's face.

"What's wrong Babe? Why you crying?" Damon said it so innocently that it made Vanessa cry even more.

Damon couldn't figure out what was wrong with Vanessa.

"Do you want to leave Babe?" Vanessa shook her head no, but in all actuality, Vanessa wanted to go to sleep and wish this was all a dream.

"I'm okay." Vanessa managed to say as she turned her attention on the movie.

Damon grabbed Vanessa's hand and they locked her fingers.

Kim was in her seat, bagging up as Martin Lawrence did his standup comedy.

"Oh My Gosh, this dude is so Fucking funny," said Kim as she began to laugh at one of Martin's jokes again.

Tyrone was laughing along with Kim as he began to hold his stomach. Tyrone snuck in a bottle of Hpnotiq so that he and Kim could drink as they enjoyed the show. Kim noticed that something was wrong with Tyrone but didn't know what it was. She thought maybe it was her, but Tyrone wasn't acting like Tyrone when they met up at the comedy club. Kim just thought she was tripping and paid it no mind.

"He going to make me pee on myself!" Kim said out loud as Martin began to crack a joke on one of the people in the audience.

"I go to use the bathroom," said Kim, a little bit tipsy off of the Hpnotiq she had been knocking back because of the place being so hot.

As Kim got up from her chair and went to use the bathroom, Tyrone slipped something into her drink, almost getting caught from the person sitting next to them.

"What? I can't put no sugar in my drink?" asked Tyrone switching drinks with Kim before returning to her seat.

"What did I miss?" asked Kim as she sat down and took a sip of her drink.

"Nothing really," said Tyrone and took a sip of his drink, wondering how long it would kick into when Kim would be pasted out.

Kim and Tyrone talked for a little bit until the next performer came on stage.

"So, Kim, how's the married life treating you?" asked Tyrone looking into Kim's eyes.

"It's going good. I love my husband and he loves me back. Nothing more, nothing less. All I ask if we can move from where we at and live somewhere else. That's our plan now, trying to buy a house."

"Oh, that's what's up," said Tyrone.

"So, how's your life treating you?"

"It's okay. Could be better if I had a wife as pretty as you," said Tyrone smiling a little bit.

Kim blushed and thought to herself. *I wonder why this Sexy Mother Fucker don't got a wife.*

"So why don't you have one?"

"Because I never found the right one for me. Seems like every girl is either after your money, your money or your money." Kim and Tyrone began to laugh at the joke.

"But I'm serious I met a lot of women; it is just I don't see myself with them for the rest of my life. You know?"

Kim thought to herself, *"When he said meant, he really means slept with a lot of women, but he was still trying to fuck everything moving, so he can't stay with none of them for the rest of his life, is what he really meant to say."*

Kim laughed to herself and said, "Nah, I don't know what you mean. I found my love of my life, but I'm sure you would find the love of your life as well."

"I found the love of my life already."

"Yeah, who is she?" asked Kim, seeming interested.

"She is you." Kim's smiling face now went straight as she turned to the next comedian.

"I love you, Kim. Can you give me a chance to show you how much I do?"

Kim now felt uncomfortable with Tyrone and knew this would be their last time going out because Tyrone caught feelings and Kim knew that they can't be friends.

"I have a husband Tyrone, you know that. So why would you even come at me like that."

Kim knew Tyrone was drunk because of the slur in his voice said it all. When Kim met up with Tyrone out front of the comedy club, she knew Tyrone was drunk and looked like he had been drinking for a couple of days, but Kim didn't say anything because he kept himself uptight and was still very respectful towards her, and because Kim really wanted to go to the comedy club was part of the reasons as well.

"I know, but it was something I had to get off of my chest and I didn't know how else to say it," said Tyrone, a little bit tipsy. After Tyrone said what he said, Kim felt like somebody punched the shit out of her because she was so dizzy.

"Oh shit. My head is spinning Tyrone. I got to get going. Like now," said Kim trying to get up from her seat.

When she did, she got up and it hit her even harder, making her stumble a little bit.

"Hold on, don't fall. I'll walk you to your car," said Tyrone grabbing Kim's hand and wrapping his arm around her shoulder.

"What the fuck was we drinking? Why do I feel like this?" asked Kim Tyrone.

"We was drinking Hpnotiq. How long haven't you drunk?"

"I always drink, and it don't put me like this. I'm fucked up," said Kim, barely able to walk.

"I don't think you should be driving. You're too wasted; you are going to get in a car crash. You're going to get killed or kill somebody.

"No, I'm good," said Kim jumping into her car.

Kim knew in her mind that something just wasn't right. Kim turned her car on after missing the ignition 10 different times.

"Are you sure you can drive? It look like you are going to get in a car accident. Please just come with me. I'll take you home," said Tyrone.

"No, I'm okay. Can you please leave," said Kim knowing Tyrone did something to her drink because she never felt like this before, especially not after a cup of Hpnotiq.

"Okay, suit yourself," said Tyrone.

Kim closed the door. *As long as she was away from Tyrone, she was okay*, she thought.

Tyrone went to his car, a couple of cars down and started the engine. Tyrone looked over at Kim's car and saw that she was passed out with her car lights on. Tyrone got out of his car, went over to Kim's car, and knocked on the window. Kim could hear the knock but didn't even have enough strength to open her eyelids. Kim heard the door open and somebody grabbed her as roughly as possible. Kim blacked out after that as she was thrown into what felt like a back seat of a car.

CHAPTER 15

Anger, Betrayal, Hatred

"Yeah Babe, I love you too. I don't want to be late, so I'm going to be there early… Yeah, and you know we are moving next week… Yeah, I got promoted!... Yeah, I start my job next week… Yeah, me too, okay I love you Babe," said JT going to his job happy as ever. He will start his new job in a new state with his soon-to-be wife. JT couldn't be more happy for himself until he looked at his phone and saw Trish calling.

"Damn, this bitch is annoying," said JT to himself as he didn't pick up her call.

JT has been dipping and dogging Trish for the past two weeks. He had about 52 missed calls, maybe more from Trish, and about 100 texted messages. JT thought if he stopped talking to her and had no communication with her, she would get over him, but if only JT knew he was in a rude awakening. JT's phone goes off again; this time it is Cameron. JT saw he had a whole lot of missed calls from Cameron as well, but he meant to get back with him but forgot to because he was always in the middle of something every time he called.

"Yo, what's good nigga?"

"What's up? About time you fucking answer your phone where you been at?"

"I know my fault; I just been busy as shit, you know I been out and about, but what's up? Talk to me," said JT closing his car door and getting ready to go inside of the state penitentiary.

"Look it's important. You got to meet me somewhere so I can tell you this; you won't believe me if I told you over the phone," said Cameron in his most serious tone. JT knew Cameron was serious by the way of his tone; he just wanted to know if he really wanted to know what was going on.

"What happen? I was just about to go to work."

"Man listen, it's a life-or-death situation for you man. Look, just meet me at the McDonald's near the Pussy House in 5 minutes; JT I'm serious Dog, come now."

"A'ight, here I come," said JT hopping in his truck and pulling off.

JT had a million thoughts and questions going through his mind that he started to get a headache. *Does he know about Trish and me? Why am I meeting him at the McDonald's near the Pussy House? Do he still want revenge on Marshal for killing Richard? Don't Ryan be at the Pussy House? What do he mean by a life-or-death situation for me? Do he know that my job gave me a license to carry a concealed weapon, and I got a. 9 mm in my glove compartment?* JT was going crazy trying to figure out what Cameron wanted with him.

JT pulled up in front of the McDonald's facing the Pussy House. From the McDonald's parking lot, JT can see everybody that's going in and going out of the Pussy House. A few minutes later, Cameron pulled on the side of him and got out and jumped in JT's car.

"What's up nigga? What is so important that you had to bring me down here?"

"Look Jay," said Cameron calling JT, Jay, as when they were in high school. Cameron sighs and then begins, "You my man, so you know I want the best for you. You messing with Shanay is a total no-no man and told you that from the gate. We had a threesome with her twice and we both fucked her a couple of times…." Cameron got cut off.

"Nigga you brought me down here for this. I told you I don't care about that. I'm a sucker for love than Fuck it; call it what you want. I don't care about her past. She with me now, so that's all that matters." Cameron looked at him like he was a smooth cold-blooded asshole.

"Look, since you want to be like that, I'm going to give it to you raw then. Your girl got HIV, she still fucking other niggas, and she still prostituting," said Cameron looking in JT's face.

JT had rage in his eyes when he said, "How do you know this?" asked JT, trying to get his head to gather after what he had just heard.

"When she got raped, one of the dudes that raped her had HIV. The nigga 8-Ball is still Fucking her till this day and she been prostituting out of the Pussy House for quite some time."

JT's world felt like it was crashing down on him, like he didn't have any more hope in the world. JT couldn't believe it and wouldn't believe it until he got some proof.

Cameron knew what JT was thinking as he said, "Watch this," said Cameron looking at his watch.

JT saw Shanay's car pull up to the Pussy House and park on the side of it. Pussy House had three floors, and 8-Ball's office was on the third floor. The Pussy House had nine bedrooms and was really a small apartment complex until 8-Ball got a hold of it.

"See look," said Cameron pointing at Shanay.

Shanay looked around the perimeter before she walked in.

"I told you nigga," said Cameron.

"I'm about to go in there and Fuck that Bitch up," said JT, furious as he could be.

"Nah man, you can't go in there; if you go in there on that hostile shit, you not going to make it out. 8-Ball got that shit vacuumed sealed in there. Just wait until she come out." JT wanted to go in there badly, but he knew Cameron was right, so he fell back and decided to call her.

"Hello," said Shanay in a sexy voice.

"Where the Fuck is you at?" asked JT, looking like her got from coming out of his mouth.

"What's your problem? Why you so mad for what the hell did I do?" asked Shanay, sounding like a little girl.

"I said where the fuck is you at?" asked JT with even more hatred in his voice.

"I'm home Babe. Now can you please tell me what's wrong? You're scaring me," said Shanay trying to sound so innocent.

"Oh, you home, huh? Well, I'm home and I sure don't see your ass!" said JT.

"Look Babe, I'm coming home now. Can you please tell me what's the matter?"

"You just said you was home; now you coming home? That's a nice try. You really had me going too. You know what…" JT paused then said, "Fuck you Shanay! You in their fucking that nigga 8-Ball! Fuck you! After all the shit I did for you and you going to do me like this?!" JT said furiously as he was about to explode out of the seat. Shanay wanted to explain her side of the story but JT hung up on her before even getting a word out.

"Good looking man. What the Fuck was I thinking about?" asked JT with a puzzled look on his face.

"I know it hurts man. I just didn't want you to walk around here looking all crazy and shit. You know I love you like my brother. I won't let nothing happen to you. We all we got." JT looked at Cameron and saw water in his eyes a little bit.

"Yeah, you right nigga," said JT getting him a dap.

"Well, I'm going to let you go my nigga, so you can go to work but make sure you go get checked out," said Cameron leaving JT's truck and hopping into his car.

JT felt bad about having sex with Trish even more now. Here Cameron is trying to look out for JT, but he fucking his girlfriend. JT felt like shit but knew there was no way in the world that Cameron would forgive him. Cameron has been with Trish for almost a decade. There was no explaining that. JT waited and saw Shanay get out of the Pussy House and fly off in her car. JT thought about following her but said, "Fuck it," as he shed a few tears going to work, reminiscing on the times he and Shanay shared.

"But it's not my fault. I told him I was sorry. 8-Ball said he was going to kill me because of that shit. I'm sorry Sabrina. Can you talk to him for me?" Sabrina was lost at all the information that Shanay was giving her.

"Look Shanay, I'm going to call you on my lunch break. I got a lot of clients and it's hectic right now," said Sabrina.

Sabrina wondered what Shanay was talking about and who the hell was 8-Ball. Sabrina had a tough day at the job and figured that she was too tired to even call back Shanay for an earful of drama. After work, Sabrina went straight home and took a shower. Omar came into the house shortly after Sabrina got out of the shower.

"Hey Babe, what you up to?" asked Sabrina coming down the steps and jumping into Omar's arms.

"Nothing missing you all day. I hope you are not going to be mad at me, from what I am about to yell you?" asked Omar dropping Sabrina so she could be on her feet.

Omar looked into Sabrina's eyes and said, "Your sister is a prostitute, and she has HIV." Sabrina knew that already and wondered now Omar knew.

Omar explained how he found out and how the whole city knows now.

Sabrina just looked in a daze and said, "That's crazy."

Sabrina knew she had her own life to worry about and a family she was about to start up after what she had found out today.

"Look Babe, sit down," said Sabrina, hype and with joy. Sabrina had a big smile on her face as she grabbed Omar's hand and sat down.

"You all happy. What's up?" asked Omar, curious as to see what was on his girl's mind.

"Well, today at work. I been feeling sick in the morning, mind you, and I been having back pains and having the urge to eat a lot. So, you know I been exercising and stuff."

Sabrina got caught off when Omar said, "Girl, just get to the point."

"I'm pregnant," said Sabrina with a smile.

Omar thought it couldn't be true. Omar tried to get Sabrina pregnant for the past year, but it was always something wrong and now Omar had his chance to be a dad. Omar got up off of the couch and jumped with joy.

"I'm going to be a dad!" said Omar playing but serious as a heart attack.

Sabrina laughed and thought to herself, *"Man, I love this man,"* as she got up and hugged her man.

Sabrina was so happy that they both fell into each other's arms; as they were getting ready to make love, an unexpected knock came at their door.

"Who the Fuck is that?" asked Omar getting up from the couch and walking to the door. Omar opened the door and saw that it was Trish.

"What's up?" asked Omar, not knowing why Trish was at their doorstep.

"Can I speak to Sabrina," said Trish calmly.

Trish looked like she was stressing about something bad as her makeup looked like it was everywhere on her face.

"Babe come here," said Omar.

Sabrina came to the door and saw Trish and the look on Trish's face seemed like she was ashamed of something.

"You want to come in Trish? Are you okay?" asked Sabrina as she stayed at the door.

"No, I'm okay. I just wanted to tell you something…" Trish paused for a minute and said, "look Sabrina, I have mad respect for you that's why I'm coming to you, but if you don't tell your sister to stay the Fuck away from my man," Trish's voice began to increase after every word, "I'm going to whip her ass! I know they been fucking for quite some time and I'm tired of this shit!" said Trish break down crying on Sabrina's doorstep.

Sabrina wrapped her arms around Trish and took her into her house as she sat her down. Sabrina felt bad that she told Shanay to keep fucking JT even when she knew that Trish was JT's girl, but it seemed like JT didn't have any girl the way he was in Shanay's house every day and now living with her.

"It's going to be alright, Trish. You don't need no nigga to fulfill yourself. Look at you, you're beautiful. And life is too short to be worried about no man," said Sabrina trying to encourage Trish the best way she could.

Trish wasn't trying to hear that shit. Trish was deeply in love with JT and she hadn't talked to him in weeks. Trish was losing her mind. Trish was stressing, growing bald in some of her hair, and losing weight. Trish was doing all of that and was still trying to hide it from Cameron.

"I know it's just I'm madly in love with this man Sabrina. What if Omar just up and left you for some other bitch and didn't talk to you for weeks? What would you do?"

Sabrina had to think about it and asked herself, *"What would I do?"*

Sabrina couldn't even imagine what she would do if Omar left her, so she tried to skip the question and ask her something.

"What would you do if you never met JT? How was your life before you met JT?"

Trish tried to remember all the happy times she had with Cameron and all the fun they had, but Trish's reality then set in when all the girls Cameron had cheated on her with and all the times Cameron wasn't there like JT was there, how JT knew her body perfect, where Cameron knew her body not as much and they been together for years. Trish knew she had to get JT back because it seemed like she couldn't live without him in her life, especially since she hadn't had sex since JT last touched her.

Cameron knew something was up but didn't know what until Trish denied him to have sex. Cameron will soon find out that Trish is sleeping with his best friend because Trish couldn't hold it in anymore.

"It was good, then it got bad, then JT made it good. Now that JT is not with me, it is bad," said Trish crying. Trish knew that Sabrina didn't know that Trish goes with Cameron, which she never brought up.

"It's going to be okay Trish. Just have faith if he really loves you, he will come back to you. If he don't, then fuck him," said Sabrina trying to lighten Trish up and give her hope at the same time.

"It's a'ight, Trish. You don't need no nigga. You are good-looking. You ain't no ugly broad that can't find no love nowhere. I'm sure you can find a man in a heartbeat that will love you and cater to your every need, and I'm telling you from a man's perspective," said Omar trying to cheer Trish up as well.

It was a knock on the door and Sabrina looked at Omar with a puzzled look.

"It's Marshal. I forgot I told him I will go play ball with him earlier."

Omar answered the door and greeted Marshal as they walked into the house. An ultimate attraction came from Marshal as he saw Trish sitting down in tears. Even with her makeup everywhere and her bloodshot red and puffy eyes, Marshal was still attracted to Trish.

"What's wrong with you sweetheart? Why are you crying?" Trish didn't say anything as Marshal sat down next to her on the opposite side of Sabrina, "You too pretty to be crying. It must be a relationship problem. What man got you crying like this?" asked Marshal, trying to get something out of her.

"She's just depressed, that's all," said Sabrina getting up from the couch and grabbing Omar's hand as they headed upstairs.

"I'll just leave you two alone for one quick second. I got to talk to Omar real quick."

Sabrina went upstairs to their bedroom and said to Omar, "What do you think about Marshal dating Trish?" asked Sabrina, eager to hear Omar's answer.

"I don't know. Marshal gets around the city and he just came home from doing 10 years. I don't know if he is ready to settle down."

"Well, it's worth a try. I mean, we can kill two birds with one stone. JT mess with Shanay so Marshal can get JT out of Trish's system, and everybody lives happily ever after," said Sabrina, hearing a knock on the door; it was Shanay.

All you could hear was banging, screaming, and yelling downstairs. Omar and Sabrina went downstairs and saw Trish grabbing a handful of Shanay's weave and punching her in the face. Shanay picked Trish up and threw her on the floor. Trish released her grip on Shanay hair and a moan of pain came out of her mouth as she felt like her back was getting ready to break. Shanay got on top of her and started punching her. Marshal finally got Shanay off of Trish and took her outside. Trish got up, holding her back with a light scratch on her lower eye and you could see that the swelling was starting to kick in on her cheek.

"Oh My God, I'm so sorry. I didn't know she was coming over here. Are you okay?" asked Sabrina walking towards Trish.

Trish didn't say anything but got up and left the house, holding her back.

"Kamiyah! You see them fine ass niggas over there!?" yelling Candy over the loud music in the strip club.

"Yeah, I see them!" said Kamiyah looking over to where Kamiyah was pointing at.

"I want the light skin one! It look like he is Puerto Rican or something!" Candy side licking her lips as the guy looked over and saw her looking at him.

"Yeah they cute! You know we only got 10 minutes left and our shift over!" said Kamiyah clapping her ass in front of some drunk young boy's face as he kept sticking ones in her panties, trying to get a feel.

"I know, I'm tired as shit. I might just go home and call my bro over!" said Candy looking at Kamiyah with a devilish grin while shaking her ass in front of the young boyfriend who Kamiyah was dancing on.

"You know he called me and told me to tell you to stop doing that shit! You know if you fuck up my brother relationship, I'm going to Fuck you up," said Kamiyah in a serious tone.

"I'm not Kamiyah. It's just your brother got a Bitch sprung on some shit," said Candy getting up from the boy's lap.

"Yeah a'ight. I'm just letting you know so Kim won't be on no sucker shit and break my brother's heart," said Kamiyah walking out of the main room and to the back where the girl's locker room was at.

Candy followed her the whole way and asked her a question when she got there. "So, you don't think if I vow my life to Aairyah that he won't choose me over Kim?"

Candy had to know and anticipated the answer. Candy opened up her locker and pulled her street clothes out as she looked at Kamiyah, which was only one locker apart.

"I mean you sexy as shit, don't get it wrong, but Aairyah is head over heels with that broad. If you don't know, they had been married for some time now."

"Yeah, yeah, I know. I promise this is the last time I'll see him on that tip again," said Candy putting her clothes on and heading out of the strip club in a hurry.

Candy knew she had to stop her little game she was playing with Aairyah, so she had her mind made up that tonight was the last night. Driving to her house, Candy decided to call Aairyah. Aairyah didn't answer.

Candy texted him and said, "If you don't pick up your phone, I swear I'll go to your house now and bang on that shit and tell Kim what's really good." Five minutes later, Aairyah called Candy.

"What the Fuck do you want?" asked Aairyah in a low tone of voice.

"Did I wake you?" asked Candy, knowing she had because she left the strip club at 3 o'clock in the morning, and it had to be a little later than 3:30 in the morning.

"Well, if I did, I'm sorry," said Candy after Aairyah didn't respond to her last question.

"Look, I'm going to make it short and sweet. If you come over now and fuck me like you never did before. I promise I will leave you alone. If you don't, then I'll make it my duty to make sure you come over here every day," said Candy.

"How I know you not bullshit'n?" asked Aairyah getting out of bed and walking to his closet.

"I told you, I swear and your sister told me you had a talk to her about it, so I promised both of y'all," said Candy.

"Oh yeah, I forgot to tell you I'm pregnant." Aairyah dropped the phone and felt like his world just ended.

"How did I get this dumb bitch pregnant? What the fuck was I thinking?"

"Hello, Hello!" was all Aairyah could hear over the phone as it sat on the floor. Aairyah picked the phone up and looked at it.

"Hello, is you still there?... I was just fucking playing Aairyah," said Candy over the phone.

Aairyah had a sense of relief when he replayed, "Why the Fuck is you playing?"

"Damn, you was going to leave me in the gutter like everybody else, huh. That's fucked up; you don't get to answer. Just hurry your ass up here before I change my mind," said Candy hanging up the phone.

Candy had an attitude the rest of the ride to her house, as Kamiyah called her. Aairyah just looked at the phone and knew that was a close call. When Candy called Aairyah, he was never asleep. As a matter of fact, he was up thinking why Kim didn't come home the other night and why she had been so disclosed to Aairyah since then. Aairyah feared that she had slept with somebody else but knew he would go crazy if she did. Aairyah threw on some Jordan basketball shorts, a white T-Shirt, and some Jordan basketball flip-flops as he headed out the door to Candy house. The feel of Aairyah not being there woke Kim up.

Aairyah went to Candy's house and went straight in the door as he already had a copy of the key form when he first started fucking Candy.

Aairyah didn't even notice his sister watching TV in the living room as he walked past the living room and to Candy's bedroom. Candy had just gotten out of the shower and was lotioning herself when Aairyah walked into the bedroom and closed the door.

"That's what I like. A man that's always on time, I'll be with you in a minute," said Candy sitting on her bed, lotioning her legs and feet.

Aairyah didn't say anything to her as he approached her and pushed her back on the bed so she could be on her back.

"I said hold on," said Candy looking in surprise at the seriousness on Aairyah's face, which turned her on even more.

"Shut up!" said Aairyah in an aggressive but sexy tone.

Candy didn't say anything but put her head back as Aairyah snatched the towel off her body, exposing her beautiful shape. Aairyah always loved her stripper shape and admired how she always kept her body tight, but he knew he had to perform well to keep Candy out of his life, so that's what he planned to do.

Aairyah wrapped his arms around each one of Candy tight with his head in between her legs. Aairyah smelled nothing but strawberries in between her legs as he licked away. Aairyah spreads candy pussy lips with his lips as his tongue begins playing soccer with her clitoris. Aairyah then put his finger in her pussy that another then another one. Aairyah had three fingers in Candy's pussy while he was still licking and sucking on Candy's pussy. In and out of Candy Pussy made Candy mean like crazy. Candy's moan made Aairyah's dick grow, wanting to burst out his Jordan shorts as you could see his print.

"AWWWWWWW, SHHHHHIIIITTTTT… DAAAMMMMMNNNNN

DADDDDDDDDYYYYYYY!” Candy moaned Aairyah rammed his fingers in her pussy even harder as he ate her clitoris, damn near biting it off.

“OOOOOOOHHHHHH YES! YES DADDY YES!” said Candy erupting. Candy's orgasm left her in a daze as Aairyah turned her on her stomach. Candy couldn't even move as Aairyah tried to make her arch her back. Aairyah smacks her ass hard as shit as she jumps in the air.

“Get your ass up!” Aairyah demanded.

Candy didn't say anything but assumed her position. Candy liked pain and felt the burning sensation on her ass as Aairyah entered inside of her giving her everything he had. Aairyah grabbed Candy's weave and wrapped it around his left hand. Every time he stroked, he pulled on Candy's hair.

“YOU GOING TOOOOOO AWWWWWWW… PULL… PULL MY HAIR OUT, AWWWWWWW!” Candy moaned.

Aairyah didn't give a fuck about pulling Candy's hair out; he was going to give her a night to remember. Aairyah smacked her ass harder and harder as he took each stroke. Candy didn't know what was worst. The pain from Aairyah pulling her hair or every time Aairyah would smack her ass. Candy didn't care because all of that excited her that a man could take full advantage of her, and not including every stroke Aairyah took felt so good to her. Candy couldn't remember how many times she climaxed on Aairyah's dick before he spits in her ass whole. Aairyah stuck his dick out of Candy's pussy and went in Candy's ass, making Candy scream with pain.

“AAAAAAHHHH SSSHHHIIITTT! TAKE IT OUT! TAKE IT

OUT!" Aairyah lets go of Candy's hair and sees a bald spot where he was pulling her hair and still had some hair in his hand. Aairyah flung the hair he had in his hand across the room and put his hand over Candy's mouth. Aairyah went harder and harder into Candy's ass, causing pain and pleasure at the same time.

After about a couple of minutes, Aairyah turned Candy around on her stomach and gut on top of her. Aairyah lifted Candy's legs on his shoulder as he began to go inside of her. Aairyah could feel. Candy gets wetter and wetter with every stroke. Aairyah could see Candy's face tightening up and could feel her pussy gripping Aairyah's dick as well. Aairyah could feel he was about 10 nut, so he hurried up, pulled out, and started jerking off his dick until he ejaculated all over Candy's stomach. Aairyah pulled his shorts up and left the room without saying one word. Candy couldn't do or say anything because she couldn't even move for now anyway. All you heard was knocking on the door as Aairyah walked past the living room.

"Who the hell is that?" asked Kamiyah. The voice of Kamiyah startled Aairyah as he looked over into the living room.

"Oh shit, I didn't even know you was here. Who at the door?" asked Aairyah, motioning at the down.

"Hell, if I know," said Kamiyah getting up from the chair. Aairyah looked at the door and saw it was Kim.

"Oh shit!" Aairyah's heart almost jumped out of his shirt as he saw his wife standing there.

"What am I going to do? It's Kim?" asked Aairyah, paranoid. Kamiyah answered the door without saying anything.

"Hey Sis," said Kamiyah with a fake smile.

"What's up Babe? What you doing here?" asked Aairyah, trying to think of a way to get out of the situation he is currently in now.

"How could you? After all, we been threw you going to cheat on me with this bitch, tho? A stripper whore. Where she at so I can fuck her up. I know this ain't your crib Kamiyah," said Kim angrily but hurtfully.

"Can you keep it down? This is Candy's man house, Kim," said Kamiyah trying to have her brother's side. Kim wanted to believe it but couldn't believe it.

"So why are you over here then?" asked Kim looking at Aairyah.

Aairyah stuttered over a few words then said, "If you must know. Candy's boyfriend is a great art designer and he throws big party's around the world. I figured since your birthday is coming up, I throw you a surprise party, but I guess it ain't no surprise no more." Kim looked into Aairyah's eyes and saw he had a straight face.

"So why you coming over here wee hours in the morning?" asked Kim with her hands on her hip, striking a pose.

"Because this is the only time that I can catch you while you're sleeping and you won't expect nothing. Like it was a surprise," said Aairyah pushing past Kim out of the house.

"A'ight Sis, I'll holla at you tomorrow. Tell Candy and her man I said I'm out," said Aairyah as he walked to his car.

"Babe I'm sorry okay. I just expected the worst." Aairyah didn't say anything, just kept walking to his car.

"Can you just hear me out," said Kim jumping in front of Aairyah so he couldn't go anywhere.

"Do I question you at any time in our marriage?"

"No," said Kim with her head down.

"Okay then, so why would you question me? Matter of fact, why didn't you come home the other night? We are married; it is no way in hell that you should be sleeping anywhere else other than our bed."

"I'll tell you when we get home. We got a lot to talk about." Kim was nervous and scared when she hopped in her car and followed Aairyah to the house.

Kim didn't know what to say or how to say it. Inside their house, Aairyah didn't what for nothing.

"So why didn't you come home last night?" asked Aairyah, wondering what the answer was to the mystery question.

"Look, first off, I really don't remember what happen. I was drunk."

CHAPTER 16

What Would I Be Without You?

"Well, why are you still mad for?" asked Kim.

Kim told Aairyah everything that happened when she didn't come home that night. She told him how she was cool with Tyrone and they had been friends for a while. Nothing had ever happened with them the whole time. She told him that they had had lunch together before and that she had gone to the movies with him. She told Aairyah that they were never on no flirting or sexual type time which Aairyah didn't want to hear anyway. She told Aairyah that she had met Tyrone at the comedy club and that they were just there to have a good time. She told Aairyah that she began feeling woozy and dizzy, so she left the comedy club thinking Tyrone had put something in her drink. She told him how she got in her car and tried to leave but fell unconscious at the wheel. She also said she doesn't know what happened after that and that she woke up in a hotel room butt naked.

Aairyah just forgave Kim after a month's time. It has been a month since Kim told Aairyah the news. Aairyah left Kim as soon as he heard the news. Aairyah was staying with Damon the whole time and decided to take Kim back now after Kim begged, pleaded, and asked for forgiveness a thousand times. Aairyah knew deep down he didn't know what to do if Kim left him, but he still was furious and had a heart in his heart because of that. Aairyah didn't really have any family except his sister Kamiyah but didn't want to bother her in his relationship.

"Why am I still mad for hhhhhmmmmmmm? Maybe because why a wife who I been married to for 5 and a half years was in a hotel butt ass naked and she don't know how she got there. Then seen a man behind my back and thought everything was all cool. Maybe that's why I am still mad!" said Aairyah putting a little bit more bass and volume in his voice in every word.

Kim was getting tired of arguing with Aairyah every day since he came back. Even though this was his first day back living together, that didn't stop him from coming over and grabbing his clothes every day. Kim was in the wrong, so she couldn't really say anything.

"I hope you got them test results back," said Aairyah looking at Kim and noticing a new tattoo on her navel that almost blended in.

"Yeah, I got them right here," said Kim walking over to Aairyah in panties and bra and throwing the test results on Aairyah's lap.

"You making it seem like I'm some bitch that fuck a whole bunch of people. Me or you don't even know if I had sex…." Aairyah cut his eye at her.

"At least I kept it 100 with you and didn't lie to you." Aairyah walked over to Kim and threw her on the bed, "so, you got a new tattoo?" asked Aairyah, looking at Kim's navel.

You could barely see the tattoo because of Kim's panties in the way. Aairyah reached down and pulled Kim's panties down so you could see the whole tattoo. Kim got Aairyah's name on her when he left her. The tattoo said, "AAIRYAH PROPERTY," with an arrow pointing towards her pussy. Aairyah smiled in satisfaction but still was mad at her.

"I got it when you left me. I'm sorry, Aairyah. Can you please forgive me?"

Aairyah didn't say anything but kept it moving out of the room. Weeks went by, and Aairyah would barely speak to his wife. Kim would just get frustrated and lock herself in the room every day after work. Aairyah would come home from work and drink all day without saying anything to Kim the whole time. Weeks on in, Kim will get even more madder, depressed, and frustrated with Aairyah.

Until one day, Kim got fed up and said, "What do you want to have a divorce or something?" Because in Kim's mind, she thought Aairyah didn't want anything to do with her.

Aairyah had finished two six-packs of Corona's and a pint of Hennessy. Aairyah was tipsy but wasn't drunk as he watched the football game on TV. When Aairyah heard Kim say that, a million things flashed through his mind, tears streaming down his face. Aairyah never turns to look at Kim as he keeps watching the football game. Kim knew what she said was strong but didn't know how strong it was until she walked over to Aairyah and saw tears coming down his face.

Kim just threw himself on Aairyah and began kissing him. Kim grabbed Aairyah face with both of her hands and started sucking on the bottom of Aairyah's lip after she got done kissing him. Kim slid down to the floor, unzipped Aairyah's pants, and pulled his dick out. Aairyah just tilted his head back and enjoyed the pleasure. Kim locked her fingers with Aairyah as she sucked his dick with no hands. Kim had her lined black skirt on with her white button-down shirt and her black heels. Aairyah pulled her up as his dick was covered with saliva and his dick was as hard as a Rock Weller bite. Aairyah pulled Kim's skirt up. Now the bottom of her skirt touched the bottom of her Brest, revealing the zebra stripe panties. Aairyah pulled Kim's panties down, showing her tattoo of

Aairyah's name, making Aairyah feel proud. The panties dropped to the floor and Aairyah leaned back on the Lay-Z-Boy. Kim put her feet on the armrests as she positioned herself to ride Aairyah.

Aairyah lifted Kim by her ass so that his face was looking at Kim Pussy head up. Aairyah began to blow lightly on Kim Pussy as he began to eat her out. Aairyah used his thumb to enter inside of Kim Pussy as the rest of his hand grabbed her butt. Playing with her clit with his tongue, Aairyah saw Kim's legs begin to shake. Kim let out a moan so loud that it could be heard in the house next door. Kim fell on Aairyah's lap, trying to gather herself together. Aairyah picked her up and sat her on his dick. Sliding down slowly on Aairyah's dick until she got to the base of it, Kim's eyes became watery. Kim leaned over so that her Brest was in Aairyah's face and he couldn't see her face. Moving her body up and down on Aairyah's dick. Kim didn't want Aairyah to see that she was crying, so she kept her head over the Lay-Z-Boy. Aairyah got up while his dick was still in Kim picking her up. Kim wrapped her arms and legs around Aairyah's neck and back like a little girl.

Aairyah walked Kim to their bed and laid her on her back. Aairyah could see that Kim was crying from the wet spots on her face. Aairyah wiped her face with his hand and kissed her ever so lightly. Aairyah went inside of her deeper, sending Kim's head and eyes back. Aairyah stroked her faster and faster, trying to hurry up and get his nut off. Aairyah could tell Kim climaxed by her moaning and all the whiteness around his dick. Aairyah nutted inside of Kim as he laid on top of her.

"Babe, your ass is heavy," said Kim laughing, pushing Aairyah off of her.

Aairyah couldn't help but laugh and got off her and laid on his back. Kim snuggled up Aairyah's arm and put her arm around his body. Aairyah turned on his side, wrapping his arm around Kim's body as they faced each other; Aairyah kissed her first.

"Babe can you promise me that we would never be like that again," said Kim looking into Aairyah's eyes.

"If you promise me that you won't go out on no dates again?" asked Aairyah feeling a little relieved about the burden he had on his back all that time.

"You have my word, my life, and my soul that that would never happen again Babe. I promise," said Kim with sincerity in her heart.

"Babe." Kim's voice started squeaking and tears rolled down her face as she began.

"Babe I love you. I wouldn't know what to do without you. You are my everything Babe and I promise that will never happen again. Just promise me Babe. Promise me nothing will come between us again," said Kim with her lip trembling. Aairyah knew Kim was sincere about every word she said.

Aairyah whipped her eyes and said to her, "Nothing would get in our way as long as we stay loyal to each other and keep it 100 with each other," said Aairyah.

Aairyah had a fuck it attitude about the whole situation because he didn't actually know if she had sex with another person, and if she did, it wasn't intentional. *Was it?* Thought Aairyah as he was recording the situation back in his head. *At least I don't know, know damn Tyrone anyway, so fuck him. I'll just let it go for now. Matter of fact, if I ever do get caught up with Candy like I almost did, I can use this as my weapon.*

Aairyah caught himself talking to himself when Kim said. "I love you Babe. I just wish we can move past this and live our lives."

"We can and we are Babe," said Aairyah pulling Kim even closer to him

as they fell asleep in each other arms.

"Damn, Babe, this crib is so beautiful," said Vanessa with sparkles in her eyes as she stared at the house in front of her.

Vanessa, Damon, and Mrs. Riley, the real estate agent, stood in front of a white and blue house.

"Well, as you can see, the house is white except the door, window panels, and roof are blue. The front yard is filled with flowers, as always, all around the house. There are three bedrooms, two full bathrooms, an attic and a basement. The house is sitting on one acre of land."

The real estate agent started walking on the side of the house, which had a path of cement going towards the backyard.

"As you can see, the white gate that covers the house stretches all the way down there," said Mrs. Riley pointing down to the white fence.

Vanessa's eyes lit up as she saw so much land in one backyard. There were two trees at the far end of the yard where the white fence ended.

"Damn, this is a lot of space. What the hell are we going to do with all of this?" asked Vanessa, acting like the house is already theirs.

"Well, I'll be lying if I said it's one full acre, but it's damn near close as you can see," said Mrs. Riley.

Mrs. Riley then walked through the back door of the house. As they entered the door, they saw a chandelier hanging from the dining room as Mrs. Riley announced the rooms as she walked into each room. Mrs. Riley walked into the kitchen and showed the kitchen off.

"Well, as you can see, there are to sinks together another one over there. A stainless-steel refrigerator with a built-in ice and water dispenser. All the cabinets are glass, and I had a microwave built between the cabinets. The floor is all wood, everywhere in the house except the master bedroom. The countertops is marble black, as you can see. Come follow me," said Mrs. Riley going towards the living room.

"We have a projector built on top of the ceiling, and if you press this button, you can navigate the whole house as well as the slide coming down from the wall. We have shelves on the side of the slide where you can put DVDs or books or whatever that fits in there," said Mrs. Riley laughing a little bit. Mrs. Riley then walks up the stairs case as ends up in the main hallway.

"There's the last bedroom here on the left."

"It's plain but kinda big," Aairyah thought.

"Here's the second bedroom. There is a walk-in closet that can fit eight people in there, not too big but not small either," said Mrs. Riley.

"Now, here's the master bedroom," said Mrs. Riley in a hydrostatic voice.

The bedroom window filled half of the wall as it came out of the house slightly. It had a bench where you can sit and look out the window and into the backyard.

"The walk-in closet can fit 20 people in it; as you can see, it has built-in cubbies for your shoes, boots, or heels," said Mrs. Riley giving a wink to Vanessa. Mrs. Riley went to the master bedroom and went inside. Vanessa's heart melted as she walked inside.

"As you can see, there are two shower heads built-in on this shower here. This is a built-in Jacuzzi right next to hit and another perfect view of the backyard between his and her sink. Mrs. Riley thought she did an awesome job at presenting her house as she gave a wonderful smile.

"So, where is the attic and basement?" asked Damon as they were leaving the bathroom.

"Well, the attic and basement is not finished, and the other bathroom is downstairs. I forgot to show you before we came up. I will be glad to show you the bathroom downstairs," said Mrs. Riley.

"Now, what is the asking price?" asked Damon.

"Well, the asking price is 490,000 dollars which is low for this house, but I'll take 450,000 thousand dollars now because of the basement and attic not being done," Vanessa whispered in Damon's ear and said, "damn, that's a lot of money Babe."

Damon ignored Vanessa's comment and said, "Okay, we will be getting back to you," said Damon.

Mrs. Riley felt like she wasted her Saturday morning on nothing and Damon knew he had gone out of his league.

"Babe, I know you want the best for us, but that is too much money."

Damon didn't quote on her comment because he had 80 thousand in the bank saved up from living in that apartment. He also had grants to go to school that calculated to 20 thousand, and his credit was good, so he could always get a loan from the bank, he thought. Damon was going to get the house if it was the last thing he did. Especially after. Vanessa told

Damon she was 14 weeks pregnant and they were expecting a child. Damon knew Vanessa was pregnant but didn't say anything until Vanessa told him and he acted like he was surprised.

"Babe, it's okay; we can have our child in answer their house it don't have to be this one," said Vanessa getting in the car and closing the door.

"I just want what's best for us that all," said Damon pulling off and waving goodbye to Mrs. Riley as Vanessa did as well.

Mrs. Riley knew for sure that they weren't coming back until later that night. Damon gave her a call.

"Oh My God, this Bitch is driving me nuts," said Sabrina talking to Omar over the phone as she was driving home from work.

Shanay has stayed with Sabrina since JT left her and never returned. Shanay has been whining, nagging, and annoying Sabrina about JT the whole time she has been at her house. When Sabrina went to work, Shanay would get a countless amount of texts on her phone as she was on duty.

"What she do now Babe?" asked Omar in kind of a chuckle as he said it.

"It's not funny. You should have seen her when I left; she looked all crazy and bugged out like the world was about to end. Then she about to get me fired, blowing my cell phone up every 5 minutes about dumb shit. So, I turn my cell phone off. Then I hear my name over the intercom saying I got a phone call. So, I think it's you, so I hurry up to the phone eager to hear what you had to say because you never call me at my job. So, when I pick it up, guess who it is?"

"Shanay," said Omar with a smile over the phone.

"Yeah." Omar started laughing.

"That shit is not funny it's annoying," said Sabrina, serious but couldn't help but laugh a little bit.

"So, what you going to do?" asked Omar.

"I don't know, but she better do something because…" Sabrina stopped as she looked at her phone and saw it was Shanay.

"Here she go again, ughh. Let me call you back Babe see what the hell she wants," said Sabrina frustrated over the phone.

"Okay Babe, but don't be stressing having my Baby messed up inside of you," said Omar

"I won't Babe, I promise," said Sabrina hanging up the phone and clicking over to the other line.

"Yes, Shanay?" asked Sabrina dragging her words out like she was tired.

"Sis guess what?" Sabrina didn't even get the chance to say what before Shanay started rambling at the mouth.

"JT didn't leave for his other job yet. I saw his car at his job parking lot. I know it was his car because I remember his license plate. So, you know what that means, right? That means there is still hope in our relationship and JT would have left me, right? Right?" Sabrina didn't say anything because she had the phone on speaker on the car's passenger seat, halfway listening to what Shanay was saying.

"I think I still got a chance, maybe; maybe not, I hope so. Well, I hope he can find it in his heart. I was only doing it because I owed him money and I didn't want 8-Ball to go to the house and kill both of us. Was I in the wrong for that? I mean, I was looking out and thinking for both of us. Then I didn't want to ask JT for that much money because he would ask for what and I didn't want him to know I was prostituting and stuff, so I had to lie to him and tell him what he wanted to hear and you know what's crazy?" Shanay waited for Sabrina to say something, but all she could hear was silence.

"Sabrina, Sabrina!" yelled Shanay over the phone.

"Girl, what!" said Sabrina grabbing the phone off of the passenger seat and putting it closer to her mouth, trying to figure out what she said. Shanay ignored the smartness that came out of Sabrina's mouth and kept telling her story.

"What's crazy is he proposed to me when we was at Puerto Rico. What I want to know is who told him all of this shit? I tried to talk to Cameron, but he didn't know where he was either.

"Who the hell is Cameron?"

"Cameron, the guy that mess with Trish."

"I thought Trish messed with JT?"

"No, Trish mess with Cameron but JT was fucking her behind his boy's back. They was best friends in Howard, but when Aairyah, Omar, Marshal, and Damon humiliated him in front of the whole school, he got transferred. You don't remember Cameron?"

"No, I can't say I do. I remember that incident happened because the whole school was talking about it the whole four years I was at Howard, but I really don't remember him like that," said Sabrina trying to remember Cameron.

"Well, you probably seen him before. Just didn't notice him because he left freshman year the first semester." Shanay only remembered Cameron because she did her first threesome with Cameron and JT, and she saw him regularly.

"Oh, I don't know where you at anyway?" asked Sabrina, changing the subject.

"I'm just now pulling up to JT's house. Hopefully, he didn't change the locks on me so I can surprise him when he get inside his house."

"How do you know if he wants to see you? Maybe he needs some time away from you right now. You know he been through some shit with you and you gave him something he has to live with for the rest of his life."

"I know that Sabrina. It's just I wish he forgave me and do as we planned. Get married, move to another state, and start our lives. That's all I want."

"You know what's crazy? Not too long ago, if I remember, you said you couldn't get married and said you don't have no feelings for no man, but here you go going crazy over one man trying to get married. It don't get boring to you?" asked Sabrina, using Shanay's words on her.

"Okay you got me. Now I know the importance about love. Now it's different," said Shanay.

"Whatever Girl. All I'm saying is let him have some room. If you don't want him to do that, then tell him how it is and hopefully, he take you back."

"I been trying to tell him how it is, but he don't give me a chance in a day to explain myself. I called him on 10 different phone numbers. Every time he hear my voice, he hangs up on me."

"Well, I don't know what to tell you, Sis."

"I know what I'm going to do. He didn't change his locks, so I'm in his house now, but some of his shit is packed. I'll let you know how everything happen when I come home. Well, if I come home," said Shanay laughing.

"A'ight Girl don't catch no charges breaking and entering," laughed Sabrina.

"Fuck you, I got a key, so peace," said Shanay hanging up the phone and figuring out a way to win JT's heart as she stood in JT having room.

CHAPTER 17

Break Up to Make Up

"Getting ready for the big day tomorrow Jay," said Lieutenant Smith walking JT to the door to buzz him out of the penitentiary. It has been a long day for JT, or as you should say, a long month for JT from what it seems like.

"Yeah Smith, trying to be prepared, so I guess I'm going to go home and go to sleep," said JT saying whatever came out of his mouth because all he wanted to do was go to sleep.

"You haven't been yourself lately. Are you okay? I mean, is it because you are being transferred?"

"No, I'm alright. Just a lot of stuff have been on my mind, that's all." JT really wanted to say was, "You don't give a fuck about me, so why are you asking."

"Alright then, I'll see you later," said Smith letting JT out of the state penitentiary.

JT walked to his car with his head down like he was all day. Before coming to work, JT got his test results back from the hospital and they came back positive for HIV. JT wanted to kill himself and found himself going through a daydream about killing himself at the hospital. Until a very attractive nurse brought hope to JT's future when he had a conversation with her at the hospital.

"Listen Jason, it's not the end of the world. You're a very handsome guy, and I know ladies love you. So please don't leave out of here and kill yourself like some brothers do. There are pills to take so you can stay healthy, and there are pills to take so you can have sex so your partner will not get it."

JT replayed those couple lines in his head repeatedly all day, encouraging himself that life wasn't over for him. JT knew deep down in himself that if he never messed with Shanay, his life would be okay for the most part.

"JT," said Trish in a low raspy voice.

JT turned around, not noticing the voice and saw Trish behind him. Trish had a white halter top that had blood stains over it, some blue jeans, and some white and blue Steve Madden heels on. When JT looked up, it didn't look like Trish, though. Trish had two black eyes, a busted lip, and what looked like a fractured nose. Before JT could say something, Trish broke down in tears.

"What the hell happen to you Trish?" asked JT, walking over to Trish, trying to comfort her.

"I told him… I told him everything about us," said Trish, weeping.

"What? Why would you do that?" asked JT, now unbracing Trish and looking her in her face with a frustrated look.

"Because…" Trish paused as she got herself together and began to go again, "because of you JT! That's why!" Trish began to be in a temper tantrum.

"You stop picking up my calls, my text messages, and my visits to your house! All over some Black Ass Ugly Bitch!" Trish lowered her voice when a car passed by them and went on their way.

"I love you JT, you can't see that? I'll do anything for you. I just got tired of Cameron shit Jay. You don't know, but he use to abuse me before and treat me like shit until you came around. Then when I met you, you treated me like a queen, JT. A damn queen. You know how that makes me feel inside Jay. I feel beautiful when I'm with you JT. I feel like nothing can take us apart. Nothing. Like, I got the world in my hands when I'm with you. Do you see this Jay?" asked Trish, pointing at her face, "he did this to me. After I told him what happened, he whipped my ass and told me to tell you that he was going to kill you if he sees you again," said Trish standing there looking helpless as she doesn't know what to do.

"Damn, Trish, what the fuck have you done." JT opened his car door and reached for his cell phone. JT grabbed his cell phone and saw 47 missed calls and 21 text messages, all from Cameron and Shanay. JT read the text messages to himself. *Babe look can you please forgive me? I'm going crazy without you. Can you please pick up the phone?* JT erased all of Shanay's text messages as he scanned through Cameron's text messages. Damn, Bro I thought we was better than that. You going to fuck my bitch though. And all this time, I thought you was with me. Well, you know what? I'M GOING TO KILL YOU MOTHER FUCKER, IF IT'S THE LAST THING I DO. THERE IS NO MORE LOVE BETWEEN US. FUCK YOU. YOU BETRAYER. JT didn't want to read any more of his text messages, so he erased them all and looked at Trish.

"So, what you going to do Trish?"

Trish looked at JT like she was about to start crying again.

"Jay, I'm going with you." Trish looked at JT's face sensing it was disapproval.

"Jay, I don't have no place to go. You know how my situation is. I can't just up and go somewhere else because I don't have nowhere else to go. Please, JT I'm begging you let me go with you," said Trish pleading to

JT as she hurried up and hugged JT to feel a sense of secureness. JT knew Trish's situation and took it into consideration when he said, "Okay, follow me."

JT hopped in his car and Trish followed behind him. JT's head was spinning because he didn't know where to go or what to do, for that matter. JT knew he didn't have any more friends in this state, and if anybody called him like Ryan or anybody else for that matter, he knew it would be a setup. JT decided to go to his house and chill there until he figured out what he was going to do. When JT arrived, he saw that the lights were on. Not noticing Shanay's car, he saw a figure go across his bedroom and he took off down the street.

JT called Trish, "Look, we are going to Motel 6; follow me."

"Okay Babe," said Trish as she hung up the phone.

JT went to Motel 6 and got a room in the back so past buyers wouldn't see their cars. Going inside their room, JT grabbed some ice from his car when they stopped to fill Trish's gas tank up. JT put the ice on Trish's face as she laid down on the bed.

"Thanks," said Trish, not bothering to wrap the ice up in anything.

JT sat on the bed and then laid on the bed with his feet still touching the floor. Trish put her feet on top of JT's stomach because JT was at the end of her side of the bed. JT didn't say anything but just wondered how he got himself into all of this and how he would get himself out of all of this mess.

"Where the hell is he at?" Shanay was questioning herself when she looked at the clock and it said 1:45 am. Shanay searched all through JT's

house the whole time she was there. Shanay looked to see if there was any trace of females there as she wandered through his house. Shanay felt helpless as she roamed around JT's house. Shanay could tell JT was there by himself because his draws were all over his bedroom floor, dishes were piled up, and the trash stunk and was filled up to the top with some trash on the floor next to the trash can. Shanay decided to clean JT's house as she waited on him to come. Shanay made JT's bed, picked up all his clothes, and vacuumed his room. Shanay then went to the living room and picked up all of the empty and half-empty pizza and ice cream boxes.

"What a weird combination," Shanay thought to herself.

After Shanay picked up all the trash, she vacuumed the living room and headed to the kitchen. Shanay's fingers were wrinkled after she got done doing the dishes. Shanay then took out the trash, headed upstairs, and looked at the clock. It read 3:55 am.

"Damn, where the hell is he?" Shanay questioned herself again, *"maybe he pulled a double trying to get that extra money like he always does."* Shanay said to herself, *"I'm just going to take a shower and go to bed; my love will come sooner or later."*

Shanay got in the shower and got in her panties and bra as she lay in JT's king-size bed. It wasn't long before Shanay went to sleep. Shanay felt like she had been asleep for 5 minutes when she was woken by a bucket of ice-cold water being thrown on her. Shanay jumped up out of shock as she got put back down by one of Cameron's punches. Shanay lip split as soon as he punched her. Shanay was shocked as she looked at Cameron and saw somebody else behind him in all black.

"A Ryan, go grab the rope and duct tape from out of the car. I guess we will need it sooner than I thought."

Ryan didn't say anything but went downstairs and went to the car.

Shanay was still in shock as she said, "Please don't rape me I…." She was cut off by Cameron, making him mad.

"Shut up Bitch! Where the hell is that nigga at?!" said Cameron with anger in his voice.

"I don't know. I was looking for him too. I was hoping he came here," said Shanay with water in her eyes as she shook.

"Bitch don't lie to me!"

"I'm not lying Cameron. Watch, I'll show you," said Shanay getting up from the bed.

Shanay got up from the bed and was back smacked back down. The smack had Shanay face burning and stinging. Shanay grabbed her face as she started crying.

Cameron came up on Shanay and stood over top of her and said, "Bitch, you not going nowhere! Keep your whore ass in the bed before I whip your ass!" said Cameron.

Shanay had nothing but fear in her heart as Ryan came into the room with duct tape and rope.

"Please Cameron, don't do this," said Shanay crawling up the bed and under the covers.

"Help me tie this Bitch up," said Cameron grabbing Shanay's feet and pulling her closer to him.

"No Please! Stop!" yelled Shanay before Cameron knocked Shanay unconscious. Cameron dragged Shanay off the bed, making her body hit the floor.

"Damn, this Bitch is phat to death," said Ryan looking at Shanay's body as she slumped on the floor.

"Remember that bitch got that shit," said Cameron as he bent over and wrapped Shanay's mouth with the duct tape.

Cameron damn near used all of the duct tape, wrapping it throughout her head, covering her mouth. Ryan tied her arms and legs together and threw her on the bed.

"What the hell we going to do now?" asked Ryan looking at Cameron.

"We wait till this bitch nigga come in. He will be here sooner or later. He love this stinking bitch here, and if he know we got his bitch tied up, he'll come," said Cameron sitting on JT's bed and laying back.

"Hit that light nigga. We going to wait for this nigga to come here," said Cameron closing his eyes.

Shanay was thrown on the floor when Ryan hit the light so he could make himself comfortable. Cameron laughed at Ryan's actions when he laid on the bed next to him.

"Where the hell you think that nigga at?" asked Ryan pulling out his cell phone.

"I don't know. I'm sure Trish got up with him by now. Maybe she told him not to come to his house because I said I was going to kill him."

"Maybe."

Cameron and Ryan were drunk when they entered the house; they dozed off in JT's bed no more than 5 minutes after laying down on it.

"Happy Birthday to you! Happy Birthday to you! How old are you now!?"

Everybody at Kim's party sang as Kim spat out, "I'm only 18!"

Everybody laughed as Kim blew out the candles as she cut the song short. Kim knew this wasn't the big surprise party that she was expecting, but she was just happy that she and Aairyah were back to normal once again. Kim blew out the candles and the whole room got dark.

"Well, is somebody going to turn on the light?" asked Kim as everybody stood in the dark.

All Kim heard as the light was being cut on was.

"You ready?"

The light cut on and Kim had the cake flying to her face. Sabrina and Vanessa laughed as they let the cake fall from her face and drop on the floor.

Kim laughed and said, "I'm going to Fuck you Bitches up!"

Kim wiped the icing from her eyes as she saw everybody laughing; Marshal, Damon, Omar, Kamiyah, Candy, and Ron-Ron was on the other side of the table.

"Awwwww, bayyyy beeeeee," said Aairyah as he kissed Kim with all the icing and cake on her face.

Ron-Ron still had feelings for Kim even today, he felt like he should be Aairyah kissing Kim right now. Ron-Ron would do anything to be with Kim. Even if it meant blowing Aairyah's brains out, he would do it. Ron-Ron had the best plan to win Kim over; he was just waiting for the perfect time.

"Thanks Babe, I needed that," said Kim smiling from ear to ear.

Aairyah walked to the kitchen to grab some napkins to wipe Kim's face but was met with Candy in there. Candy pushed Aairyah to the refrigerator and started kissing him.

Candy grabbed Aairyah's dick and said, "Let's get it in right here."

"Bitch is you crazy! What if my girl walked in on us and saw you do that shit!? Fuck is wrong with you!"

Nobody could hear their conversation because Damon turned the music up, and everybody was being loud. Aairyah grabbed the napkins, moved Candy out of the way, and left the kitchen. Aairyah left and could her Marshal and Damon's conversation in the back for just 3 seconds.

"You see, that nigga is slick. I got to give it to him."

Aairyah looked back and Marshal said, "I see you Player."

Aairyah knew Marshal was real and he wasn't going to say anything to his sister about it, but he just wished he hadn't seen it. Aairyah got to Kim and whipped her face off as she talked to Vanessa.

"Yeah Girl, the Gucci bag is nice wait till you see this thing Girl; you are going to fall out," said Vanessa wiping some of the cake off of her face as well.

"Yeah right, you know her shit is bogus," said Sabrina as they all laughed.

"Sike Nah, I got my present and Shanay present in the car. Omar brought his present in already, I believe."

"Okay that's what's up. Where is Shanay at anyway?" asked Kim looking around the room.

"She couldn't make it, I guess. I didn't talk to her in like two days, but she left me her gift at my house. We went shopping for you weeks ago," said Sabrina looking for Omar.

"Well, well, well, look who we got here," said Marshal, not noticing the White girl in the corner next to Marshal and Kim's mom, Mrs. Sasha.

"Who the hell is that?" asked Marshal, pointing at the White girl talking to Damon and Omar.

"I don't know. Go find out she talking to your mom," said Damon as he took a sip of his Hennessy on ice. Marshal walked over there, hoping Candy or Kamiyah didn't cock block his swagger.

"Hey mom. I see you got a new friend," said Marshal as he hugged his mom.

"Hey Baby. This here is Cindy; she works at the hospital with Sabrina. She's a very nice lady."

"I bet she is," said Marshal licking his lips and staring at her.

Cindy smiled as she looked at Marshal, not trying to blush too hard.

"Damn, this nigga is diesel. I know he can pick me up and spin me around every way he can."

"Hey how you doing?" Marshal reached his hand out so Cindy could shake it.

"My name is Marshal; I'm Kim's brother."

Marshal knew he had her because when she stuck her hand out for him, her hand was shaking as her hand met his.

"Do you mind if few go on the front step and talk? It's kind of loud in here," said Marshal trying to get Cindy all to himself, without nobody interrupting or cock blocking their conversation.

"Yeah, that's fine with me," said Cindy as Marshal grabbed her hand and escorted her out of the front door.

Marshal looked at Cindy up and down. Cindy was 5'6, 150, with blonde hair with a Black girl body. Cindy was a little bit overweight if you saw her chubby stomach.

"Nothing I can't fix with a little cardio and exercises I have in mind; she will be in the best shape of her life, " Marshal thought to himself after he closed the front door behind him and started his conversation.

Back in the house, Aairyah could feel the animosity coming from Ron–Ron as he stood at the far end of the room. *Do this dude still got feelings for what I did to him or what? Fuck is he keep staring over here for? Who even invited this dude? Whoever did must not know I don't like this nigga, or he wouldn't be in here. Most likely, his sister invited him. I would fuck the shit out of his sister now that I think about it.* Aairyah started to lust over Vanessa as he had pictures in his head of fucking Vanessa. Candy stopped his lusting by grabbing his dick in front of Kim. Aairyah looked at Kim before looking at Candy. Aairyah saw that Vanessa saw it, but Kim couldn't because she was still whipping the cake icing off. Aairyah gave Kim a look like, please don't tell my girlfriend on me. Vanessa just turned her head and wiped Kim's face as if nothing had ever happened.

"So, what we doing tonight?" asked Vanessa as she took the icing out of Kim's hair.

"I don't know. What do y'all want to do tonight?" asked Kim waving Damon over to them.

"I don't know, let's go to a party or something. I heard Club 723 is going to be jumping tonight."

"Can you get me another glass of Hpnotiq Bro?" asked Kim as Damon came over.

"Me too Babe," said Vanessa hurried up and drowned the rest of her drink that she had in her cup.

"Sure ladies," said Damon sarcastically.

"I don't know about Club 723. You know what happened last time," said Kim as Sabrina stepped off to use the bathroom.

They both laughed a little and Vanessa said, "Girl be quiet, and I'm just saying the ladies out. You know, like a ladies' night out."

"Hold on, ain't you pregnant Bitch?" asked Kim.

"Yeah, what you thought was Hpnotiq was a blueberry blast. I'm on my Hawaiian Punch shit," said Vanessa as they both laughed.

"Just because I'm pregnant don't mean I can't have fun," said Vanessa grabbing her drink from her man, as well did Kim.

Sabrina came back and said, "What did I miss?"

"Nothing, just we going out. Meaning all of us. A girl's night out. So, everybody, please ask your man can you go out tonight because we are leaving in a half-hour."

Sabrina rushed to Omar just as fast as Vanessa rushed over to Damon.

"Babe, can I please go with Kim tonight? It's a girl night out to celebrate Kim's B-day please," said Vanessa.

Damon really didn't want Kim to go but said, "Go ahead Babe. Just make sure you bring your ass home at a decent time," said Damon.

Vanessa kissed Damon and said, "Thanks Babe," as she ran back over to Kim.

Sabrina came back to Kim with a frown, the opposite of what Vanessa had on her face. Kamiyah and Candy didn't have to anybody because nobody would love them enough to wife them up, so they were already there waiting on their response.

"What's the matter Sabrina? What Omar said you can't come?" Sabrina just shook her head from side to side, not saying anything.

"You pregnant any way Girl. You'll be alright, stop feeling down," said Kim.

Kim got up and called Damon to the kitchen.

"Babe, me and the girls are going out to celebrate. Is it alright if I go with them?" asked Kim with puppy dog eyes.

"Yeah, go ahead Babe. I had a surprise, but I'll wait till tomorrow."

"You want me to cancel it. You know I'll stay here with you Babe," said Kim using her index and middle fingers as legs and walking them up Damon's shirt.

"No Babe, go have fun. I'll see you when you come back," said Damon kissing her and smacking her ass to let her know she could go.

Aairyah came into the kitchen.

"Yo, this bitch is crazy. She just grabbed my dick in front of Kim, but Kim didn't see it; Vanessa saw it and the look on her face looked like she was going to tell Kim."

"I'll got you. I'll make sure she won't, but the girls are going out tonight. You know what that mean, right."

"The Pussy House," said Aairyah.

Damon rose his eyebrows up and down with a smirk on his face. The party was over, and everybody was leaving the house except Ms. Mellisa, who was guarding the house until Marshal and Vanessa came back for her. Kim didn't mind letting Mrs. Mellisa stay there because she was passed out in the corner anyway. When everybody left the house at once, they could see Marshal's Truck moving back and forth. Damon was the only one who had enough balls to open the back door. When Damon opened the back door, Marshal had Cindy in the doggy style, smacking her ass. Everybody laughed, including Marshal, as he kept stroking. Damon shut the door as everybody left in different cars. Everybody laughed and talked about the incident the whole way to wherever they were going.

"You fucking prick. One of your stupid dumb ass whores gave me HIV and I swear I'm going to kill that Bitch. If you get in my way, I'm going to kill you as well."

8-Ball was wondering what bitch he was talking about because he almost fucked all of his girls or a regular, and he was scared that he might have got it, but 8-Ball didn't take threats lightly, so he put his I'm going to kill you look.

"Listen here punk. I don't know who you are talking to pointing that fucking pee shooter at," said 8-Ball poking the boy in his chest and taking the gun from him in a blink of an eye.

"But look here. I'll kill you with my bare hands."

The guy's eyes were bulging as he saw 8-Ball pointing the same gun at him as he was just pointing it at 8-Ball.

"Now tell me who you fucked so I can get to the bottom line of this."

"Sunkiss, I fucked her a couple of days ago. I fucked my wife and everything. I went to get tested and they said I had HIV."

"Are you sure your wife didn't have this shit and you gave it to Sunkiss," said 8-Ball because he made sure every one of his girls gets tested every week.

"Yeah, I'm sure. I been married to my wife for 13 years and she has never cheated on me. Dog check that bitch before I kill her," said the mysterious guy. 8-Ball went to his office and called Sunkiss in there as he got in. Sunkiss came storming in and looked at 8-Ball.

"Yes Daddy," said Sunkiss.

Sunkiss was 5'11, 170 pounds, with a cinnamon complexion. Sunkiss looked like Lauren London, but Lauren London didn't have shit on her.

"Let me see your checkup sheet from last week."

Sunkiss bounced her sexy ass out of the room and came back 3 minutes later. 8-Ball looked over it and saw everything was negative. Today is Wednesday. I fucked Sunkiss Sunday; maybe Monday or yesterday, the dude must've fucked her. 8- Ball thought, trying to calculate the moments that happened in his life.

"Did you fuck a Black guy? He about 5'6, 140 pounds. He got glasses, he married as well."

Sunkiss thought about the guy and said, "Yeah, right, before my break. My two-day break anyway. You know I just punched in a couple of hours ago and you messing my money up; that's why I came ramming in here."

"Who else did you fuck?" asked 8-Ball.

"I fucked you and him. You know I don't fuck nobody on my days off, so it this is some shit trying to make extra money without you knowing, you can save it," said Sunkiss.

"No, it's nothing like that. You know what? Go get tested now."

"But how am I going to make today's pay if I don't work?"

"It's alright. I got you; just go get tested," said 8-Ball shoeing Sunkiss off with his hand.

8-Ball had to get to the bottom line before it got worse.

CHAPTER 18

Something Got to Give

"So, you know our anniversary is tomorrow? What do you want to do?" asked Damon while he was driving home from the hospital so that Vanessa could get another ultrasound.

Vanessa was bobbing her head to the music and flipping through a magazine as she answered Damon's question, "I don't know. It's funny you said that because I'm reading an article about how most men forget about their anniversary but I don't know what to do. What do you want to do, Babe?" asked Vanessa flipping through the magazine.

"I don't know. Do you want to do something romantic or do what we did last year and give out gifts," said Damon pulling up to their apartment complex.

Damon got out and opened the door for Vanessa.

"Well, we can't do nothing too romantic since I'm pregnant. Let's just exchange gifts," said Vanessa walking up to their apartment and opening the door.

Damon swept her off of her feet and took her to their bedroom. Damon laid Vanessa down on the bed and started taking Vanessa's clothes off. It had been a daily ritual for Damon for the past month since Vanessa was six months pregnant. Damon has been doing everything under the sun for Vanessa, trying to make her life stress-free.

"Well, I already got one of my presents here already and two more tomorrow," said Damon as he got Vanessa butt naked and took her to the bathtub and ran the water.

"Yeah, what is it? Can I see?"

"Yeah, you can see. Wait till you done washing up. I got you."

Damon turned the water off when it got high enough. He made sure he had bubbles in there as she liked it. Damon then grabbed Vanessa's rag and started washing Vanessa's whole body. After washing Vanessa's body, Damon got up and grabbed her towel. Vanessa stood out of the shower and Damon wrapped her body up with the towel. Damon sat her on the bed and dried her off. Damon then lotioned Vanessa's whole body down, even between her toes and up to her face. Damon then clothed her and sat her in the living room in front of the TV.

"What do you want to watch Babe?" asked Damon looking through all of the movies they had.

"How about a porno." Vanessa started laughing.

"Yeah, I got a porno for you, alright." Damon started laughing as well.

"I don't care Babe; put whatever you want to watch."

Damon grabbed his favorite movie Big Daddy.

"Babe, why we always got to watch Big Daddy every time I say I don't care."

"One because I'm the daddy and two because you don't care," said Damon running to the bedroom and coming to the living room with two boxes.

"What is it? What is it?" asked Vanessa, hype like a five-year-old child on Christmas.

Damon handed it to her. Damon could tell she was struggling, so he opened it for her.

"Watch out, Babe, stand up for me." Vanessa stood up as Damon sat the present on the couch.

"Okay sit down… Here," said Damon handing Vanessa the remote to the massage chair. Damon set everything up and told Vanessa how to work it.

"Oh My God Babe, this feels so good," said Vanessa getting a massage.

Damon then set up the foot massager. Next thing you know, Vanessa's had her feet in some water as it massaged her feet and back at the same time. Damon hurried up to the shower. He took a quick shower and hurried up and got dressed. He got the popcorn ready and poured two ice-cold Sprites for them both. Damon came into the living room with the bowl of popcorn and two big glasses of Sprite. Damon didn't realize that Vanessa was halfway asleep when he brought her the popcorn and soda.

"Babe press play."

Damon saw she had the remote in her hand when Damon looked out at Vanessa, Vanessa's head was tilted back and her eyes were closed. Damon didn't even bother waking Vanessa up. Damon pressed play on the DVD player and watched the movie by himself. After the movie was over, Damon turned both of the massagers off and grabbed Vanessa off the couch. Vanessa woke up when he placed her on the bed.

"What did I miss."

"Nothing," said Damon drying off her feet and then hopping into bed with her.

Vanessa thought to herself, *"Damn, I love this man. What can I do to make all of this up to him? Only God knows what's he got in store tomorrow."*

"I love you Damon."

"I love you too Vanessa." As they both closed their eyes and fell asleep.

Vanessa woke Damon up with licking the top of his dick, making it harder by the second. Before Damon could wake up all the way, he exploded inside of Vanessa's mouth.

"Now get up. I got a big day ahead of us, and our appointment is at 11:00 on the dot."

"To where?" asked Damon.

"You'll see when we get there," said Vanessa running out of the bedroom and into the kitchen.

Damon got out of bed and got dressed as his phone began to go off. Damon looked at the number and saw that it was Omar; and he wondered what the hell did he want but didn't answer the phone as he let it go to voicemail.

"So where are we going at Babe," said Damon as Vanessa headed out the door.

"You'll see."

"But I didn't even brush my teeth yet."

"You don't have to worry about that; just bring your ass."

Vanessa was joyful to take Damon to the massager parlor called 2 in 1. When Damon looked at the building, it didn't look like anything; it looked like a regular building until they stepped in there. Vanessa and Damon looked at all the Korean women posed as they took their positions.

"Hey, how are you?"

The little old Korean lady came up to Vanessa and Damon.

"Good, I got an appointment for 11:00, for my husband, of course."

"You don't get no massage?" asked the old Korean lady speaking and pointing at Vanessa.

"No, I'm pregnant. I'm okay, just him for right now," said Vanessa, pulling her wallet out of her Coach bag.

"Okay whatever… You go pick you two females to give you massage," said the Korean woman putting her two fingers up and then pointing at the woman.

Damon looked at Vanessa first, getting the okay, and then he went to all of the beautiful Korean women in front of him. Damon picked a short Korean woman with a pink and navy-blue bathing suit on. She had pink eye shadow on with her long silky black hair touching her butt. She was a time to be Korean, with her sizes being 30-18-28. Damon thought her body was the shit that's why he picked her. Damon's second pick was a tall Korean woman at 5'11, 165 pounds; this Korean woman was thick in all the right places. Damon fell in love with her legs as soon as he saw them.

"Okay, you got your pick; now go in the back room and let them do the rest," said the Korean lady laughing a little bit.

After taking Vanessa's money and sending the girls back with Damon, the old Korean lady said, "It's not likely you see a man's wife in here with him as he gets it done."

"It's okay. I'm not the jealous type of person, you know," said Vanessa sitting in the waiting area.

"Oh, that's nice must be a special day today."

"Yeah, it's our anniversary today and I want to make it special."

"Oh, I see. Good present, good present," said the old Korean lady. As soon as Damon hit the room, the tall Korean girl said.

"You have a whole hour with us; what do you want to do." Damon was kind of surprised, thinking that he came here for a massage.

"What do you mean what I want to do?"

The short Korean sucked her teeth and dropped Damon's boxers and pants at the same time. The Korean then started sucking Damon's dick, stroking the base of his dick while she played with the head. The tall Korean put one of her legs on the massaging bed and started to play with her Pussy. Damon's back was against the wall as he was getting head. The only thing in the room was the massage table, a sink and two cabinets on top of the sink. Damon lifted the short Korean up from sucking his dick and placed her on the massage table. The short Korean untied her panties to her bathing suit showing her shaved pussy. The tall Korean opened the cabinet and pulled out the Baby Oil and a box of condoms. She then opened one of the condoms and placed it in her mouth. Bending down and swallowing Damon's dick whole as the condom got on every inch of Damon's dick. The short Korean then turned herself around, laying on her knees and forearms. Damon had a perfect view of the short Korean pussy as her ass cheeks were spread from the tall Korean. The tall Korean then began to eat the short Korean pussy from the back. After a couple of minutes of watching, Damon couldn't take anymore, as his dick began to drip of pre-cum. The tall Korean then began to put Baby oil all around the short Korean ass making her ass shiny to the light.

The tall Korean got undressed out of her bathing suit and said, "What are you scared of some Korean pussy?"

Damon laughed a little bit and then got behind the short Korean and entered inside of her going slow so he could remember this anniversary. Stroking harder and harder while smacking the oil of the Korean girl's ass, Damon could feel the Korean orgasm over his dick as her Pussy clinched up on him. The tall Korean was getting her Pussy a ten on the other side of the massage bed when the short Korean said.

"Oh shit, that's enough, that's enough."

The tall Korean got out of her spot and switched places with the short Korean. This time Damon had the tall Korean on her back, with her long legs over Damon's shoulders. The short Korean stood over top of the tall Korean and squatted over her face as the tall one began to eat her Pussy. Damon grabbed the bottle of Baby Oil and poured it over both of the girls as he started stroking. Damon knew his boiling point and it was coming up as he started to shake a little. Damon tried to hold it in as long as he could but burst inside the cherry red condom he had on.

"You came already?" asked the tall Korean girl with a surprising look, just getting into the rhythm.

"Yeah," said Damon watching his dick get smaller by the second.

"Oh well, see you next time," said the tall Korean getting up and putting her bathing suit on.

"I thought I had an hour? It only been 20 minutes."

"Up to an hour, until you nut. No longer than an hour," said the short Korean girl.

"You got to look at the fine print," said the fall Korean.

When they were all finished wiping themselves off and heading out, the short Korean girl said, "Do your girlfriend know this is just more than a massage parlor?"

"She might, I don't know," said Damon walking to the main lobby and meeting Vanessa.

"Well, if she does, you should keep her," said the short Korean girl smacking Damon's ass as she left.

Both of the Korean girls laughed as they left the main lobby. Vanessa picked up her head as the two Korean girls laughed and walked.

"While them two girls laughing for?"

"I don't know."

"They laughing like they just got fucked instead of giving a massage."

"You know them Chinese people always laughing about something," Vanessa laughed and they both left the building.

Driving off in the car, Damon asked, "Where did you find this place at?"

"Kamiyah told me about it. She said that all men loved it there and I should take you. She said their special massages are the best, that's why I paid for the special massage. But what I want to know is what's so special about it?"

It didn't seem special to me except it was two women, but I enjoyed it; thank you Babe," said Damon giving Vanessa a kiss.

Damon told Vanessa where to go next and she winded up going to the house that they had looked at before.

"Babe, why did you make me pull up to the house we were looking at before?" Damon dug in his pocket and pulled out a house key.

Vanessa's face lit up as she saw the key.

"NO NO NO NO, you got to be playing."

"Where else are we going to raise little Damon."

Vanessa jumped back and forth in her seat as she hugged Damon. Vanessa couldn't stop screaming while she was hugging Damon.

"Is you going to scream in my ear or is you going to check the house out one more time. Vanessa didn't want to be overreacting, but she couldn't help herself. Vanessa ran out of the car and into the house. Spinning like a ballerina with her hands spread in the air. Vanessa went to every room saying.

"I love it."

Where Damon got the money from, Vanessa didn't have any clue. She was just happy to be with Damon in the new house instead of that apartment that they were living in before.

"So, when are we able to move in?" asked Vanessa after she toured the house twice and they left.

"Whenever you feel like it."

"So, we can move in today?"

"Yup."

"Well, you know I'm packing up as soon as well get home."

"Be my guest," said Damon as they pulled up to the apartment.

It took Damon and Vanessa a whole week to get everything out of the apartment and into the house. Surprisingly, Vanessa did most of the work while Damon worked doubles at his job. A week into living in the house, Vanessa and Damon talked in the living room.

"So, are we going to have a housewarming this weekend Babe?" asked Vanessa while Damon turned the TV on.

"I thought the baby shower was this weekend?"

"It is, but that's on Sunday and we can have the housewarming on

Friday."

"I thought you was suppose to have a housewarming as soon as you move in. It's been a week since we moved in."

"So what? We still can have it."

"Whatever you want, you can have," said Damon with a look like go to your mom's house already.

"Thanks Babe," said Vanessa, happy as ever when she kissed Damon and got up from the couch.

"I'll be back Babe; I'm going to run to mom house real quick and see if she needs anything," said Vanessa as she grabbed her keys and headed out the door.

"Be safe, and drive safe," said Damon as he changed the channel of the TV.

"I will love you," said Vanessa shutting the door.

"I love you too," said Damon in a whisper because Vanessa shut the door on him before he could say anything.

Damon sat there looking at a Best Buy magazine, wondering what he would buy for the house, when the doorbell rang. Damon was surprised to hear it because nobody knew where they lived at. When Damon got to the door, he saw a UPS shirt and hat with a White guy wearing it.

Damon opened the door and said, "Can I help you."

"Yes, I'm looking for a…." The UPS man looked at his clipboard and said, "Mr. Damon Banks?" asked the UPS man in curiosity to think it was him he was talking to.

"Yeah, that's me," said Damon looking at the box he held under his armpit and the clipboard in his hands.

The UPS guy made a couple of X's on the sheet.

"Ok, can you sign by the X's and that will be it?"

Damon, signed by the X's and the UPS guy, handed Damon the box that was held under his armpit.

"Who's it from? It doesn't have a return sender," said Damon as he scanned the box with no returning address on it.

"I don't know man; I'm just the guy to get it and deliver it. Have a nice day," said the UPS guy and left off of Damon's steps and headed to his UPS truck.

Damon closed his door and sat on his couch. Damon studied the handwriting and knew it wasn't Vanessa's handwriting, so he opened the box and inside the box was a videotape. Damon looked at it and was curious to find out what the hell it was. Damon got up from the couch and put the videotape in the DVD/VCR that was hooked up to the TV. Damon pushes play and you couldn't see anything at first, just black and white fuzz going up and down the screen. Damon fast forwards it to where he could see somebody talking. What Damon saw next, he broke down in tears. Rage filled his mind as he left out of the house with one thing on his mind. Revenge!

CHAPTER 19

Trust

"What the fuck Babe. You are really getting on my Fucking nerves with this shit. You are so overprotective like I'm pregnant. What could I possibly do? Huh? You tell me," said Sabrina talking to Omar sitting on the couch, not even listening to Sabrina.

"Babe come sit down. You are working yourself up for nothing. Calm down. You are going to stress my baby out," said Omar rubbing Sabrina's stomach as she came and sat down.

"The only reason why I don't let you go nowhere is because I don't want you to get hurt. Anything can happen to you, Babe, and God gave me a chance to make another little Omar or another little Sabrina after I thought I couldn't caught me by surprise. I'm so happy that you are pregnant Babe. Sorry for being overprotective; I'm just scared of losing the baby, that's all," said Omar kissing Sabrina. Sabrina felt bad for arguing with Omar now that he said that to her.

"It's okay Babe; I understand where you coming from," said Sabrina looking into Omar's eyes as she now kissed him.

"Listen Babe, you hear that?" Sabrina stopped moving and eventually stopped breathing to try to hear what Omar was talking about.

"I don't hear nothing Babe," said Sabrina in a whisper, still trying to figure out what Omar was listening to if he was listening to anything.

"That's right nothing. Your phone not going off or nothing, right? That's the best sound in the world. Your sister is nowhere to be found that's what I love about her she knows when to dip," said Omar as he chuckles a little bit.

"Now that you said that, I didn't hear from her since she said she was going to JT's house. Did she come get some of her clothes lately?" Sabrina asked Omar with a confused look plastered on her face.

"No, didn't see her in a couple of days; maybe JT took her back and she up his ass now instead of ours," said Omar flicking through the channels as he landed on Sports Center.

"Maybe I should call her then," said Sabrina grabbing her cell phone off the table and started dialing Shanay's number.

"Hold up," Omar said as he reached for Sabrina's phone and took it away from her.

"Once you call her, it ain't going to be non-stop calls from her all over again."

"I just want to make sure she is okay."

"She's okay Babe. She's a grown woman; she knows how to handle her own."

"But she don't even got no clothes with her. She would have at least took some clothes and made a note or called me. She would have did something to let me know something," said Sabrina worried about her sister.

"Babe, she probably got clothes over JT's house. If I know what I think is going on, she probably don't even got no clothes on anyway." Sabrina playfully hit Omar on the shoulder with a smile.

"Shut up, stop trying to play my sister."

"It's true Babe, and I'm not playing her. I'm proud that she found somebody to take care of her and love her for who she is."

"Yeah, yeah, save the sob story for her," Sabrina said, knowing Omar was Full of Shit.

"I'm serious Babe. You know I don't really like your sister like that, but I am happy that she found one person to be with. I look at it like she is the aunt of my unborn child and not some whore who is related to my wife," said Omar giving Sabrina her phone back as he spoke again, "look, Babe Shanay is fine. I'm sure JT wouldn't let anything happen to that girl. Stop worrying so much, it's okay."

Sabrina heard the convincing words of her husband, but that still wasn't enough for Sabrina. She had to make sure that Sabrina was fine.

"But Babe, it's not like her to not call or text. She would have been blowing my phone up at least to tell me the good news."

Omar now wished he hadn't mentioned Shanay's name now. Sabrina could feel that something was wrong because she knew Shanay would have come to the house by now.

"Babe, she's okay, damn," said Omar getting frustrated.

"Well, I'm going to go see then because I know my sister. I'm going to go to her house and if she's not there, I'm going to go to JT's house." At this point, Omar didn't care anymore; all he wanted to do was relax, with or without his wife.

"Okay, then go ahead," said Omar with an attitude.

"You not going to come with me?"

"No Babe I'm not. I know she is okay; you just going to be wasting your time."

"What if something happen to me? Are you going to go out and look for me, or are you going to sit here on the couch?"

"First of all, it's not you. Secondly, you don't even know if something is wrong with her. You just making assumptions. Thirdly, you are overreacting, so calm your ass down before you get started," said Omar looking at Sabrina standing in front of him in a pose, bouncing her leg up and down to let Omar know she's getting mad.

Sabrina didn't say anything but just kept staring at Omar until he gave in.

"Damn, you get on my nerves. Go get my…" Omar got interrupted by the doorbell ringing.

Omar got up and saw that it was Fed Ex at his door. Omar opened the door and said, "What's up?"

"Are you Omar Simmons?"

"Yeah, why what's up?"

"I got a package for you then," said the happy White guy dressed down in a Fed Ex button-up, blue khakis, and some Jim Bean boots on.

The Fed Ex guy handed Omar a shoebox wrapped up in a Christmas present. Omar looked at the address from the return sender and didn't know anybody named Harold Paterson.

"Is this some type of joke?" Omar asked as he shook the box and threw it on the floor.

"No, it's not a joke Sir. Can you sign right here and right here," said the Fed Ex guy as he handed the clipboard to Omar.

Omar signed the sheet of paper and fled the Fed Ex guy off because he was already mad for having to leave the house. Omar kicked the box in the living room and walked to the car. Sabrina walked behind him, shutting the door.

"Babe, what the hell did the Fed Ex guy drop off at the house?" asked

Sabrina as she got in the passenger seat and closed the door.

"I don't know," said Omar with an attitude.

"Look, if you got a problem, you can stay here. I'll go by my damn self."

Omar was already mad as he stopped the car and reversed it all the way to the house. Omar didn't say anything as he took the house key off of his key chain and got out of the car.

"You get on my damn nerves!" yelled Sabrina as she got out of the car and walked around to the driver's side.

"Yeah, you get on mine too," said Omar under his breath as he opened the house door and shut it without looking behind him.

Sabrina just looked as the door shut, and she drove off. Her first stop was at Shanay's house. Ten minutes later, Sabrina pulls up in front of Shanay's house. Sabrina didn't see Shanay's car, so she pulled off and went to JT's house. Sabrina was happy to see Shanay's car in front of JT's house, so she decided to park and knock on the door to see if Shanay was okay. Sabrina got out of the car, walked to JT's house, and knocked on the door. After sitting there waiting for a couple of seconds, Sabrina started banging on the door.

"Where the fuck is she at? What the bitch sleep?" Sabrina said under her breath.

"Shanay! JT!" Sabrina yelled out.

If only Sabrina could hear Shanay screaming under all the duct tape wrapped around her mouth, she would have gotten help.

"Shanay!" Sabrina yelled one more after she stopped banging.

Sabrina said fuck it, after a couple of minutes and went to her car.

Inside her car, Sabrina started calling Shanay's phone. No answer. Sabrina called again. No answer. Sabrina then texted Shanay and told her to call her as soon as she got her text message. Sabrina drove off from JT's house and started joyriding. Sabrina didn't want to go back to her house because she didn't want to hear Omar's mouth, so she called Vanessa. No answer. Sabrina then called Kim. No answer.

"Damn, what the fuck is up with everybody today? Nobody's picking up when a sister needs them the most."

Sabrina's stomach started to growl. She didn't know if the baby or her had made that noise. Sabrina forgot she left her purse at home and she surely wasn't going there no time soon to hear Omar bullshit. So, she decided to go to Shanay's house.

"Let me see if this bitch got something to eat at her house," said Sabrina out loud to herself.

Sabrina drove to Shanay's house in a hurry trying to beat that 5 o'clock traffic she knew she would have caught if she was going slow. Sabrina pulled up and squirmed out of the car as if her stomach weighed a ton. As she stepped to the door, cramps started to come to Sabrina's stomach. Sabrina, already having a key, opens the door and gets inside. Closing the door and the door flings back at her. Sabrina turns around and sees a fat Black dude standing in the middle of the doorway.

"Can I help you?" Sabrina said with an attitude as she grabbed the door and tried to close it on him again.

The fat man puts his arm out and grabs the door before she tries to close it.

"Where Shanay at?" the fat guy says.

"I don't know. I haven't seen her, so if you can leave, I will gladly appreciate it," said Sabrina, now standing behind the door.

"How about I stay," said the fat guy as he rams open the door and Sabrina falls to the floor.

"Listen, I swear I don't know where she at. I been looking for her all day," said Sabrina pleading to this fat guy right in front of her.

The fat guy closed the door behind him and said, "So that's why you come around here the first time, huh?"

"Yes," said Sabrina realizing that this guy was outside plotting the whole time.

"Well, look here, your sister owes me money, and she gave me HIV, so you know what?"

"What?" asked Sabrina as her body trembled in fear.

"You better try to get a hold of her right now before I give it to you."

"I'm telling you the truth. I don't know where she's at," said Sabrina, with tears coming down her face at the fact that this guy might rape her.

"Listen Sir, I'm pregnant. I don't want no problems. Whatever my sister owe you, I will pay for it out of my pocket."

Sabrina started to get up from off the floor. The fat guy saw the slight stitching of Sabrina's panties as she got up. She's wearing a thin all-white summer dress with blue and green sunflowers around it. It was easy for the fat guy to see with his perverted eyes everything he wanted to see. The guy's mouth got watery as he licked his lips and looked at Sabrina's silky-smooth legs.

"So, you say you her sister, huh? Well, that makes it even more better for me to do what I am about to do."

The fat guy lunges at Sabrina and grabs her by the hair. He throws her on the couch in the living room.

"PLEASE, DON'T DO THIS! I'M PREGNANT! HELP!" Sabrina screams as she asks anybody to help her out of this situation.

Thoughts run through her mind as she knows that this guy has HIV.

"Look, I have 50,000 dollars saved up. You can have it all. Just please don't rape me."

The fat guy feels no remorse for Sabrina because Shanay didn't have any remorse for him when she didn't tell him she had HIV. He gave it to his wife; now, they are split up because of that and now his life is over. Not only as a pimp but as a husband as well. His wife wouldn't even let him see his son anymore because she moved to a different state and lost all contact with him. The fat guy's life was like it was over, so he didn't have any sympathy for whoever he gave it to, especially if you are related to the person who gave it to him.

"Shut up Bitch!" said the fat guy as he back smacked Sabrina off the couch.

When Sabrina hit the floor, the stinging sensation she felt as he smacked her went away as hope filled her heart as she planned on running away, thinking she could get away. Sabrina got up and ran to the back door. Not fast enough for the fat guy tho.

"You must not know me. My name is 8-Ball Bitch and I'm use to chasing bitches to get my money," said 8-Ball grabbing Sabrina by the hair and yanking her to the floor.

Her falling to the floor made her dizzy as she came down headfirst from 8-Ball, pulling her backward. 8-Ball jumped on top of her and pulled her sundress over her head.

Sabrina pulled it back down and said, "Stop, please! Don't do this!"

As Sabrina tried to get up, 8-Ball punched her back down, knocking her out cold. 8-Ball then pulled Sabrina's panties down and flung them across the room. 8-Ball was figuring out how he would position himself after looking at Sabrina's stomach. He knows two big stomachs couldn't do it from the front, but that didn't stop him from trying.

"You don't think that nigga will call cops and tell them we in here, do you?" asked Ryan as he passed the bottle of Hennessy to Cameron.

"Nah, he wouldn't do that. Besides, he don't even know we here," said Cameron as he flicked through the channel; they had Shanay on the other couch tied up watching TV with them.

"He must have some type of idea if the nigga didn't come to his own crib already. It's been 48 hours and no show. For all we know, he can send the cops over here, and we going to be surrounded. We get a kidnapping and a gun; we can do at least five years. I say we leave this crib," said Ryan trying to figure out what Cameron wanted to do.

"You do got a point, but where we going to take this bitch at?"

"Let's take her to your crib."

"Hell no, let's take her to your crib."

"My girl and kids at my crib. You don't got no girl or kids at your crib."

Ryan was saying this; he knew he lit a spark into Cameron because Cameron's body language switched up. Ryan thought fast about something to say, so he said the first thing that came out of his mouth.

"Let's take her to her crib." Ryan saw Cameron's body change up and kept going with it.

"So even if the cops do show, we can say we visiting her upon her demand."

"Yeah, that do sound better than staying in this bitch; let's dip," said Cameron as he got up from the couch.

Shanay's hands and feet are tied up as well as her mouth. Shanay looked up at Cameron with hunger and pain in her eyes.

"We can't take her out the crib like this. We got to untie her, so we don't look suspicious carrying this broad out tied up," said Cameron as he hovers over top of her.

Ryan then pulls a pocket knife and begins to cut the tape that is around her mouth.

When the tape was fully off of her mouth, Cameron said, "Listen, if you make any loud noise or scream for help or any bullshit like that, I'm going to fuck your whore ass up. You got that?"

Tears rolled down Shanay face before she spoke, "Yeah, I got you, but why are you doing this to me. Me Cameron, why?" asked Shanay, basically pouring her heart out to Cameron.

"I thought I told you already. I want revenge on this Mother Fucker and you are the only thing that he got. Since I can't fuck your ass, I'm going to make you and him suffer."

"But he doesn't even mess with me no more. He found out I got HIV and he left me.

"Yeah, he left you and went with my girl. Now my girl probably got HIV and I can't even deal with her because of you."

Shanay was speechless, and she didn't know what else to say she just wanted this nightmare to be over with already. After Ryan cut the duct tape off Shanay and untied the rope, Cameron, Ryan, and Shanay were on their way. Cameron felt a little bit of sympathy for Shanay, so he stopped by Burger King on his way over to her house. Cameron bought himself, Ryan, and Shanay something and left. The cashier at the drive-through window knew something was up when Shanay was saying help in the back lower than a whisper. She saw Cameron driving and Shanay and Ryan in the back like they were getting chauffeured in Cameron's S550. Ryan didn't notice Shanay saying it to her because he was too caught up talking to his girlfriend, trying to explain why he wasn't home for the past two days. As they drove off, the cashier that was doing the drive-through took down Cameron's license plates and what type of car it was and began dialing 911. Cameron arrived at Shanay's crib after getting directions from Shanay. Cameron grabbed Shanay by the hair and threw her into the house. They saw 8-Ball and Sabrina on the couch when they got in the house.

"What the Fuck is y'all doing here?" asked Cameron as Ryan shuts the door.

"There she go. The star of the show. Thank you gentlemen, for getting her for me," said 8-Ball as he got up from the couch and walked over to Shanay.

Sabrina was crying when they walked in, but as soon as she saw Shanay, her frown turned upside down, thinking that her sister had died. Sabrina was wondering *why the hell Mitchel was bringing Shanay in the house by her hair. Is Mitchel hired by 8-Ball? What the hell is 8-Ball going to do to us? How am I going to get out of this?* So many questions ran through Sabrina's mind as she was stuck on the couch in shock.

"Why the hell is Sabrina here for? Did she get my tape already? Do she even know who I am yet?" Cameron asked himself before 8-Ball got close.

"Hold up 8-Ball she with me and I need her for a special occasion."

"Listen, I want her dead. How much money do you want for her?" asked 8-Ball as he looked into Shanay's eyes. Shanay is scared half to death after hearing that and all she wants to do is make this nightmare stop.

"After we done with her, you can have her, but you can't have her until we done."

"I need her now. Fuck that, I got 20 thousand for her right now."

Ryan's face lit up as he wanted to say take the bitch, but he knew Cameron was in charge. All Ryan really wanted was Marshal that's why he tagged along in the first place. Cameron told Ryan he would help him get Marshal if he helped him get JT. 8-Ball knew Cameron wasn't budging, so he drew his gun.

"Fuck this; the Bitch is mine," 8-Ball said, pointing the gun at Cameron's head.

8-Ball grabbed Shanay by her dreads and pulled her closer to him. 8-Ball didn't know that Ryan was behind Cameron with a gun pointed at him.

Cameron sees the gun pointed at 8-Ball from the corner of his eye and he says, "So, what do you want to do, 8-Ball? You want to die or give the bitch up?" 8-Ball's head started sweating as he didn't know what to do next.

"Mitchel!" Sabrina yelled in the air. Everybody looked at Sabrina and wondered what the hell she was talking to.

Cameron smiled and said, "Yeah?"

"I'm pregnant with your son? This Fat Mother Fucker just raped me," said Sabrina.

"Yeah right. You pregnant with my son; that's like Santa Claus is real."

"I'm serious, my husband can't have no kids, and you are the only one I slept with. I'm not going to lie to you. I'm almost six months pregnant. Now count how far we had sex and do the math. If you don't do it for me, do it for your son."

Cameron calculated the time they had sex, and it wasn't too far off, but to have a possibility of the kid beginning his brings hope and joy to his life. He no longer felt that revenge, hatred, and anger inside his chest no more. Then just how fast it left, it came back to his heart, now feeling the same thing only towards 8-Ball this time.

"You raped her nigga?"

"Nah, she gave me the pussy." 8-Ball laughed but was telling the truth at the same time.

"Fuck you, you Fat Bitch you raped me," said Sabrina as she got up. 8-Ball could see the anger in his eyes as he let go of Shanay.

"What you got a problem with me now Nigga?" asked 8-Ball as he steps in Cameron's face.

Knock, Knock, Knock, Knock.

Ryan went off of his reactions and said, "Who is it?"

"It's the police. Can you open the door?"

It was music to Shanay and Sabrina's ears, but the same music to their ears put fear into Ryan, Cameron, and 8-Ball's hearts. The next thing Sabrina did could cost her her life, or it could save her life as she…

CHAPTER 20

I Won't Tell If You Won't Tell

"So, what we doing tonight Babe?" Kim asked Aairyah as she was getting dressed.

It was Aairyah's 25th birthday and Kim wanted to do something special for him. Every year they celebrated their B-days together because it was only a couple of days apart, but since Kim almost caught Aairyah having sex with Candy, he decided to let Kim have her own birthday party.

"I don't know Babe. What you want to do? I'm not really in the mood for anything," said Aairyah.

Aairyah couldn't tell Kim why he really didn't want to do anything because it will break her heart. Lie after lie, Aairyah was telling Kim every time he came home like he was about to now. Aairyah kept getting blocked mail every day after work. Candy would call him every time he came off of work, demanding that he sleeps with her. When Candy would call, Aairyah would try to ignore it, and when he did, she will a text message threatening that she would tell Kim everything.

One day, Aairyah tried to call her bluff and said he wasn't going; go tell. When he came home, Candy was in his driveway about to park. Aairyah then knew he had a psycho on his hands. Aairyah has been getting calls all week from Candy and it's been draining him every time he comes home, not being able to perform with Kim as much as he wants to.

Aairyah forgot that he said he was going to celebrate his birthday tonight instead of last week because Kim's birthday they celebrated early and now they are going to celebrate Aairyah late. Aairyah has been telling

Kim that he has been working late now and the job has been working his ass off so Kim wouldn't wonder why he has been coming in late and why he seem like he is always tired. Aairyah is drained once again today after having sex with Candy again. Candy wouldn't let Aairyah go until she was fully satisfied with herself. Candy will call Aairyah every time she wakes up, usually 3 or 4 in the afternoon since she works at the strip club and tells Aairyah to come over. If Candy could have it her way, she would strip at night and fuck Aairyah during the day. After Candy found out how Aairyah really was in bed the night he came over, she wanted Aairyah even move. Candy caught feelings for Aairyah throughout the time they had been fucking, but she knew she wouldn't be with him, but it didn't hurt to try.

"We can just go to dinner if you want to. I don't really mind," said Kim looking in the mirror as she did her makeup as Aairyah likes it.

"That sounds good to me. Let me take a shower, then we can go," said Aairyah reminding himself that he got Candy scent all over his manhood.

"We going to go now? It's only 6:30." Kim turned around and saw Aairyah going to the bathroom.

"We can catch a movie as well."

Kim tried to go in the bathroom with Aairyah, but he shut the door on her. A strike of pain hit Kim's heart as she wanted to cry. *It's not the same no more.* Kim said to herself, making herself want to cry even more.

Knock, Knock, Knock, Knock, Knock.

"Babe, can I come in?"

"Babe, I'm taking a shower. I'll be right out." Aairyah assured her.

Kim knew their relationship was falling because Aairyah didn't even want to have sex like he used to. Now little things start to add up in her head, like not letting her do her makeup while he was in the shower. Kim puts her thoughts to the back of her mind as her phone rings. Kim went to get her phone, and when she did, it hung up. Kim looked at the missed call and saw it was Sabrina. Kim decided to call her back until Aairyah called her name.

"Kim!... Babe!"

"Yeah!" Kim yelled back to Aairyah can you get me some more soap out of the closet.

"Yeah, I got you Babe!" said Kim as she went to the hallway closet and got a box of soap off of the shelf.

Kim went to the bathroom and knocked on the bathroom door. Aairyah opened the bathroom door a little bit, grabbed the soapbox, and said, "Thank you," as he shut the door in her face for the second time.

Kim felt hopeless in her marriage as she turned around and went to the living room. Twenty minutes later, Aairyah was out of the shower and dressed for the occasion.

"Somebody got their birthday suit on," said Kim, admiring how Aairyah put his gear into order.

Aairyah had a Gucci skully, with a Gucci shirt that matched the tan, dark brown skully. Aairyah had some navy-blue jeans and butter timberlands. Aairyah went back to the room and grabbed his Gucci scarf to set it off. He had early birthday presents from Damon and Omar, so he decided to wear their presents today.

"Yeah, something light, something light," said Aairyah as they both laughed at the fact.

"You crazy Babe," said Kim as they headed out.

"What is this place called?" asked Kim as she go out of her car as Aairyah helped her out.

"Steak House. You never been here?" asked Aairyah, trying to think back if he had ever taken his wife here or not.

"Ummmm... Nope," said Kim trying to be funny.

"Well, let me show you a little something then," said Aairyah as he walked hand and hand with his wife up the steps to the restaurant. The restaurant looks like a big teepee. The restaurant holds up to 200 people, with a VIP section that holds 25 people. Aairyah had booked a reservation to the VIP section earlier that day, so he already knew where he had to go, but as he tried to go up the steps to the VIP section, a guy had stopped him.

"Where do you think you are going?" asked the heavyset White man that stood in front of him.

"I have a reservation for two, or seat numbers are 40 and 41," said Aairyah as he remembered what the lady said over the phone.

"Well, you got to check in first," said the White man as he pointed to the long line of people waiting to get their tables in order.

Aairyah turned and knew what the guy was pointing at before turning around. Aairyah saw the line when he first stepped in and tried to avoid it, that's why he tried to go up the steps and avoid waiting in line.

"Damn," Aairyah whispered under his breath as he went to the back of the line.

"Babe, I got to use the bathroom real quick. The reservation is under my name if you get to the cashier first."

"Okay Babe," said Kim as Aairyah kissed her.

As soon as Aairyah stepped into the bathroom, Kim felt somebody tapping on her shoulder. When Kim turned around, she was surprised, angry, and scared as she saw the person that was now in front of her.

"I thought that was you. I can never forget them legs," said the man as he smiled.

"Monroe, what are you doing here?" asked Kim looking Monroe up and down.

Kim met Monroe in college. They both went to Penn State and they both had most of the same classes. Monroe was dating one of the Penn State cheerleaders at the time, one of Kim's friends in college. While Kim was still dangerously in love with Aairyah at the time, she was head over heels for Monroe on the D-L. Flashbacks came to Kim's head as she remembered the night of the college party she will never forget. It was about 3 in the morning and the party was still live as if it was 12 o'clock at night. Kim was pissy drunk as she stumbled into the kitchen trying to find Courtney (Monroe's girlfriend and her friend in college). As she stepped into the kitchen, she saw Monroe talking to all his boys as they were in a deep conversation as Kim walked in.

Everybody turned to see Kim as she said to them, "Have any of y'all seen Courtney?" Everybody shook their head no, so she walked back to the party until Monroe spoke up.

"Kim." As he followed behind her and grabbed her arm, Kim felt a tingling sensation run through her body as he turned her around.

"Look, you look pissy drunk and there is no way you can go back to your room like this. Let me help you get there. Courtney said she was going to go to her room already; you just missed her."

Courtney and Kim were roommates, and she didn't believe that Courtney would leave without her, but she knew she couldn't make it home without Courtney or Monroe, so she accepted his offer. When they got back to the room, Courtney was nowhere in sight.

"Who the fuck is this guy?" asked Aairyah coming up on the side of Kim breaking her train of thought.

Monroe knew exactly what Kim was thinking, so he didn't bother her and let her mind take her back to the past, where he wished he could be.

"Hey, I'm Monroe. You must be Aairyah?"

Monroe knows all about Aairyah, just that Aairyah didn't know about him. Aairyah was shocked when he said his name wondering if his girl had just told him.

"And who the fuck is you?" asked Aairyah catching an attitude.

"My name is Monroe; I went to Penn State with Kim. We were just catching up on old times."

"Oh, a'ight then Nigga I'll see you another time then," said Aairyah putting on his gangster's voice and letting him know it was time to go.

"Okay then, bye, Kim. I guess I'll see you another time then," he said as he extended his hand and shook her hand; Monroe pulled out a business card and handed it to Kim.

"Here are my numbers. My law firm is not too far from here. The big building that says Monroe and Law Firm."

"Okay, I got you," said Kim as she grabbed Monroe's card and placed it in her purse.

"Okay, bye now," said Monroe as he left the restaurant and went out of sight.

"You better throw that Mother Fucking card in the trash," said Aairyah. Kim looked at Aairyah and saw anger in his eyes.

"He's just a friend."

"What the hell did I say," said Aairyah while his teeth were clenched so he wouldn't make a scene at the restaurant.

Kim didn't say anything but pouted her way to the Trash can as if she was a little girl. Kim dug in her purse and threw the business cord in the Trash can as she headed to the line with Aairyah. Aairyah knew she was mad but didn't want anything to do with Monroe as he remembered the name somewhere but couldn't pinpoint it. Aairyah grabbed Kim's hand to let her know he still loved her and gave her a look to let her know to stop acting like that. As the line finally came for their turn to get checked in, Aairyah checked both him and Kim in as they went to the VIP section. After they got done eating, Aairyah and Kim went to the movies. On the way to the movies, Kim wanted to tell Aairyah about Monroe because they were done telling lies to each other and she didn't want to keep anything back from him. Kim decided not to because she knew Aairyah would question her why she wanted to keep the card for if they were messing before. She also didn't want to get into a big argument with him because she knew Aairyah would snap if she were having sex in college while she was at home. Kim made a mental note to tell Aairyah when she thought the time was right. As they pulled up to the movie theater and parking, Aairyah's blood began to boil.

"Now I know who that mother fucker was," said Aairyah as he thought about the name for the longest.

"That's the Mother Fucker who you went to school with, huh? The same Mother Fucker when I went to your room, he was coming out!? The same Mother Fucker who had blushing when I come pick you up he was always somewhere around. So that's the Mother Fucker, ain't it?" Kim didn't say anything as she just put her face down.

"Ain't it?"

Aairyah said even louder as he began to get angrier by the second. Kim tried to quickly come up with a lie, but her mind was completely empty, and she didn't know what to say.

"Oh, so you star struck, huh?"

Kim still couldn't put the words together as she tried to get her lies. Kim said forget it and told him the truth.

"Yeah, that's him," Kim said with her head down and tears began to fall.

"Don't fucking cry now. You wasn't crying when he was all up in your face. Please don't tell me you Fuck that nigga?" Aairyah waited for a response and when he didn't get one, he already knew what that meant.

"So, you fucked that nigga, huh? After all that bullshit you was telling me, and you had the nerve to tell him about me. So, what was y'all talking about then? What did you tell him? That if you ever see me to act like everything is cool? You told him to act like y'all was friends if I ever came around?"

Kim still didn't say anything, which got Aairyah's blood boiling even more. Kim had her face buried in her hands as she let the tears roll down her face.

"Can I at least explain before you accuse me of doing this shit?" asked

Kim as she picked her head up.

"Shit, you going to do a lot of explaining once we get to this fucking house," said Aairyah driving to their house.

The car was silent the whole ride to the house. As soon as Aairyah got in the house, he back smacked Kim, sending her to the floor.

"You tried to make me look like a Fucking Sucker in front of that nigga. Like I wasn't going to find the fuck out. Dumb Ass Bitch!" Kim face lit up in shock as soon as she hit the floor, not to mention Aairyah calling her a bitch was out of the line now. Kim got up and started swinging on Aairyah with everything she had.

"You Fucking Bastard! You going to fucking smack me like I'm some type of whore or something! You Punk Bitch!"

Kim was too weak for Aairyah; as she was swinging, Aairyah was dipping all of her punches until he grabbed her. Aairyah picked her up and put her in her arms. Kicking and screaming all the way upstairs to the bedroom, Aairyah threw her on the bed. Kim tried to get up and Aairyah backed smacked her back on the bed.

"Don't get the Fuck up!" Aairyah barked at Kim.

Aairyah felt bad for putting his hands on Kim, but he knew she was in the wrong, not him. Kim saw fire in Aairyah's eyes as she crawled to the top of the bed and cuddled up with one of the pillows. Aairyah ripped the strap off of the stilettoes that Kim was wearing and threw them on the floor. Aairyah pulled Kim's legs to him, unbuckled her jeans, and ripped them off as well as her panties.

"Babe can you…" Kim was interrupted by Aairyah.

"Shut the Fuck up," Aairyah said without even looking at Kim.

Aairyah picked Kim up on his shoulders and began eating Kim Pussy. Kim didn't know what to do as she moved her hips back in forth because the pleasure was getting too much to handle.

"OH SHIT DADDY! AAAAAAAHHHHHH HOLD ON, HOLD ON!" screamed Kim as her orgasm exploded over Aairyah's face. Kim was slumped with her breast on top of Aairyah's head and the rest of her body dangling on the backside of Aairyah's body; Aairyah threw her on the bed.

"Turn your ass around," Aairyah said with an attitude as Kim did what she was told.

Aairyah dropped his pants to the floor and stepped out of them. Aairyah got behind Kim and slid inside her slowly as he saw the white cream around her pussy. As Aairyah slid his whole 9 inches of dick inside her, he started fucking Kim like a jackrabbit. Having no remorse if Kim was in pain or not. Aairyah fucked her harder and harder until he knew her Pussy was hurting. Kim didn't know how many times she orgasmed as her body hit the bed and her Pussy was aching.

"I'm not done with your ass yet," said Aairyah as he jumped on top of Kim and put his dick inside of Kim's ass whole.

"BABE WHHHHHAAAATTTT THE FUCKKKKK!" screamed Kim as Aairyah pumped faster and faster as he felt fluid on his dick.

"TAKE IT OUT! AAAAAAHHHHH SHITTTTT! BABE, PLEASE TAKE IT OUT IT, HHHHHUUUURRTTT!" Kim screamed at the top of her lungs as Aairyah kept stroking Kim.

Kim tried to run, but Aairyah pinned her down on the bed. Aairyah nutted inside of Kim's asshole as he laid beside her. Kim was in pain as

Aairyah got off of her. Kim tried to move, but her body wouldn't let her. Aairyah looked down and saw that it was blood on his dick and Kim's ass as she was still laying on her stomach.

"Why would you do that?" Kim said in tears.

Aairyah knew Kim was in tears the whole time he was fucking her in her ass, but he didn't care as much as he does now.

"I told you don't Fuck with me. You did it to yourself," said Aairyah looking into Kim's watery eyes.

"Look, I'm sorry I just blacked out when I hit you, but it still ain't change that you fucked that nigga while you was in college." Kim knew she was wrong, but all she could feel was pain coming from between her legs.

"So, you not going to comment on that?" asked Aairyah after a long pause.

Kim put her head down and just looked at Aairyah and started crying.

"I'm sorry," said Kim in almost a whisper.

Aairyah didn't hear her but could read her lips. Aairyah got up and went to the bathroom. Kim could hear the water running and tried to get up, but she couldn't.

A few minutes later, Aairyah came and picked Kim up from the bed. Aairyah took off Kim's shirt and bra before taking her to the bathroom butt naked. It smelled like apple cinnamon as soon as Kim got in the bathroom. Aairyah laid Kim in the bathtub, which was filled with bubbles, and stepped out of the bathroom. When Aairyah got back to the bathroom, Kim was pasted out in the tub. Aairyah grabbed a washcloth and some body wash and washed Kim's body. Kim woke up when Aairyah started washing her coochie.

"Not so hard Babe it still hurt down there," said Kim as she closed her eyes again.

After Aairyah got done washing Kim up, he got her out of the tub and dried her off in the room. Aairyah lotioned Kim down and tucked her in bed. Aairyah took a quick shower and cuddled up right with Kim as he went under the covers and fell asleep.

The next morning, Aairyah woke up, went inside the kitchen, and started cooking breakfast. Kim was woken by the smell of cheese eggs, scrabble tater tots, and toast. Kim loved when Aairyah cooked breakfast for her. She just hoped that the incident last night would go past them and they could just live their lives. Kim knew that she would eventually see Monroe; she just wished she didn't see him with Aairyah. Kim got up from the bed and went to the bathroom. After brushing her teeth and washing her face, Kim walked downstairs. As she was about to speak, the doorbell rang.

"I'll get it," said Kim as she walked to the door. She opened the door and a guy wearing a UPS shirt and hat was standing in front of her.

"Yes," said Kim.

"Yeah, how you doing? Can I speak to a mister Aairyah Washington?"

"I'm his wife. Is there something I can help you with?"

"Yeah, I have a delivery for him and I need his signature."

"Well, can I sign for him? I mean, I am his wife."

"No, sorry. They specifically need your husband's signature."

Kim looked at the guy with puppy dog eyes as she pouted with him.

"Oh well, I mean, I guess they wouldn't know. It's not like they check for IDs anyway," said the UPS guy handing over the clipboard with the white and pink sheet on it so she could sign.

Kim signed the paper and the UPS man went on his way.

"Who was that Babe?" asked Aairyah as he finished pouring two glasses of orange juice.

"The UPS man, he gave me a box," said Kim as she walked into the kitchen with a box in her hand.

Kim opened it and it was a tape and a note on the inside of it.

"Who the Fuck sent it?" asked Aairyah as he watched Kim pull out a videotape and a sheet of paper.

"It doesn't have a mailing address on it," said Kim picking up the note and reading it.

Aairyah saw Kim's facial reaction change and went over towards her. Aairyah got behind her and started to read the letter with her.

Dear Aairyah, What's up Nigga? I hope when you see this tape; it brings you a world full of misery. I know you are wondering who this is, so I'll just say it. Cameron. Yeah, the same Cameron you and your boys pulled that stunt off in school. My reputation was shot. I had to move out of the town. I couldn't even go to schools in the same state. That's how much embarrassment you brought to me. But I plan to bring much more embarrassment, anger, and betrayal to your life. You will soon find out the pain I endured this whole time. Ever since that day, I haven't been the same. You thought you was crazy then; wait till you watch this tape. It will drive you insane.

Stay Tune Till Love will Drive You Insane.